BATTLE

— OF —

WILLS

BOOK 1

MAROLYN CALDWELL

NEWMAN SPRINGS PUBLISHING
320 Broad Street
Red Bank, NJ 07701

First originally published by Newman Springs Publishing 2021

ISBN 978-1-63692-668-1 (Paperback)
ISBN 978-1-63692-669-8 (Digital)

Printed in the United States of America

*For ancestors on both sides of my family
who came to this country seeking freedom,
a passion for fair play embedded in their genes.
They served in the Continental and the Union Armies
and worked in the deepest of silence on
the Underground Railroad.*

CHAPTER 1

*Going on midnight, Friday, July 18, 2014; poolside
at the South Wind Conference Center located in
mountain country near Marietta, Georgia*

Something was moving out there in the darkness. Poised
midstep on the pool deck before dimly lit vending
machines, Lorie Manning paused, listening intently.
Something large was clawing its way up the steep brushy slope
just below the mesa where the Center's lovely swimming pool
had been cunningly constructed—moving directly toward
the place where she was now standing, coins in hand!

Sliding the coins back into her pocket, she edged quietly around the side of the sturdy machine and backed as
far as she could into the darkness of the narrow space left
between the machines and a facing half-wall studded with its
unfathomable jumble of plugs and heavy wires, leaving only
enough room for necessary maintenance.

Only now did she recall the warning poster she'd
noted, with a twinge of alarm at the time. She'd seen it as
she and her aunt Carol were passing through the Center's
gates at the completion of a grueling full-day odyssey from
their Mississippi River hometown in northwestern Illinois—
where folks lived in comfort and safety—to central Georgia

where it seemed they didn't! "TAKE CARE!" that poster had proclaimed. "BEARS IN THE AREA!"

A sinking feeling growing in the otherwise empty pit of her stomach, Lorie now realized that the only thing even remotely resembling a barrier between whatever was arising out of that mountain darkness and herself was an old-fashioned split-rail fence posted with signs, also printed in capital letters, cautioning visitors away from the edge of the cliff! Why had she not remembered either or both of those warning signs before stepping out of her room at midnight, searching desperately for something to eat?

She had left the door to her suite propped open a crack—should she try to make a dash for it?

Too late! Through the quivering shadows of undergrowth appeared human arms covered by dark sleeves, bare hands grasping toward low-hanging branches. A shaggy head, pale hair flashing golden in the sparkling light emitted by the pool, lifted resolutely above the brow of that steep slope. Lorie froze. This was a different species of night intruder— infinitely more dangerous than bears!

As he levered himself upward, his lean torso could be seen silhouetted intermittently against the glimmering lights of vehicles headed northward along a curve of the distant Interstate highway rising mountain-bound from Atlanta. He paused for a moment when he finally reached the top of the ridge—then bent over, wheezing, pulling hard to catch his breath. With even greater effort, it seemed, he fully uncurled his body and rose tall against the raw edge of nothingness, mist swirling about knee-high boots as if ethereal fingers were reaching toward the hem of his long button-studded jacket, trying to drag him back into the darkness from which he had just emerged. Illuminated only by the glowing shimmer of the motel pool's underwater lights, he seemed to be a young man, relatively clean-shaven.

Thanks to the many Atlanta Campaign Sesquicentennial posters Lorie had noted since she and her aunt had come into Georgia, she recognized the officer's uniform as Confederate. Almost as a reflex, she frowned. A sheathed weapon seemed to be dangling from his broad belt. A reenactor, perhaps? If so, he was either late getting to the party, or lost! Or something else was happening…

Without warning, a coin meant for the machine slipped from her pocket and bounced off the hard surface of the deck. She gasped, horrified! The intruder turned instantly, wrenching open a nearby gate in the only barrier that still stood between them, a split rail fence.

Abandoning her few meager purchases, she pushed herself free from her hiding place and bolted toward the hotel and her open doorway.

She heard a soft, quick oath. An icy chill penetrated her sleeve from behind. One hand missed. The other caught her, spun her into the crook of a muscular arm. Frigid fingers clamped across her mouth. His body was army hard! "Silence, boy!" A hoarse whisper. "The Yankees are primed to fire!"

Her struggles were useless. But as his arm shifted upward, it caught against her breast. She heard a quick oath, felt a cold puff of breath on her cheek. The fingers loosened, but only by a fraction.

It was enough. "Let me go or I'll scream!" Her words were soft but deliberately sharp.

A deep, tremulous voice. "My apologies, ma'am—but we must find cover while there is still time. Federal troops are moving up! They will fire if they hear us speak."

A sudden spasm caught him, crippling him instantly. Recognizing it for what it was, she wrenched away and bolted toward her doorway.

She was no more than two steps from sanctuary when she heard the soft, anguished moan—a sound with which she had grown far too familiar across the past two years. Skidding to a halt, she turned back. His knees were buckling. Face distorted, eyes pleading, he spoke softly. "Help me. Please…"

Instinct kicked in. She captured his cold outstretched hand, held it tightly as he sagged to the ground. Even in the dim light she could see dark stains growing on the back side of his gray jacket. Flooded suddenly with remorse and a surge of adrenaline, she encouraged him to regain his footing.

His breath rasped hard with every halting step. It was her strength alone that propelled the two of them through her hotel doorway. She shoved the door shut, waited only to hear the reassuring click of the lock, then directed his stumbling footsteps through the large room toward her aunt Carol's bed, the only surface in the room not presently stacked with sorted legal documents and ancient letters.

How close behind were his pursuers? She had heard nothing she recognized as gunfire. Nor had she seen or heard anyone else nearby. As she ripped the covers away, he sank onto pristine white sheets—instantly bloodied. She guided his head to a fresh pillow, lifted his legs to a height where she could deal first with the boots.

Dimming the lights, she pulled the draperies tight and turned back to focus on working off his muddy footwear. Making quick work of it, kicking the boots to one side, she swiftly wrapped his bare feet with the red woolen sweater she had earlier tossed across a chair and shoved a rolled blanket beneath his lower legs. It wouldn't halt the crimson flow now staining the left breast of his jacket in an ever-widening ragged-edged circle but might—with great good luck—slow it down a bit.

Only then did she grab her cell phone from the bedside table and punch in 9-1-1. "I have a gunshot victim bleeding profusely from the chest," she told the dispatcher sharply. "One of the Atlanta Campaign reenactors."

Instant attention. "Where are you?"

"The South Wind Conference Center—just off the old highway from Marietta to Atlanta." Quickly she added, "I didn't hear shots. But he seems to think gunmen are chasing him." She paused and cleared her throat, dealing now with unexpected emotion. "He's badly hurt! Bleeding out, I suspect, if he doesn't get immediate help! I'll do what I can."

A hurried voice—had she seen his assailant?

"No, but his injuries are not self-inflicted. It's likely someone is hunting him. Room 12, back side of the hotel. Ground level—facing the pool."

As the phone slid into her pocket, she brushed at the sudden tears coursing across her cheeks and forced her attention to the belt. "Need to see what we're dealing with, friend! I'll stash that sword in a safe place."

"Saber!" Barely a sound, but crisp. Authoritative!

Quick first assessment: how many people would care about the distinction between a sword and a saber? West Point alum? Army brat? A small smile briefly curled her lips. "Friend," she said softly as she detached the weapon from its belt and slid it under the bed. "We have a lot more in common than you know."

Blood, too much of it, was welling from his mouth now, trickling across his lips and chin. *Focus*, she admonished herself sternly, fighting once again her most troublesome problem. *You know how to do this, Manning! Stay strong!*

Racing to the bathroom, she moistened a clean washcloth and brought it back to wipe his lips. Gently! Gently! The police would need any information she could get before he passed out. Or worse yet, died! "Who are you?" she asked urgently. "What's your name? Who attacked you?"

"Federals. They're bivouacked nearby."

He's delusional! Work faster, Manning!

"How near are we to the river?" He was looking directly at her now, understandably anxious. Framed by dark eyebrows and long lashes, his eyes were an unusual shade of blue. She could almost feel the pain expressed in those eyes.

"The Chattahoochee?" She paused, thinking. "It's somewhere south, I suppose. I'm not that familiar with the terrain—I've never been here before. The owner of this place, Jon Randolph, he's a good friend of my aunt… Don't worry, an ambulance will be here shortly. You can ask the drivers."

"Jonny owns this place?" Puzzlement and apprehension showed on his face before his eyes disappeared into another agonized grimace.

She paused for a brief second—this man knew Jon Randolph? Was he kin? Poor soul—finding the person he was seeking just as the old gentleman was dying! But of more importance right now, where was that ambulance?

Breathing hard, she worked the damp coat sleeves down his arms alternately, across muscular hands, long fingers, trying to ease the heavy garment from beneath his body without causing further pain. Another soft groan. She gave a firm jerk, and the coat came free. Letting it drop, she kicked it out of her way. It skittered across the floor, disappearing halfway under the TV table with a resounding *thunk*.

"I'm sorry." She sighed. Her aunt Carol, physician assistant extraordinaire, would have had both coat and shirt off by now. "There's always been someone around to help! I'm still a student…was a student. Long story," she mumbled under her breath, indicating a stopping place. His troubles were far more serious than hers—even on a bad day.

"Jonny Randolph?" The voice was reedy, the question sharp!

She didn't have to reveal anything more about Jon Randolph either or the reason she was alone at the hotel. "I'm cutting your shirt off. Sorry, but I need to do this." With fingernail scissors—the only tool she could find in her purse—she snipped frantically at the soft gray cloth, folding it back as it peeled free, ripping it where she could!

As she worked it away from his body, blood pumped onto the sheets. Her stomach started to churn. "Hang on," she whispered—to herself!

Taking deep, deliberate breaths now, she hurried again to the bathroom, came back with a stack of towels, and pressed them tightly across the torn flesh of his left side. Deep, angry wounds. "Bloody mess," she said softly. "Where is that blasted ambulance?" And then hoped those soft words had not sounded as dire to him as they did to her!

She heard another deep moan. Deliberately ignoring the impending nausea, she encouraged him to roll slowly onto the towels, letting their bulk compress his wounds, hold back the flow of blood. So he couldn't slump backward, she propped him from behind with a barricade of pillows. *Focus,* her stern inner prompter instructed her. *Stay strong, Manning!*

She covered his muscular torso and arms with a soft blanket retrieved from the closet shelf and again moistened his lips with cool water. Once he seemed a fraction more comfortable, she strode to the window, pulled back a portion of the drape, and peered into the darkness. Where were those red-flashing lights—a distant siren? Nothing yet!

"When did you last see Jonny Randolph?" The soft tone was insistent, the cadence of his words firmly proclaiming his Southern roots. "I was told he had perished in the Wilderness of Virginia. Is he yet alive?"

The drape slipped from her hand. She turned back to him, puzzled. "Just barely." Wilderness? Virginia? What was he talking about? And in what world did he know old Jon Randolph—no one, not even her aunt, had ever referred to that elegant old patriarch as "Jonny."

"Tell me about him." His voice sounded grim. It was clear this man was part of the "Georgia mess," as her aunt was now branding it. And this meeting was no coincidence!

"Jon Third, everyone calls him," she began softly, wondering how much she could reveal if he were somehow on the other side of the conflict that had brought them to this place. "Lovely old gent, the way my aunt Carol talks about him. A little confused right now because of his age. My aunt's cousin called from Randolph City just as we got here this evening, saying they needed her immediately. I stayed here at the motel to get our paperwork organized. I haven't heard from her for a while. But if he's dying, it's in his own home."

He lay quiet, frowning as she approached him. He seemed to be examining her face, again with a puzzled expression. "Is Jonny Randolph family to you?"

"A family friend. My aunt knows him well. Her cousin—the person who asked us to come—he's related to her somewhere on the other side of our joint family…" She paused. "I'm sorry—it's a complicated relationship! Anyway, I've never had the privilege of meeting him."

He grimaced as another wave of pain swept across him. She gripped his hand. "Hang on," she said softly. "I've called 9-1-1. Someone will be here any minute now."

Increasingly anxious, she hurried again to the bath-room, this time bringing back a warm damp cloth to stroke his forehead and cheeks—wash away some of the blood. This man's connection to Jon Randolph had to be quite close!

He sighed at her touch, and his eyes fluttered to a close. Judging by his physique and the scarring she could see on his body, she pegged him for someone far more experienced in the ways of warfare than an ordinary reenactor. A career soldier, likely. She'd only treated a few of them during her previous short-lived medical career. All had proved daunting!

His eyes opened again. He stared at her, frowning. His voice came almost as a whisper. "You resemble someone I know quite well. Who are you?"

"Oh, I'm sorry. I should have said. My name is Lorena Manning."

"Manning?" There was surprise in his tone, almost as if he knew the name. "Why are you here, Lorena Manning?"

"Everyone thinks Mr. Jon Randolph is dying. My aunt Carol is a specialist in nursing older folk, and she felt she could offer some crucial help. I'm her backup driver. We're jointly doing research on family history." She hoped she wasn't speaking out of turn. He seemed intensely interested, despite his physical distress. "Our family and Mr. Jon's family are related," she went on, "although my direct family isn't blood kin to him. We have a mutual kinship, though—with some of Jon Randolph's other living relatives—of which there seem to be many!" In response to the increasingly puzzled expression on his face, she added, "So we're doing computer research and hands-on historical digging: museums, libraries, courthouses, and the like…"

Silence. Had he understood anything? He was frown-ing. He seemed bewildered. She wasn't sure that even she could understand all the nuances of the extended family. It would take a detailed family tree to work it all out—something she was trying very hard to pull together before it was too late, and decisive court papers had been filed. In any case, she was beginning to suspect that this man knew nothing useful.

"This history you are working out," he finally said, very softly, "does it record the name of Marshal Manning? Captain Marshal Manning?"

She straightened up abruptly. "Marsh? He's my brother! He's just finished his yearling year at West Point—going into his junior year if you don't know the jargon. Are you a West Pointer, too? Do you know my brother? Are you related to Mr. Jon?" A new doorway was about to open, she thought—maybe more than a crack.

Or maybe not! His body suddenly stiffened. His head fell back. He started to gag as if all the air were being sucked away. Lorie reached two fingers into his mouth, raked out a clot of thick blood that had settled in his throat. Opening his mouth wide, she blocked his nose and melded her lips to his.

Two quick breaths. A pause. More air. Over and over, forcing her breath into his starved lungs. He pulled it in deeply each time, expelled with a sigh. With all the blankets she had just tucked around him, how could his body still be so cold?

A cough! He sucked in another breath—this time, thank goodness, on his own!

She lifted her head to find his attention focused hard upon her face. He couldn't possibly miss the relieved tears now streaming across her cheeks. "I almost lost you…" Her voice broke, whether or not she wanted it to. "But I'm not going to lose you, mister," she said to him softly, wondering if he could hear as acutely as he could stare with those beautiful eyes. "I won't ever forget…" She stopped talking for a moment and closed her own eyes. Almost under her breath, she went on, very softly, "That even though you had to be hurting like hell, your first instinct was to protect me—a stranger! People like you are rare, Friend, and I promise you right now—I'll do everything I can to keep you safe.

"But just this minute, I have to do everything I can"—another near-miss on those tears—"to keep you alive!"

He drew in another lungful of air—under her touch she felt his chest expand. He seemed better, strangely enough. She felt the gentle touch of his hand on her fingers and was gratified that at last his flesh was beginning to warm. She felt new strength as well as he gently squeezed her hand. "Thank you, Miss Lorena Manning," he whispered. "I am humbled." Evidence enough that he had heard her.

He cradled her bloodstained fingers against his cheek, and she did not stop him. With her other hand, she stroked his forehead and pulled the damp strands of pale hair away from his eyes. "Where is that blasted ambulance?" She said it rather crossly, trying now not to bawl with the relief she felt.

What was wrong with her? She had gone well past the reactions of a trained emergency room nurse. This had become real personal. Not at all proper!

She had to think. She strode to the window, peered out, saw nothing but darkness, and shook her head.

The sudden sound of a bell cut through the room. The startled expression on his face surely reflected hers. Once again the bell pealed. Not the motel phone—it was her cell phone! What was wrong with her? She ripped it from her pocket and put it to her ear. "Aunt Carol, thank goodness it's—"

"He's dead, Lorie. I'd just walked out of the room. I wasn't gone more than two or three minutes. Such a shock when I got back!" It was evident Carol had been crying.

Still was. "He's dead. I tried. I tried every way I could! But I couldn't get him back. They're going to get the town now!" Then all Lorie could hear was crackling inside the phone.

"Carol, say that again, I can't hear you—bad connection. Please try again."

"The developers are going to have a field day here, Lorie." The words came as if from a very far distance. "All Mr. Jon's properties will be on the auction block if Rolf Maratti gets them."

That was something she hadn't needed to hear! "Oh, Carol, I am so sorry." This was the worst-case scenario Carol had not been willing even to consider during their intense road trip. "And you didn't find out anything? About the will, I mean."

"Nothing yet." The voice dissolved once again into the crackling ether. When it came back, she heard Carol saying, "that you got something to eat, hon, and that you're not bored to death with that never-ending family tree. I won't be here much longer. I just have to find out what Sue and Sid are planning for tomorrow. Funeral plans and so forth. Are you okay, Lorie? I'll be on the road in just a few minutes. I'll see you in forty-five minutes, an hour tops—there's a lot of fog, I've been told, so I'm being careful. Will you be okay?"

"I'm…fine, Carol. I do have kind of a problem to deal with, but…" She sighed deeply. "It's nothing I can't handle. Don't worry about me. Do what you need to do, and I'll tell you all about it when you get here." The words tumbled forth without thought as she disconnected.

She turned to look at the frowning man on the bed, then toward the windows—once more hoping to hear sirens. Nothing! "The great Jon Thomas Randolph Third has died," she mumbled. "I hope they can find his will! So much depends upon it!" Suddenly alarmed that she might have revealed too much, she looked back at her patient.

Too much information? No. It was obvious he hadn't understood a thing she'd told him—nor did he seem to care. His puzzled gaze was shifting around the suite. A frown wrinkled his forehead as he spotted the muted TV screen with its talking news anchors. Then very softly, he said, "You asked me who I am, Miss Manning. My name is Jefferson Richard Preston. Major, Army of the United States. I find I need more help than I at first believed. Will you help me?"

She sighed deeply, relieved. She had been correct about his army connection. And now she had a name. "I will help you in any way I can, Major Preston!" A solemn oath!

Suddenly the wail of a nearby siren blew away the silence of the night.

CHAPTER 2

Lights went on everywhere and startled guests at the convention center popped out of doorways, holding robes and blankets around themselves as the ambulance, sirens finally winding down, backed into place in front of her doorway. Lorie didn't fault them. She would have done the same.

With quiet efficiency, two policemen who had arrived simultaneously with the paramedics encouraged onlookers to retreat. She held the door open for a variety of emergency personnel and their gear.

The expression of puzzlement—fear, she thought—in her patient's striking eyes confused her. Professional help had finally arrived. She wished she could ask him more questions, maybe even hold his hand. But the two paramedics, a young man and an older woman working in perfect sync, were too busy treating his horrific wounds to put up with any nonsense. They asked her somewhat curtly to "move out of the way, please"; they'd let her know if they needed her.

Understanding, she stayed well back, watching with relief their competent hands go about stabilizing the life force of a patient whose care required far more skill than she could offer. "Your immediate first aid clearly saved his life," the female paramedic finally said to her with an approving smile. "Bravo, young lady. You've had excellent training! Well done!" At Lorie's responding nod, she gave a reassuring wave. "We'll take good care of him, honey!"

And then, with sirens again at full cry, they were gone, patient and all, with only two grim-faced uniformed policemen left to get what answers she could give. Officer Tim Murphy. Officer Randy Ross. Marietta, Georgia Police Department. The business cards they handed her reflected the nametags they wore on their chests. Their questions were curt and to the point. She wished she had more to tell them. Her own questions about what had just happened ranged far beyond any they might consider.

In response to a query from one of them, she turned toward the bed. In that brief moment, she became all too aware of the damp blood still soaking into the bedsheets. Blood had spilled onto the rug—she saw spatters everywhere she looked. *Focus*, she screamed frantically to herself. But her legs had already gone all wobbly. "Not again!" she mumbled. Her mind turned to mush. In that brief moment, everything disappeared.

When she regained consciousness, feeling a little sick, she found one of the officers—the one with freckles and sandy hair—kneeling, holding her in his arms. She looked up into a concerned young face, kindly brown eyes. Not just a policeman. A concerned human being. Officer Randy Ross. "I'm sorry," she managed to say into the nametag now pressed across her nose. "For some reason, I've developed an insane sensitivity to blood."

"Don't apologize! It happens. Take it easy."

She touched her forehead, still feeling the rapid throb inside her skull. "But I'm a nurse!" she confessed with chagrin. "I've never had a problem with blood before. But now, for some reason..." She sniffled a bit, holding back tears with difficulty as she let him help her to her feet. "It's cost me my job—my career!"

"There's no doubt you saved this man's life, Miss Manning," he answered very gently. "Everything worked when you needed it to. Why don't you just relax on that couch over there while we take a quick look around the area? We'll be back. It won't be long."

A quick glance passed between the two men—brief nods. They excused themselves, reassuring her that they weren't going away, they simply needed to begin the investigation.

Making certain the door closed securely behind them, they left, giving her time to pull her embarrassed self together. *True Southern gentlemen*, she thought gratefully. After a few minutes lying supine on the couch, trying to stave off incipient nausea, she slowly pushed herself up. Humiliated by this uncharacteristic weakness, unwilling to wait for whatever material help the hotel night clerk had just promised over the phone—clean sheets, towels, and so forth—she took a deep breath and looked around.

She didn't need fresh sheets. Not yet. What she needed was time to gather together all those important papers she had tossed so recklessly into the wind. If what her aunt had been telling her was borne out by facts the other part of the family was compiling, most of what she had been doing recently would at this point be considered highly classified: Family names! Addresses! Phone numbers! It seemed clear: as of tonight, most—if not all—the people she had already identified had to remain anonymous! She called the manager and told him to hold off bringing sheets and so forth for at least a half hour as she needed some time to get organized.

First, strip the bed, roll the blood-soaked bedding into a bundle with all the other towels and so forth that had previously gone willy-nilly onto the floor, and cram everything into the closet so her aunt wouldn't stumble over odd stuff when she came in. Or to be quite truthful, so her aunt wouldn't freak out! That cluster of small tasks took only a few moments.

Second, carefully gather up her "guest's" bloody clothing, the belt, and the lethal weapon he had so specifically designated as a "saber." These needed to be got out of the way quickly.

She piled everything into a generalized stack on the floor. Authorities would require them, and Carol wouldn't see them! She was as curious as the dickens about what was in the pockets of garments she had removed from his person, but she also knew that law enforcement required first crack at that. She thought she might ask them to let her know what they had found after they took their own look.

Thinking about it, she shook her head. That wouldn't happen in a lifetime! She'd go a different route. She'd find out what hospital they had taken him to, and she'd just go there and ask him straight out what he'd been carrying. If he were still alive and was unwilling to tell her, she probably didn't need to know.

Third, she retrieved the coverlet she had earlier tossed across the room, flung it over the mattress she had just cleared, and arranged all the pillows against the headboard. What she was going to do right now was to lie down! She'd be darned if she'd let this unaccustomed stigma beat her!

Since when had she become so sensitive to blood? Since *never*! There was something else going on in her cluttered brain. She felt it—but she wasn't quite sure what it was.

She did need to huddle for a while, though, to wind down—do some mental processing. He was part of it all. He had to be—this man who called himself Major Preston. He could be an integral player in the problems Carol had told her were happening in Randolph City. She couldn't guess how he might fit into the scheme of things. But that there was a connection she had no doubts whatsoever!

She had made a promise to him: to protect him to the best of her ability. He was stuck with her!

If she could find him again.

But that was really important! He needed to be briefed on what was happening in Randolph City, just as she and Carol had been. If he were really a part of the mess Carol had told her about, it could mean life or death—to him! If what had just happened to him was the first attempt at assassination, there might be a second.

Only now did she recognize how much catching up she herself had to do. "Sue wasn't aware that Mr. Jon was going downhill so quickly," her aunt had told her during an earlier phone call, one she could almost recite *verbatim* because it had been so alarming: "He's been rambling aimlessly all day about conspiracies, his mind in and out. We're still hoping he'll have a moment of clarity, recognize one of us, tell us where he put the will—if there even is one. Maybe he doesn't know himself.

"There's a labyrinth of hidden compartments in his old mansion, Lorie—and Sue has no idea where all of them are. They tell me Mr. Jon had been going from one hiding place to another, shuffling things as if he's looking for something. The will? We don't know. Diamonds? He keeps rambling on about a diamond…or diamonds. Sue wasn't sure which.

"I have to stay for a little while longer. Sue and Sid are frantic. If they don't find that will, Randolph City and its big, bold plans are toast! Lorie, thank you for digging in and helping with this relative search. We'll need it now more than ever. You're my hero, niece. Always!"

She had realized after that conversation that, as much research as she had already accomplished, she was truly coming into the middle of this drama as a complete novice. She didn't know enough about the situation even to respond. It had all seemed so melodramatic while Carol was briefing her during their very long southern journey. Conspiracies? What kind? Why?

In view of what had just happened, perhaps that was a topic demanding several more very intense discussions with her aunt!

She hoped Carol had at least found something to eat! Her own stomach was growling. Trying to ignore it, she went back to her own organizing chores.

When a sharp, authoritative knock came again shortly after 1:30 a.m., Lorie closed the laptop on which she had simply been deleting useless emails, pushed herself out of the nest she had created on the couch, and hurried to the door. It was the same two officers who had arrived with the ambulance. As the door shut behind them, tension virtually shimmered in the room.

"I'd like to know what you've found," she said, "if you can tell me."

"Not much," the first officer admitted. "Yet! We have to get lights out there and down below the cliff, too." The tag on the officer's shirt said "Tim Murphy." Neat prematurely white hair framed a serious rugged face—but she realized now that he was younger than she had first thought. A kind man altogether.

How did she know that? Her sudden assessment of this policeman jolted her. She'd never been so certain about things like this before.

What was going on here? At first there had seemed to be an odd dreamy feel to this whole scenario. She had chalked it up to her weariness. But something else was happening to her now. Her senses seemed to be sharpening, her recall far more acute!

Her arrival with her aunt in Georgia a few hours before had certainly begun on an odd note. Was it something float-ing in the air? She sniffed. Nothing there but a sweet scent of honeysuckle that had drifted in from the courtyard as Officer Ross shut the door firmly behind himself. She watched Officer Murphy consult a small notebook. He was counting, his mouth moving soundlessly. "Twenty-two rooms occu-pied," he finally said. "No one seems to have heard a shot or even a scuffle."

"I didn't either until I was out at the vending machines on the patio." Lorie was reluctant to recount her short per-sonal scuffle—at this point, it didn't matter. "But there was no question about his being shot. Two entirely different kinds of bullets, judging by the severity of the individual wounds. Blood everywhere. Well, you saw it!"

"The blood trail made it easy to see where he came up from the ravine," the other policeman said. Officer Randy Ross, wiry, compact, no more than a head taller than she was—the picture of competence despite a sprinkle of boyish freckles across his nose and cheeks. Someone who liked to laugh, it seemed to her, although he certainly wasn't laughing right now. "Lots of broken branches and displaced ground-cover," he continued. "As clear a blood trail as you can find from the base of the ravine to the place where you say you first saw him.

"The crime scene investigators will take a closer look at first light. But right now, we're thinking he fell or was pushed down that slope somewhere else, managed to get this far, and then pulled himself back up when he saw the swim-ming pool lights above him. Little mix-up out there, huh?"

He grinned at her enthusiastic gratitude as he handed her the can of fruit juice she had dropped earlier and her bag of vending machine trail mix. "You were lucky." Once more deadly serious, he said, "Bringing him inside was a gamble. You're a brave lady, Miss Manning."

Officer Murphy nodded. "But next time, for your own safety, call us first!" Giving his head a small shake, he asked, "Did he appear to have been drinking?"

"No." Lorie said it as authoritatively as she could, chagrin sweeping through her. Had she taken too much of a chance? To her way of thinking, there had never been an option! "He was bleeding profusely from his chest, so when he started gasping for breath, I gave him mouth-to-mouth resuscitation. No smell or taste of alcohol. And no indication of drug use. Believe me, that's something I would know!"

Murphy's eyes narrowed. "And you'd know that—how?"

"I'm a licensed nurse. I've been working in the hospital emergency room back home for most of the past six months. Well…" she looked up into two surprised faces, "blood has never been a problem for me. Until recently. Now I'm being told I'm overly sensitive. Too empathetic! 'Keep some emotional distance, Nurse.'" She said the despised words in a singsong pattern, remembering all too well the faintly mocking voice that had thrown them at her at least one time too many. "But as you can probably imagine, when I started fainting at every gory sight, I got my walking papers. I've never been 'too empathetic' before. It's a curse!"

"No wonder you know so much about emergency procedures." Murphy's tone had shifted subtly from surprise to respect. "They tell us your rapid response saved his life, Miss Manning. I don't know what your plans were when you got here, but we'd like to ask you to stick around until we can sort out what's going on, see if your presence is part of a broader picture. Do you want us to arrange a clean room for you to move into?"

"You think we might be targeted, too?" she said, startled by the thought. She wondered now if her aunt's contacts had notified the Marietta police a few days ago, at the same time they had talked to the police in a different town, one called Randolph City—named for Mr. Jon's' family, no doubt—about unusual "incidents" that seemed to be going on around Mr. Jon's mansion. "And 'no' on the 'clean room,'" she finished. "There's way too much stuff here to shuffle to another room. I'll be fine now, gents. Thanks for all your help. I'll just get some rest right here until my aunt gets back, and then we'll make more permanent plans."

"Since we're going to be around for as long as it takes," Officer Murphy said agreeably, "we're okay with that. But double-lock and chain the door the minute we walk out of here. Keep in mind, if he were trying to escape from someone, it's more than likely he's being tracked. Don't open that door unless you know exactly who's standing there. We've asked for another black and white. Two officers will be sitting out there in the parking lot, keeping an eye out. Feel free to call us personally if you have any other problems. If you go elsewhere, please let us know where we can find you. And above all, don't take any more chances!"

By now, Lorie was thoroughly alarmed—as she strongly suspected was his intent. "Could you tell me, please, where did the ambulance take him? I made him some promises that can't be kept unless I know where to find him." *To keep him safe! To keep him alive!*

"We can find out for you," Officer Ross said rather vaguely. "Don't worry about him, Miss Manning. Those emergency people are good. They also told us he was damned lucky that someone with your particular skill set was on the scene. Look, don't worry about passing out, either. It happens all the time! Are you sure you're okay now? We won't leave if you need us to stay until your aunt gets here." Aside from the little "comfort" game he was playing, he seemed genuinely concerned.

Again she felt a flush come to her face. "Yes. Yes. I'll be okay. Thank you again. I'll let you know where you can locate me once I know that myself!"

So decided, the two policemen collected the bloody clothing, the boots, and the archaic weapon her patient had seemed so concerned about, logged and bagged them, and left. She locked the door behind them and slipped the chain into place.

Now taking a very deep breath, she looked around: daunting perhaps, but not as much of a disaster as she had feared. Before stripping out of her soaked sweats, she mopped up as much of the blood as she could with the less-saturated towels, threw the whole mess into a cold water soak in the bathtub, and shut the plastic curtain against them. She washed herself in the sink and changed into a clean flannel nightgown. Pulling her red sweater across her shoulders, she crawled wearily into the nest she had created for herself on the bed. If someone did come from the office with fresh sheets, she'd deal with it. If they didn't, well, she was okay—as long as that door remained locked! It didn't hurt, she had to admit, to have policemen stationed just outside!

Sitting quietly now inside her wall of pillows, munching the sweet-salty trail mix, and washing it down with fruit-flavored liquid, she tried to pull her thoughts together. The snacks took the edge off her hunger—leaving behind a great calm. At this point, she wasn't much interested in food anyway.

The wounded man: Jefferson Richard Preston. Major Preston. US Army.

A brief contact only. And yet for some inexplicable reason, she had promised her loyalty to him. Moreover, she fully intended to keep that promise! Why?

Perhaps it was because she was now convinced that his appearance had not been coincidental. The name Preston had come up at least once in the computer research she'd been doing for Carol: she'd been creating, with pen and ink, endless tombstones to tack onto the giant bulletin board her aunt had been developing for Cousin Sue before Sue's frantic call for immediate help had overtaken all.

Lorie glanced at the big chart that almost overwhelmed the bed she was using as its base. She leaned the chart against the headboard. This would be a terrifically useful genealogy tree for use not only by her family but by all the "relevant relatives'" families. Rows of neat little tombstones were now beginning to display, in easy-to-understand terms, all that was left of three centuries of human lives. Entire lives, Lorie mused sadly. Each reduced to two lines: a name, two dates. She sighed.

Life boiled down.

Her aunt had tried to explain to her just yesterday how her ancestors and Jon Randolph's family had intersected. Carol always referred to Sue as her cousin. And without question, Sue was related to Jon Randolph, hence the connection to her aunt and herself—even if it weren't by blood. "We have to search out everyone living now who might be related to Jon." Carol had repeated that mantra several times during their long journey south as if Lorie should memorize it.

Lorie's assignment, however, had actually been outlined in somewhat more sketchy terms. "In case Jon Randolph dies intestate—without a will—we'll want to have a lot of people on our side." Carol had sighed. "We strongly suspect that there are other legitimate heirs. Sue has a lot of ancient letters in her attic. We could spend days sorting them, trying to ferret out something about the people who wrote them. The problem is, Sue's never been able to locate any of those people. Now it's become imperative that we find them before anyone else does! We've got to warn them of the dangers involved and ask them if they'll help us save at least some of Mr. Jon's legacy for the people we know Jon wants it to go to."

"Danger?" Lorie's alarm had risen to her hairline.

"We seem to be dealing with a shadowy underworld, hon. You've heard me talk about Rolf Maratti. He was born in Italy during the Second World War to a woman who helped Mr. Jon when his plane went down over the mountains somewhere between Italy and Switzerland. There's no question Rolf is Jon's legally adopted son. I've seen copies of the adoption papers.

"Which means that whether or not the will is found, Maratti will get a big chunk of the estate. But the word is getting around lately that Maratti is gang-connected. There's a lot of money and property involved here. Cousin Sue says Maratti is in Randolph City already. With a bodyguard, if you can believe that!

"If other descendants come with claims on Mr. Jon's estate without being warned, they may run into a hornet's nest of trouble. We'll check them out to see if they're legitimate and then try to run interference if we can."

"Oh-kay!" There was definitely more to this family tree search than mere curiosity. Jefferson Richard Preston, in fact, might have become simply the first victim of Mr. Jon's legacy—with more to come.

Pulling herself out of her cozy nest, she stepped across to Carol's bed and tipped up the poster-board chart to see what tombstones she had thumb-tacked to it so far. A cursory search wasn't showing any Prestons in the mix other than Jon Randolph Third's grandmother, Sara Preston, born in 1846.

Hardly a factor here. Her children wouldn't be named Preston. They'd bear the surname of her first husband: Jon Randolph. The first Jon Randolph. Here was the second Jon Randolph. And here lay the third, the one who had just died. All the same name. Jon Randolph. No Prestons.

It was frustrating to search when so many names were exactly the same. The only differences: birth dates and death dates. What did that say about the Randolph family? Blind family loyalty? No imagination? Sighing, she made a firm decision on the spot: her children, in the unlikely event she ever had any, would never include a "Junior."

Well, maybe it was time to get out the computer. She charged it up, opened the genealogy program, and entered the Randolph family tree. Perhaps she could branch off Grandmother Sara Preston's name. Find a brother.

Settling herself back inside her cozy nest, she typed in the name: *Sara Preston*. Data came up on the screen. Birth: 1846. Death: 1940. Ninety-four years, a long life. She zeroed in on Sara's history and quickly discovered why her aunt, and herself by extension, was involved in this family dilemma. This, in fact, was the very link Carol had wanted her to search out. Bravo for Carol!

Sara Preston was the pivot point. Her first husband was the contemporary Jon Randolph's grandfather—a.k.a. the first Jon Randolph. Sara Preston's second husband, however, had been a gent named Marshal Manning. "*Our* link!"

In her surprise, Lorie actually said it aloud. The senior Marshal Manning was one of her own many-great-grandfathers, and his name had ping-ponged through her family tree hit or miss throughout the years until it ended up attaching itself to her younger brother—whom her accidental new acquaintance somehow seemed to know.

Puzzled but feeling a more personal connection now, Lorie examined Sara's tree in greater detail.

It seemed that the original Marshal Manning was already father to a young son when Sara married him. That youngster was called Harry, for Harrison, the surname of the mother who had died giving him birth. So the Harrisons were part of her own family, too, along with the Mannings.

Sara Preston Randolph and Marshal Manning's joint son—second child for each parent—had been named Preston. His first name, not his last.

Opening further windows, Lorie further confirmed family links. Sue Bailey, née Manning, Carol's cousin (and hers, one further step removed), was one of Preston Manning's descendants; indeed, she was the "Sue" in "Sid and Sue."

Lorie and her aunt were not related by DNA to Jon Randolph Third. But Cousin Sue was. One of the potential heirs, something Carol had already confirmed.

Computer access to family trees, Lorie mused, could become almost an obsession—all the more fascinating since computers enabled relatives from any part of the country to view the tree and add branches to it. If one needed to check out more history, one simply clicked!

She clicked on Sara's name.

The list of Sara's siblings opened. Seven of them. Tragically, only Sara and one brother had lived to adulthood. That brother's name?

The words emerged as a single surprised breath from Lorie's throat: "Jefferson Richard Preston?"

Information on Jefferson Richard Preston? Not much! Birth date: January 11, 1837. Death date? A side note: *Likely killed July 18 or 19, 1864, during Atlanta campaign. Body never found.*

Lorie glanced quickly at the computer calendar: "July 19." A single-date wall calendar hanging within plain sight of Lorie proclaimed "July 18." Her spine tingled! The first Jefferson Preston apparently died one hundred fifty years ago yesterday or today—somewhere near Atlanta. *Body never found?*

She gave a nervous little laugh, saying to herself, "Don't go there, Lorena." A gentle whiff of honeysuckle suddenly tickled her nose, and a light glimmered somewhere in the darkened room. Honeysuckle? A reflection of car headlights? Carol returning earlier than she had planned? She hoped!

She pushed herself up, strode to the tightly closed window, and pulled away a portion of the drape. The whole area outside their suite was dark, quiet. No movement anywhere. Even the police car was sitting dark, two policemen on a silent watch to prevent a possible further crime. She looked at the clock. The hour hand had just passed midnight.

The sweet scent lingered. Why? Well, that wasn't hard to answer—the pool shelter was wrapped in honeysuckle vines. Honeysuckle seemed to grow like weeds on this campus, and she'd had the door propped open for a long period of time. Perhaps she'd just been too busy to focus on that familiar scent until now. She laughed uneasily.

Then there was the other thing. Had she really seen what she had thought was a flash of light in her room? Or were her eyes just getting too tired?

She looked at her watch again. It was late, and she was drooping with fatigue. That's all it was: fatigue! Or maybe the chart was making her buggy-eyed. She put in a call to her aunt. "Did you just pull into the parking lot and go the wrong direction?" she said when Carol's tired voice answered.

"Not there yet, hon. I'm on my way back, though. No point my staying with Sue. The coroner's coming so he can sign off on the death certificate. I'm just in the way. Another half hour and I'll be back with you."

Vaguely troubled. Lorie didn't quite know what to say. She finally blurted out, "Carol, something happened tonight you really need to know about."

"What is it?"

She thought again. Darn it all, the whole encounter was too complicated to explain to anyone and especially to a grieving woman driving her car through a dark foggy night. "Never mind. Family tree business. It'll wait till you get here."

Lorie returned to her tombstone task. Still troubled, she had just finished attaching another tombstone to the family tree poster when again she saw a gleam of light. She looked around.

Like before, it disappeared. The scent of honeysuckle had disappeared as well. And a moment later, a brisk knock sounded on the door. She hurried toward the peephole. It was a policeman, her aunt Carol standing right behind him, eyes wide, a shocked expression on her face. "Do you know this person?" the young officer asked her when she opened the door.

"She's my aunt!" She smiled her profound gratitude. "And I'm really glad to see her. I expect you guys can go home now. We've got this!"

"We'll stick around for a while." Smiling politely, he turned back to the police car.

Once the door closed, Carol stood quite still. She was quiet. Unnaturally quiet. Then almost under her breath, she said, "What the hell is going on?"

"I met someone tonight," Lorie said hastily. "I think he's part of this whole thing, Carol. I just have this funny feeling..." Her voice trailed off.

"You met someone, Lorena?"

She had never heard that tone in Carol's voice before. "No, no, no, Carol! You know me better than that. Sit down and let me explain."

Carol sighed. "I'm sorry. I do know better and I apologize. I'm just tired! And really upset about this whole mess. Okay, young lady, let's start over again. Whom did you meet and why the police presence?" She dropped her handbag and her briefcase and lowered herself into the embrace of an overstuffed armchair.

Her aunt looked exhausted: eyes large with deep circles beneath, makeup dissolved in tears whose tracks could still be seen on her cheeks. No mascara. No lipstick. Her short dark hair looked clumpy, like something had been pulling at it. Even her once-crisp khaki slacks and white shirt were wilting. Lorie had never seen her appear quite so defeated. Or so old! Would a hug help?

At this point, probably not!

Lorie settled herself on the edge of the bed next to Carol's chair. "I went out to the pool to get some juice and stuff from the vending machine"—maybe she could just gloss over the dangerous part—"and encountered a person... well, he'd been shot." She said it very quickly and moved on. "I gave him first aid and called for help. The important thing is, I think he's a relative, Carol. He seems to know Jon Randolph."

But Carol had already come to her feet at that one problematic word. "*Shot!* My God, Lorie! I'll have to call Sue. Warn her! What's his name? Why do you think he's a relative?" She reached for her phone.

"Jefferson Richard Preston. Major, US Army. At least that's what he told me." Carol again looked up sharply and Lorie hurried her narrative along. "I remembered seeing 'Preston' in my research, so I looked. It doesn't go anywhere. It kind of ends. In 1864." She paused. Nuts! Coincidence was just coincidence! And there was the other thing. Sudden relief, as with a sigh, she remembered. "He asked me about Marsh. I think he's family. Or family friend, at least."

"Major Jefferson Richard Preston"—Carol was staring at her—"asked about your brother Marsh?"

"There must be a Preston connection to Jon Randolph's family," Lorie said lamely, "that didn't get entered into the family tree program."

The continuing silence was disturbing. Carol was standing as if in shock, as if she were searching her mind and not at all liking what she found there. Her mouth opened and closed. Then, all of a sudden, she said, "Where is he?"

"The ambulance took him to the emergency room at the hospital."

"Which hospital? How hurt is he?"

"The policeman wasn't sure. But the man was obviously shot. Blood everywhere. I managed to get most of it cleaned up—"

"I'm calling Phil." It was as if Carol were suddenly switched on, once again her cool, efficient self. Well, maybe a little manic, under the circumstances! "He can contact the hospitals and ferret out everything we won't have access to. Lorie, get yourself dressed. Stat!"

More than surprised, she rooted through her bag and pulled out jeans and a yellow T-shirt, with a long-sleeved flannel shirt to guard against the chill of the drizzly night. "Phil who?"

"Dr. Philip Barnett. You've met him a couple of times when he and his family visited me in Illinois. He's the doctor who was first on the scene all those long years ago when your uncle Bill and our baby were killed in the accident in Atlanta, and I was so banged up. He's why I soldiered on afterward to become a physician assistant. He runs an orthopedic clinic now, to help wounded vets."

"Wow," Lorie said softly. "'Old friend' is right." That devastating tragedy had happened twenty years ago. Even though she'd just been five years old, she clearly remembered the trauma of it all. It had echoed down all their lives. "Where are we going?"

"Phil will let us know."

Carol was on her phone while Lorie, with a gratified sense of anticipation, scrubbed her face, dabbed on a little lipstick, and quickly pulled a comb through her short cut.

They stopped by the police car to tell the waiting officers they had to go out. "Don't leave town without letting us know," they were told. "This is an ongoing investigation."

"I understand," Carol answered. "We're meeting someone who might shed light on what's happened. If we find anything pertinent, we'll bring it to you immediately."

"We'll be here," they promised and handed her a business card. "Call if you need help."

CHAPTER 3

From the front, the South Wind Conference Center resembled the movie version of a southern mansion, a colonnaded portico spread across its width. Carol maneuvered the car expertly through vehicles lining the back parking lot, but as she pulled into the lot adjacent to the portico, she stepped on the brakes. Wordless, she pointed left toward the highway. A dark-colored van that had just split off from the four-lane was approaching the motel along the access road. "It's kind of late for someone to be checking in, don't you think?" Lorie whispered, sensing what Carol was thinking. "The police warned me someone might be tracking him."

Her aunt sat silent for a moment and finally said, "Let's wait. Hopefully, it's police related."

Increasingly uneasy, Lorie watched the van slow and turn onto the long motel driveway. It made a left turn toward the South Wind office at the far side of the portico. In backlight, she caught a quick glimpse of two figures in the front seats. The vehicle passed even more slowly beneath the porte cochère outside the office. Not stopping, it made a right turn toward the back parking lot.

"A registered customer." There was a note of relief in Carol's voice.

Lorie saw momentary flashes of headlight on bushes that rimmed the back area. "Maybe not. I think they're turning around."

The van reappeared. Slowly it crossed in front of the center, gave Carol's idling Escort a wide pass, and turned toward the back side of the building—the side where a police car was conspicuously parked. Lorie watched as headlights briefly illuminated yellow crime scene tape strung around the far bushes by the ravine. For a moment the area went dark. Once again Lorie saw the moving glow of lights on trees beyond.

"Not customers." Lorie's heart was suddenly in her throat. "Or the law, either. They're coming back. I bet it's someone searching for my soldier."

Releasing the brake, Carol turned the Escort smoothly out to the service road and from there onto the highway. She accelerated gradually to the posted speed, keeping an unhurried pace. Lorie watched behind long enough to realize that her nagging apprehension was fast becoming reality. The black van had quickly wheeled onto the service road behind them. A few minutes later, it followed their lead onto the dark highway. Its lights remained steady about two car lengths behind as they headed toward Marietta. "What now?" Lorie asked.

"This," Carol responded, "is very disquieting. It never occurred to me that someone might associate us with a police investigation."

As with everything about her aunt, Carol's car was efficient and understated. No fancy electronic gadgets, great gas mileage. As long as the air conditioner worked, Lorie found no problem with the old-fashioned stick-shift and thought the car was fun to drive. But it was no muscle car. If there were to be a race, it would be an uneven contest. "What's the plan?" she asked her aunt.

"First, call the cops, Lorie. Tell them we think this van is stuck to us and ask if they noted its license number. Whoever these people are, I don't think we've given them any reason to connect us with the 'goings-on' back there. But if we are their target, I think I know how to cool this whole thing down."

Lorie called the number on the card she had been handed. The officers had spotted the van, she was told, but the plate had not been visible. No tag lights. Suspicious, on the face of it, the officer added, allowing that she and Carol might be in trouble. "What shall I tell him?" Lorie turned to her aunt. "He suggests we come back to the motel."

"That would only serve to confirm these folks' suspicions that we're involved. Tell them we're headed to the nearest twenty-four-hour drug store. Hopefully there'll be surveillance cameras inside and out. At best we can get some pictures. Let's see what these guys are up to."

Lorie passed the message to the officer and turned back to Carol. "He says there's an all-night pharmacy at the second exit north. They want an update when we get there, and they're calling for someone to meet us. What now?"

"Not sure yet. Let's shake these guys first. Then we'll start doing the rounds. There are dozens of hospitals around here. In the case of gunshot wounds, security will certainly be required. I asked Phil to find your Jefferson Richard Preston and see if he could treat him at his clinic." As if in chorus with Carol's words, her phone rang. She put it to her ear and, after a brief conversation, said, "Then you got him? Thanks, Phil, that's great."

In the dim light from the dashboard, Lorie could almost see the glow in her aunt's eyes. Carol closed her phone, saying, "The emergency people stabilized your friend, and Phil got permission to transfer him by ambulance to the Barnett Orthopedic Clinic. He emphasized its isolated location, its treatment of vets, its staff of former army EMTs, and the gated fence around the facility—and got quick police approval! Major Jefferson Richard Preston, or whoever he is, is safely in our hands now, Lorie. If anyone's thinking further of finishing him off, they've got another think coming."

Lorie breathed a sigh of relief. He would be okay. And more to the point, he was real! There! She'd said it…one of the many vague possibilities her tired mind had been playing with. Since she had just promised him her undying assistance, "realness" seemed essential.

The second Marietta exit opened to them, and Carol headed without hesitation off the highway toward a still brightly lit mall advertising the presence of a twenty-four-hour pharmacy. To Lorie's ever-increasing dismay, the van also made the turn, staying about half a block behind. Carol slowed and pulled the Escort into a parking space directly in front of plate glass doors. The van cruised through an almost empty parking area well behind them, looped back toward the exit, but paused as it approached the roadway. It was situated, Lorie realized, where its occupants could easily see through the pharmacy door. Its headlights went off.

"Stay here to watch them. Count people if they get out," Carol said briskly. "And lean on the horn if anyone approaches you." She stepped out of the car and entered the store. Lorie made herself as small as she could and watched, heart pumping wildly, as the dark vehicle continued to wait near the entrance to the highway.

Carol shopped casually along the aisles, always staying in plain sight, first selecting one product, inspecting it, reading the label in great detail…then another…then another.

No emergencies in this woman's life. Only a head cold that required medication. Or a sleeping aid of some kind.

Suddenly another van, identical to the first, turned into the parking lot. Lorie's heart did a quick flip. She called Carol's cell. "They have company. The drivers are consulting."

"Call the cops," Carol said sharply.

Lorie put in the call. "They're on their way," the dispatcher reassured her. "They'll be on-site in two minutes."

As a police car turned into the driveway, the first van's dimmed headlights suddenly blazed. A motor roared back to life. The vehicle accelerated abruptly, wheeled onto the exit road, and moved out toward the four-lane, retracing its route heading south. The other van quickly looped through the parking area and took a northbound exit. The police car moved in beside Carol's Escort. The driver, an older gent with a soft Southern accent, asked Lorie if she was okay.

"I think so," she answered, still feeling a little shaky. "Did you get license plate numbers?"

"They didn't let us get that close," he replied, sounding annoyed.

Carol came out immediately, offering profuse thanks to the responding policemen. The driver told her not to hesitate to call if there were any further hints of something amiss and waved as he pulled away. Her aunt then handed Lorie a cup of hot coffee and a package of small sugared doughnuts. "Eat up. It's going to take us some time to get where we're going. Phil knows what's happening."

Carol cruised slowly through the quiet streets of Marietta, watching for any indication they were being followed. With a slight shake of her head, she wove through a series of dark, upscale suburban neighborhoods she seemed to know very well and at last back to the high-speed road.

Half an hour later, she turned the Escort off the freeway onto a quiet country road.

"That scared me," Lorie admitted. She didn't remember having tasted the doughnuts as they went down, but the bitter coffee was bracing.

"Likewise," Carol confessed. "We'll be a little smarter next time."

It was around 3:30 a.m. when at last they reached their destination. Lorie spotted a sign for the clinic, and moments later, their headlights illuminated an open gate not far ahead, beyond which a large square white building blazed with lights. At the front door, an ambulance stood open. It was empty.

"Now," Carol said, "let's see what this is all about."

Lorie swung her legs out and stood up, stretching, finally experiencing fatigue and a sudden case of nerves. "I need some serious updating, Auntie!" At least he wasn't a ghost. Lorie chuckled to herself. What a relief!

He'd been seriously wounded, Carol had told her after fielding a phone conference with the doctor a short time before they arrived. But he was holding his own. So many questions: why had he been wearing a Confederate uniform? How many people outside the family knew the will was missing? On top of everything else, what kind of danger had the two of them gotten themselves into?

"Let's go inside." Carol picked up her briefcase and handbag and strode toward the door.

The drivers were just leaving. Lorie saw behind them a tall, well-built man wearing dark trousers and a white shirt, sleeves rolled up to his elbows. Carol put down her bags, gave the man a hug and a kiss on the cheek, put her arm around his waist, and brought him to meet Lorie.

"You've grown," Smiling, Dr. Phil Barnett extended his hand, and to her credit, Lorie remembered him. She had liked this rugged-looking man the first time she'd met him at Carol's small house down the block from her family's home in Illinois. She recalled his intriguing Southern accent and the songs his family and hers had sung together on a soft summer evening accompanied by the sweet strains of an expertly played guitar.

"It's been a few years. I remember you, your wife, and two gorgeous boys who were both in college and way too old for me."

"Beth died of cancer some time back," he said matter-of-factly. "And the boys have scattered to the winds, both doctors now with young families of their own. I understand you're training to be a nurse, Lorie."

She wasn't sure how to respond. Her aunt spoke for her. "Probably the wrong profession, Phil."

"I've discovered that I faint at the sight of blood." She found herself mumbling the words somewhat under her breath. "And cry at the drop of a hat."

Phil's bushy eyebrows raised momentarily. "What happened?"

"The last one was a really bloody head wound," Carol explained. "When they wheeled the patient in, Nurse Manning dropped like a rock. Don't worry, the patient survived!"

Phil snickered once and then let out a big booming laugh. He put a kindly hand on her shoulder. "Sorry, Lorie. It happens."

"It's humiliating."

"You'll find your own path. Maybe right back into medicine."

"She's researching for me right now on this family prob-lem," Carol said. "Not everyone is cut out for front-line med-ical service." She grinned at Lorie. "I'm told you did okay tonight, hon, blood and all. What more can we ask?"

"How is he?" Lorie asked eagerly, now back in safe territory.

"Sedated," Phil replied. "Very pale. Not unexpected, given the amount of blood he seems to have lost. He's got a somewhat rare type, so we're simply stabilizing him until we can locate a pint or two. I'm going to let him sleep. We've got monitors on him, and one of my best aides will babysit him tonight." He turned to Carol. "You ladies are staying with me over at the house for the duration. I need to be briefed. And I can see how tired you both are. Your encounter with those vans scared me even more than it did you. No more adven-tures until you get some sleep."

"Sounds good," Carol said with a deep sigh.

It was a short drive to the doctor's old homestead, nes-tled comfortably in a substantial wooded area near the clinic. The kitchen was large, old-fashioned, and comfortable, mirroring the remainder of the house. They sat at a round wooden table under a Tiffany-style lamp, unwinding, drink-ing, as Carol described it, "warm milk with a little tea and honey in it."

"'Calm' in a cup," the doctor had said, offering it to them. "Now, can you give me an update in about fifty words?"

Carol's laugh was sharp. "Make that a hundred and fifty…mostly profane!" Her smile had faded. "I guess you know Mr. Jon died tonight."

"Sue called me. She also told me his last words were gibberish. What were you expecting?"

"We can't find his will. We were hoping he could tell us where it was. I tried everything I know to help jog his memory, but in the end, nothing worked."

"That's strange. He was nothing if not organized."

"Exactly what Sue said. Except he'd been moving things around lately. Without telling her. When she couldn't find the will in the bank safe, she opened the vault out at Randolph House. She found everything she expected—except the will. Worst case: if Mr. Jon hadn't tucked it away in one of the secret compartments for some reason, we think someone might have taken it out of the safe before we had a chance to look."

"Who?" The doctor frowned.

"Whoever is causing all the trouble over at Randolph City." Carol looked at Lorie as if apologizing again for the anger in her voice. "Sorry, hon. I'm beyond rage right now. I'm inclined to blame Rolf Maratti, but he couldn't have done it himself. Who is he working with?"

Lorie had been listening carefully, but she still didn't feel she had a firm handle on what was going on. "Tell me more about this Rolf Maratti," she said.

"Mr. Jon's adopted son? Long story, tinged with tragedy. It's too complicated to get into right now. Let's just say that there has been bad blood between them for years, at least on Rolf's part. Why did he show up in town the day before yesterday? Someone must have tipped him that Mr. Jon was failing badly and likely to die. He came with a formidable-looking escort."

"I know someone is saying Mafia. Do you suppose...?" Phil Barnett frowned, and Lorie thought with increasing discomfort about their followers in the dark van.

Carol hesitated. "Phil, I just can't picture Maratti as a gangster. I met him several years ago and was impressed by the way he handled himself. But everyone else in town thinks the person who came with him is either a hit man or a Sicilian bandit. A guy with a hooked nose and lots of dark hair. Always beside Maratti wherever he goes. They haven't said 'boo' to anyone. Just checked into the hotel. Waiting. Like vultures. Scaring people."

"Waiting for what?"

"If there's no will and no other close descendants, Maratti will get the bulk of the estate. He was legally adopted. Right?"

"I'm no expert on Georgia probate law," Phil murmured, "but that sounds likely."

"And even though he hasn't talked with Sue or Mr. Jon's lawyer, he has been seen talking to the developers at Randolph City who—rumors once again—want to put up a hotel-slash-resort where Randolph House now stands. They flock around him and follow him everywhere he goes."

Phil Barnett stared long at Carol. "You're kidding?"

"Unfortunately not."

The doctor rose to his feet and started to pace around the kitchen, rubbing his hands together, staring intently at the floor. "What a disaster. Does anyone know what Jon intended?"

"Everyone knows he was leaving most of his property to the Randolph City Historic Development Foundation so they could move ahead with their project. It would bring lots of people to the area and make jobs for everyone in town. Theoretically."

"Theoretically?"

"Ah, there's the rub. Randolph City is an out-of-the-way place at best, and this historic town thing they've been planning seems like 'pie in the sky' for a lot of people, including some of the council members. On the other hand, a posh hotel for folks with deep pockets who want to visit the mountains and lakes of northern Georgia is a proven moneymaker, bringing rich tourists and creating jobs. We have the perfect stalemate in Randolph City. The arguments are beginning… and creating deep divisions among the good people of that pretty little town. Old friends aren't speaking to each other right now! It can only get worse."

"Unless the will is found."

"You see the dilemma."

Phil sat down again.

"What gibberish?" Lorie said evenly.

"What?" Carol raised her eyebrows. "Oh…what Jon said before he died?"

"What did he say that was gibberish?"

"I tried to memorize it as he was speaking. It was kind of hard to understand because it didn't make any sense. So bear with me: 'Give my son the letter that's in the green box in the clock room. Tell him it's a little late, but all the answers he's looking for are there. Tell him his own children have a far better father than he did.' And then he said he was sorry they had run out of time to talk about it."

Lorie was silent for a moment, thinking. "That doesn't sound quite like gibberish to me," she murmured.

"Clock room?" Carol said with barely controlled frustration. "What the heck is a clock room? Sue didn't have any idea what he was talking about. And Tommy, his real son, died in Vietnam. Years ago. Unmarried."

"Oh."

"And then there's Rolf." Phil put in.

"There's Rolf," Carol repeated. "The estranged stepson who came as baggage with Jon's second wife, the beautiful Maria Maratti. He brought her here from Italy after his first wife died."

Lorie pressed her. "And?"

"Maria died of unknown causes a number of years after they married. Tommy and the stepson, Rolf, never seemed to mesh. And after Tommy went away to the Military Academy, Rolf and Jon had a big falling out. Rolf left home and never came back. He was an angry teenager then. The way I heard it, which may or may not be accurate, was that Rolf just walked out, no reason given. But there's always a reason, isn't there? Real or perceived. He was hell-bent on finding his 'real father,' whoever that was. I don't know if he ever found his father. Probably a casualty of the Second World War.

"Rolf never changed his last name despite the fact he was adopted by Mr. Jon. So maybe he did find the guy. And maybe that guy was part of the Italian Mafia."

"Here's a thought," Phil put in. "Jon traveled a lot after Rolf left, and Tommy was killed in one of our incessant little wars. Is it possible he had a love child somewhere? If it could be proved, with DNA or something, a natural child might take precedence over an adopted child in the absence of a will."

"Unlikely, Phil," Carol answered. "But worth a call to a probate lawyer. Maybe that's where this Jefferson Preston comes in. Lorie, how old do you think he might be?"

She thought about it. "My age probably. Mid to late twenties." The doctor quickly affirmed her estimate.

"About the right age bracket to be a grandchild of some degree," her aunt said thoughtfully, "if Jon weren't simply speaking gibberish."

Phil swore. "I think we have to consider everything up for grabs now, don't we? We probably should consult a lawyer about these things."

"First," her aunt answered, "we've got to chat with this man Lorie saved for us."

There was now no doubt in her mind that Jefferson Richard Preston and Jon Randolph were related, either by blood or by circumstance. Perhaps tomorrow would bring some answers.

How could she sleep? She wanted to see him now, to confirm he was still alive.

But Dr. Barnett had shown her the way to the guest room, and the bed was so comfortable, and she was so very tired. She stripped out of her clothes, slipped into the oversized T-shirt Carol had handed to her in lieu of her nightgown, sank into the bed, and snuggled under the coverlet. She would think on things.

CHAPTER 4

Saturday, July 19, 2014

Lorie awoke to the mouthwatering aromas of sizzling bacon and freshly brewed coffee. Her eyes popped open. She gazed around the unfamiliar room. All soft green, pink, quilted, pillow-spattered, and country-style, with century-old furniture and quaint framed pictures on the walls. Where in the universe was she?

She remembered with a start, pushed herself out of the pillows, and put her bare feet to the gleaming pine floorboards. The sun was up, slanting its golden rays through an open window. It was still early morning, quiet except for birds singing their hearts out in the surrounding woodlands and the rise and fall of a cicada chorus. She was eager to be up and about. In the large immaculate guest bathroom with its claw-foot tub and fat bath towels, she splashed water on her face. She dressed, pulling on jeans and a clean shirt, and ran a comb through her short, tousled hair. Quickly slipping her feet into her moccasins, she hurried through the wide hallway, spun down the stairs to the front hall, and from there made a one-eighty-degree turn into the kitchen.

Over two steaming coffee mugs, Dr. Philip Barnett and a much-refreshed version of Carol Kendall were engrossed in a grave discussion about the battle shaping up in Randolph City. They looked up as she entered.

"How is he?"

Phil smiled a bit quizzically. "Better than we had expected. Here, have a cup."

Lorie grabbed a mug and let him fill it. She seated herself at the table, eyes intent on the doctor.

"I've checked him out thoroughly," Phil told her. "He has scars and bruises all over his body, but he's in pretty good shape for all that. There's a fairly serious slash wound across his forehead that seems to have recently healed. We're wondering if that figures into his apparent amnesia. He's definitely been shot. We're thinking now it might have been a shotgun. Fragments of lead everywhere. A bullet went through his upper arm as well. Nicked a bone. No break. Lots of blood-letting, a few deep wounds in his side that needed stitches, but nothing lethal. He should be okay in a month or two if he takes it easy. Bruised ribs, no doubt. He'll be slowed down. Sure as hell. The danger is infection. We'll keep a close eye on him. This one has been around the block a few times. I'd guess he's a soldier in real life."

"That was my guess, too. Have you told the police?"

"We have," her aunt replied. "They'll be here to interview him this afternoon. In the meantime, they're still doing their investigation over at the convention center. They promised to give us a briefing when they're finished."

Lorie's mind had been prepared for tragedy. It seemed almost illogical that he was still living. "You're thinking the weapon was a shotgun? Wow, it seemed a whole lot worse than that to me. But what really puzzles me is why he was wearing a Confederate uniform."

Across the table, both faces registered shocked surprise. "You didn't tell us," Carol said into the silence.

"Oh," Lorie said, feeling she'd just drawn a blank. "Why didn't I? My first thought was that he was a reenactor who had gone missing from a sesquicentennial event. He seemed so worried about 'the Federals,' and he thought they were camped nearby. Then he showed a strong interest in Jon Randolph's name. By the time the emergency squad left, all I could think of was genealogy and discovering a link to Jon Randolph."

"A Confederate jacket?" Phil repeated. "Maybe there's an identifying mark on it somewhere. Or something in the pockets. We didn't find any ID in his trouser pockets."

"Does he remember anything?" Lorie asked.

"Only you." The doctor smiled. "You made a big impression on that young man. Let's go over to the clinic and talk with him. See how he is. If he's feeling better, we'll get him up and bring him back to the house for a good hearty breakfast. He looks like he could use some fattening up."

They took the doctor's red minivan, a conveyance rigged for a wheelchair. Made sense, Lorie thought…for an orthopedic clinic. The narrow road wound through shadowy woodlands and terminated in a fenced parking lot at the back side of the clinic.

"Mostly we do out-patient work with our soldier clients," the doctor said, holding open the heavy back door for his guests, who quickly entered the air-conditioned building. "But occasionally we need hospital beds for more seriously injured folk, so we have a few available. It was useful last night."

He led them through a maze of short hallways to a door that opened into a long brightly lit corridor. Halfway along the corridor, a muscular, balding young man in a white jacket sat outside a windowed door, reading a medical manual.

"Hi, Chris," Phil said. "How's our patient?"

The young paramedic looked up, smiled broadly when he saw them, and rose to his feet. "Hi, Doc, ladies. From what I can see, he's doing fine. Not talking much."

"We're thinking of taking him over to the house. Are his vitals stable enough?"

"For someone who's gone through what he has, I'd say he's in pretty good shape. Don't ask him to run any marathons in the next week or so."

"Thanks, Chris." Phil smiled at Lorie and her aunt as he knocked at the door. "Are you fit for company, son?" Hearing a soft positive response, they entered.

"My dark-haired angel!" His face lit with a smile. He was resting against pillows, partially propped up by the articulated hospital bed frame, wearing the ubiquitous patterned hospital gown, wrapped in a glow of light. Lorie blinked. There were no windows in this room to capture sunlight. Perhaps her eyes were more tired than she realized. She blinked again, and the perception was gone.

Still, she could not quite believe how different he looked this morning. His now clean-shaven face was deeply tanned, his hair sun-bleached to near white. A pale scar cut across his forehead. It was the eyes, though, that once again grabbed her attention. Eyes as blue as the sky. In a striking face. She walked slowly to the bed and stood beside it, focusing on those eyes, that face. "How do you feel?"

"I feel much better. Now." His soft, deep voice was musical with the accent of the south. His gaze never left hers. "Thank you for finding me, Lorena Manning."

"I made you a promise. Did you hear me?"

"I heard you," he said softly, "and I never once doubted you!"

She didn't know how to respond. Tears were forming already. When he held out his right hand, she took it. It was warm. Last night, when he had caught her arm, that hand had been cold as death itself.

Now, however, he didn't seem to want to let her go. Very gently, with a smile, she pulled away.

"We brought you something to wear." Phil Barnett opened the large shopping bag he had carried from the house. "My tallest son left these in his dresser. I think they might fit you." He pulled out a worn pair of jeans, a belt, and a yellow polo shirt. "There's some skivvies in there for you, too. And some deck shoes and tube socks. If they fit, they're yours. Let's step out, ladies, and let Chris get the young man out of bed. What do you think, son? Do you need a wheelchair?"

He turned to Lorie as if he were seeking her advice. A little flustered, she nodded. He turned to the doctor and nodded as well.

"Thank you again," he said softly.

"Well, my word!" Carol said after the door had closed behind them. She whistled. "I think that's just about the finest looking dude I've seen since I was fifteen and fixated on movie stars."

Phil laughed. "He cleaned up well, I'd say."

Lorie couldn't comment. It was the eyes that drew her. So much was in those eyes. Most of it questions, she thought. And she had plenty of questions to ask him. As soon as the wheelchair and patient were secured in the doctor's van, he turned the car onto the country road toward his home.

Lorie sat next to Jefferson Preston in the shortened van seat. She could see his face in the rearview mirror. She half closed her eyes so he wouldn't know how carefully she was watching his face. He was trying for "stoic," she thought. But she could sense fear.

As they drove on, however, fear faded first to unease and, as he gazed outside the windows of the van into the forest surrounding them, to curiosity. Finally, as the doctor turned the van onto the main road and her patient had a broader view of the surrounding countryside, his attention indicated true excitement.

"Who are you?" Lorie asked him quietly.

The blue eyes focused now on her. "I'm not sure."

"You told me 'Jefferson Richard Preston.'"

"That has always been my name." He spoke very carefully, trying purposefully, she thought, to moderate the broad Southern drawl she had heard in his voice before. "I don't know if that tells you who I am. I am going to have to think about it myself."

She fell silent, reluctant to ask what exactly he meant, a little uneasy about what he might conclude. He resumed his gaze out the window.

"There," he said suddenly, peering through a break in the trees. "I thought I saw it. Kennesaw Mountain."

"Right, son," the doctor replied. "My property lies close to the national park. I'm relieved to see you're beginning to remember where you are."

"*National* park?" Jeff repeated softly, emphasizing the word "national" as if the term were an unfamiliar concept to him. Lorie ticked off another anomaly. They were beginning to pile up. But to what end? She didn't want to ask...not right now, at least, when she thought he was finally beginning to come to terms with reality. As the talk went on, he seemed to relax.

At last, Phil turned the van into the driveway of his lovely home. Moments later, at the touch of a button, the wheelchair was lowered from the van. The doctor pushed his visitor up a wheelchair ramp Lorie had not noticed in the dark of night, around a spacious porch and through wide front doors. "Breakfast before anything else," he said. "Let's stoke up before we get too involved in business."

"What shall we call you?" Carol asked the visitor.

His smile glowed. "My friends call me Jeff."

"Jeff it is," the doctor said cheerfully. "And I can tell by the way you talk, you're a native Georgian. I'm Phil, this is Carol, and you already know Lorie." He busied himself at the stove, and in only a few moments, a hearty breakfast appeared on the table, delicately scrambled eggs to go with the rasher of bacon already there, crisp toast with softened butter, a coffee cake pulled from the warming oven, orange juice in stumpy little glasses, and fragrant coffee with cream and sugar to suit any taste.

The conversation was general and cordial: weather, hospital gossip, amusing anecdotes—carefully, Lorie noted, avoiding any mention of the trouble brewing in Randolph City. Jeff Preston ate as if he had not eaten for a week and then lingered, almost worshipfully, over a large mug of coffee, smelling it, sipping it, turning the mug around and around in his long slender hands. He remained for the most part, however, silent, watchful, intensely interested in the continuing banter.

"Jeff," Carol finally said directly to him, "Lorie says you were dressed in a Confederate uniform. Do you remember why?" When he didn't answer, she pressed him. "The sesquicentennial of the Battle of Atlanta is coming up in short order. We're thinking you might be here doing work as a reenactor. Does that ring a bell?"

"Sesquicentennial?" he repeated. "What is that?"

"The one hundred fiftieth anniversary of an event," Carol said evenly.

Under the table, Lorie felt him grasping for her hand. She took it and he hung on with an almost desperate grip.

"One hundred fifty years?" Although he was trying to suppress it, she could not miss anguish in his voice. One more oddity to add to the others.

"I don't want to press you, but it just seems likely that you might be part of the celebration. One of the Confederate actors. Perhaps you were injured in a practice battle."

"No," he said. "I am not an actor. Nor a reenactor. I would never practice at war as a game—war is not a game!"

Phil looked at Carol. She nodded. "We have to talk. Please excuse us for a while. Lorie, why don't you take Jeff out to the porch to get some air before it gets too hot to be outside?" She waved toward the back door. "That porch is screened. It's a lovely place to sit."

It was clearly a dismissal. They were going to discuss Jefferson Preston and try to make sense of his presence—make some phone calls. He needed to be shuttled out of the way for a while.

"Do you want to be pushed in the chair?" Lorie asked him. "Or do you feel up to walking?"

"I can walk." With Jeff gripping her arm, they went slowly out the back door onto the spacious wraparound porch with its spectacular view of Kennesaw Mountain.

"A great battle took place there," Lorie said. "Perhaps you know of it. When it looked like the Rebels might win, the Yankees just waltzed around them and on into Atlanta."

"I wonder if it were as easy as all that," he said slowly, and she realized he had been consciously suppressing his soft accent until just now.

"Then you do know of it."

He shook his head. "I heard people talking. Do you know where I might find something, an account, a book...to tell me what happened here?"

"Of course," Lorie said. "Once I retrieve my computer, you can search out anything you want to know."

She directed him to a porch swing, and when he was seated, she sat beside him, careful not to make direct contact. As they rocked in silence, he reached for her hand, drew it to his lips briefly, and looked into her eyes. "I am very much a stranger here, Miss Lorie Manning. I need your help." The distinctive Georgia drawl was strong now.

A little shaken, she finally managed to say, "I'll be glad to help you in any way I can, Jeff."

"There may well be danger."

For a long moment, she was silent. Then she smiled. "If that's the case, I may have to take my promise back. If there's any hint of danger..." Gently she retrieved her hand and finished the sentence, "I faint." His eyebrows had raised. "It's true." She looked away, trying to suppress the giggle she knew was bubbling up the more she thought about it, but it slipped out, and finally, she told him what had happened to her three times while she was trying to be an emergency room nurse.

The skin around his eyes crinkled, and then, although she knew he was trying to hold it back, laughter erupted. She joined in. Her odd malady, the affliction that had caused so much upheaval in her life, just didn't seem that important anymore.

"Guess I'll have to think of something else to do," she said, finally taking a deep breath. "Like skydiving or mountain climbing."

"I understand mountain climbing, but what is skydiving?"

"With parachutes. From airplanes."

His face remained expressionless.

"Up in the sky?" Smiling, she pointed upward.

"Oh!" Chagrin, and then an expression of concern. "Lorie, you are going to find me as much of a puzzle for a while as I find you. Will you indulge me in those peculiarities?"

"Peculiarities?"

"Look over there." He pointed to the three cars sitting in the driveway. "I don't know what to call them."

"The cars? The black one's a Lincoln Town Car. The little blue one is a Ford Escort. I'm afraid I don't know what brand the red minivan is. Maybe another Ford. They all look alike to me. They're either trucks or jellybeans."

"Cars." He chuckled. "Trucks. Jellybeans? Do you know how to work them?"

"Yes."

"Could you show me?"

"Sure. I'll ask Carol if I can borrow the Escort. Any particular place you want to go? Kennesaw Mountain? Atlanta?"

He hesitated. "Do you know the town of Roswell?"

"I know that it's not that far from Marietta," she said. "I'm a good map reader. Anything in particular you want to see?"

He was quiet for a time. "I'll know when I get there."

"Good!" It sounded like he was beginning to remember. Something. She guessed it might be difficult to recall car brands. She couldn't tell one car from another herself.

But skydiving? She wasn't clear as to why it made her so uneasy that he didn't seem to know what skydiving was. Why the heck had she mentioned it in the first place? Peculiarities? Well, this could be an interesting experience, she thought, dealing with his peculiarities. The intrigue won out.

CHAPTER 5

Permission was easily obtained, with the proviso that they be back before their two o'clock appointment with the detectives. "Don't let him tire, Lorie," the doctor warned. "And on your way back, pop by the South Wind if you will and pick up your luggage. It's infinitely safer if you folks stay here with me. They probably have Carol's license plate number traced by now, and your aunt's connection to Jon Third is no secret."

Carol nodded, her expression grim. "Keep a sharp eye out," she added. "If you see anything suspicious, don't even stop. Call the police immediately."

Lorie felt a jolt of the same fear that had caught her up the night before. "I'll keep my cell phone handy," she replied quietly, slipping it into her pocket.

He was standing beside the Escort when she came back outside. He watched eagerly as she unlocked the car doors. He settled himself into the passenger seat, looking around with great interest.

"Put the seatbelt on," she said, pointing. He found it and drew it across his chest, then sat a moment, faltering, seemingly wondering what to do with it. Remembering that his arm had been injured, she hastened to assist him with the latch.

She folded the big map expertly to the Atlanta-Marietta area and handed it to him. "You're the navigator today," she said. "This is my first time in Georgia, so you can help me with the route."

He examined the colorful paper with its multitude of small place names. His eyes widened as they moved from one side of the state to the other. She pointed to their approximate location. "Okay," he said, "now I see." He moved his finger. "Here is where I would like to go, if you don't mind." It was an area somewhere east of Roswell.

"If this jaunt will bring your memory back, sir, I am at your service."

He was watching her intently as she started the car, backed out of the driveway, and headed northeast on a gently winding two-lane road. "How fast were we going?" he asked a short time later as they were paused at the entrance to the Interstate.

"About forty miles an hour. The speed limit on the big highway is posted at seventy." As they entered the flow of traffic, she noticed his quick, eager smile.

Everything about him, as he had said, was puzzling to her. Perhaps not this! She stepped on the gas and saw his eyes light up. Grinning broadly, he turned back to watch the scenery flash past—large houses and small, occasional billboards, farm fields, wooded lots. Conversation was minimal. She was surprised until she realized he was once more concentrating on the map. Shortly he pointed to a sign. "Roswell Road."

She turned off onto a two-lane road. "Where from here?"

He looked back at the map. "Northeast."

"Into town?"

"No, several miles farther. I'll tell you where to make the turns."

She followed his directions. Still there was silence in the car, her passenger following the map with intense concentration. "Slower," he said once and, a moment later, pointed to an upcoming intersection. "Turn right onto that road."

It was a gravel road leading past open fields into what seemed an otherwise unbroken forest. Though the sun was high in the sky by now, little sunlight had made its way through the foliage. She cut back on the speed and lowered her window. The cool air seemed pleasantly fresh. The birds were rejoicing. It was a lonely place, she thought, but quite beautiful.

"Are you sure this is the way you want to go?" she finally asked. They had traveled at least two miles from the highway, and the gravel road appeared to be petering out. Tall grass almost hid the tracks. No one had been on this road for a very long time.

He nodded, not speaking.

Lorie kept the car moving but at increasingly reduced speeds as the roadway effectively disappeared. When one of the wheels dropped into a shallow hole she'd missed seeing, she began to worry about mufflers and other obscure car parts and even more about her companion's sense of direction. After another jolt, she stepped on the brakes. "This can't be the right way."

"It is decidedly the right way—and it's not much farther. Do you mind walking, Lorie?"

He now seemed so determined. She knew she could not refuse. If the key to refreshing his memory were here, it was a chance worth pursuing.

"Lead on," she said.

The old roadway was rough. Hiking boots would have been more appropriate than her flexible driving shoes, but she didn't want to go back to the car to get them. When she stumbled, Jeff took her arm.

She straightened up, saying abruptly, "You shouldn't be doing this at all, Jeff. You can't be well enough for all this exertion."

"With you beside me, I feel quite fit," he said, sounding now relatively cheerful. "You can pick me up if I stumble, and I will do you the same favor with great pleasure." Giving her a big grin, he turned back to the road. Sensing it would be futile to argue, she fell in behind.

"It's not much farther," he said a moment later. "See there. The gateposts."

Two stone columns stood in the midst of nowhere, crumbled and worn and almost hidden by heavy vines. A sign was posted on one. When they came nearer, Lorie read it aloud, her voice rising with surprise. "'No Trespassing. Property of J. T. Randolph.'"

She stared at Jeff Preston. There was no way he could have known about this remote place unless he had been here before. He was standing motionless, staring intently past the gateway. What was he looking for?

There were signs of a trail leading into the deep woods beyond but no indication of recent use. He turned to her, blue eyes pleading.

Relieved, she grinned, feeling the excitement build. "I wouldn't miss it for the world. If you're still up for this," she added cautiously. Good grief, no one healed that fast! Sensing her growing reluctance, he turned and began to walk, letting her know by his actions that he would not be dissuaded. She followed.

They kept to the pathway as best they could, pushing through brush and tangled vines, painstakingly circling fallen tree limbs wanting to block the way. When Lorie wondered whether the trail had disappeared, Jeff Preston pointed it out with no hesitation. His stride was one of purpose, his expression now surprisingly grim. It would have been a most pleasant hike, in fact, except for his haste and his increasing show of concern. He didn't seem to have any pain or discomfort now, nor, rather surprisingly, did he seem aware of the beauty surrounding him!

To Lorie, the beauty was mesmerizing. She paused. Great pines swept upward like cathedral spires reaching for the sky. Morning sunshine shafted shimmering gold across leaves and spiky needles. Ground squirrels scurried about in the fragrant rust-red dirt of the forest floor, hunting cones and seeds, darting quickly away when they sensed the presence of intruders. The air was cool, and the pervasive aromatic fragrance gave Lorie a growing sense of physical contentment she had not had since childhood. Everything sparked with life. Lorie looked ahead, saw the pathway quite clearly. He was far ahead of her, and she hurried to catch up.

Suddenly they came out of the shade of the trees into the hot glare of sunlight. A massive clearing lay before them, scattered with bushes and brambles in sharp contrast to the surrounding woodlands. Lorie paused, shocked.

"It was a peach orchard once," he said softly. "The sheep liked to come in for a nibble." He stood quite still, as if perplexed. Breathing hard from the unaccustomed exercise, Lorie wondered, in contrast, how her companion still seemed so fresh.

A dark cloud crossed the sun, and in its dull shadow, the field began to seem a dismal place, out of joint somehow in the greater scheme of things. A vague depression touched her. And what was that sound she was hearing?

It was a rustling. A moaning. Tree branches high above were swaying. A storm blowing up? Lorie had seen many such storms in Illinois. She was scared of them. They always left damage behind. Gray shadows through the trees seemed somehow darker. The damp, motionless air below the tight forest canopy now seemed oppressive, even menacing. There was something very odd about this place.

Jeff Preston was now far ahead of her on the forest path. He had paused to let her catch up, but for the first time, she questioned her willingness to follow him. He was watching her now with an expression she simply could not read.

She really didn't know him at all, did she? Why had that thought not occurred to her earlier? Quietly he said, "It's not much farther."

What wasn't "much farther?"

She moved slowly toward him. He took her arm, helped her through the weeds, across downed trees. A hedgerow suddenly brought them to a complete halt—tall tangled bushes concealing what might be beyond. He skirted the shrubbery until he found a ragged opening. Parting the foliage, tearing some of it out of the way with a show of strength she could scarcely believe, he passed through and held the branches apart so she could follow.

As the foliage fell into place behind her, the noise of the wind diminished—ceased altogether. In the profound silence, Jeff Preston stood absolutely still.

At the end of a long rutted roadway, overgrown walls rose in tall ragged patterns. A century and a half ago, Lorie knew, without asking, those walls had defined a gracious brick home spanned at either end by broad chimneys. Shafts of weedy grass stood quite still at the base of those crumbling walls as if they were expecting something to happen. A partial window cut through one side, its blank eye open to desolate ruins beyond of similar brick and timber outbuildings.

Eddies of air began to whistle down the open chimney shafts. Tree branches above and around the ruins swept forward and back, scraping against each other, rasping, moaning. The soft sound reminded Lorie disturbingly of human voices crying out in distress. She stood motionless, increasingly uneasy—a bit frightened, perhaps.

A puzzled voice, soft. "Who would have done this?"

She turned to him, and all questions crumbled. She could tell he had expected to find something here. But not this! The light that had been to this point animating his eyes, was shuttered. "What is this place?" She said it very quietly, not certain she really wanted to know.

"Riverside Plantation." He remained motionless as the wind continued its strange dissonant song. It was as if he were listening to voices she could not quite hear.

During the wholeness of this expedition, she had not felt fear—until now. "Talk to me, Jeff. Please."

He spoke without looking at her. The words were chilling, coming in a dull monotone. "I sent Sara here. Captain Manning and the boy told me they would bring her here."

The wind rose then, wailing, sighing, filling the air with a deep sadness. In her mind, Lorie repeated the name he had spoken. Sara: the pivot point of the joint family tree.

With a sense of rising panic, Lorie realized that everything she had learned about this man was beginning to coalesce. There was only one more question to ask: "Who is Sara to you, Jeff?" She said it very softly, fearing the answer. When it came, she didn't quite know how to handle it.

"My sister."

Shivers rose on her arms.

"I left her with Captain Manning," he continued softly, to her even greater distress. "I asked him to bring her here to our father. She was already in premature labor, and she would have had help here." He was quiet again, then said softly, "She met fire and death not once that night, but twice…at homes that should both have been safe havens for her." Tears were rolling freely across his cheeks.

She wished she did not know what he was talking about. "Jeff," she tried briefly, hoping for the return of sanity, "the Yankees burned this place a hundred fifty years ago!"

"The general ordered his troops not to destroy personal homes." He said it forcefully. "General Sherman knew Riverside was my father's home!" The expression on his face hardened. "The Yankees would not have done this. It was someone much nearer home."

Again the hair rose on Lorie's neck and arms. She spoke very softly, with hesitation, trying hard to bring his words back to sanity. "Sara who?"

His eyes flickered, turned to hers. They were shuttered. Dark. Then a light sparked as if he had come quickly out of a trance. "Sara Preston. Randolph. You know of her. Her name was on the big family tree you were building. What can you tell me about her?"

There it was! He was back in this world now with a logical answer. He'd seen the family tree posters she was creating for Carol while he was looking around her room at the conference center. They'd been right there in plain sight. "What do you want to know about her?"

"Whatever you have gleaned. Anything."

She spoke quietly. "Sara Preston was Jon Randolph's grandmother. She had two husbands. The first was Jon Randolph Sr. He died in the Civil War. Quite young."

A ragged sigh issued from deep within him. "And the second husband?"

"That would be Marshal Manning. The first. The ancestor my brother is named for."

Jeff Preston turned away from her suddenly, his face buried in his hands. She saw his shoulders heaving and again heard deep emotional sobs. How could she help him? When he turned back to her, tears were still streaming down his cheeks. "Sara survived." To her surprise, it was relief resonating in his deep voice now. "Thanks to Captain Manning, she and Jon's child lived. What of my father?"

Stunned, now unable to speak, Lorie simply shook her head.

"I am beginning to discover why I am here, Lorena Manning." His words broke. When he reached out for her, she didn't resist. He held her for many minutes, weeping openly, his tears blending into her hair.

She wrapped her arms around his tightly bandaged torso, smelling the freshness of him, feeling the life that was there. She pressed her cheek against his chest. A heart beat strongly inside him. With quiet but desperate sobs, his lungs were pulling in the fresh aromatic air of that forest wilderness and breathing it out onto her cheek.

He was solid, real—no more a ghost than she was. It was his words that were confusing. Or irrational. It was obvious he thought he was a Confederate soldier resurrected from 150 years ago. What should she say to him? What *could* she say? It had to be something helpful!

She remained silent.

At last he released her and stepped back, his eyes glistening, his cheeks still damp. In silence he led her to a low moss-cushioned brick wall facing the old ruins. He seated himself and waited for her to join him. She sat, too, keeping a respectful distance.

Again she gazed at the old ruins. It was the setting, the odd weather, his injuries; everything had combined to affect him adversely. Perhaps his mind was projecting him into a scenario befitting the history of this place. In any case, there was no question now of his relationship with Jon Randolph. He was clearly not an outsider.

The sun had returned, the clouds had passed, and the breeze was gentle, only a sigh in the treetops. Birds chirped and warbled as they circled the tall chimneys and their nests inside. Why had everything seemed so frightening to her when she first came through into the clearing.

"It's beautiful here," she said softly. "Even if it's just a ruin."

"It was very beautiful once." He wiped at his eyes before he turned to her. He moved closer and captured her hands. "Lorena Manning, I know you don't want to hear this. But honesty between us is paramount." He waited. Finally, he said into her silence, "Did you hear them…speaking to me?"

Startled, Lorie stared into his face. The expression there held her motionless. His hands tightened on hers. A tremble of confusion, and fear, caught at her once again and constricted her throat. "It was the wind," she whispered.

"Voices…telling me that a force intending great evil is gathering strength. It tried to destroy my family in the past, but your ancestor intervened, and for nearly one hundred fifty years that evil was held at bay. If we cannot find and unmask the people behind this conspiracy, Lorie, everyone and everything my family cared about will be destroyed."

She stared at him. Whoever had attacked him had done serious damage not only to his body but to his mind. Especially to his mind!

It was pretty obvious that he was part of Jon Randolph's family. But he had obviously also suffered brain trauma along with the rest of his injuries. Until that was taken care of, it would be very difficult to see where he fit into the whole picture.

She looked up into his solemn face. If they could wait until his body and his brain were repaired, the delusions would disappear. Until then, she would do whatever it took to protect this vulnerable man from further harm.

But given what had just happened, she thought, just a glimmer of a thought, what if…No, that was crazy. But what if…? Darn it! That was not even a possibility!

It would sure be interesting, though. Wouldn't it?

She pushed that thought aside. *Pull yourself together*, she said silently and turned to the most important task she could think of right now—getting him back to a safe place.

CHAPTER 6

The hike back to the car was made in absolute silence. Lorie's mind was working overtime, reasoning, wondering, rejecting, calculating. She could hardly focus on time or place. When occasionally she stumbled, he was there, his hand supporting her.

Was he crazy? Or was she? Because against all logic, against all the training she had in the natural sciences, she really wanted to believe him!

It could only be a delusion. He needed medical, if not psychiatric, care. Still, there had to be something behind the delusion if only access to family histories.

Then they were at the car, and as she reached out the key to unlock the driver's door, he came to stand beside her. She turned to face him, and he put his hands gently on her shoulders. "Do you believe me?" he said very softly. "If you do not, I am lost in your world, with hidden evil all around us."

She was quiet for a long time, looking up into his luminous blue eyes. "What makes you think there is evil?"

"I realize now I would not be here except for the evil. I was brought here to join you in the battle against that evil!"

Lorie shook her head, trying again to resolve her thoughts, wondering what to say. And then she knew. This she could say without equivocation. She took a deep breath. "Jeff Preston, I promise with every fiber of my being that we will stand together against this evil."

He sighed. "Thank you, Lorena Manning."

"Don't thank me yet," she said, almost under her breath. "I'm not sure I'm that reliable."

"Lorie, Lorie, Lorie," he said, suddenly with laughter in his voice. "You are so incredibly honest! I promise...if you faint, I will catch you and put you back on your feet."

She felt a little ashamed of herself for allowing him to think she really believed him. "Let's get going. Don't forget your interview with the police."

"I think we will find out more from them than they from us."

She glanced at him, surprised. That thought had not occurred to her, but he was right. Let the police do their job, and perhaps some answers could be found. The benefits of reality!

She had turned the car and was coaxing it carefully along the rough roadway when he asked the question. "How did you know about Sara Preston?"

"I pulled her name up on my computer last night."

There was a long silence. "I have no idea what you mean."

"It's obvious you saw her name on my chart. Didn't you?" She thought about it. Perhaps his memory would come back when she showed him the laptop. "Wait till we get back to the South Wind."

She could scarcely endure the silent, urgent ride back to the hotel.

Lorie parked the car under the office porte cochére. "Wait here," she told her passenger. "We're checking out."

With her credit card, she paid the bill to a polite but indifferent young man who didn't seem to care one way or another that the life-or-death emergency which had occurred the night before had originated in the suite she shared with her aunt. When she told him she would leave the key cards in the suite, he simply nodded. On leaving the office, she scanned the parking areas for dark vans. To her great relief, the preponderance of parked cars remaining in the back parking lot was police vehicles, and in the distance, at the edge of the ravine and beyond the yellow crime scene tape, she could see the hustle of active police presence.

The room facing onto the pool had not been disturbed since she and Carol had left it. She checked her watch. Noon. Detectives would be meeting with them at 2:00 p.m. at the doctor's house. She'd see to it that she and the man in her charge weren't late getting there, but there were a few things she had to find out first. Privately.

Jeff joined her in the room and stood to one side as she quickly packed Carol's bag and her own.

She didn't realize until she pulled the blood-soaked sheets and pillowcases out of the closet where she had dumped them the night before that somehow a very heavy packet the size of a notebook had gotten caught in the jumble. She worked it out of the still damp linens and looked at it. It was lumpy, wrapped in what seemed to be black oilcloth, and tied securely with a cord. Carol had brought a lot of old books and documents with her, but Lorie didn't recall having seen this one before.

She thought about it for a minute. "I bet this is yours," she said, turning to Jeff.

At his perfunctory nod, she slipped it into one of her aunt's tote bags. The police would definitely want a look.

Identification was forthcoming, she bet, and it wouldn't have anything to do with ghosts.

"Back in a minute," she then said to Jeff, who was trying hard to stay out of her determined way. Hoping not to attract undue attention, she layered everything into the opened hatchback, secured the huge family-tree bulletin board atop everything else, and rejoined him inside. She shut the door and slipped the lock chain into its slot.

She had left the laptop on the table. She showed it to him. "Computer." She flipped it open, hit the on switch and, whirling moments later, clicked onto the genealogy program.

Seated now at the table beside her, Jeff watched silently. She typed the code that would activate the family tree and turned the machine so he could see the monitor images more clearly. "There's my name. There's my date of birth. Here's my mom and dad, here's my grandpa Henry, my great-grandpa Robert, my great-great-grandpa Harrison, and my great-great-great-grandpa Marshal Manning. It says Colonel Marshal Manning, so he must have seen some service." He looked at her, silent, questions ready to be asked. But not yet.

"Here's Sara Preston," Lorie said, clicking on the name.

"Where are her parents?"

"See this blinking symbol? It means someone has entered information on her. Let's see what it says." She activated the graphic. Names unfolded on the monitor. "Isaac Preston is her father. He died on July 18, 1864." She heard a quick intake of breath and turned to the man seated beside her. Words crumbled on her tongue. Isaac had died on the same day his son had disappeared and most likely perished. Jeff had seen the dates already. His eyes were closed, hands clenched. He seemed once more on the verge of weeping. Lorie saw the ruined plantation house in her mind's eye.

She knew now without a doubt the date of its destruction!

A sharp jolt of awareness swirled around her, almost overwhelmed her. She sat back, staring into darkness, breathing very fast. This man thought he was the real Jefferson Richard Preston. She had just informed him casually, as if it were nothing of note, of his father's death—in his frame of reference that was less than twenty-four hours before! How would she feel to be told that everyone in her family, everyone she knew, her childhood home, her whole world as she had known it, had vanished in the blink of an eye?

More tragic yet, getting a sense of what had transpired on the actual day of destruction might prove to be even worse. She closed her eyes. If he really were the person he thought he was... She shook her head sharply. *Don't you be going irrational now.* She said the words silently. Someone had to remain sane.

She heard him speak then, very softly. "His wife was Rachel Brooke. She died in 1850."

"Seven children," Lorie continued, trying to get past the moment, focusing on the monitor, stumbling a little over the names. "William, Jefferson..." She stopped speaking, unable to continue!

"Will was the oldest." Jeff cleared his throat and took a deep breath. "Born in 1834. Died in 1850."

"Oh dear God," Lorie said very softly, wanting desperately now to protect him from the names on the diagram. "It's showing that five of these children died during the same year their mother died. There must be a mistake here. Sometimes people get careless with their dates. Matilda and Susanna—"

"Mattie was twelve. Susie was almost eleven. Tommy was seven. Carl was five. It was an unnamed contagion. Deliberately brought from Africa to destroy my family."

She looked up at him with increasing distress. Who would know these things other than someone who had been there? She turned abruptly back to the monitor. "Sara Anna Preston. Look, she lived until 1936."

"And her brother?" Jeff asked softly. "What date is recorded for Jefferson Richard Preston?"

Not looking at him, she said under her breath, "You already know."

"One more thing." His voice was deep, harsh. "Sara's first husband, Jon Randolph. Does it give a date for his death as well?"

"May 5, 1864. The note says: 'Probably killed in the Wilderness of Virginia.'"

She could sense anger rising. She would ask him about it later, not now. Please not now. But he didn't hear her silent plea.

"The letter Sara got was clearly not from Jon." Though they were soft, his very precise words expressed rage. "Someone meant all along to kill Sara. And Moses." The fierce expression on his face set firm. "They didn't reckon on Father having enough good sense left to send Rastus to find me. And the captain…Captain Manning and his young healer…these villains could never have predicted their presence!" He moaned softly then as if he had faced something so terrible he couldn't press it out of his mind, and he rubbed a weary hand across his eyes.

All Lorie could think was that she was grateful she hadn't fainted. Or burst into uncontrollable tears. She felt suddenly overwhelmed. "Let's get back to Phil's house. After the police tell us everything we need to know, we've got a lot to talk about."

They reached the old farmhouse in time to sit down to a lovely delayed lunch with her aunt and the genial doctor. A fresh fruit salad was offered, a savory omelet laced with fragrant herbs, and sweetened iced tea. Lorie and Jeff Preston ate ravenously. Neither spoke, except in generalities, about the very long journey they had made. As Carol was clearing off the table, a black car pulled into the driveway.

"Company," she said. "I'll start a pot of coffee."

Phil Barnett brought three men into the kitchen, pulled up more chairs, and offered seats around the big table. Cups were distributed and hot brew accepted.

Detectives Alan Macdonald and Dean Harris, decked out in suits and ties, were new to Lorie. But the compact, good-looking young man with a scattering of freckles across his face looked quite familiar. Today he was wearing tan slacks and a black knit shirt under a tweed sports jacket. He held out a hand to Lorie. "Randy Ross. I met you last night."

"I recognize the freckles." She grinned. "Thanks for picking me up."

"I actually caught you before you hit the ground," he said with a chuckle. "Any time!"

She noted Jeff Preston following the exchange with intense interest.

"Randy wanted to tag along," Detective Macdonald said. He was a middle-aged man, trim, with intelligent hazel eyes. Sparse hair was plastered to a high forehead, and the remainder of the hair was dark and neatly cut. He smiled brightly at the young policeman and grinned at Lorie. "Aside from the obvious, I'll let him tell you why."

"Spooky stuff," Detective Harris said lightly with a big grin. His manner was convivial, friendly, calculated to put people at ease, Lorie thought. He was quite black, tall, and probably a little more overweight than was good for him, with grizzled white hair. Mature he might be, but Lorie could see he was solid muscle where it counted.

At Harris's mild jibe, Randy Ross looked a little embarrassed. "I'll fill you in later."

The two detectives got down to business quickly, questioning Jeff Preston as to his reasons for being at the South Wind and trying to elicit any recollections he might have of what had happened to him.

"I really wish I could help you." He frowned. "But except for the occasional pain, this whole world remains a mystery to me."

At least he knows to keep quiet about the delusions, Lorie thought with relief.

"Doctor?" Macdonald turned to Phil Barnett. "What can you tell us about his wounds?"

"There's the scar on his forehead, obviously recent, which may be related to the amnesia. The gun…possibly a shotgun. Not like any wound I've seen before. I don't know what the cartridges might have been loaded with. I've kept the fragments for you to look at. If he weren't the athlete he obviously is, he'd be laying in a bed over at my clinic, still on life support. The arm wound is from another type of gun. I have that bullet, too."

"Have you checked to see if any reenactments are taking place in the area?" Lorie asked the officers.

Harris pulled out a notebook and turned the pages with quick, efficient fingers. "Smart of you to think of that. Lots of Civil War reenactment groups are pulling themselves together for the big one. It's almost time to refight the Battle of Atlanta. Related activities going on everywhere. We're putting out inquiries. Not getting many answers. No 'missing person' reports on lost participants. Not yet, anyway."

"We haven't found anything current down there in the ravine," Macdonald said. "All we're gathering up is a lot of genuine old Civil War stuff nobody ever stumbled across before. Fragments of shells. Occasional spent cartridges. A water canteen, Federal issue. Must have been a lot of activity in that area during the Federal's push to Atlanta." He turned to Jeff. "We brought the uniform with us, sir. We have a number of questions to ask you about it."

Harris had gone out to the car, and now he reappeared, bearing a large box which he placed on the quickly cleared table. He opened it and removed the first item. "Long gray jacket. Confederate cavalry officer. One star on each side of the collar denoting the rank of Major. Many pockets inside and out. All empty." He laid it carefully across the box and looked hard at Jeff. "Do you remember where you got this jacket, Mr. Preston? Our people tell us it seems to be a pretty good reproduction. Maybe even authentic. Hand stitched. Possibly taken from an old trunk or borrowed from a museum."

Jeff shook his head. "I'm sorry." Lorie breathed a sigh of relief.

"What about the wool shirt?" Harris held up several tattered pieces of soft gray cloth.

"I cut it with fingernail scissors till I could rip it apart, in case you're wondering why it looks kind of like a dusting rag," Lorie said apologetically.

With a grin, Detective Macdonald returned the shirt remnants and the jacket to their evidence bags. He looked at the doctor. "Trousers?"

"Over at the clinic," Phil Barnett put in. "And some skivvies that smacked of army issue, although I didn't see any ID markings on it. We can get everything for you."

Next, Macdonald pulled the sheathed saber out of his box. "What they won't do for authenticity." After donning thin latex gloves, he pulled the blade free of its sheath and looked hard at Jeff. "This isn't a toy, son."

"No," Jeff replied softly. "It is not a toy."

"A belt. I guess the saber was attached to this." The officer lifted it from the box. "And knee-high boots. That's the lot."

"Cavalry boots. I hadn't seen these before." Randy Ross, hands now gloved as well, reached for the boots. He turned them over and over, examining each one carefully. He whistled. "Whatta you know?"

"What?" Detective Harris looked up sharply.

"Custom-made. Union officer's boots. Authentic, I'd say. In pretty good shape considering their age. Nobody makes these anymore. Probably from a museum. Look at this. Straight toes. A hundred fifty years ago, toes for both feet were cut exactly the same, square. Over time, with wear, they kind of began to look shaped. These seem to have been well used. If they match our new Jeff Preston's feet, we've got a shot at tracing them backward to the source and maybe finding a purchaser's name."

"What makes you think they're not reproductions?" Harris asked.

"This mark here. The manufacturer." Ross showed it to the detective. "I've done a little reenacting myself." He looked up, frowning. "This isn't such a good thing. Damn! In fact, it's pretty bad news, now that I think of it! We've got a Confederate officer here wearing Union boots. Unless it's just a slip-up in costuming, someone who shouldn't know maybe knows just a little bit too much."

"What do they know?" Jeff asked quietly.

"That our Confederate Jefferson Preston was really a Yankee."

Harris looked up sharply at Randy Ross. "A spy?"

"A loyal long-time Union man, working undercover against secessionists," Ross said firmly. "One of the early abolitionists, Dean. Someday I'll tell you all about him. But first we've got to figure out who this Jefferson Preston is."

"We've found another clue," Lorie put in hastily. "When we went back to the motel, I found a packet that must have fallen out of Jeff's inside pocket when I took his jacket off." She hastened to retrieve it from Carol's luggage. "May I?" she asked Jeff, and when he nodded, she handed it to Detective Macdonald.

Still with gloved hands, the detective untied the cord and began to unwrap the oilcloth. From inside the first fold he pulled a large water-weathered card. He looked at it and in grim silence handed it to Randy Ross, who took a long hard look and turned to Jeff with a frown on his face.

"'Jefferson Richard Preston,'" Ross read softly. "'Riverside Plantation, Roswell, Georgia.' Damn! This is beginning to look pretty much like you were targeted, mister."

Lorie felt a chill creep across her. This was not going as she had hoped.

Macdonald unfolded the oilcloth a little further and whistled. "Look here." From a tin waterproof container, he drew out a beautiful pocket watch, its gold case ornately engraved. A gold watch chain hung from it. "Engraved initials. JRP."

Ross sighed deeply. "Someone has gone to a lot of trouble."

"And lots of cash here," Macdonald went on, holding it up. "Somebody robbed a bank!" He fanned a sheaf of bills out across the table.

Harris's hearty laugh broke the tension. "Georgia issue. Confederate money. I don't think that's legal tender anymore, folks."

"But wait," Macdonald went on. "There's more." He snapped open a leather bag he had brought from the deep interior of the oilcloth. Coins spilled out onto the table. A long low whistle issued from his lips, echoed by Ross and the doctor. "Maybe the Confederate money isn't legal, but this is. Or used to be.

"Good God! A fortune here in gold. Union gold." He turned to Jeff. "Please tell me you know where this came from."

"I'm sorry," Jeff said softly, shaking his head.

"Well," said Harris, "This will go into the evidence cupboard for a while…probably with an armed guard! I guess it's a good thing we brought Ross with us. Okay, Randy. Tell them what you told us. Maybe it's not so wacky after all."

"I don't think any of this is a coincidence," Ross said, frowning, "since Major Preston's body lies somewhere on the South Wind property. That's why my ears perked up when I heard you were checking reenactments."

The detectives both sat back, eyes widening. "You didn't tell us that!" Harris said.

Lorie tried to conceal the fact that she was finding it very hard to breathe and fainting just wasn't an option. Not right now.

"Murdered?" Harris asked.

"Shot by Yankee soldiers," Ross's quick answer. "That area where the South Wind is, that's sacred ground to my family."

Carol's exclamation was sharp. "What do you know about it?"

"A lot." He turned to her. "I'm from Randolph City, Mrs. Kendall. My folks keep me in the loop. I got a call the minute they heard that Mr. Randolph had died, and they also told me Rolf Maratti was seen in town. I think our victim here," he indicated Jeff, "is a first warning from Maratti or whoever he's associated with. A shot across the bow. A warning to you Northern folks to stay out of their business or get hurt."

"Randy!" Detective Harris said. "Calm down. Pure speculation."

"I don't know who you are," Randy Ross said directly to Jeff Preston in a combative voice, "but you talk like a Southerner. So either you were recruited, or...oh, I don't know...you're a random victim they picked because you sure as hell look right for the part."

Harris spoke quickly. "He's the victim here, Ross. Settle down."

"I'm pretty certain he's a relative of Jon Randolph," Lorie put in just as quickly. She hadn't told Carol even that much, and she saw a small frown cross her aunt's face.

"That makes it even worse!" Ross's voice moderated, became contrite. "Whatever happened, sir, you're in someone's cross-hairs. I suspect they really meant for you to be dead when someone found you."

Carol interrupted. "You said 'sacred ground'? What did you mean by that?"

"This is the spooky part," Harris put in with a hint of a smile on his face.

Ross glared at him. "My grandfather told me the story. We have papers to prove all of it." He turned back to Carol. "Back during the war between the states, my grandfather's great-grandfather, Master Sergeant Ben Ross, rode with Major Jefferson Preston." He tipped his head toward Jeff, whose face remained impassive. "They were a team."

"Go on," Carol said.

"On the eighteenth of July 1864, one hundred fifty years ago yesterday actually, while the Yankees were moving down toward Atlanta, Major Preston and my great-great-great-granddad Ben accidentally stumbled into a Yankee hornet's nest they couldn't escape from. Granddaddy Ben got killed first. Major Preston might have been able to get away. But instead of that, he carried Granddaddy Ben's body to a place where the Yankees would find him and give him a decent burial. Because of that courageous act of loyalty, Ben's wife, Ellen, was allowed his pension checks from that moment onward so she and the kids could survive." He stopped, cleared his throat, and continued. "That's true friendship! So that's sacred ground to my family."

Phil Barnett frowned. "Why would the Yankees give a pension to a Confederate widow?"

"They weren't Confederates," Randy Ross said firmly. "That's what I'm trying to tell you, folks. They were loyal Union soldiers. Always had been. They were killed by 'friendly fire,' I guess you could call it, because the Yankee soldiers they got mixed up with didn't know those two Rebs weren't what they seemed. Since my family stayed in Georgia after the war, we've kind of kept that part private. So I'm trusting you guys not to tell.

"Major Preston and Ben Ross were the leaders of a bunch of Southern Unionists pretending to be an irregular Confederate company. It started out as a way to keep Union sympathizers from being impressed by the Confederate recruiters. After a while, when people started getting hungry, with the help of Union brass, Preston and Ross organized fake raids on the railroads and the big Union wagon trains so people could eat. They got pretty good at that, Grandpa said. The mountain people loved them. We think that in this case, though, they were carrying out their main task: intelligence. They were probably on their way to Atlanta to scope out the lay of the land for Sherman."

"What happened to the officer?" Harris said, obviously impressed.

"No one knows," Randy Ross replied. "A picket on duty saw him bring Granddad Ben's body right into a bivouac area. He knelt over the body and for a time seemed to be praying. The picket said he didn't shoot because he wouldn't shoot a man at prayer. Then Major Preston disappeared. He was presumed dead. But his body was never found."

"But," Lorie's aunt added, much to Lorie's surprise, "Jon Randolph thought he must have fallen close by that Yankee campground. Years ago, when he realized that same area was being developed, he purchased all the acreage to keep as a wilderness preserve. The only structure left there is the South Wind, the place we're staying, which was a pretty active motel at the time he bought it, and he's made it into an even more upscale convention-related hotel. The cash it generates helps pay for upkeep on the preserve. I hate to think what might happen if Maratti gets his hands on that property."

"Aunt Carol," Lorie exclaimed, feeling a little betrayed, "you knew all along about Jefferson Richard Preston. Why didn't you tell me?"

"Sorry, honey," she said, not smiling. "I wanted to call Cousin Sue first. Find out what she knew."

"Well?" Detective Macdonald's eyebrows raised.

"She's as puzzled as we are."

As they were speaking, Jeff's eyes had closed. Now he drew a hand across them.

"Are you ill, hon?" Carol said to him, touching his arm lightly. "All this talk about shooting and killing…"

He reached for one of the dinner napkins and wiped it across his face. "Just a little pain. I'll be all right." With some effort, he seemed to be pulling himself together, but Lorie thought she saw a glisten of tears in his eyes. He glanced at her briefly, cryptically, and then turned to the policemen. "What can I do to help you?"

"Be careful. Stay out of the way," Randy Ross said passionately. "You'll probably be as safe here as anywhere."

"We don't have any authority in Randolph City," Alan Macdonald said to them. "But we can put out a few feelers to friends we trust. In the meantime, we'll let our forensics people take a look at the evidence and see if we can find out who you are. I'm betting this bundle was part of a grave our new friend here stumbled over in the dark. And I bet if we search long enough, we'll find some spare bones."

"I've got some time coming," Randy Ross said. "I can arrange to take off and do a little on-the-ground research. I know Sue and Sid Bailey pretty well. They probably wouldn't mind if I moved in with them for a few days. Give them protection if it comes to that."

"They've been nervous, I can tell you that," Carol said. "I like that idea. You know we were followed last night?"

"I do," he answered. "I'm glad you're staying here."

"Well," said Harris. "Our usual kind of case. A jigsaw puzzle with half the pieces missing." He turned to Jeff. "Look, son, do you mind if we call you Jeff?"

"I don't know any other name," he said quietly.

"Okay, Jeff. We'd like to take your fingerprints."

Jeff gave him a sharp apprehensive glance.

Lorie spoke up quickly, hoping he wouldn't say anything out of place right now before she could get a handle on what was really happening. "We think you might have been a soldier, Jeff. If so, they can compare what your fingerprints look like to those of other soldiers in the database, and maybe we can find out who you really are."

"In that case, do what you wish," he said hesitantly. Detective Harris excused himself to get a kit from the car.

The process was quick. Lorie brought a soapy cloth from the bathroom so Jeff could clean his fingers afterward.

"Very interesting," he said softly. Lorie noted that he was taking a careful second look at his hand and fingers. He didn't seem to remember some very basic things. *He's a real person, not a spirit,* she reprimanded herself silently.

The two detectives rose from the table. Macdonald spoke first. "I think we have our work cut out for us here."

Harris agreed. "Please keep in touch with us. And, Preston, I suggest you stay in hiding for a while until we get a handle on this stuff. We will be in touch. Randy?"

The young policeman had been involved in an animated conversation with Carol Kendall. He turned and joined the detectives as they returned to the black car. "I'll see you in Randolph City," he told Carol. "You'd better believe we'll get to the bottom of this."

"I like that young man," Carol said, as the car turned out of the driveway. "I'm glad he's on our side."

Phil Barnett put a protective arm around Carol's shoulders. "We'll not let Mr. Jon Randolph's legacy be stolen away."

Jeff rose from his chair as the lawmen departed. "Good people, all!" He motioned Lorie to follow him, and they went out to the porch. She sat beside him on the swing, careful not to touch him.

"It's obvious you know a lot of family history," she said very quietly.

He smiled at her. "You don't believe I am who I claim to be, do you?"

She was silent for a time, looking down at her hands. "Would you believe me if I came up with a tale like that?"

He seemed amused. "Maybe not right away."

"Nevertheless," Lorie conceded, "what you've told me sure ties in with what I'm hearing from other sources. You have to be related to Jon Randolph."

"The more the police look into the mystery of my appearance, the more information they will uncover about the mischief being planned against Jon Randolph's family and friends." He turned to her, reached for her hand, and then seemed to think better of it. "You will find yourselves arrayed against some formidable foes. I will help you to win against them."

"If you really can't remember the 'modern world,'" she said into the uneasy silence that now lay between them, "you need a jump-start. I'm going to let you use the computer." She hastened to retrieve it from the car.

While her aunt and Dr. Barnett made multiple phone calls in the kitchen, Lorie sat on the porch swing beside Jeff Preston, showing him the intricacies of the laptop. He was fascinated and was also a quick study. Soon he was fully immersed in the vastness of knowledge held in a small electronic box made of plastic, silicon, steel, and copper, drawing information about the world through wires and the air itself.

The remainder of the day, Lorie opened relevant programs for Jeff. Finally satisfied with his progress, she realized he was doing what he really needed to be doing, working hard with his damaged mind. If he kept this up, judging by the expertise he was displaying, his recovery should come soon. By the time dinner was called, she was feeling much easier. He was so good with the computer, in fact, she felt she could dismiss the irrational conclusions her mind was still playing with.

CHAPTER 7

Sunday, July 20, 2014

The next morning, lured by the smell of fresh coffee, Lorie quickly stepped out of her nightgown into her underwear, pulled on jeans and a T-shirt, and raked a comb through her hair. Still barefoot, she hurried down the stairway into the front hall. She made a quick turn into the kitchen and skidded to a stop, surprised. Jeff Preston was sitting alone at the kitchen table, still working with the computer, still wearing the same clothes the doctor had loaned him. It didn't matter that they didn't quite fit. Nothing could take away from his athletic build and the scarred and weather-tanned face, haloed by thick straw-colored hair. He was without question a fine-looking man.

He glanced up from the computer and smiled broadly. "My dark-haired angel approaches." The words resonated with warmth.

"How are you feeling this morning?" she asked, unaccountably flattered. "Did you sleep well?"

"I'm not sure." His blue eyes twinkled. "I wasn't awake long enough to notice."

She fell silent, mouth open, then sorting out what he had said, immensely relieved, she grabbed a kitchen towel, balled it up, and lobbed it at him. He caught it, laughing. Grinning back, she selected a cup from the cabinet. "A joker! You're as bad as my brother. He does that to me all the time!"

"Wonderful food, beautiful home, pleasant weather, amiable people. Even hot running water for my bath. I am content, Lorena Manning. And here I now sit, surrounded by what the good doctor calls 'kitchen gadgets' that do all my work for me. How can I not be happy?"

"*Carpe diem,*" she answered.

"Seize the day." His smile broadened. "*Quam minimum credula postero.*"

"Excuse me?"

"'Trusting as little as possible to the future.' The time to eat, drink, and be merry is now."

"You are a well-educated man."

"Greek and Latin. Some Hebrew. European languages. Philosophy. Geography. History. Mathematics. Natural and biological sciences—"

His mind was clearly beginning to reassemble. "Stop. I'm impressed already." She seated herself at the table. "But I don't think I can *carpe diem* very well this morning until I have some of that." He filled her cup, and she took a careful sip. It was just the right temperature and delicious. He then offered her a perfectly browned piece of toast, buttered, with jam spread generously across the top. She thanked him with a smile.

"Ambrosia," he whispered, licking the remnants of jam from his fingers. "And an angel beside me. I never believed in heaven before."

Carol came into the room just then wearing white slacks and a stylish blue overshirt.

Lorie looked up at her. "What's the occasion?"

"Phil and I are headed to Randolph City to help Sue arrange for Jon's memorial service. Lorie, Jeff must remain in hiding until we figure out what's going on. Will you stay here with him, please? There's lots of food in the fridge. We'll be back as soon as we can."

Lorie glanced at Jeff Preston. His full attention had shifted to her, the expression in his eyes hopeful, a sweet crooked smile on his lips. "Sure," she said and realized with a start that this time she didn't mind being asked to stay behind.

It was a quiet morning. She answered computer questions for Jeff and put some needed time on Carol's family tree bulletin board. When she tired of tacking the endless tombstones to the chart, she began to explore the house. The doctor's study was large and lined with bookcases. Aside from an antique roll-top desk, it was furnished with comfortable modern furniture: lounge chairs, lamps, and side tables. The book collection was extensive. She saw many medical books, including some basics she recognized, as well as books on related branches of science. Classical literature lined one wall along with mysteries, westerns, and contemporary novels. Another series of shelves contained political expositions and histories with an emphasis on volumes relating to the Civil War.

With a quiet "ah-ha," she pulled an ancient-looking book from the shelf and walked back into the kitchen, scanning its pages. "Jeff, this should give you some idea of what happened here. Campaigns of the Civil War...Atlanta." She handed it over to him.

"General Cox wrote this!" Jeff said with some surprise, glancing at the cover. He took it with enthusiasm, now eagerly abandoning electronics for the printed word. Following her back into the study, he settled himself into a comfortable armchair by a sunny window. "Jacob is a dedicated aboli-tionist and an honest man," he said. "His assessment will be even-handed."

"He died a long time ago," she answered drily.

He glanced up at her, flashed his crooked little grin, and winked. He was joking with her again. He had probably been doing that all along. She smiled back, unsure, but hopeful.

For a while, the house was very quiet. Lorie curled herself into the corner of a comfortable couch and opened an old Agatha Christie novel. Across the room, Jeff seemed totally absorbed, turning pages swiftly, sometimes checking the index, skipping from map to map, then sitting quiet, once more engrossed. She was not as equally tied to her book. Instead, she spent a great deal of time studying the mysteri-ous visitor, trying to figure him out.

He was certainly good to look at. Laugh lines played around his eyes, although he was not laughing now, deeply involved as he was in a history book concerning terrible events. From what little she knew of him, he seemed a kind person. Even when he was teasing her, there was a smile in his deep voice. And she had seen him weep. She knew his injuries had made him very vulnerable.

But nothing quite made sense about him. She had to admit it: it was as if he were a foreigner who had come to a place with which he was completely unfamiliar.

She had thought she was good at reading people. She had often been told her initial perceptions were right on the mark.

Not so long ago, however, she had been cruelly deceived. Stunningly so. By someone she thought she was going to marry. Dr. Stan, everyone called him at the hospital where she was training. Brilliant. Handsome. Not too patient, espe-cially when he was in the operating room dealing with people he perceived, often wrongly, to be incompetent. But she had thought he was, for the most part, a kind person. And that he loved her.

She had been wrong on both counts! She was now a little more wary and mistrustful of initial impressions.

In the quietness, Lorie wandered into the kitchen and browsed through the refrigerator. She made sandwiches, cut up some fruit, and poured iced tea. Putting everything on a tray, she took it back into the doctor's study.

Jeff looked up from the book. He seemed older to her now, grave. "So many deaths," he said. He accepted the food graciously, seemingly grateful for the interruption.

"It was a terrible war. I hope it never happens here again."

"The slavery question has been settled, hasn't it?" he asked sharply.

Here we go again, Lorie thought. He hadn't quite come back into the real world. "By Constitutional amendment," she said patiently, "as the war ended."

He was very quiet for a time. He looked down at the book and then away. "Moses would have liked that." She thought she saw the glisten of tears in his eyes once again.

"Moses?"

"Moses was a good friend." He said it softly, his eyes almost closed. He swiped at his face with a napkin, then pulled himself up and turned back to his book.

Sometime later, he asked softly, "Would your computer be able to tell us if any Southern towns refused to join the Confederacy?"

"Well," she said, mystified by the abrupt change of topic, "we can try. It's just a matter of asking the search engine the right question the right way."

He immediately rose from his chair, retrieved the computer from the kitchen, and handed it to Lorie. "How shall we frame the question?" she asked him as he reseated himself.

"Frame it?"

"Make a sentence even a dumb computer might recognize."

"It lacks nuance, does it?" He thought for a time. "What Southern towns rejected the Confederacy?"

She tried the phrase. "Nothing relevant," she reported, then scanned the items that appeared, opening and reviewing a few of them.

"What towns seceded from the Confederacy?" Jeff offered.

"What about states? West Virginia split from Virginia." She typed his words into the search engine and read through a number of sites. "Nothing helpful. Anything else?" She tried a few more of Jeff's suggestions and some of her own, but nothing close to what Jeff was asking came back. When she saw the disappointment on his face, she said, "Let's ask the doctor when he gets back," and she added, "What exactly are you after?"

He answered in a soft voice. "It's something Officer Ross mentioned."

"About the historical Major Preston being a Union man?"

"That. And some other things."

A car turned into the driveway just then, and shortly thereafter, the house was livened by the reappearance of Carol Kendall and Phil Barnett, bringing in bags of groceries. Lorie joined them in the kitchen, Jeff following closely behind. She noticed that he watched with careful attention as food and supplies were unpacked and shelved or placed in the refrigerator. He asked Phil questions about a few of the items and received an effusive response.

"Young man, I sense in you the heart of a cook. Let's do the 'he-man' thing and prepare dinner for the ladies tonight." Phil turned to Carol and Lorie, smiling. "Our treat," he said expansively. He reached into the refrigerator for a pitcher, set it on the countertop, and pulled some tall glasses from one of the cupboards. "Iced tea for the ladies. Now go on out to the porch, beautiful ones, and relax. Jeff and I will whip up some delicacies you won't believe until you are eating them."

Tender steaks sizzling from the grill, garlic mashed potatoes, and a tossed salad filled with fresh garden produce were served in due course. And then, the real conversation began, starting with plans for the memorial service. Lorie listened quietly. Only a few of the names she heard were familiar to her. She would meet the owners of those other names soon enough.

When it seemed appropriate, she broached the question Jeff had asked earlier. "Do either of you know of any Southern towns that wanted to opt out of the Confederacy?"

"As a matter of fact," the doctor said, leaning back in his rocking chair and taking a sip of cabernet from his wine glass, "there were some people in Mississippi, Jones County, who didn't like the idea of rich slave owners requiring poor men who didn't abide by slavery to fight a war they didn't agree with. So the Jones County Rebels hid in the swamps and fought the recruiters." He took another sip of wine, considered the setting sun for a time, and finally continued. "When I was on a trip to Alabama a while back, I saw a statue of a soldier in front of the county courthouse—half Union, half Confederate. Let's see, where was that?" He was quiet for a time, thinking. "Winston County. That was it. There again, Unionists refused to be recruited. According to what I read, there was a lot of trouble in Winston County, neighbors fighting neighbors. People having to leave their homes and hide in the hills."

"What about here in Marietta?" Lorie watched Jeff's face carefully.

Again Phil Barnett paused for thought. "I read a quote once," he said slowly, "from the diary of someone who lived here in Marietta during those days. Matthew Williams. West Point graduate and teacher. A dedicated Union man. I don't remember his exact words. But as I recall, he implied he would never have fought for the Confederacy.

"On the other hand, he refused to shoot at his fellow Georgians. The war destroyed him. His only son, daughter-in-law, and grandchild took refuge in southern Georgia to escape from the war. All died of cholera. When Matthew found out, his mind slipped over into insanity, and the diary ended."

"It was a bad time to be living in Georgia," Jeff said under his breath.

"And what about that town we visited once…just east of here?" Carol said, reaching out her hand to the doctor. "Madison, wasn't it? Quite a nice town. It was spared by Sherman because the inhabitants were largely Unionists."

"I don't think Southerners like to admit their 'noble cause' wasn't universally accepted in the South," Phil said.

"Noble cause?" Jeff's voice took on a sharp edge. "Slavery is not a noble cause!"

"States' rights," Phil said. "That's what they argue now."

"A thin excuse," Jeff growled, "to keep people shackled and the gold those people represent locked away in iron vaults by men who would be kings. What about Jon Randolph's town?"

"Randolph City?" The doctor turned to Carol. "Do you know anything, honey?"

She shook her head. "No one's ever said anything to me. Randy Ross's account was the first I've heard of it. Southern Unionists? Those people seem so proud of their Southern heritage. We'll have to ask Sue."

Lorie thought Jeff seemed a little depressed as the topics of the Civil War and slavery ebbed and flowed around him. When she moved from cleanup detail to the swing, he came to sit beside her, saying, "Do you mind?" He reached for her hand. She felt an unexpected thrill at his gentle touch and cautioned herself. He had not been flirting with her. This was not personal. He was not seeking romance. He needed comfort.

This man had been seriously injured. She was all too aware that he didn't quite know who he was right now. It wouldn't be fair to him, or to her, to let a romance develop. For all she knew, he had a sweetheart or wife somewhere else. But still, while she wouldn't admit it to him, his hand felt so good on hers. And when his arm went around her, she moved just a little closer into the warmth of his shoulder. Be careful, she warned herself again! He just needs to know someone cares.

They sat rocking for a long time, quietly listening as Phil and Carol's discussion moved to the situation in Randolph City. The sun went slowly down, shadows got dark and darker, and fireflies flickered across the grass and through the woods. Lorie didn't want the evening to end and found herself feeling a little sad when Carol said it was time for bed.

Carol left shortly thereafter, followed closely by Phil, and still Jeff kept his arm around her. Then his other arm completed the circle. He held her tightly against his chest, resting his face atop her head, buried in her hair. She understood. She had seen it at the hospital. Children whose parents had been injured. People whose loved ones had just died. They reached out for the nearest sympathetic soul. In her short career, she had held and cried with too many people. It was always shattering.

Jeff had lost everything, his name, his family, his background. Instinctively, she had already wrapped her arms around him in a comforting hug, trying not to put pressure on the bandages covering his yet unhealed wounds. "Everything will be okay," she murmured. "We will find out who you are, Jeff. We will get you back to your family."

What she hadn't reckoned on, however, was her own reaction to his need for the human touch. A great wave of affection welled up inside her. She had seen nothing to make her feel he was duplicitous or deceitful. He was gentle, courteous, a complete gentleman. *Oh my God!* she thought. *I don't need to go through this all over again.* She realized now that almost against her will, she had developed the deepest of feelings for him. In utter despair, she knew she was completely smitten. Every atom of her body was responding to his gentle embrace. And so she didn't break away until finally he raised his head.

"Thank you for being my friend," he said softly, and she knew she was lost.

CHAPTER 8

Monday, July 21, 2014

The next morning Carol woke Lorie early, coming into the bedroom elegantly clad in a white silk blouse, gray slacks, and high heels.

"We're going over to Randolph City this morning. Sue is waiting for us. Both of us. Now don't get all grumpy on me, young lady," she said when Lorie mumbled that she didn't want to go anywhere. "They're your cousins, too. Put on something a little dressy. We're probably going to be talking with people in high places."

Carol stepped out into the hall, and Lorie heard her speaking to Jeff. "I'm sorry we can't take you with us, hon, but in view of all that's happening, we really need to keep your whereabouts unknown."

"I am happy to remain in hiding," she heard him say. "I have become one with this little computer machine, and I will be satisfied tapping into its contents during the next few hours, if not the next few days."

"Where's the doctor this morning?" Lorie asked as she came out of her room wrapped in her robe. She followed Carol downstairs and into the kitchen. Jeff had reached the kitchen ahead of them and was expertly placing aromatic grounds into the basket of the coffeemaker. He was still wearing secondhand clothes, but to her right now, he looked outrageously attractive. Her heart gave a little leap as he looked up, saw her, and smiled.

"Phil was called over to the clinic early." Carol reached into the refrigerator and pulled out a bowl of freshly cut fruit. "Sunday breakfast. You have a choice this morning. Cereal with fruit and milk or cooked oatmeal."

"Try the cereal," Lorie called out to Jeff as she headed back upstairs with a cup of microwaved tea in one hand, a cinnamon roll in the other, knowing she had to leave his presence quickly or reveal the attraction she felt toward him. "Only Scots can abide oatmeal."

Jeff laughed, saying something about things never changing.

Lorie chose formal white slacks and, since the weather was warm, a short-sleeved red silk blouse, a simple gold chain, and small gold earrings. Remembering how drab she had felt in nurses' scrubs, she applied eyeliner, a little blush, and a dab of rose lipstick. She slipped her feet into white high-heeled sandals, grabbed up a small purse, and hurried back downstairs. The look on Jeff Preston's face when he saw her was a reward in itself. As she and Carol left the house, she smiled back at him over her shoulder. "*Carpe diem*," she said, and he grinned.

Carol had told her that Randolph City was a good hour's drive north from Marietta at interstate speeds. But her aunt didn't keep the little hatchback on the interstate for long. Soon she left the highway and cut northeast on a two-lane country road, headed toward mountain country. "As far as I know, we aren't being followed," Carol said. "But if we take the scenic route, we disappear."

"That screened porch is a great place for picnics." Lorie leaned her head back against the headrest, almost content. Thinking about the previous evening, she wished her almost obsessive feeling for Jeff Preston would subside. Life was already too complicated.

"It was lovely," Carol laughed. "But it's the company that made it special. Phil pulled off a great dinner with Jeff's help. He likes cooking for people. Your friend is very quiet, I notice. He listens a lot. I don't think he misses a thing."

"Life is very confusing to him right now."

"No memory yet? He must have taken a powerful blow to the head. Sometimes the brain doesn't reorient right away. Don't worry, honey. He should recover, given time. He's a healthy specimen if I ever saw one."

He sure is, Lorie said to herself. She gazed out the window, trying to distract herself. The farther northeast they traveled, the more winding the road became and the denser grew the trees. Small hills swelled to large, large hills plunged deep into forested valleys. Crystal lakes mirrored the red earth and green foliage gleaming in the fresh light of morning. Lorie felt the beauty about her as a powerful source of peace. Someday when she was rich and famous—well, rich maybe—she would buy herself an acre or two in a setting like this and just let nature take its course.

Carol interrupted her reverie. "I'm glad you're with me today, hon. You'll like the Baileys. I do wish you had been able to meet Jon Randolph, though. He was a practical idealist. You would have liked him."

"There aren't many of those anymore." She sighed. "Now it's all about greed."

"Idealists crop up everywhere," Carol said. "They come from every source, and there's never been a clear majority of them, but if you look hard, you're bound to find some close by." She slowed the car and turned onto a graveled road cut through the forest. "I'm going to take you into town by way of the scenic route. If any spies are watching the highway for us, they won't know we're coming until we're there."

Occasional splotches of sunlight broke through the leafy archway above the road, but for the most part it seemed a woodland cathedral, a setting of infinite beauty. Eventually the forest gave way to farmland, and the car came out finally into sunlight, which spilled onto the meadows with sparkling gaiety. They had broken through a time barrier, Lorie thought with delight, for from that point on, it seemed that the pages of history were turning gently back to the nineteenth century.

A few houses on the outskirts of Randolph City were Victorian in style with the distinctive gingerbread trim so common to an earlier era. Homes seemed freshly painted, some sparkling white, some brilliantly decorated in rich antique colors. They were sheltered by huge trees, hugged by honeysuckle vines, and embellished with magnificently varied flower beds splashed from a painter's pallet. Past these dwellings, architectural styles showed the simplicity of even earlier days—small frame houses covered with narrow clapboard siding and chimneys at either end, big brick houses with comfortable porches and white shutters, and here and there a larger dwelling dignified by graceful columns.

"It's wonderful." Lorie knew she would have to explore on foot to appreciate the uniqueness of so many interesting homes.

"I knew you'd like it."

Carol slowed before one of the larger houses, a white brick two-story with a simple columned porch spread across the front. "We're here." She turned onto the graveled driveway. "And there's Cousin Sue."

The Manning gene was strong in Sue Bailey's face, a slightly older, gray-haired version of Carol. The rest of her derived from a different genetic mold. Clad in a well-fitted blue denim dress, she was shorter and a bit plump. But she was just as elegant as Lorie's aunt.

"Well, here you are at last," Sue said, coming down the steps toward them. "Lorie, I've heard so much about you..."

Lorie glanced quickly at Carol, who said softly, "Nothing about blood or fainting."

"And I've been eager to meet you. Come on in."

The minute Lorie got out of the car, she was swept into a big hug. "Come on in, dears. We've got iced tea and cookies, and so much to talk about."

Sue had Southern hospitality to spare, but unlike Phil Barnett and Jeff Preston, her voice did not reflect a Southern origin. "Oh no," she said when Lorie remarked on it. "Sid and I are Northerners, just like you folk. We came here a goodly number of years ago to help Jon. He was approaching his late seventies, and he was ready to hand some of the responsibility over to his younger kin. It's been so interesting, especially this historic town project. I hope we can still do him justice now that he's gone." She looked away for a moment. Tears filled her eyes. She dabbed at them with a tissue, cleared her throat, turned back and smiled. "I have to remind myself that he's gone. I just keep expecting to see him walk through that door."

She ushered them into the house and showed them around. It was a beautiful old dwelling, comfortably authentic. High ceilings kept the spacious rooms cool; large windows made them airy and bright. The air conditioning was unobtrusive and welcome. Furniture, while obviously of the period, wasn't of sufficient museum quality to make Lorie feel uncomfortable about touching it.

Sue invited them into her sun-sparkled kitchen. Lorie seated herself next to Carol on a bench at one side of the long, polished pine trestle table. Their hostess brought a plate of home-baked cookies, poured iced tea for both her guests, picked up her own glass, and sat down to conversation.

Topics of discussion were far-ranging, including updates of Sue's two grown children: Jim, a successful architect, and Marianne, a high school science teacher. Sue had the same warmth and connectivity Lorie already knew in her own family, and she felt instantly included.

"Now," said Sue finally in a tone that meant business, "let's talk about our new version of Jefferson Richard Preston."

"Not much to say," Carol responded. "His memory hasn't returned. He's almost a blank slate."

"Except," Lorie put in, "he seems to know a lot about the family. Yesterday he wanted to check out a place that, strangely enough, belonged to Jon Randolph."

Sue and Carol came to abrupt attention. Carol asked, "Where did you go?"

"Somewhere beyond Roswell. He pointed out a country road that took us to an old burned-out plantation house. We had to walk the last mile or so."

"Oh my word!" Sue said. "Riverside Plantation. However in the world would he have known about that?"

"Riverside Plantation?" Carol turned to her cousin.

Sue gave her head a shake. "Nobody goes there. It's a graveyard, basically. But it's another of Jon's wildlife preserves. He thought someday he'd make a park out of it. For now, he's just keeping it out of the hands of developers."

"Who lived there?" An uneasy feeling began to creep back into Lorie's mind. Perhaps she shouldn't have mentioned their little side trip.

"Well," Sue said, "for one, Major Preston." Lorie had been afraid she would say that. "And his sister, my great-great-grandmother Sara. They lived there with their father when they were children. The house was unfortunately burned by Sherman's troops as they swept through Georgia, and the senior Preston was killed there about the same time Major Preston disappeared."

Lorie interrupted. "It wasn't the Yankees who did that."

Sudden silence. Two sets of eyes staring at her.

"Uh, Jeff said it wasn't the Yankees. He said the general would have known—" Okay, it was time to shut up!

"That the Major was working with the Yankees," Sue finished softly. "My word, Carol! It sounds like your young man is aware of some of the more closely guarded Preston/Randolph lore. He must be part of the family."

"But what part?" Lorie's aunt said. "Phil and I were talking about it. Remember what Jon said the other night as he was dying? 'Tell my son…' Phil and I are speculating that Jeff might be the product of a secret love affair. He could be an unacknowledged grandson. Or even a great-grandson."

Distractedly, Sue Bailey picked up another cookie and started to munch. "Maybe," she said. "Mr. Jon spent many years working for the government. Like his father before him, there was much he couldn't talk about."

"Was he a spy?" Lorie asked, now intensely curious.

"Maybe," Sue repeated carefully.

"Tell us." Sue now had Carol's full attention. And Lorie's.

"His father was also an intelligence officer for the government. Long, long ago. Did you know that, Carol?"

"I had no idea."

"Sara's first baby, the first Jon Randolph's son—we all call him Junior—was a West Point graduate, just as Major

Preston was. He did government work for many years. One of his jobs was checking out rumors of German espionage and sabotage in the States before America came into World War I. He died coming home from one of those missions."

"Tell all," Carol said and now silent, she and Lorie both leaned a bit closer.

"Okay. I'll start at the beginning. There are only two very long generations here, so it isn't really complicated. Junior was born during the Civil War right there at Riverside Plantation, where you were yesterday, Lorie. That was a terrible time because the plantation house had just been burned to the ground and Sara's father, Isaac, murdered along with the farmhands and household help who weren't able to escape. By person or persons unknown, I now have to presume. A terrible massacre."

She paused, thinking. "You know, I'm relieved to think it wasn't the Yankees who did that. It was brutal. I've been told Grandma Sara wouldn't ever talk about it. Well, anyway, I'm getting ahead of myself.

"The people who were caring for Sara that awful night," she went on, "were afraid neither she nor her baby would live. Losing everything, just like that, was, of course, a terrible shock. But at the last minute, Junior let out a big yowl, and there he was. And his mom had to stick around to take care of him." Sue took Carol's hand in hers and squeezed it. "Guess who the midwives were."

"One of 'em," Carol said playfully as if it were a kid's guessing game, and she was delighted she could give the correct answer, "could have been a relative of Phil's. Right?"

"Dr. Phil Barnett?" Lorie was completely taken by surprise.

"It's how we know Phil, Lorie," Carol said. "One of his ancestors was a healer from the mountain country. Elijah

Benning was his name. He was just a kid when this happened, not quite sixteen, but he'd been the caretaker for
everyone else in his family since he was small because his
dad wasn't around much, and he had a real knack for knowing what was wrong with people. He helped Sara through a
difficult childbirth and basically saved her life. Our family,
the Mannings, sent him to medical school after the war, and
most of his kids, including a few daughters, carried on the
tradition. Phil is one of that pack."

"That's wonderful!" Lorie said.

"And the other midwife?" Sue prompted.

"Our joint ancestor...Marshal Manning." Carol
laughed with delight, reaching across the table to give her
cousin a quick hug. "I know this part of the story from the
Manning side. How he took complete charge of her and the
baby. And when they found out for certain that the baby's
father had been killed in the war, they ended up falling in
love and getting married."

"And having another baby," Sue added, laughing. "But
we'll ignore my multi-great-grandpa Preston Manning for
now and stick with Sara's firstborn, Junior. Because he was
our Jon Randolph's father."

Lorie blinked but didn't have time to react as Sue
plunged ahead.

"Junior didn't marry until his thirties, not just because
he was busy, but because he was waiting to meet exactly
the right person. Then he found Penny, who was ten years
younger and simply gorgeous, and it was love at first sight.
They traveled and did all kinds of exciting things. But when
they got tired of circling the globe and tried to have their
own baby, it didn't seem to work out. Then when she was
well into her forties, when she wasn't thinking about it anymore, Penny got pregnant.

"Back in those days, because of her age, it was a chancy pregnancy. So Junior bought an airplane—remember those old bi-wing open-cockpit things?—so he could get home to her fast if he needed to. That happened. Some kind of crisis. He was on his way back from a meeting in Washington, DC, when his plane went down. Somewhere over the Shenandoah Mountains, they think. No one ever found a crash site corresponding to the presumed facts, but plane and pilot never showed up from that time forward.

"That was a horrible blow. Penny was in premature labor, and they thought for a while she was surely going to lose the baby. But Great-Grandma Sara, who'd been through it all herself, wasn't going to let that happen. She got on Penny's case and kept her on task. At the same time, Mr. Jon Third was just as determined to be born. He snuffled and sniffed a time or two when he entered this world, a tiny little thing, and then he let out a big old yowl, and he didn't give up that wonderful life spirit he had in him until last night.

"They never found Junior's body—Junior being Mr. Jon's father. But Mr. Jon was always intrigued by the stories about his father. I think that's what persuaded him to go into government work, too. And flying. That's why he built a runway and a hangar on Randolph House property. Mr. Jon loved to fly. And Tom was a flyer, too."

"Who's Tom?" Lorie asked.

"Mr. Jon's first son. His natural son. Tom died in the early years of the Vietnam conflict. Such a waste of a good young life. Why do we have these cruel useless wars that take our brightest and bravest?"

"Okay, tell us what you know about the other one," Carol prompted.

"Rolf," Sue said it as if it were an oath.

"Strange name," Lorie ventured.

"An Italian name. Rolf Maratti came to America as a child with his beautiful Italian mother, Maria. There's a big oil portrait of her out at the house."

"She was his second wife, wasn't she?" Carol asked.

"Correct. Tom's mother was Sylvia Mitchell. Jon and Sylvia were married before the war started, back in 1938. Mr. Jon was also a West Pointer, already doing secret government work back then. OSS, I presume. That's what they called it then. He never talked about it. I don't think Sylvia liked it much. Well, who would? But she had little Tommy to care for. So she was kept plenty busy."

"What happened to her?" Lorie wanted to know.

"Breast cancer. She probably would have lived if she'd been born a generation later. Such a tragedy. Tommy was about six when his mother died. He grew up with a series of nannies. Until Mr. Jon went back to Italy to find Maria."

"Do we have to urge you to elaborate on that?" Carol laughed, and Sue grinned and continued.

"During the war, sometime in '43 or '44, Mr. Jon was flying a mission over northern Italy when his plane was hit by flak. He tried to get back over the border to Switzerland but knew he wasn't going to make it, so he parachuted out. He was fearful he'd be picked up by the Nazis or Italians and put into a POW camp. More likely shot on the spot because he wasn't in uniform. Obviously a spy. The Resistance found him first, thank goodness, and spirited him across the border. Maria was his guide."

Carol refilled her glass with iced tea. "Were there sparks?"

"Good heavens, no! He was a hundred percent devoted to Sylvia. And Maria was married, too, to a folk hero of the Resistance. But after Sylvia died, Mr. Jon thought about it and finally decided he'd try to find Maria. When he discovered she was a widow and nearly destitute, he brought her back to the States, along with little Rolf. And fell in love."

"And the boys didn't like each other," Carol said. "I've heard that much."

"I don't think it was that they didn't like each other so much as it was they didn't have anything in common. Tommy was at least six years older than Rolf, and the only language Rolf could speak when he got here was Italian.

"Poor little fellow. They were living in a posh suburb of Chicago then, but despite that, Rolf was subjected to the worst kind of discrimination. Don't forget, Italy was one of the Axis countries. Many people still thought of Italians as the enemy. Tommy was an athletic kid, a football star headed for West Point, and even he never really warmed up to this poor little waif he was now supposed to call his brother."

"I think I feel sorry for Rolf already," Lorie said quietly.

"Mr. Jon did, too." Sue nodded. "That's why he moved the family to Randolph City once Tommy left for the Academy…to get Rolf away from the people who were giving him such a hard time." Sue paused and took a breath. "The town wasn't called Randolph City then, of course. Its original name was Oak Hill."

"Another revelation!" Carol said.

Sue nodded again. "It was a small town then, tight, almost locked away in time. But the people were good solid folk, and they really liked the Randolph family. They took Maria and Rolf to their hearts and tried to make up for all the bad things that had happened to them during the war. It was a good town then. Not fractious like it is now. Maria died when Rolf was fifteen. Such a tragedy. He was inconsolable."

"So Jon Randolph built the house when they moved here?" Lorie asked.

"Oh no, no, no. Randolph House was here already. It was one of the many properties Mr. Jon inherited from his family. It wasn't called Randolph House when it was built, any more than the town was called Randolph City. Originally it was called Oak Hill Plantation. Major Preston's summer home. There were all kinds of stories about it."

A shiver ran up Lorie's spine. She held her breath, waiting for more.

"He's the one who built the house, don't you know. It's rumored within our family that even before the Civil War, he ran an operation from here that transported escaped slaves up north via the Underground Railroad. But no one can prove that one way or the other. The way some people around here tell it, he was a Confederate hero. Those of us who know see it exactly the other way 'round. He was a major player on the Underground!"

Lorie was silent. This is what Jeff had been wondering about, she thought, when he asked if any Southern towns had resisted the Confederacy. Apparently people still didn't like to take sides. Too many friendships might get tangled up in controversy. Officer Randy Ross claimed that Major Preston had been working with the Yankees, but he also was a bit reticent about revealing that as confirmed fact!

"Do we have time to go out to the house?" Carol said. "Lorie needs to see it before people start dismantling it."

"Let's hope it never gets to that point. But sure, let's go. I'd like to pick up some of my things from there, and I'd also like to do another search for the will. Will Purdy knows where some of the hiding places are, but Mr. Jon didn't tell him about the rest. I don't think he trusted Will Purdy that much."

"Will Purdy?" Lorie asked.

"Jon's lawyer."

"He didn't trust his own lawyer?"

Sue smiled. "Will was the other half of Neil & Purdy LLC. It was Mike Neil who did Jon's legal work, including all the wills he ever wrote. Mike died a couple of years ago in a car accident. Sudden heart attack. He was only in his sixties, but these things do happen. Anyway, much to our disgust, Will inherited all Mike's clients and the files. Good for Will, I guess. Not so good for some of Mike's clients. Will's a pleasant enough fellow but not the brightest flicker in the chandelier." Sue looked at her watch. "It's about ten thirty now. We're meeting with Maratti's lawyer, Arthur Ehrlich, and good old Will at two o'clock to talk specifics about these developers who are showing up in town. We have plenty of time to give Lorie a quick tour and get back to the meeting on time."

"Let's go," Carol said.

Lorie settled herself in the back seat of Carol's Escort, and they headed out of town along a winding two-lane road through unbroken woodlands. "It's about five miles," Sue said. "All of the property from this side of town out to Randolph House belongs—sorry, *belonged*—to Mr. Jon."

"Did you say," Lorie asked Sue, "that the developers wanted to replace the house with a hotel?"

"That's the rumor. Kind of like the conference center near Marietta."

"But that's a modern building," Lorie put in. "And five miles away from town seems a little distant for that kind of operation?"

Sue made a rude sound, and everyone laughed.

"The lure of easy money makes people stupid," Carol ventured. Spirited conversation flowed from there, generally about plans that were in the works to attract tourists to Randolph City. "Sid and I have reconstructed the old-time pharmacy," Sue told Lorie. "It even has an old-fashioned soda fountain. But it's a real working drug store, too."

The road meandered around hills and through narrow, wooded valleys where vines grew wild along the roadside, climbing trees and utility poles and hiding smaller brush completely. "Kudzu," Sue said with disgust. "Much like the developers that are coming to town. Taking over everything." And then she said, "Slow down. Here's the turn-off."

Carol turned onto a graveled road and drove more slowly into a forested area. Ahead, stretched across the road waist-high but standing open, was a wrought-iron gate embedded with a stylized "JTR."

"That's odd," Sue said. "Someone forgot to shut it. I don't remember a planned delivery, but maybe someone has sent flowers, and they were delivered up to the house."

"Are you armed?" Carol said darkly.

The black van had sharpened her aunt's sense of caution, Lorie thought uneasily. She didn't think Carol was kidding.

But Sue had not been recently followed and didn't realize the fear that kind of threat evoked. "With our killer charm, who needs guns?" Her voice was bright, unconcerned. Everyone laughed, but Lorie also remembered Jeff's allegation about evil. And Officer Randy Ross, too, in his way. She would keep an eye open. And her cell phone at hand.

Past the gate, the road made a gentle arc to the right and straightened into a tunnel of enormous moss-encrusted oak trees, seemingly as old as the hills.

"Lorie," Sue said. "When we turn back to the left and start up to the crest, take a look out the right window. You'll see why we don't want to lose Randolph House."

The sun was bright on the road ahead at the curve, where trees were spaced more generously. As the car made the turn, the exclamation that came from Lorie's lips was quite involuntary.

Backlit by the late morning sun against dark forest pines, it stood proudly at the summit of a steep grassy rise, a Greek temple transplanted intact to the New World.

The trees and vines grew tight again, and Lorie lost sight of the house until the car curved once more to the right and up over the hill to a level lawn and a broad parking area. She stepped out of the little car onto gravel and stood still, awed by the perfect symmetry of the building. Tall fluted columns surrounded it on three sides. A wide stairway led the few steps up to the portico and served to direct attention to a hanging balcony of white filigree iron over the front entrance. The many windows facing onto the portico were huge, extending from floor level to a point high above Lorie's head.

"If someone's here," Lorie heard Sue saying to Carol, "they had to have walked. I don't see another car."

The older women had reached the portico. As they moved to the front door Lorie heard an exclamation from Sue, almost like a yelp. She hurried to join them.

"What's up?"

Sue's face was the picture of exasperation. "What in the blue blazes? There's a hasp padlock on the door."

"And on all the windows," Carol said. She walked quickly from side to side across the portico, examining each window in turn. "This is freshly done, Sue. There are drill shavings here on the porch."

"And the drapes are drawn tight," Sue said angrily, "so we can't even see in. Who would do this?"

"Maratti!" the two women said together. Sue added, "He probably thought we'd strip all the valuables out of the house before he could see what was there."

Sue dug into her purse, brought out her cell phone, and punched in a number. "Sid," she said a moment later, "call Will Purdy, will you? Someone locked us out of the house." There was a short pause. "I didn't say it that way, dear, being a lady, but you've touched my sentiments exactly. We'll want to check in with Will and get our ducks in a row before we go into that meeting. Thanks, honey." Another pause. "No, it won't be long. I want to show Lorie the gardens, at least, before we get home. She's never been here before."

"Let's go around to the back." Sue herded Lorie and Carol down the steps and around the south end of the portico. They followed a garden path to the rear. The broad backyard was beautifully groomed. At the far side, backed up to a boxwood hedge, stood a solitary stone building, seemingly extending from an enormous chimney.

"Summer kitchen?" Lorie asked, her eyebrows rising.

"Indeed," Sue said. "Besides the summer heat problem, our ancestors always used open flames, and the threat of fire was fearfully present. This summer kitchen, unlike some, had its own water supply. Quite an innovation for the day and probably the practical reason the kitchen is so far from the house. It's used for storage now. Mr. Jon has a lovely kitchen inside the renovated house, as you might imagine."

"What about the hedge behind the summer kitchen?" Carol asked. "I've heard it's a maze."

"Oh, I forgot, Carol," Sue replied. "This is your first time in the gardens, too, isn't it? Well, the maze is large and very tricky. If there's a pattern to it, I've never figured it out. I finally started taking a ball of twine with me. I think most people do. It's super fun."

"I'd love to explore." Lorie looked around her. The mansion had proved to be vastly beyond her expectations. The grounds were superbly cared for. Everywhere she turned were views of incredible beauty. "This would make a grand tourist attraction or even a convention center. Why should anyone want to destroy it?"

"'Rehab' takes more money than 'rebuild,'" Sue said. "At least that's what they keep telling me, even though I don't think it makes any sense at all. Okay, let's head this way to the formal gardens."

Comfortable footpaths wound past gazebos luxuriant with hanging blossoms, through vine-covered passageways fragrant with potted plants and lined with benches, around sparkling pools and fountains and past plots of blooming roses, wildflowers, and bushes of every conceivable variety. "Who takes care of these?" Lorie wanted to know.

"When we got here, it was my kids and all their friends," Sue answered with a chuckle. "But now Mr. Jon uses… Excuse me…I'm sorry, I keep forgetting." She pulled a tissue from her pocket and dabbed at eyes which had suddenly filled with tears. A moment later, she cleared her throat and continued. "Now Ginny Clark comes with lots of big trucks containing her multiple redheaded nieces and nephews and they take care of it in no time at all." With some effort, it seemed, Sue tried to make her voice a little more cheerful. "One more thing, Lorie, before you go. You really must visit the monument."

She looked around. "Monument?"

Sue went on as if there had been no break in her narrative. "Sara Randolph put the monument here nearly a hundred fifty years ago. Everyone visits it. I don't know why, but they say it brings them good luck if they rub it. Poppycock, but the story has taken on a life of its own." She pointed. "See that hedge over there? There's a hidden door there into a secret garden. Old-timers all know about it, of course. That's where the monument is."

Dutifully, Carol and Lorie followed Sue across the lawn. "You first, Lorie." She pointed to a garden gate draped with vines, cleverly concealed in the hedge. Lorie opened it, passed under a trellis, and came into what had to be the most wonderful garden she had ever seen, fragrant with blooming roses of many varieties. In the center of a green lawn, a small fountain sprayed sparkling water into the air. The air seemed cooler, the birds more melodic.

"Fabulous," she murmured to Carol as her aunt came through the doorway. "Is that the monument? The fountain?"

"The monument's back by the hedge." Sue's voice from outside.

Carol, who had come in behind Lorie, called back, "There's just the fountain, Sue."

Lorie heard a sudden gasp. As Sue emerged through the passageway, she came to a complete stop. Wordless at last, she pointed toward a gentle green mound at the far side of the space. Around the area lay shards of shattered stone. She hurried across the grass toward the mound, followed closely by Carol.

What apparently had been an imposing monument lay now in random slabs on the grass. "Sledgehammers," Lorie said, looking around. She pointed to the pieces of a fractured tool, partially hidden under a bush. She looked up at her aunt, not knowing what to say. "Hatred!" The word issued itself.

Sue burst instantly into tears. "Who would do this?"

Lorie had heard that same anguished cry only yesterday from another source. She found the echo startling.

A deep angry male voice rose just behind them. "What are you ladies doing here? If you don't leave at once, I will have you arrested as trespassers."

Lorie whirled to confront the intruder. His tanned face was stern, his hair jet black, his eyes dark and menacing. He was wearing a tailored summer suit almost the same hue as his face, a crisp white shirt and a dark tie. Of more importance, his large body was blocking the only way out.

CHAPTER 9

Sue Bailey rose to her full height, not so much—and dignity, full bore! "Mr. Arthur Ehrlich," Sue said sternly, with perfect composure despite the tears still glistening in her eyes. "We have far more right to be here than you do. I've worked with Mr. Jon Randolph for years. You had no right to seal the house without giving us notice.

"It's my office!" Now her voice became as testy as his. "Nor did you and Mr. Maratti have cause to destroy the monument. It's been here for well over a century. It's part of the history of this community."

He looked startled. "Monument?"

She pointed to the evidence.

He stepped forward. The stern visage softened in an instant to one of genuine distress. "I can't imagine who would want to do that. Certainly not Mr. Maratti!"

Sue was momentarily silenced. "Then who?" she finally asked, her voice still sharp.

He shook his head. "I don't know." Ehrlich turned to Sue, the tone of his voice now completely transformed. "Mrs. Bailey, I must apologize for my rude outburst. I didn't recognize you right away. I am aware of your relationship with Mr. Randolph, and I'm genuinely sorry for your loss, which must be grievous." He stepped forward and took Sue's plump little hand gently in both of his big ones. As he did so, Lorie's initial evaluation of the man began a subtle shift.

That small gesture and the expression of regret in his dark eyes made her consider quite seriously that he might not be the villain some were assuming him to be.

Obviously surprised, Sue pulled the worn tissue from her pocket and again blotted at tears. In a more subdued tone, she said, "Mr. Ehrlich, this is my cousin, Carol Kendall. And her niece, Lorena Manning. They've come from Illinois for the funeral."

"And the reckoning, I expect," Ehrlich said with a sigh, offering his hand to each in turn. "Whose grave was desecrated here, if I may ask?"

"It's not a grave," Sue Bailey said. "It was a monument."

"To Mr. Randolph's parents?"

"No. It's much older than that." Sue carefully lowered herself to her knees beside one of the broken pieces of stone and, with some effort and a quick assist by Lorie, rolled it over. "You can't read it now," she pointed to the mud-smeared inscription, "but this stone was placed here well over a century ago by Mr. Jon's grandmother to honor the man who built the house: her brother. Jefferson Richard Preston."

A magic name. Startled, Lorie was coming to new conclusions every moment about the owner of that name. If he had been allowed to survive, she thought, he would have been known as someone of note: a man very much missed, even now. Maybe he was deserving of more than just two lines on his tombstone—if he still had a tombstone!

"Why would anyone want to destroy it?" Ehrlich asked, clearly puzzled. "Senseless vandalism. I wish we had placed a lock on the gate as well as the house."

At that, Sue's expression hardened. "Why didn't you warn us you were locking up the house? At the very least, we deserved a chance to move personal belongings."

"An order was presented to the judge," he said almost apologetically. "And the judge signed it. I thought you would have been notified."

"Who asked for the order?"

"Mr. Maratti did," he admitted. "He had his reasons."

"What reasons?" Sue's voice rose.

"Mrs. Bailey, why don't we discuss this when we meet with Mr. Purdy this afternoon?"

"Is the judge going to be there also?"

"I don't believe so."

"Which judge would sign an order like that?" Sue's voice was rising again. She came to her feet in full indignation.

"Sandy Cragin."

Sue went silent. Then querulously she asked, "Why Sandy? He was Jon's friend. He's a friend of ours. He should know better."

"It was necessary." Lorie had the immediate perception that Ehrlich wanted to expand on what he was saying, but legal ethics precluded further discussion. "Ladies," he continued, "I must get back to town. I apologize for the question, but could you please tell me when the funeral is being held? I'd like to be there."

"Tomorrow morning," Sue answered rather sharply. "At the community church on Main Street. It's a memorial service as Jon wanted to be cremated. I had hoped we could scatter his ashes here, but perhaps we'll have to rethink."

An expression of genuine regret crossed the big man's face. "Let's see if we can work something out," he said gently. "Please bear with us. And if you don't mind, could I rely on you folks to pull the gate shut when you leave? I'll arrange for a lock right away to make sure something like this doesn't happen elsewhere on the property. And I'll personally make sure you get a key."

Tense and silent, Sue stared at him. She sighed. Her shoulders relaxed. "Of course. I didn't think it would be necessary, but obviously it is. Thank you," she said and then inquisitively asked, "Where is your car?"

"It's in the parking lot now. I was driving out in the fields behind the house to check the status of the property. I see there's a nice-sized airfield back there."

"You could have asked me about the status of the property." Sue's tone was sharp. "I keep the records. And I have surveyor reports."

"I'm sorry. I was just following orders. But next time, Mrs. Bailey, I assure you I will keep you in the loop."

He turned and left.

"'Driving out in the fields' indeed," Sue sniffed. "Mr. Ehrlich was most likely looking for fresh land to develop."

Lorie's attention shifted to the column of broken granite at her feet. She knelt and, with a wad of tissues and occasionally her fingernail, scraped away as much as she could of the grass and soil driven into the markings by the impact of the stone with the ground. She read aloud softly, "To honor my beloved brother Jefferson Richard Preston, 1837–1864." She looked up at Carol. "He was twenty-seven when he died." Deep inside, Lorie felt a tremor.

"No verse?" Sue asked.

"Not here."

"Maybe we can find it." Carol was looking around. With effort, she turned over a larger piece. "Here it is."

Lorie joined her and again read aloud. "'So young, so fair of form and face. We weep, for we'll not see him more. Gone is his smile, his wit, his grace. He's left to seek a brighter shore.'" She thought about the brilliant smile and quick wit of the man she only knew as Jefferson Richard Preston, and the words became suddenly too personal. What if she hadn't been able to save him the night she'd met him?

She saw now the danger she'd been warned about by all her medical supervisors. Too much empathy for her own good. Getting too close to patients. She turned away, tears welling in her eyes. That old bugaboo—sudden tears!

Not at all professional. She didn't want Carol to see.

But as her aunt continued reading, Lorie strained to hear the soft voice. "'He was our anchor and our guide. He brought us courage, healed our pain. Remember him with love and pride. We will not see his like again.'" Carol, her face wet with tears, looked up at Sue. "We'll have another monument commissioned. If we can't place it here, we'll find a suitable spot. They're not going to get away with this!"

"But we don't know who they are."

"We'll root them out, Sue." Carol stood and put her arms around her cousin. "Let's get back to town and find something to eat. I need something in my gut to build up a proper head of steam."

"So that's Mr. Arthur Ehrlich," Lorie said as they walked back across the lawn to the parking area. "Is that the guy you described as a Sicilian bandit?"

Sue nodded. "Very scary."

"No, he's not," Lorie said, wondering why anyone would think so. "He's tall enough to be pretty normal, in this day and age. And he doesn't have a hooked nose at all. It's just a little larger than noses on some of the other people around here. And what's more, how many Sicilians are Jewish? Just a snap judgment here, but I'm sure he's a lot nicer person than you were led to believe. People are using racial slurs to divide old friends!"

"Jewish?" Sue said, frowning at Lorie. "Then why is everyone saying he's Mafiosi."

"Where do these rumors get started anyway?" Carol put in, now obviously irritated. "We're going to have to get very aggressive about tracking down half-truths and untruths. They're not helpful."

They met Sue's husband back at the house. Gray-haired Sid Bailey was a tall, spare man with a pleasant narrow face and a high forehead. Casually dressed in tan slacks, his white sport shirt open at the collar, he had prepared a quick meal for everyone, ham sandwiches with lettuce and fat tomato slices and everything that went with them. He paused when they walked in, iced tea pitcher in his hand. "Hi, ladies," he said in a surprisingly deep voice. "I understand you had some problems out at the house." He spotted Lorie. "Glad to meet you at last, young lady. Come join us and let's get an update on the unfolding disaster."

"Oh, Sid." Sue gazed up at him as she seated herself at the table. "I just turned all watery. I wasn't tough at all. I'm so ashamed."

"She behaved herself admirably!" Carol offered the words with pride.

Sid bestowed a genuinely loving glance on his spouse. "She always does."

Between Carol and Sue, the story was soon told. Sid sat stoic, listening to each in turn, asking occasional questions. At the conclusion of the narrative, he remained still. Lorie noticed a red flush creeping up his cheeks. Suddenly he rose from the bench, strode across the kitchen, yanked open the door, and disappeared outside, closing the door securely behind him. Lorie heard loud words coming from the back porch. Most were unintelligible, but some were very clear.

"I won't let him swear inside," Sue whispered.

"He's doing it very well," Carol whispered back. "I haven't heard some of those words before. Not sure what they mean. Maybe I should take notes."

Lorie grinned, approving the sentiment. Tension broke in the room.

"Okay," Sid said in a modulated voice when he finally reappeared. "We've got an early meeting with Will at the hotel. Let's go meet the lawyers."

A satisfied smile lighting her face, Sue said, "Let's go!" She fished a set of keys from her purse and led the way outside to the garage where brooded the family minivan beside a well-buffed vintage car much more in keeping with the historic nature of the town. They took the van.

The meeting, Sue told them, was to take place at the Imperial Hotel. "The only hotel in town," she explained. "By default, the best. And the worst. Take your pick." It was located on Main Street in the heart of downtown between one of the local banks and a dry goods store, both, Lorie decided, restored to look like something off a movie set. Delightful and decidedly tourist-worthy—to her eyes, at any rate.

The Imperial was still undergoing renovation as part of the "historic town" district. Scaffolding and paint-spattered drop cloths littered the lobby. Updated air conditioning was being installed, and high ceilings were being refurbished. Someday it would be a showplace.

Not today.

The desk clerk, a harried young woman with a deeply tanned face, dark eyes, and frizzy blond hair, looked up, saw Sid Bailey, and smiled. "Hi, Sid, what's up?"

"Afternoon, Judy," he said. "Is Will Purdy here yet? We're meeting with him in the Victorian Room."

"He's up there, Sid. Look, I heard what happened to the Major's monument. That's a crime. I'd sue if I was you."

"How on earth did she hear about that?" Lorie over-heard Sue whisper to her husband as they walked along the darkened corridor to an elevator at the end. "We didn't tell anyone. And I don't think Arthur Ehrlich would have gone around tattling. He was very upset."

"Remind me to ask her later," he answered thoughtfully.

"We have to find out," Carol concurred. "If someone is out there bragging, or even gossiping, we need names. Things seem to be getting out of hand here."

They came out of the elevator on the second floor and walked halfway back along the corridor to a room with a heavy double door, one standing open. As they entered, Lorie beheld a large Victorian-style parlor—dark woodwork, heavy pieces of furniture, elaborate ornamentation. An old couch upholstered with colorful needlepoint sat against the far wall. Another wall was dominated by a massive glass-fronted bookcase filled with ancient volumes.

A man rose dispiritedly to meet them from the depths of an overstuffed armchair near the couch. If there was such a thing as a "medium man," Lorie thought critically, Purdy was it! Medium in height, medium in weight, medium in age, medium in looks, probably medium in intellect—but she would hold that judgment in abeyance until she knew more about him. He was wearing a dark suit which might fit, she thought, if he added a few pounds. His salt-and-pepper hair hadn't been cut any time in the past month. His tie was lopsided, and his shoes didn't quite seem to match. Her impression: he was acutely distraught.

"Hi, Sid. Afternoon, Sue." He reached for their hands. He frowned at Lorie. "Who—" he began, but Sue interrupted before he could say another word.

"Will Purdy, this is my cousin Carol Kendall. And our niece Lorie Manning. They are here for the funeral, and anything you have to say can be said in their presence."

"Please be seated," Purdy responded meekly, recoiling from her intensity. "What's the nature of this meeting?"

"We were locked out of the house this morning," Sue said, her voice rising. "Did you know about that?"

"I'm afraid I did."

"Why the hell didn't you tell us?" Sid said, rather more forcefully than his wife.

"I called this morning," he said softly, "but no one was home."

"Both Sid and I have cell phones," Sue snapped, "and you have the numbers."

"Sorry, Sue," Purdy mumbled. "I would have fought it, but as I understand it, everything has to be secured until there is a complete accounting of the estate assets. It's only fair to the heirs, especially when they're coming from far places."

"No one's coming from far places," Sid Bailey grumbled. "They're here already."

"I work at the house, Will," his wife said forcefully. "Work! Do you know what that word means? Randolph House is my office." Again her voice rose. "How am I supposed to conduct business when my office is locked up tighter than a drum?"

"And where is the will, Will?" Sid's voice had turned menacing. "We know there was a will."

"I looked everywhere," Purdy protested weakly. "Everywhere. I know Mr. Jon talked about a will, but I don't think Mike ever had it typed up. I haven't even found copies."

"Claptrap!" Sue erupted. "Mr. Jon indicated to me that everything was signed, sealed, and delivered."

Purdy spoke as if he were profoundly tired. "I'm sorry, Sue. Until I find any sign of the will, even a copy of it, I have nothing to work with."

Sue crossed her arms in front of her tense sturdy body and stared at the lawyer as if her gaze could propel a beam of fire and burn him to a crisp. He took a quick step backward.

Her husband had left the room. He was talking to himself in the hallway. Lorie recognized a few of the words from his earlier recitation.

A moment later, Sid returned, accompanied by two men. One was Arthur Ehrlich, who reached for Sue's hand, then Carol's, then Lorie's. He smiled at her, and she thought the smile was a little sad. "So nice to see you ladies once again." He turned to Will Purdy and acknowledged him. But Lorie noticed that his hospitality did not extend in Purdy's case to a handshake.

It was the third person, however, who dominated the room from the moment he stepped through the doorway. Lorie was fairly certain he was taller than she was but not as tall as she had expected him to be from all the larger-than-life comments she had heard about him. He looked younger than she had envisioned as well, although he had to be well into his sixth decade. His was a commanding figure, however—slender, straight, and neat. His skin had the same Mediterranean richness as Ehrlich's. His full head of hair was black, streaked with gray at the temples. His eyes were a beautiful shade of brown, lashes, and eyebrows luxuriant. His face was clean-shaven, his nose long and straight, his lips beautifully shaped. With the exception of Jefferson Preston, Lorie had to admit, he was one of the most handsome men she had ever seen. She didn't know why that fact was so jarring. Had she been expecting to see a villain? What might a villain look like, anyway?

He seated himself gracefully on the Victorian couch, crossed his legs, adjusted the crease of his dark blue trousers, and looked up directly into Lorie's eyes. "And who do we have here?" There was only a hint of an accent in his voice.

She already knew what to do. She approached him deferentially, smiled, and reached for his hand. "My name is Lorena Manning. I'm Mrs. Kendall's niece." His eyes widened a fraction. He obviously knew the Manning name. "I'm delighted to meet you at last, Mr. Maratti. I just wish it had been a happier occasion." His handclasp was firm but brief.

He turned quickly to Carol. "Mrs. Kendall. How nice to see you again." Again he extended his hand without rising.

"Hello, Rolf. Please call me Carol. I'm so sorry Mr. Jon is gone." Taking her cue from Lorie, her aunt spoke warmly, extending both hands. He blinked. This time Lorie was not surprised.

He had not been expecting the friendly greetings or sympathy. His return smile was instinctual and quickly suppressed. Interesting. While he seemed intent on maintaining his superiority, it did not appear to be in his nature. Was he playing a role of some kind? Why?

Still seated, he turned to Sue Bailey and offered his hand. "Mrs. Bailey. I remember meeting you and your husband a few years ago at some occasion for my stepfather."

"His eightieth birthday party," Sid grumbled, but loud enough for everyone in the room to take note. "And his ninetieth, ten years later!"

"Let me tell you," he said, obviously ignoring Sid's comments, "why I decided to join you today." When Ehrlich tried to stop him, he waved his hand. "Art, this is between friends." He turned back to the Baileys. "I understand you are having trouble producing Jon Randolph's current will."

Sue spoke over Purdy's attempted response. "We know a will was written. Your stepfather spoke about it many times with both of us. I was going to look for it out at the house, but someone put locks on the doors."

"The locks were necessary," Maratti said smoothly, "but I regret your not having been notified first. I've also been informed that damage has been done in the garden." Lorie noticed the tone of his voice changing ever so slightly as he spoke of the damage as if he were more disturbed by the incident than he wanted to let on. "The judge has suggested that guards be employed, and for my part, I've agreed to it. They will patrol day and night. You can be assured that nothing else will be damaged."

"Guards?" Sid burst out.

"If you need anything during this time," Maratti interrupted before anything more could be said, "just ask my friend, Art, who is a firm advocate on your behalf. He will make sure you are escorted into and out of the mansion. You can retrieve anything you like so long as it's your own personal property or related to the day-to-day business you are handling for the estate. In the meantime…" And now the tone of his voice went a half step lower as if he had something very important to divulge. Lorie glanced at Carol and raised her eyebrows.

"What?" Carol mouthed.

"Something big," she mouthed back silently and then realized Maratti was looking straight at her, frowning.

His eyes still focused on her, Maratti went on more slowly, almost as if he did not want to say what he had to. "In the absence of a current will, I have in my possession an original will, which my stepfather wrote many years ago. I regret to say I took it with me when I left his home. I was seventeen and not too bright. However, it's signed and witnessed, and

I'm assured that it is perfectly legal if a subsequent will cannot be found. Mr. Ehrlich will file the will for probate this afternoon. It leaves everything he owned to his named sons and their heirs. I am the only one of his named sons surviving, and I have a number of heirs."

Lorie glanced at Will Purdy, who seemed strangely nonreactive. His mouth had formed the shape of an O.

The silence in the room spoke volumes.

Maratti looked at Sue. Then at Sid. "Please contact Mr. Ehrlich, and he will make arrangements for you to retrieve your personal possessions and any business files you have been working with. I have a room in this hotel in case you need to get hold of me. Thank you, ladies and gentlemen. We will meet again." He rose, made a summoning gesture to Arthur Ehrlich, looked Lorie squarely in the eyes, frowned, whirled, and left the room. Ehrlich trailed dutifully behind him without saying a word.

The silence lingered.

"How did you know it would be something that important?" Carol said to Lorie quietly.

"The tone of his voice changed."

"I think," her aunt said, still very quietly, "that you are unusually perceptive, young lady!"

"Well," Sue said, "there goes the idea of finding a love child." She glared at Purdy. "Did you know anything about this?"

As if he were in shock, he remained very still. After a moment, he said, "I've been trying to prepare for dispersal of property to blood relatives in the absence of a will. So you can inherit something, Sue. And your kids. I'm afraid this doesn't leave me much wiggle room."

"Zero," Sid said. "Unless you can find that other will. Folks, let's go home."

But once they were seated in the minivan, Lorie's aunt had another idea. "Let's go right to Phil's place, people," Carol said. "I'd like you to meet the twenty-first-century Jefferson Preston. Let's try to figure out where he came from."

"Great idea," Sid turned the car toward the highway out of town. "We need to get some fresh air. Far away from this town."

Sue leaned back with a deep sigh. "It's been a rough day all around. Who invited Maratti to our meeting?"

"What's his game?" Lorie asked.

"Game?" Carol frowned. "You really think he's playing a game?"

"He's playing something very close to the chest."

"Besides the will? If it's proved legal, he gets it all. I don't see that we have a chance now."

Very little conversation took place in the Baileys' minivan as it journeyed southward toward Marietta. Carol had called ahead to alert Phil to the change of plans.

He had a pot of coffee ready when they entered the kitchen from the back porch. "Welcome, friends," he said. "Come in, sit down, unwind. Tell Uncle Phil all about it."

"Very grim," Carol said, standing for a long moment in the circle of his arms. "A bad day all round."

Lorie busied herself, bringing cups, saucers, and cutlery to the table, as well as cream and sugar. The doctor handed her a plate of freshly baked peanut butter cookies and said to her softly, "He likes to cook."

"Is he awake?" Carol said. "I'd like the Baileys to meet him."

Phil laughed. "I finally tore him away from the computer long enough to do a little shopping. Then he made the cookies. And now he's doing some reading in my study. He seems to think it's easier to read from the printed page than from a computer screen. I can't say I disagree." He called down the hallway, and a moment later, Jeff Preston entered the kitchen, the picture of health. Taller than anyone in the room except Sid Bailey, he was wearing custom-fitted blue jeans and a white woven shirt over the tight bandages that did nothing to conceal his trim, muscular torso. On his feet were soft leather moccasins. His blond hair was finger-tousled, his blue eyes shining with cordiality.

When he saw Lorie, those eyes burst into life. Lifting her hand gently to his lips, he held it there a long moment before releasing it. The warmth of his greeting flooded her with…what? A passionate desire to be alone with him in a secluded place?

Oh my goodness, she thought, this wasn't right! She had been warned repeatedly about the empathy she experienced with her patients, but this was something very different— very dangerous!

He released her hand, gave her a conspiratorial wink, and mouthed, "Carpe diem." He moved to greet Carol with a quick hug and a peck on the cheek and then zeroed in on the Baileys, who by this time were mesmerized by his charm. They rose to greet him and shake his hand.

"By God, you must be Jon's kin," Sid Bailey exclaimed. "I've seen that face somewhere, I swear."

"I've seen it, too, and I know exactly where." Sue took his hand in both of hers. "It's Great-Great-Grandma Sara's face! And her eyes, sure enough. You are kin all right. And you and our son Jimmy, almost like two peas in a pod. Don't you see it, Sid?"

Lorie was startled by Sue's words, although even she had begun to assume Jeff was a blood relative. To have it confirmed so affirmatively was somewhat of a shock.

"Would there be old pictures at the house?" Phil asked. "Taken before you folks moved here?"

"Yes, dammit," Sid said firmly, and Lorie's initial alarm turned to amusement when she spotted Sue's warning glance at her husband. "The house is locked up tighter than Ft. Knox," Sid continued. "We can't get in to work or anything except with an escort." Between the two of them, with occasional comments from Carol, they related the whole sorry tale of the morning's encounter with Arthur Ehrlich to the meeting with Rolf Maratti in the afternoon.

"What house are you speaking of?" Jeff said into the silence when they quit speaking.

"Randolph House," Sue said. "It's where Jon Randolph lives in Randolph City."

"Did it ever have another name?"

"Well, before Mr. Jon moved back there with Maria and Rolf, it was called Oak Hill Plantation. Is that what you mean?"

"Oak Hill?" His eyebrows rose with his quick smile. "And the town was also called Oak Hill, I presume?"

"Randolph City?" Sid said. "Sure. Jon became so much a part of the town they officially changed its name, years back, in gratitude for his generosity."

"Does the summer kitchen still stand at the plantation?" Jeff asked, his voice very animated now. "And the boxwood maze?"

"Yes." Sue's voice held a question.

"What do you want to find at Oak Hill? Write out a list. Tell me where the items are. We can go in the back way tonight. Lorie and myself." He looked at Lorie, now grinning broadly. Was he serious?

When she looked around her, she saw other faces staring at Jeff in astonishment. For a long while, no one said a word.

"You've been there?" Carol asked.

"Many times in years past. If the plantation's traditions have been honored, I'll be able to find my way around quite easily."

"Then you know a lot more than we do about it," Sue said. "There will be guards."

"That is of no importance. What do you wish to find?"

"The will," Sid said after a long silence, "would be helpful."

CHAPTER 10

In the lingering silence, Jeff's eyebrows rose. "The will? Where was it last seen?"

"I looked in the vault," Sue Bailey answered. "The will wasn't there. Jon talked about a green box. He said it was in the clock room. We don't know what he meant. So we wanted to search some of the hiding places we know about."

"I know them all."

"The clock room?"

"I have an idea what he meant."

"You've been in Randolph House?" the doctor said, finally closing his mouth.

Jeff answered, "It was many years ago. But I remember it well."

"Lorie tells us you found Riverside Plantation," Sue Bailey said.

"Yes."

"Then you are beginning to remember."

"Some things."

"Bring personal stuff back," Sid said excitedly. He pulled a small notebook out of his pocket, fished the stub of a pencil from another, and began to write, speaking aloud. "Photo albums. Letters, journals, things like that. Mr. Jon kept them organized in file cabinets and on his library shelves. Any photos of you that you can find."

"If it's there and we find it, we will bring it back. Lorie? Are you with me?"

Not trusting her voice, Lorie nodded. She had promised to stand beside him if he needed help—a promise she was determined to keep. And this was only his first request! Why was she beginning to tremble?

Sue and Sid huddled together, making lists, indicating places where items could be found. "You'll have to take a backpack or a duffel bag," Sue said, lifting her head and looking at Jeff.

"For the first trip, we'll focus on the most important items," he told her. "Only as much as we can carry easily."

"The first trip?" Lorie whispered, wondering how many further trips were anticipated.

"It sounds too dangerous," Carol said quietly, echoing some of Lorie's hesitance. "What if the guards are out there already? And what if they're carrying guns?"

He reached for her hand. "My dear friend Carol, they won't know we are there."

"You're sure?"

Lorie saw his anticipatory smile and wondered again what she had signed up for. "And perhaps my entry into Randolph House," he then added, speaking now to Lorie, "will bring back more memories. Useful memories."

"How will you do it?" Sid wanted to know.

"Do you have a map of the property?"

"The computer you were using," Phil Barnett said. "Bring the computer. Let's get a satellite view."

Jeff brought the laptop to the table and spent the next fifteen minutes exploring the capabilities of satellite cameras. "This is astounding. I can see that some of the original trails remain. We will need someone to transport us to this position, right about here." He traced a fingertip across the monitor. "Is the estate fenced?"

"Split rail yesterday," Sue said ominously. "I can't speak for today. Mr. Jon had a gate put across the drive to discourage casual tourists, but he didn't mind bird watchers and hikers. If they came up to the house and knocked, he served them mint tea and cookies. If Maratti's people are serious about locking up the property, though, you might be facing barbed wire."

He looked at her, frowning. "Barbed wire?"

"Let's carry a blanket," Lorie suggested hastily, recalling something she had recently read...that the now ubiquitous "barbed" wire had not been invented until a few years after the end of the Civil War. A discussion at this point could become, well, awkward! "If we have to climb over barbed wire, it will be useful." She would explain it to Jeff if need be.

"Have the trails been cleared recently?"

"Occasionally." Sid Bailey was now caught up completely in the unexpected venture. "And I see what you're getting at. Not many people use the trails nowadays since our kids and their friends went away to school. But occasionally Mr. Jon sends...sorry, sent people out to clean up and make sure serious hikers had access. That place you indicated as a drop-off—it's as close to the nature trail as you're going to get from the road."

"You are indeed knowledgeable," Jeff said.

"So are you, mister," Sid replied. "And it's clear you know what you're talking about."

"We'll need flashlights," Lorie suggested quickly, hoping Jeff would not bring up the idea of lanterns.

"Done," said the doctor, who rooted through one of his kitchen drawers, pulled out two small LED flashlights and handed them to Lorie. With a sigh of relief, she tested them and then slipped them into her purse.

"We need dark clothing," Jeff said.

"Hooded sweatshirts and the like?" Phil asked. "I've got closets full of those."

While the Baileys and Jeff further planned the expedition, Lorie joined the doctor and her aunt in preparing a meal. A big bowl of tomato sauce laced with fresh sweet onions and garlic was placed in the middle of the table along with shredded Parmesan cheese. Texas toast came hot from the oven. A fresh vegetable salad was forked into salad bowls. And ready for serving was steaming hot pasta liberally splashed with olive oil.

Everyone but Lorie was feeling much better by the time dinner was done.

Sue Bailey sat back and lifted a glass of cabernet in an informal toast. "Jeff Preston or whoever you are, where have you been all our lives?"

"Someday perhaps I can tell you that."

As daylight faded, tensions began to mount.

"Shoes?" Jeff said to Lorie.

"My hiking boots are in the trunk of the car." She headed out to get them. She had already changed into jeans and a long-sleeved black shirt donated by the doctor and for that reason somewhat too large. She rolled up the sleeves. Grabbing the flashlights from her purse, she shoved them into the back pocket of her jeans.

"I have blue greasepaint," the doctor said, "left over from a play I was in. Want it for your faces?"

When Jeff realized what it was, he nodded. "Far kinder than mud, I suspect." He looked around. "We need something in which to carry the treasures we're fetching back."

"My youngest son's Scout backpack," Phil said, handing it over.

"Bug spray," Lorie said.

The good doctor nodded. He walked out of the room and brought back an aerosol can. Lorie sprayed herself liberally, then turned the spray on Jeff.

"What...?" She grinned at his sputters.

"Trust me! It will protect you from chiggers, ticks, and mosquitoes."

He put up with the indignity of being dosed front to back and returned her playful smile. "Are we ready now?" He turned then to Sid. "Have you been in the summer kitchen lately?"

"About a week ago."

"Is the door locked?"

"The kitchen's long been used as a storage shed, so the door has a padlock on it. But the old windows are easy enough to unlatch if you have a long wire and don't mind climbing in through spiderwebs." Lorie shuddered a little, but Sid's eyes were alight. "There's a tunnel, isn't there? I always thought there must be. But I've never been able to find it."

Jeff grinned broadly and gave a wink.

Sid went off to find a wire coat hanger and put himself to the task of making an appropriate tool.

In the meantime, his wife was on the phone. She came back into the kitchen, very excited. "Judy, over at the Imperial Hotel, tells me she overheard several strangers talking together this morning about how the monument had been destroyed."

"Strangers?" Phil Barnett said. "I guess she'd know, wouldn't she?"

"She knows everyone in town," Sue concurred. "Anyway, she saw them again later talking with Judge Cragin, and rumor has it that these guys have been hired as guards out at Randolph House."

"You mean," Lorie asked with growing indignation, "that the same people who broke the monument are going to be paid to guard the property?"

"We don't want to jump to conclusions about their guilt," Carol said hastily.

"How many men did she see?" Jeff asked.

"Five or six."

"Uh-oh," Sid said. "Perhaps we should call this expedition off."

"I can assure you they won't see us." Jeff shrugged a black turtleneck sweatshirt over his head and pulled it down around his hips. "Did she say anything else?"

"That they seem to be Southern boys from the way they talk. Country boys, she thought, although they were dressed pretty sharp. She said they look tough."

"Sid," Jeff asked him, "do you have any qualms about transporting us to the property line?"

"Not a bit," the tall man exclaimed. "After I drop you off, I'll go on home and wait for your call when you're ready for a ride back. Sue, I'd like you to stay here with Carol. Don't worry, I'll keep in touch."

"Jeff," the doctor put in, "your hair stands out like a beacon. Here's something." It was a knit black cap with a gold stripe around the rim. The words "West Point" were embroidered above the stripe in a stylistic script. Jeff looked at it, grinned again, and pulled it down across his fair hair.

He winked at Lorie. "Ready, Captain Manning?"

"Since when did I get promoted to a position of responsibility?" she grumbled. She took the rough woolen khaki blanket Phil Barnett handed to her and walked out into the darkness.

She rode in the back seat, relieved she didn't have to do the driving. She was beginning to feel a bit sick. Was this what it was like to be a soldier? Nervous? Dry-mouthed? Jumpy? How had she got here anyway? Jeff and Sid Bailey were conversing softly, still coordinating times and places, running through possible snags. Escape scenarios were discussed briefly. And then, too soon, Sid slowed the minivan and braked to a stop at the side of the road. When he turned off the headlights and the engine, Lorie thought the night had never been so dark.

She unlatched her door very quietly, as Jeff was doing in front. The interior car lights went on, an anemic glimmer surrounded by utter darkness. Jeff stretched free, pushed his door gently into the click of the latch, and reached for her hand. In the forest, cicadas and tree frogs were doing an admirable task of masking small sounds.

"The backpack?" he whispered. She handed it to him, tucked the blanket under her arm, and shut the back door as quietly as Jeff had earlier. The lights went out as he was slinging the backpack over his shoulder.

"Greasepaint?" she asked him. She had already applied some to her cheeks and forehead. In the darkness, she reached out and transferred the small bottle into his hand. A moment later, the pale white oval of his face disappeared. She pulled a dark scarf from her pocket and wrapped it around her hair. She didn't like spiders. Not big ones. Not little ones. Especially not webs with all kinds of yukky things stuck in them. "Here's your flashlight." Dangling the khaki blanket around her neck, she switched the light on briefly to show him how it worked.

"Damnation," he said, seemingly startled. "This would have saved my life and Ben's a couple of nights ago."

The words jarred her! Could she opt out this late in the game?

Too late! Lorie heard the minivan's engine quietly turn over and watched red tail lights move ever more quickly, almost silently away from them down the quiet country road.

Jeff switched on the small flashlight and led her through the high weeds lining the road. They had not gone far before they found the fence, no more than a split rail barrier. With seemingly little effort, Jeff picked Lorie up, set her across, and followed in one quick movement. There was no way now but to finish what they had begun.

He flashed the light around for a moment and suddenly held firm. "There's the trail," he said. "Now stay very close. I'll use the light only to get our bearings."

There was no moonlight, but stars were brilliant in the sky. She could see him ahead of her on the path as a shadow against shadows. He was walking with such quiet footsteps that she might never have known he was there. Her booted feet, on the other hand, scrunched.

She tried walking more quietly. *Scrunch. Scrunch. Scrunch.* It wasn't working. He turned back to her and whispered, as if he knew what she was thinking, "Don't worry. No one will be out here in the dark, and the tree frogs are collaborating nicely. We're a long way from the house. I'll warn you when we're close."

The hike seemed interminable. *Scrunch. Scrunch. Scrunch. Scrunch.* There were rustlings in the dark, mysterious depths of the deep woods, unfamiliar sounds, and drifting mist. Surely animals were watching them. What kind? If it was bears, she didn't think she wanted to know. She needed to keep up with Jeff and moved a little faster. *Scrunch. Scrunch. Scrunch.* He stopped suddenly, and she almost ran into him.

"We're about to come out of the woods," he said very softly. "See there ahead. A light."

She did see it and felt a sudden burst of panic. He reached for her hand and squeezed it, and then his arms went around her, and he pulled her tightly against his body in a reassuring hug. She felt his breath on her cheek, felt his lips brushing super-sensitive skin, and then she heard his quiet voice in her ear, "Stay here. I'll scout ahead and return for you in a very short time. In the meantime, put these on." He handed her some soft, pliable shoes with thick innersoles. Real Indian moccasins?

Her heart was beating wildly, and now it wasn't just the darkness of the night. She was reminded once again how little she knew about this mysterious man. Much as she liked him, why in heaven's name had she said yes to this crazy expedition? And then she realized with a surety she had never known before that she didn't want to be any other place right now than where she was.

Quickly she removed her boots and replaced them with the soft moccasins. They fit as if they were custom-made.

He was back as suddenly as he had left. "They're all at the house. Three at the front, two in back. We're leaving the trail right now."

"Where are we going?"

"Into the maze. An orchard used to grow behind the maze. It is long gone, nothing left at all, but it's dark enough if we take care."

He held up their mission for a long moment at the edge of the woods, listening for any sound that would indicate human presence nearby. A good hundred feet of open ground lay between the trees and the tall boxwood hedges.

Lorie followed him as he sprinted across the lawn. It seemed they were silent as shadows against the backdrop of black woodlands. Still, it was with a great deal of relief she realized they had reached the wall of glossy boxwood unseen.

She felt his hand at her waist. A quick whisper. "Stay very close." He moved ahead of her, reached backward with his right hand to grasp hers, and led the way through a narrow opening into an aromatic tunnel of leaves. Except for an occasional glimpse of stars far overhead, Lorie felt, for a panicky moment, she had gone blind.

He traversed the tight passages without hesitation, always brushing their joined right hands against the leafy wall. He seemed utterly confident. Still Lorie could not shake a sense of unease. How long had it been since he'd been in the maze? How often did mazes get changed? Did they ever get changed? *Stop it*, she chided herself sternly.

A moment later, he paused and dropped, pulling her down beside him. He switched on the flashlight for an instant, flicked the beam across the lower branches to her right, and as the light just as quickly went out, she saw he was pressing those branches downward and apart. A moment later, he touched her back, very gently, but clearly indicating that she should crawl through to the other side.

In for a penny, in for a pound. Leaving the blanket in his care, she squirmed as quietly as she could through the narrow opening he had created. With minimal movement, he bundled the blanket and backpack and handed them into her keeping. Finally understanding what he was attempting, Lorie reached for the branches and held them apart—and mere seconds later, he was beside her. A quick flash of his light beam showed that they were now sharing quite a deep recess carved out of the back wall of the stone summer kitchen next to the broad chimney. Another short flash of light illuminated parallel rows of iron pegs driven into the wall at body-width, hand-hewn toeholds constructed between them, leading upward. A virtual ladder!

Keeping his hand across most of the lens, Jeff directed a narrow beam of light upward. Lorie saw their chosen entry point—a small dark window placed in the stone wall beside the fireplace. When she stood tall, the sill of the window just brushed hair at the top of her head. The window sash itself ended at a point somewhere far above.

Again the light went off. Jeff moved swiftly upward and Lorie could hear him working with the window. The bottom of the sash shifted outward with a loud grinding sound. She froze.

From the distance came a low murmur of voices. Beams from two flashlights bounced across tree branches above, twinkled along a high ridge of boxwood leaves, and were finally cut off by the building itself. Lorie wondered if the hollow beating of her heart could be heard that far away. Shortly the lights went off, and the voices subsided.

Again Lorie heard Jeff working with the reluctant window sash. It opened outward from the bottom, pivoted up, and with a gentle *click*, was captured high above by a metal latch imbedded in the overhanging roof. The noise was diffused by the rise and swell of the night creatures' songs. He hoisted himself through the window, and she heard the muffled thump of his feet hitting the floor inside. She handed up the blanket and the backpack. He took them. Then standing on something inside, he leaned out the window, reached for her hands, and helped her to pull herself up the makeshift ladder. Once she was on a level with the opening, it was easy to worm her way across the sill. He caught her under her arms, lowered her quietly to the floor, and seconds later, joined her.

They stood very still, close together. Lorie's nerves were sparking. Had those unavoidable scuffling sounds been heard? No cry of alarm resounded from the direction of the house.

In the softest of whispers, Jeff finally asked for the blanket. He walked away, and when the dim rectangle of a front window went darker, she knew where he had hung it. He then knelt and made use of the flashlight.

Garden tools, lawnmowers, and yard furniture seemed to have laid claim to the old building. It was damp and cobwebby. Instinctively Lorie brushed at her hair, whipping away the scarf she had wrapped about it. Quickly she retrieved the scarf and stuffed it into her pocket.

Jeff touched her hand and put his light into it, motioning for her to move backward. She stepped behind him, keeping the light on his hand. He knelt, pushed three fingers through a knothole in a large plank of floorboard, and twisted. He then reached for a similar knothole about two feet away and did the same thing. Taking a firm grasp, he pulled upward. That plank, roughly three by five feet, was half of a hinged covering to smooth subflooring in which was embedded a large metal ring. He levered the ring to an upright position, twisted it, and pulled. Nothing happened. He rose to his feet, angled around to get better leverage, and this time used both hands. A large rectangular section of subflooring moved slowly upward at right angles to its concealing cover, groaning as it came. The odor of murky dampness drifted up from below.

"Lights off," he said. She doused the flashlight, and they waited.

Minutes later, hearing nothing, Lorie once more switched on the flashlight. Light gleamed on rungs leading downward into darkness.

Even with two flashlights directed into the hole, it seemed awesomely forbidding. Jeff indicated she should go first. She drew a deep breath, knelt backward at the opening, and holding firmly to his outstretched hands, gingerly reached a leg downward until her foot was firmly set on the first rung. He held her as she lowered herself onto the ladder and began her descent.

He remained above for a moment. She heard the scrape of moving wood. Finally, he stepped down onto the top rung, then the next, gripping a knob on the trap door above him, letting it rest on his arm as he descended one step at a time. As he reached a midway step, the panels above closed with a sliding sound and a soft double thud. Lorie's foot hit solid earth. She was down.

The blackness of the deep musky tunnel nearly swallowed their narrow light beams. Almost out of range, a bright-eyed creature scuttled away. The seeping walls, slick with moss and mold, were constructed of roughly cut stone blocks welded together by some version of cement. Sturdy wooden planks dark with age formed the ceiling. At intervals, heavy timber framing assured that nothing short of a major earthquake could destroy what man had built.

They walked cautiously along the slimy floor through the darkness, dodging puddles and startled creatures, ducking now and then to avoid water leaking resolutely through from above.

The tunnel ended at a wooden door gleaming damply in the two beams of light.

"What now?" Lorie whispered.

Jeff released a catch on one side of the door and pulled hard. It pivoted open with a groan, allowing entry into pitch darkness. Sudden light, Jeff's flashlight, showed the space to be a storage area lined with unused shelves. When they had come through, he returned the door to its original position. That area appeared now to be no more than a rough brick wall, its utility unknown to any but its builder.

She flashed her light around the modest-sized space with its odor of mildew and age. Rows of wooden shelves lined two walls. Home-canned goods were stacked high.

Jeff turned his light up to an electric bulb in the ceiling. "The root cellar has changed." He pulled at the hanging cord, and light flooded the room.

Lorie was startled. "Is that safe?"

"No windows. Let's enjoy the light while we can."

He was right. There was something quite reassuring about it. She could see his smile, the brightness of his eyes, and the greasepaint smeared across his handsome face.

"You have cobwebs in your hair." He grinned as he took a handkerchief from his pocket and worried the webs away.

"Thank you, kind sir." She took a deep breath, thankful she hadn't inadvertently released that cowardly sound lurking so close within her throat!

He wiped the soles of his moccasins carefully on a pile of rags in the corner of the room and had Lorie do the same. He then readjusted the backpack hanging from his shoulder. His light went off.

Again they were a part of the darkness. Behind the next door lay a large mechanical room, not remotely crowded by a large boiler, two water heaters, and overhead, many pipes spread like the legs of giant spiders across most of the ceiling. Close by, sturdy wooden steps rose to an upper door. Jeff went first. At the top, he leaned against the door, listening.

"It's quiet," he whispered. "I don't think anyone is in the house."

At that thought, Lorie's heart skipped. She felt a trifle dizzy. She had never been as sure as her companion that all would go without incident.

He pushed the door open. "The pantry," he said. Lorie flashed her light around and saw that it was a fairly large room—about the size of her mother's spacious kitchen. Each of the four walls was covered from top to bottom with cabinets, except for areas where standard-sized modern doors had been cut through.

Jeff opened one of the doors and looked into the next room. "Kitchen." He pulled the door shut. His light moved to a swinging door on the adjacent wall. "This should lead to the dining room." He opened the next. "The hallway. The fastest way to get to the drawing room. Follow me."

He used the light sparingly. She stayed as close behind him as she dared. They moved along a broad hallway with doors at either side, some open, some closed. At the end of the hall, he paused, listened, and very gently turned the knob his right hand was touching.

She could tell from the swirl of air that it was a large room. All she could see clearly in the narrow beam of her swiftly moving light were two couches and several armchairs grouped comfortably before a large fireplace set into an interior wall.

He stepped inside, turning his flashlight around the room as he did so. "It's just the same, in a way." His voice was rather sad. "But it looks so…worn."

Lorie flashed her light around as well. Worn? A curious word for priceless antiques.

She moved her light across several pictures hanging on the wall. Over the fireplace hung the likeness of a beautiful woman dressed in a delicately draped black chiffon evening gown. She was seated. Her long slender hands lay gracefully in her lap. Her black hair, pulled severely back from a pale face, was crowned with a tiara of sparkling gems. Her dark eyes were large and lustrous, and at her throat, she wore an elaborately entwined necklace set with diamonds.

"A lovely woman," Jeff whispered, directing his light toward the same picture. "She looks like a queen."

"Maratti's mother," Lorie responded. "Judging by the fashion of the time, it can't be anyone else."

She moved her light to the next portrait…that of a man dressed in a dark business suit reminiscent of the late '50s. Faint shadings of gray at his temples gave him a distinguished appearance, but his blue eyes seemed to twinkle with suppressed humor. His face was strong, and the expression on it spoke of determination as well as compassion. Jon Randolph Third himself? Lorie wondered, but before she could ask Jeff, he swept the flashlight from her hand and doused its light.

"Someone's on the portico."

She heard it, too. Footsteps just outside the window. Muted voices. She froze.

Words came dimly through from beyond the draped windows. "There's someone in that place, I tell you."

Jeff's arm came around her. She huddled close to him, holding her breath.

"So what do you want me to do about it?"

The first voice spoke again. "You're in charge, Moultrie. You tell me."

"Look, Daniels, there's no one out there. Now will you just leave me alone?"

Lorie let out a big sigh of relief. It was the summer kitchen they were speaking of. Jeff's arm tightened in a triumphant squeeze.

"I heard noises," the first voice persisted.

"Yeah? What kind of noises?"

"Well, you know...groans...rattles. You'd have to hear them!"

"Ghosts!" Moultrie laughed out loud. "Big tough guy. Ghosts? Damn!"

Daniels stood his ground. "I did hear something!"

"Was the padlock broken?" Moultrie asked sarcastically, and upon receiving a negative response, he said, "Did you see anything when you shined the light in? Real or unreal?"

"Couldn't see in," said the sullen, petulant voice. "Could be anything."

"Nobody told us to look out for the storehouse," Moultrie snapped. "It's prob'ly a raccoon. We're here to keep people out of the mansion. Now you git back out there where you can keep an eye on the perimeter of the house. And remind Klein he's bein' paid to keep a sharp eye out, too."

There was a scraping sound on the portico as if a chair were being moved across the floorboards. Moultrie had apparently settled himself just outside one of the big windows. "Everything okay out there, Leeds?" he called. From the distance came the reply that all was clear.

Jeff switched his flashlight back on. An elegant antique glass-fronted cabinet stood against one wall. It contained a display of ancient clocks and watches. A small gaslight fixture jutted out from the wall close beside it. Jeff reached for the fixture and gave it a quick twist one direction, then two twists backward, and the whole cabinet turned smoothly out into the room.

Lorie exhaled very quietly. The clock room.

He didn't have to ask her twice to join him in the concealed room beyond. He closed the wall silently behind them and flashed light around. A cord hanging from the ceiling came into view. He pulled it. Florescent light flooded the room.

"Splendid," he said softly, smiling. "Jon Randolph found my special room. I was hopeful he would have." He released the backpack and pulled the West Point cap off his tousled hair.

"Your special room?" She frowned at him. "Jeff, you know exactly who you are and what you're doing here. Don't you?"

"I do," he said. She waited for an explanation. Instead, he looked around. The room was long and somewhat narrow, small compared to the spaces Lorie had glimpsed from the hallway. But it was far too large to be considered a closet. Stacks of framed paintings, some covered loosely by old sheets and newspapers and some not, lay on the floor or leaned against the walls. A spinning wheel stood in one corner of the room next to an ancient dough box. Other household objects of varying degrees of antiquity were either stacked on shelves which lined one of the walls or lay about the room in neat, separate piles. None were in good repair, and Lorie surmised that they were being stored for eventual restoration.

Jeff touched her arm and pointed toward one of the more dimly lit corners of the room. On a battered paint-stained cigarette table sat a large green metal box. "I think we have found what we seek." He opened the box, picked up a document or two, scanned them briefly, and put them back.

Lorie looked up into his face. "The will?"

"Yes. But, Lorie, there is something else I must show you before we examine what we have found."

"You're sounding very serious, Jeff."

"This is very serious, my dear love."

"Serious"? "Dear love"? She suddenly felt a little light-headed.

"You saw my wounds the other night."

"Of course. And I continue to wonder how you have the strength to do all this physical stuff. I'm sometimes afraid you're not being careful enough!"

He stood silent for a moment, then stripped off the black shirt. Next, he lifted the white tee shirt and pulled it over his head. As she stood motionless awaiting his explanation, he proceeded to peel away the bandages. She held her breath. A moment later, he stood before her bare to the waist. His muscular torso rippled in the bright fluorescent light. "Look at my right side, Lorie. Feel it."

She had quickly closed her eyes, not wanting to look. Even the thought of that torn flesh brought her to the brink of tears, but she was a nurse, or had been. She opened her eyes. And she realized what he meant.

"No wound? Jeff...?"

"No scar. No bruises."

"What...?"

He turned to one of the larger covered paintings leaning against the wall and slowly pulled away its soft white shroud. Created in oils, it was the full-length portrait of a Confederate soldier. His strong, handsome face was tanned by the sun, his blond hair was rumpled, his sparkling eyes were blue as the sky, and the smile on his scar-cut face was boyish and infectious. He was wearing a double-breasted gray jacket trimmed in gold. There was a star at each side of his stiff upturned collar. Lorie had seen that jacket before—had taken it soaked with blood from the man who was standing in the room beside her. Glowing.

"Oh crap!" she said as darkness enveloped her brain.

CHAPTER 11

When she regained her senses, a little sick to her stomach, he was kneeling, holding her in his arms. Her cheek was cradled in a warm place between his bare shoulder and his chin.

"I'm sorry," he said contritely. "I didn't expect that! I couldn't catch you. You're going to have a hell of a headache later, I'm afraid. I'm so sorry, Lorena. Here." She knew he was trying hard, but it only made things worse. "Put your head down between your knees. That should bring the blood back."

She leaned over. What humiliation!

And then she started to cry!

"Sweet girl," he whispered, securing her once more against his sturdy bare shoulder. "It's okay. Really it is. It must be hard to have to deal with this." His eyes were so kind, his voice so soothing. He leaned back against the nearby wall, stretched his legs out along the floor, and brought her tightly into the embrace of his arms against the warmth of his bare chest, his hand in her hair. And then his beautiful lips sought and found hers, and she couldn't cry anymore, even if she wanted to. She wrapped her arms around his shoulders and pushed her fingers up through his hair, and they both slid to the floor. He made short work of the shirt she was wearing, and her bra came with it, sliding easily up her arms and over her head.

"My God," he said a few exquisite moments later, "I'm so sorry, Lorena. I didn't mean to pounce like that!"

He didn't seem very sorry, she thought. And she realized she wasn't sorry at all!

His lips were brushing hers very lightly even as he spoke. They had just passed over her cheeks, her neck, and her ears, raining gentle kisses. They moved down to her breasts. He stroked her arms, her sides, and her back and played around the waistline of her jeans, as if wishing to seek out a greater treasure. "It's just...well, I'm almost consumed by...urges I can hardly resist. I can't keep my hands away from you." He lifted his head and looked down into her face. "But we have a task. They'll worry about us if we're gone too long."

"I quite understand," Lorie said breathlessly. "I guess we'd better get busy." She stretched up and backward for the shirt and her undergarment, both of which she supposed were somewhere on the floor near her head. The effort again melded her upper body to his. Every place skin touched skin she burst to fire, flesh trembling at the touch of his fingers and his lips.

But dammit, he was right. This was not exactly the optimum time.

Did she care?

Well, she knew Aunt Carol would worry if they didn't check in soon. She grabbed her clothes and sat up beside him. With a deep sigh, he brought her gently back into his embrace.

"I don't remember having put greasepaint...right there," she said a moment later as she lay again beneath his loving gaze. She indicated a particularly sensitive spot. "Nor there."

"Nor do I remember putting it here." He lifted her hand onto his warm chest, and she felt the accelerated beating of his heart. "But we are moving a little too fast, I do think." Very gently, he began to wipe greasepaint from various parts of her body with the scarf she had brought for her hair.

Once again, their lips came together in a magical burst of heat and passion. It was all she could do not to divest herself of the rest of her clothing.

"Oh, good grief," she said after a time. "Was there something we were supposed to be doing here?"

"Damnation," he said, sounding equally frustrated, "they'll be waiting for us, won't they?" He was quiet for a long moment. "Lorie, in case you're wondering...I don't usually..."

"Neither do I. Really!"

"But it just seemed so...right...somehow!"

"I know."

"I've never felt like this about anyone. No one but you, Lorena!"

"Neither have I," Lorie said, in what she considered the greatest understatement of her life. "But what bothers me"— she hesitated as she sat up, as he fumbled to help her fasten the bra behind her back—"is how I think...even if I didn't want to..."

"You sensed that what I had told you was the truth. From the beginning. I thought you did. How the devil does this thing...? Oh, there it goes."

"I tried not to know..." She felt again like she wanted to cry. Needed to cry!

"I know. But, Lorie, you have a rare gift. You are unnaturally perceptive. Or you would still disbelieve..." He turned her toward him, cradled her face in his hands, gave her another kiss, then helped her with her pullover.

"Being perceptive in one way seems to have lost me a career," she said pensively as her head reemerged. Tears began to form. "But if you're right…and to get back to the reason we're here…besides this…" Another passionate kiss, and she added breathlessly, "I'm not sure I'm perceptive enough to understand what else is being played out here."

"Tell me what you think is happening, Lorie."

She leaned against him, looking up into his face. "Besides something or someone trying very hard to bring us together, you mean?"

Very gently, he brushed her tears away with gentle fingers. He pulled her tightly against him and buried his face in her hair. "I do believe that. I do believe we were destined to meet. But give me your first thoughts, my darling dark-haired angel, on what's happening in Oak Hill—Randolph City, they call it now. I find I trust your conclusions more than any others I've heard."

She thought about it for a time. He really wanted her assessment. Under the circumstances, that was a huge responsibility. She knew so little. Nothing, compared to her aunt Carol and the others. Could she really help him? She said softly, "All I know is that Mr. Rolf Maratti is playing some kind of game with all of us. And a good man—his lawyer, Arthur Ehrlich—is backing him up. I don't think they are the enemy. But they may be forced into working for the enemy. Or something else is being played out here entirely.

"That's real definite, isn't it? I'll try to help, but Jeff, I just got into this game."

Chuckling, he pulled her to her feet, then reached for the sham bandage and his own two shirts, white and black.

"I don't doubt you at all, having observed with wonder the logic that flows from your sharp mind." With her help, he was soon dressed again, preparing to refresh his facial camouflage.

"But, Jeff, what I do isn't magic. I watch. I listen. I put two and two together. Like I…somehow…knew…dammit!" Feeling her knees go wobbly, she sank onto a chair that had been drawn up beside the cigarette table. Frowning, Jeff knelt before her on one knee, supporting her. She reached out to him and touched his face gently with her fingertips, his lips, the deep scar on his forehead. "Major Jefferson Richard Preston, I've fallen head over heels in love with you! You feel like a real living human being. You act like one. But you can't be, can you? Am I going to lose you when this mission of yours is finished?"

The expression on his face was very solemn. He took her hands into his. "Lorie, those lovely green eyes of yours, your sweet laughter, they've dominated all my dreams. I knew you were to be my guide the instant I saw you. Finding the will may be only part of the reason for my presence here. I don't know what else might lie ahead. But I agree. We are meant to be together, at least for now. Perhaps we will have the good fortune to make our own future. But we must both be aware, dear one, we must both also be prepared for loss."

"How can I lose you now?" The tears started again. She tried to find a tissue somewhere, couldn't find anything, lifted her shirttail, and mopped at her face.

He rose, pulled her to her feet, and wrapped her into his warm arms. "We might never have met at all if you had not come here with your aunt. Something much larger is at play here, Lorena, with many implications. I think the loss of your nursing career is part of a greater plan. I don't know how much time we have. But we can make the best of that time. We have had these few private moments. We will make time for more, much more before this is done."

She wiped at her eyes and, finally successful with her tissue search, blew her nose. "I will like that, Major Preston." Suddenly swept with a vision of how barren her life would have been if she had never met this man, she folded her arms tightly, possessively, around his body. She buried her face into his shirt, took comfort from the smell of him, the feel of him—and felt his strength surge through her.

Finally gathering in her emotions, she took a deep breath and reluctantly turned back to the cigarette table upon which the green file box rested. She reseated herself. "Okay, then!" She looked up at him. "In that case, let's see what else we have found for all our worried relatives."

As he had done earlier, she opened the unlocked lid. "It's the will, all right." She held up a rather bulky document, spread out the long pages, and started to read. "Last Will and Testament of Jon Thomas Randolph III." It was dated quite a number of years in the past. She flipped to the last page. Jon Randolph had signed the will personally. But the names and addresses of the witnesses were typed rather than handwritten. Obviously this was not the original copy.

"But it is proof," Jeff said to her reassuringly, "that there is a will. This should count for something."

"And now we have the names of the witnesses," she said with a nod. "That should count for something, too."

Lorie returned the document to the green box, closed and latched it. Jeff placed it into the backpack and slung the backpack over his shoulder. "They'll be wondering what happened to us," Lorie said. She looked up again into Jeff's face, once again covered with greasepaint.

He pulled her into his arms and kissed her most tenderly. Then with gentle fingers he smoothed the transferred black substance across her cheeks and forehead. Every inch of her body smoldered at his touch. "May these memories last forever," he whispered. He switched off the light and opened the hidden panel. "And now it's time to call our friend, Sid, and have him waiting for us at the fence."

They heard Moultrie's voice. He was talking to someone right outside the front window. Silently they crept through the drawing room, the hallway, and the pantry. Behind a series of closed doors, Lorie pulled out her cell phone and made the call. Carefully they descended to the mechanical room and moved directly to the root cellar. The stone wall gave way fairly easily once Jeff relocated the hidden latch, and then they were back in the dark, damp tunnel. Jeff took Lorie's hand, and with the help of the small flashlight, they traversed the distance rather more quickly than when they had come into the house.

He ascended the ladder first and tried to raise the trap-door. For a moment it stuck. Then suddenly, it broke free and moved upward with a deep groan and an annoying scraping sound.

A voice sounded from close outside. "Moultrie, get out here!"

"Quick!" He reached for her hands and pulled her bodily up the steps. The trapdoor closed silently. Jeff set the floor panels into place with even more haste, then hoisted Lorie up to the escape window. She squirmed out, made a half-twist, and descended silently to the ground. He handed out the backpack and was beside her an instant later, closing the window as he exited.

Footsteps pounded across the lawn. "Moultrie," Daniels called from in front of the summer kitchen, "I heard it again. Someone's there."

"This better be good."

Lights flashed around the summer kitchen. Lorie flattened herself next to Jeff in the stone recess behind the bushes.

Jeff bent over quietly, seemingly searching the ground, then rose and tossed something over the tall hedge—a stone, she guessed. It landed with a *crack* deep inside the maze. He hunched down and pulled her down beside him.

"There. You see?" Daniel's voice was excited.

Moultrie was more cautious. "Where was it?"

"Over there. In them bushes."

Again Jeff rose and threw something into the leafy maze. At the *thump* the two men spoke again, this time with voices that were soft.

"I think you're right."

"I looked at those bushes yesterday, Moultrie. There's only one opening. You stay there, and I'll go in and chase him out to you."

Lights flashed over the branches. Daniels had started into the maze. "Hey, Moultrie, there's more bushes here than I thought. I'm not sure which way to go."

Jeff put a hand on Lorie's shoulder and let it rest lightly.

A beam of light suddenly shone through the bushes directly at them. Jeff's hand tightened. Black clothing and dark greasepaint served its purpose. The light turned, and Daniels moved on.

"Is he out yet?" Daniels sounded somewhat anxious.

"Nothin' here."

For many long minutes, they heard the man tramping about. Finally, he called out again. "Moultrie?"

"Yeah?"

"Any luck?"

"You'd have known it if there was."

There was silence for a few minutes. Then a plaintive voice. "Moultrie, I think I'm lost."

"What?"

"Well, there's this kind of big open space. I've been here twice already. Maybe three times."

"Oh, for God's sake, Daniels."

"Get me out of here, Moultrie."

"Okay, just hold it where you are. I've got some fishing line in my car. I'll follow it in and get you out. Gawd!" They heard his heavy footsteps retreating across the lawn.

"Now," Jeff breathed. They wormed their way with no more than a rustle between stone and tightly thatched greenery to the freedom of the lawn. Like shadows, they glided across the grass, reentered the woods, and within seconds found the path.

She kept an eye open for her boots, found them sitting where she had left them on the trail, tied the laces together, and slung them over her shoulder.

Voices could be heard back at the maze, one plaintive, one angry.

"They'll be at it for a while." Jeff was chuckling softly.

When they came out of the woods, the Baileys' mini-van was parked by the side of the road, dark and quiet. Jeff flashed his light, and headlights flashed back. Sid stepped out of the car. "Any luck?" he whispered.

"We found the will," Lorie said. "Not an original, but good enough to put up a fight."

"Hallelujah!" Sid said. "Look who I found waiting for me when I got home." The passenger door opened, and Officer Randy Ross emerged from the car.

"Good to see you again," Randy said, reaching for Jeff's hand and then Lorie's. "If you hadn't called when you did, we were prepared to bring a posse out here to rescue you."

"I wouldn't let him do anything so rash," Sid chuckled softly. "I figured you'd find a way to call if you ran into problems. Okay, let's get outta here."

Lorie slipped into the back seat, shoved her boots under the front seat of the car, and pulled the backpack onto her lap. Jeff joined her. His arm went around her, and in the darkness, she leaned her head against his shoulder, ignoring Randy's crisp "Seatbelts, everyone." She remained quiet during the trip home. Jeff answered questions in simple declarative sentences, unembellished, indicating that they didn't yet know what they had, but it was bound to be interesting.

Carol ran out to the driveway an hour later as Sid made the final turn into the doctor's parking area. "Oh my dears," she said, obviously distraught. "Is everyone okay? We've been just frantic. We should never have let you go."

Jeff stepped out, offered his hand to Lorie and she emerged from the car. She handed the heavy backpack to Sid and went into her aunt's protective arms. "It's okay, Aunt Carol," she said tiredly. "No one saw us. And for what it's worth, we have a copy of the will."

"Oh, thank goodness, thank goodness. Then it was worth it. I was thinking what a foolish old woman I was to let you go into that kind of danger. If your parents had called—"

"You're neither old nor foolish," Lorie chided gently. "It had to be done, and we did it."

"She has proven to be one of the bravest women I know," Jeff said warmly. "You should be very proud of her."

"I am," her aunt said. "I am very proud of her. And thank you for saying that, Jeff. Well, let's get inside and see what you found. And you two might want to wash that stuff off your faces now."

Sid had lifted the green metal file box triumphantly out of the backpack, and it was now sitting in the middle of the round table in Phil's kitchen. Still standing, the tall man was opening it just as Lorie and Carol joined the others. He pulled out the will. "By God, this is it! I knew it had been typed and signed."

"Who were the witnesses?" Sue asked. She turned back to the coffeepot and gathered up some mugs.

Sid seated himself and flipped to the last page. "Mike Neil, of course. His lawyer. Here's a name I don't recognize. Ewen Taylor." He looked up. "Anyone heard of him?"

"Taylor Electronics," the young policeman said, pulling up another chair for himself. "Big name in Atlanta. He's what you might call a computer systems entrepreneur. Into a lot of things. Airline industry. Staging for rock shows. Devices for entertainment parks. You name it, he does it. Big bucks."

Lorie looked up as Jeff came into the room, his tired face now as clean as hers. "Is he honest?" he asked Randy.

Randy made a rocking motion with his hand, palm down. "He's involved in a lot of lawsuits. Very pushy guy. Doesn't make him crooked, though. I've met him, and I'm inclined to like him. He lives in Marietta, and recently he's been calling us, claiming someone's been following him, likely trying to do him harm."

Lorie glanced at Carol and met her startled expression.

"Are they?" Phil Barnett asked.

"Don't know. We can't quite get a handle on it."

"What happened to Jon Randolph's original lawyer, Mike Neil?" Lorie was suddenly very curious. Jeff held a chair for her and then seated himself beside her, reaching for her hand under the table and giving it a quick squeeze.

"He had a heart attack at the wheel of his car," Sue said as she handed a mug of fragrant steaming coffee to Jeff and another to Lorie. "A couple of years ago."

"Was he autopsied?" Lorie asked.

"I don't know. Mike was known to have had heart problems."

Randy Ross glanced at Lorie. "It wouldn't hurt to check that out," he said thoughtfully. "I'll take care of that."

"Any other witnesses?"

"Don't need but two. But Mike's secretary signed it. Louella Simmons." Sid checked the signature page. "She retired when he died. I think she left town. Sue, do you know where she went?"

"Not a clue. We can ask around, though. Someone might know."

"Okay, folks," the doctor finally said, "It's getting late, and a few of us need sleep. Do you all want to stay here?"

"No," Sid said, looking up. "We have to get back. The memorial service is tomorrow morning, and we both have to be at the church early. You will be there?"

"Of course," Carol said. "If you need any help at all..."

"What's the next step?" the doctor asked.

"I guess we'll have to tell Lawyer Purdy we found a copy of the will," Sid said, "and have him make an appointment with the judge. But not until after the funeral."

"Don't tell him where we got it," his wife said fiercely.

"Of course not! If they ask, we'll say it was under stuff in the pharmacy lockbox at the bank. What more do we need to say?"

"What are the provisions?" Carol wondered.

"Just what we knew already," Sid answered. "Some specific bequests, notably for Rolf Maratti. Jon left us something, too. But generally, a lot of funding for Historic Randolph City. I can see why some people are so worried. Jon gave personal loans to a lot of businessmen to upgrade their stores. From what I've seen so far, Jon was forgiving most of those loans on his death. I know more than a couple of people who are worried sick that Maratti will foreclose on them if they miss a payment or two. I always said Jon would never have done that. This just confirms what I told them!"

"Nothing in there for a stray grandchild?" his little wife asked.

"I don't see anything here. But it's a long document and maybe as I go through it, I'll see something relevant. I want to look at everything else in this box, too."

"Sorry, Jeff," Sue said. She put a comforting hand on his shoulder. "I really thought we'd find the letter Mr. Jon talked about at the end."

He smiled at her. "We may find it yet."

It was nearing midnight when the Baileys left, taking Randy Ross with them. Lorie was beginning to sag with fatigue.

"Get to bed, honey," Carol said. "Your eyes look terrible." She thought a bit and said hastily, "Tired, I mean. Tired."

"Thanks a lot, Auntie!" She grinned and gave Carol a hug and a kiss. With a warm hug for Phil and a quick glance at Jeff, who was watching her out of the corner of his eye, she dragged herself up the stairs and into the bathroom, intending to make full use of the claw-foot tub.

She poured something from a bottle into the rushing water, and when she lowered herself into its warmth, fragrance erupted around her. It was wonderful. She leaned back, luxuriating, but contemplative. Twenty minutes later, mostly dry, she crawled under the covers of her guestroom bed and sank into softness.

She didn't know when he came into her bed, but he smelled fresh and masculine, and he held her in his arms and kissed her quite thoroughly and then lay beside her with his arms still around her as she fell back into deep renewing sleep. He was gone when she woke in the morning, and it was almost as if it had been only a dream.

CHAPTER 12

Tuesday, July 22, 2014

Tuesday morning was frantic for everyone but Lorie, who had slept surprisingly well and felt fresh and rested. Humming to herself, she pulled from her bag the black dress her aunt had suggested she bring. Made of some slinky undefined fabric, it was knee-length with capped sleeves, a deep V-neckline, and a soft black belt. Perhaps a little dressy, she thought, remembering she had purchased it for nights on the town. But a dark-red and black patterned silk scarf flung around her neck and fastened with a jade broach atop her shoulder would hide all signs of frivolity during the service. Black stockings, shiny black heels, black pearls at her ears. She was ready.

She walked downstairs carrying a small black handbag, and all eyes turned to her.

"What's wrong?" She stopped on the next to last step.

"Not a thing!" Phil Barnett said with enthusiasm. He was formally dressed in a black suit, with the requisite white shirt and a blue tie, which matched his eyes. He was standing in the hallway, munching a chocolate-frosted doughnut, trying to deal with crumbs.

"You look beautiful, Lorie," her aunt agreed, handing the doctor a napkin. She was also wearing black, a summer linen suit with a creamy blouse, pearl earrings, and necklace.

Jeff Preston's mouth had dropped open. "It's so...you take my breath away!"

She blew him a kiss. "You may not have seen them before, but I do have legs."

A variety of quick breakfast items had been placed on the kitchen table. Lorie cut a piece of sweet roll and had poured only a half cup of hot fragrant coffee when her aunt said briskly, "We'll have something after the service if you can manage until then. But we really have to get on the road if we're going to get there on time."

Lorie looked back at Jeff. Now she realized that he was formally dressed as well, in dark-blue trousers that fit him to perfection. A crisp white shirt clung to his upper torso, and Carol was busy adjusting a blue tie that matched his eyes. The suit jacket was draped across one of the kitchen chairs. Shiny black loafers awaited his attention. "You're coming with us?" She turned to her aunt. "Do you think that's wise, Carol?"

Carol held up some dark glasses. "He's going to have an eye problem today. And for the record, he's your fiancé, and his name is...Bruce."

"Bruce?" She thought a moment, shook her head slowly.

Phil glanced up from his coffee cup. "How about Tom...it fits with Jefferson?"

Carol said, "We couldn't persuade him to stay home. He wants to see who comes to the service. Someone may look familiar."

Lorie nodded one way and then another. "Tom Jefferson? That's not the way to avoid being noticed! How about...Richard Jefferson?" She grinned. "By the way, Rich dear, how long have we been engaged?"

"You just met me, and it's a whirlwind engagement."

"Hmmm," she said. "I sound a little rash, even though I have immediately accepted your offer."

"And I have given you a ring to declare my undying love." Smiling tenderly, he reached into the pocket of his new trousers and retrieved a small box. "Your hand, my lady."

As she extended her left hand, he slipped a ring onto her finger. It sparkled and flashed in the morning light, and all of a sudden, she couldn't catch her breath. "Good grief, Jeff. What is this?" Set in a band of yellow gold, the large diamond was oval cut, flanked by two small exquisite rubies on each side.

"I found it in the box in the clock room." He took both of her hands into his and said softly, "It was my mother's wedding ring. It fits you perfectly, Lorie. Will you accept it?" She couldn't speak. "Please don't faint," he added, no longer smiling, grasping her hands a little tighter.

As was intended, Carol had missed the private conversation. Now she looked up and saw the ring. "Perfect. I think our story will hold water." And then, as Lorie held out her hand, her aunt took a closer look at the ring. "Jeff, where did this come from? It's gorgeous! It's probably worth a fortune. Lorie, for goodness' sake, don't lose it."

"I'll…not lose it, Auntie."

She took a deep calming breath and looked up again into Jeff's expressive face. She saw great longing there—and hope.

"For always," he whispered, an eternal promise.

"For always," she whispered back, engulfed within his love.

No church service could ever have been more solemn or binding!

With Phil driving his black Lincoln Town Car, the trip was made in luxury. Carol and Jeff kept up a constant conversation during travel time, she looking back over the seat at him while checking a small notebook she was holding in her hand. "The names of the council members? Okay, here they are: Martin Dewey, Oliver Jennings, Lyman Thomas, George Garnett, Sam McIntire. Sandford Cragin, otherwise known as 'Sandy,' was mayor last term. But when the elected probate judge got sick all of a sudden, Sandy was appointed to an associate replacement position and had to give up being mayor. All of these people should be at the church. If you recognize any of them, give me a thumbs-up. If you don't, I'll sort them out for you."

"Who's the mayor now?" Lorie asked.

"The president of the Chamber of Commerce, Archer Hood. Called Archie, I understand. Another upstanding member of the community."

Jeff's breath suddenly released with a whoosh.

"Problem?" Carol said.

"That name is familiar to me," he said, "in a negative sense."

"Okay," Carol answered briskly. "We'll put a star beside that name. Any other names sound familiar?"

"How many of these council members have deep roots in the community?"

"All of them except Sandy," Carol answered Jeff, "but Sue tells me he came to Randolph City so many years ago he's almost been accepted by now. He's certainly one of the most respected people in town. He apparently started out life as a lawyer, but he made himself so valuable here by doing historic restorations on the side, including the Bailey's house, that he finally got into the restoration business. Some of these other guys have been council members forever, according to Sue. Like their fathers before them."

"Any mothers?" Lorie asked dryly.

"Occasionally," Carol laughed. "But it's a 'good ol' boy' town, Lorie. Not as liberated as you're used to."

"Which were related by their mothers?" Jeff asked.

Carol looked down at the list. "Martin Dewey and George Garnett. First cousins. I've met both their mothers. They're collectively called the Franklin sisters by everybody in town, regardless of the fact they're both many years married. One of them used to serve on the council."

Jeff chuckled.

"What?" Carol said.

"Good people all," he answered. "I don't know Cragin. But as I think back, I have no bad feelings about any of the rest."

Carol scowled. "Why are they all fighting with each other then?"

He was silent for a moment. "Perhaps someone is deliberately trying to tear this town apart."

"Who?" Lorie asked. "And why?"

Jeff frowned. "Crucial questions, I expect."

Phil Barnett looked at Carol. "What are you going to do about the will?"

"We're going to grab Sandy Cragin after the funeral," Carol said, "tell him what we have and ask him friendly-like why he didn't tell us he was going to lock up Randolph House. Sue's already asked him if we can chat with him, and he said yes, in his chambers after the funeral service."

"If he signed the order because Maratti asked him to," Lorie pointed out, "then he already knew there was a will."

"True."

"And I bet he won't tell you anything, even if there are now two wills. Because I bet judges can't talk about their cases any more than lawyers can, even if they're personal friends."

"Which certainly complicates things," Carol said. "But it won't keep us from trying."

"I wonder," Lorie asked, "if Mr. Maratti will be at the funeral with his friend Arthur Ehrlich."

He was.

Bells were pealing from the steeple of the lovely little white community church when Phil turned the car into the overflow parking lot. People were approaching the church from every direction. Many of the women, dressed in summery prints, were wearing hats, something Lorie hadn't seen since she was a child. She was touched by the turnout for Jon Thomas Randolph Third.

She saw Maratti standing at the church doorway surrounded by several well-dressed men, speaking to one or the other occasionally. He stood straight, dignified, and a little aloof. They all shook hands, and he turned to Ehrlich, motioning that they should enter the church.

Lorie came into the church on Jeff's arm. As they had decided previously, if anyone asked, he had a serious eye problem and had been instructed not to remove the dark glasses. Carol and Phil came in behind them. Sid and Sue Bailey were waiting for them in the narthex. Several fine-looking younger people were guarding them, and Lorie was introduced to Jim and Marianne, the Baileys' grown children, mixed clones of their parents, and their respective spouses. Jim Bailey was as tall as Jeff, she saw, remembering Sue's comment on his genetic likeness. He wasn't quite a clone of Jeff Preston, but if they hadn't been standing together, they surely could have been mistaken for one another. Jim's eyes were quite different from Jeff's, however, hazel and largely hidden behind correcting bifocals. Marianne's face was almost the spitting image of her pretty mother, but like her father, she was tall and willowy. A lovely family, Lorie thought warmly, wishing now she had been able to get acquainted with them many years earlier. Spouses and several children were standing nearby. They had been warned to stay close, Lorie was told softly, and was relieved they had been let in on the potential for danger. Nothing now could be taken for granted.

Jeff was introduced as Richard Jefferson, but it was obvious the Bailey kin had been briefed. "We've saved a place for family," Sue said softly. "Second pew from the front. Go on down the left aisle and fill in to the center. Mr. Maratti and Mr. Ehrlich are on the other side of the center aisle."

Lorie noted both Maratti and Ehrlich watching her as she led the way along the front of the pew. She nodded brightly to both and received a warm smile from the lawyer and a brief semi-friendly nod from Maratti. His eyes suddenly fixated on Jeff, who had moved in behind her. Maratti frowned as if he could almost remember who the young man was, as if he had seen this person before but wasn't quite sure where or when. He also let his gaze pass over Sue's family, with a lingering and quizzical glance at Jim Bailey. He turned to Arthur Ehrlich then, spoke briefly, and shook his head as if there were something he could not quite put together.

The service was short and moving, with two ministers, a thin elderly man in a black robe and a robust younger man in white, speaking of their love and respect for the audacious Northerner who had descended on them with big ideas and who had invested so much of his energy into a small town that it began to blossom. Songs were sung and scriptures were read. It was the eulogies that took time. One after another, people came to the front of the church to testify in what ways Jon Randolph had been special to them. Every one of the council members came forward to say something about the project upon which they had embarked, thanks to Jon Randolph, and how much they personally would miss his robust leadership. The young mayor, Archie Hood, a neatly bearded businessman, also stood before the congregation. His memories, he said, were brief because he had been away from town for so many years that he really hadn't gotten to know the man that well. But he did appreciate the effort that Mr. Jon had made on behalf of Randolph City.

Even to Lorie, Hood's complimentary words sounded forced, and when she turned her head to follow his retreat to the back of the church, she saw a number of folks talking behind their hands. It was clear the contentiousness in Randolph City had sowed unpleasant seeds of discord, apparent even at the funeral of a respected, if not beloved, member of the community.

Sue and Sid Bailey gave the final eulogy as a couple, talking about the old man's character and his generosity and the pleasure they had derived from working with him.

The service finally came to an end, and as organ music swelled, everyone descended to the church basement to partake of a sumptuous pot luck luncheon. Tables had been set out on the lawn to handle the overflow, and many people were headed back up the steps with full plates of food.

"Where's the judge?" Lorie asked. Carol pointed him out. Sandy Cragin was a fine-looking older gentleman with a patrician nose, a firm chin, and a tanned face. At his temples, gray hair was reaching through the original red, giving him a very distinguished appearance. The confidence he had in himself seemed manifest. He stood straight. He wore tailored and expensive clothing. He was born to be a "somebody," Lorie thought. People would always respect and trust this man. No wonder he had been elected mayor and, more recently, appointed to the post of associate probate judge.

He was talking with another man, someone physically larger, to whom the judge was apparently attempting to give his full attention. The second man had a full head of frosted brown hair and a fleshy face, which might once have been handsome. Well dressed, it was obvious he loved the good life. A slim cigar hung from his lips, unlit because of the church's ban on smoking. A person used to making his own rules, Lorie thought. She pointed him out to Jeff, who immediately turned away.

"Someone you recognize?" she asked softly.

"I think so."

"He won't recognize you, Jeff."

He breathed a little easier. "Of course you're right. He reminds me too much of one of my own father's business partners. Even though it was illegal, Jacob Macoby still brought slaves in from Africa. I hated him, but I suspect he had a tight hold on my father. I know he didn't live in Oak Hill, but this man certainly bears a strong resemblance to him."

"Maybe we should inquire into his connection with the judge, if any."

"A wise suggestion, my love."

"What about the others?"

"Their great-great-great-grandpas all rode with me." He grinned. "But they didn't all ride at the same time. For the safety of all, Ben and I didn't let one part of the movement know about the others, although I'm sure they all suspected their neighbors were of the same mind." He looked around. "I see many faces that look surprisingly familiar. People would be touched, I think, if they knew how brave their ancestors were in their commitment to the abolition of slavery and their unswerving loyalty to the Union. I would venture to guess no one ever bragged of it after the war, though. It could have left them in serious peril."

"That reminds me, Jeff. Have you seen our friend Randy?"

"Ben's great-great-great-grandson. Ben would have been so proud of him. Randy is sticking very close to the Baileys."

"I'm relieved," Lorie said with a deep sigh.

"I also saw his partner, Tim Murphy."

"Why's Tim here?"

"Ask him," he said.

Officer Murphy was headed their way. He was in civilian clothes—a dark suit, white shirt, neatly patterned tie—wearing a grim expression on his face.

"Mr. Murphy," Lorie said brightly before he could call out Jeff's name, "I'd like for you to meet my fiancé, Richard Jefferson."

Quickly picking up on the game, the white-haired officer reached out, smiling, to shake Jeff's hand. "Congratulations, Richard. That's wonderful news." Then his voice softened. "Be very careful. Ewen Taylor called this morning. Claimed he'd been followed again. He was planning on coming to the funeral, but this freaked him out. He's sticking close to home, and we've got guards on him. We hadn't known before last night that he was a witness to Mr. Randolph's will, so I'm afraid we weren't giving his complaints the proper attention. Now that we have two and two, it's possibly adding up to multiple murders."

"Can you expand on that?" Lorie felt a chill run through her, deep inside.

"After Randy called, we asked a friend to dig out the autopsy report on Randolph's lawyer, Mike Neil. He had enough sleeping medication in him to knock out a horse. He may have had a heart attack, but it was after he fell asleep and hit the bridge abutment. The police department here really dropped the ball."

"Damn!" Lorie hissed under her breath. It was one thing to suspect foul play, quite another to have that suspicion confirmed.

"And the secretary? She came into some big bucks right after Neil died. She's long gone. We haven't been able to find her, dead or alive."

"This has been a long time planning," Jeff said softly.

"It appears so," Murphy replied. "Get out of here as soon as you can. Especially if you see someone who might recognize you."

"Sue just told me we're chatting with the judge in about half an hour, Tim," Lorie said. "In his chambers."

"Where are his chambers?"

"In the courthouse."

"Go upstairs," Murphy said, urgency arising. "Right now. They tried to take you out once. Let's not take chances again, Preston. These stairs lead up to the narthex. I'll go warn Randy and then join you. Once I escort you two to the judge's chambers, I'll come back for your aunt."

Jeff said with a broad smile. "It's Jeff. Or you can call me Rich, if you like."

Murphy laughed out loud. "Okay, Rich. See you soon."

Jeff took Lorie's arm and hurried her upstairs. "You realize," she said softly, "that no one is really out to kill you. Us, maybe. But not you. They don't know who you are."

"That's precisely why they might try," he said seriously. "They are looking and talking, all wondering who I am. I may be dangerous."

"It's because you're tall and handsome and wearing dark glasses. They probably think you're a movie star."

"A what?"

She stopped at the doorway to the narthex and looked up at him. "You're not quite up-to-speed in the modern world yet, mister. We're going to have to spend many hours together—"

"I like that idea." He put his hands at either side of her face and leaned down to give her a kiss. Could anyone see the sparks flying from every hair atop her head? His lips lingered, not breaking away until steps could be heard coming up behind them. Again it was Tim Murphy. "I got directions, you lovebirds," he said with a chuckle. "Let's go."

They hurried across the church lawn to the sidewalk and turned toward the heart of town. The street they were following dead-ended three long blocks later in the city square. A large red brick building sat boldly at the center of an acre of careful landscaping. It boasted a high tower set above two imposing rows of tall windows. The stars and stripes were fluttering brightly on the flagpole in front of the building. Jeff paused. He looked long at the flag, then gave it a quick salute, his eyes shining.

Murphy hurried them up the steps and through the heavy glass doors. The building smelled of furniture wax, cleaning solvents, and old documents. It had high ceilings and black and white tile floors. To the left, at the end of the hall, was a solid wooden door on which a plaque was affixed. "Judge's Chambers," he read aloud.

He pushed the door open. The space inside was an antechamber to a series of offices. Each door bore a name. Judge Cragin's office was at the far right. Murphy turned the knob. No luck.

Lorie glanced around the large antechamber, which obviously served as a waiting area. Chairs lined most of the wall space. A gracious old plush couch held its place of honor against the wall to her left. In the corner beside the couch a large floor pot of greenery added a spot of color. At the other side, holding a lamp and a variety of magazines, sat an interesting mahogany table with intricately carved legs.

Lorie heard a gasp. She turned to Jeff. "What's wrong?"

He moved closer to the table, knelt down, felt the legs, examined them. He looked up at her, his face drained of color. "What is it?" she said again. Murphy was watching him, equally concerned.

"Sara's wedding present. From Moses. And from…her brother."

Another anomaly. Lorie glanced at Murphy. "It's an antique that shouldn't be here."

Jeff finished the sentence softly, "Because it should have been destroyed by fire in her house the night Moses was killed."

Officer Murphy was instantly alert. "Another murder?"

Jeff stood up. She saw he was trying very hard to compose himself. "A murder that was committed a century and a half ago," he said haltingly. "I know the story from old records." It was as if he were trying to cobble words together quickly to explain how he knew so much about the unique piece. "Sara Preston was our Jon Randolph's grandmother. She got married when she was very young. But her husband, the first Jon Randolph, was forcibly impressed by the Confederate recruiters and had to go off to war. She moved back to her father's house until she got a message she thought was from her husband asking her to return to their farm because he was there, seriously wounded, and needed her help.

"Her father couldn't keep her from going. Moses, the faithful retainer who had taken care of her from the day she was born—he went with her, he and two other Africans, members of the Zulu tribe, as was he. It was a ruse, an ambush. Raiders were lying in wait. Moses told her to run away into the woods to save herself and the baby she was carrying inside her. He told her to hide in the cave where many escaping slaves had already found refuge. When her brother finally found her there, he had to tell her that the house had been burned to the ground and her friend Moses and his two friends had been tortured and killed." When Lorie put a hand on his arm, she realized he was trembling. "This table," he said, "was the wedding present her brother and Moses had jointly created for her. We...she thought it had been destroyed in the fire along with everything else."

Lorie looked up into Jeff's face, aghast. She saw a hardening in his features. In his frame of reference, these events had only just happened.

"I think we'll have to find out who brought this table to the courthouse," Murphy said softly, understanding what had been said, although he had no idea of the immediacy of the crime to Jeff. "There is no time limitation on murder. Is this another piece to the puzzle of Jon Randolph?"

"Yes," Lorie said softly.

Someone else came into the anteroom, Randy Ross, followed by the Baileys. Carol and Phil arrived next with Jon Randolph's lawyer, Will Purdy, who was dressed a little more formally today in a black suit.

"Problem?" Carol said quietly when she saw Lorie.

"Civil war contraband," Murphy said, indicating the table. "Does anyone know where this came from?"

Sue examined it. "I haven't seen this piece before," she said, "but I haven't had much occasion to be here. Everyone has been given a holiday today. We'll have to wait till tomorrow to find out."

"We may have to make some calls, Sue," Lorie said. "It used to be in Sara Randolph's house. The one that was burned during the war."

Sue was obviously shocked, as was her husband. "How do we know this?" Sid asked grimly.

Lorie looked at Jeff. "He recognized it from—an old record."

"It was a book. A journal I was reading. There was a sketch of the table leg, African animals carved on it." He paused. "And a sketch of the mechanism for a hidden compartment in the drawer."

Attention now riveted sharply toward the table. Jeff opened the deep drawer and lifted out a stack of contemporary magazines, which he set carefully onto the floor. He pulled the drawer out almost its full length, pressed with both hands at the back of the base, and a slender panel of wood popped free. He lifted it out. The hidden compartment below contained a large journal with a gray cloth-bound cover. "Here." He handed the book to an obviously astonished Murphy.

Will Purdy stared at Jeff and then the journal. He plunked himself quickly onto one of the chairs as if he might otherwise faint.

Randy Ross was likewise flabbergasted. "How did you know about that?" He took the book and paged through it. "Household accounts. Journal entries. Written in a woman's hand and dated 1864." He looked up at Jeff. "You read about this in a journal?"

"As I recall."

"We've got some work to do here. Keep this quiet, please." So saying, Randy asked Jeff to replace the panel and the magazines. It was done in a moment. He looked around for a place to hide the journal.

"In my briefcase," Carol said. She had brought it with her. He slipped it into place just as the door opened, and several men walked in, Judge Cragin among them.

"Sue. Sid," he said amiably, "you asked to see me?"

"Yes," Sue said, more than a little distracted by now. "Yes. We were looking over some of the pharmacy papers in the bank and found a copy of Mr. Randolph's recent will. I'm not sure how it got there, but here it is."

He frowned. "Recent will? I've just seen a copy of a will that appears to be a legal document written some time ago, and now you say there is a more recent will?"

"Right here, Sandy." Sid Bailey showed him the papers. "This is a copy. The original of this is back where we found it in our lockbox at the bank. Now what do we do?"

The judge's eyes widened. He frowned backward at the three men who had come in with him, businessmen from the looks of two of them, Lorie thought. She had seen both of them earlier at the church talking with Rolf Maratti. The other was the tall, stocky man who had had the judge cornered in the church basement, the one Jeff had been nervous about. "I won't be more than half an hour," he said to them, "if you're willing to wait here." Cragin unlocked the door to his chambers and turned to the businessmen. "You three can wait for me here."

He glanced back at the crowd in the anteroom. "There are too many of you to fit comfortably in my chambers. We've got enough chairs in the courtroom for everyone." He led the way back to the hall and opened the next door into a relatively large room. A judge's podium and leather upholstered chair were displayed on a raised dais at the far side of the room, against two large windows. To the left of the dais sat a highly polished table and several chairs. To the right, sitting by itself as a showpiece, was a massive, beautifully embellished roll-top desk, closed. The matching ornate desk chair held its own place of honor against the wall beside the desk. Most of the remainder of the room was filled with chairs arranged to form several concentric rows.

Face frozen, Jeff took Lorie's hand and directed her to a chair in the front row close beside the desk. He beckoned to Randy Ross, who quickly moved up beside him. "I need a diversion," Lorie heard him whisper. "I need to get the judge and his visitors out of the room for about two minutes, maybe three. Think you can do it?"

Randy grinned. "You got it, boss."

Jeff took off his dark glasses and handed them to Lorie. Her heart was racing now.

The three strangers were standing at the inner door of the judge's chambers, staring into the courtroom. Cragin asked the Baileys to seat themselves at the table. They handed him the document. He pulled glasses out of his pocket, put them on, and started leafing through the pages.

Lorie watched as Randy looked around, saw the men standing in the doorway between the courtroom and the judge's chambers, and strode purposefully toward them. She held her breath.

"This is private business," she heard him say in his cop's voice. "Back off! Get outta here!"

They stared at him, startled. Two of the men stepped back. The big man holding the cigar held his ground. "Nobody said we couldn't be here." He looked toward the judge.

Judge Cragin, who had been reading the document with intense interest, looked up and frowned.

Randy snapped the cigar out of the large man's fingers. His voice racked upward, again the too-vigilant policeman. "And no smoking. This is a courthouse. Can't you read?" Upon landing, the cigar skittered across the floor.

"Come on," the man protested. "Can't you see it's not lit!"

The judge rose to his feet. "One moment." His voice was smooth and unperturbed. "Let me take care of this." Placing the document carefully on the table, he walked to the door and went through it, talking softly to the men as he went. They turned to follow him, and the door came shut.

Jeff was up in a flash. He knelt under the kneehole of the roll-top desk and pressed the back wall with his hands. A panel snapped free. Lorie saw him pull out a small book and two more journals of the same size he had already retrieved. Another seemed to be adhered to the back of the compartment. He left it there and handed what he had to Carol, who was instantly at his side, briefcase open. In seconds, he had replaced the panel.

He was seated again, breathing only a little harder, dark glasses once more hiding his blue eyes, when the judge walked back into the room.

Feeling much like a spectator at a fast-moving ping-pong game, Lorie glanced at Carol, whose face was very red. Carol pulled a tissue from her purse and mopped at her forehead. There was no emotion on Jeff's face whatsoever. Lorie drew in a deep breath and waited.

"I'm sorry," Judge Cragin said, and then zeroed in on Randy. "I don't know who you are or what connection you have with these people, young man, but you had no right to behave that way. If you make one more sound, you're out of here."

"Yes, sir." Randy's voice was properly contrite. He sat down next to Carol. Sue Bailey turned to see what was going on, her face ashen.

Not a sound had issued from Will Purdy. Lorie searched for him and found him sitting alone in the back row. His eyes were round, his mouth slack. He moved slightly, shook his head, and let his hands flop into his lap. She had never seen a more abject figure.

Cragin turned back to the document. He nodded a time or two, shook his head once, and kept turning pages. "Very interesting," he said finally, raising his eyes to the assembled watchers. "This may indeed be the will people have told me about. However"—he paused for effect—"it's not witnessed."

"Jon signed it personally," Sid Bailey said. "I recognize his handwriting, and I expect many of us would."

"No witnesses have signed this document," the judge repeated.

"We can bring them in," Sid protested. "There are several names."

Cragin looked down at the names. "I suppose there's enough evidence to bring this into question. Why don't you all meet me here on Thursday, around nine thirty in the morning, let's say, and we'll talk about it informally. I'll have Mr. Maratti and Mr. Ehrlich present, and we'll see where we can go from here."

"Thanks, Sandy," Sid Bailey said.

Cragin rose to his feet and walked briskly back to his chambers, closing the door behind him.

Lorie looked around. The doorway to the hall was behind her. So was Will Purdy, the late Jon Randolph's lawyer, sitting slumped over in his chair, his hair hanging into his face, the picture of utter exhaustion and defeat.

"I'm a dead man," he said softly.

CHAPTER 13

Lorie saw the Baileys talking quietly together on the other side of the room. They had not heard the exchange. Jeff turned to face Will Purdy and said in a soft voice, "Please repeat what you just said."

"I'm a dead man." The lawyer's demeanor echoed his words. He was sagging.

"Would you explain?"

"No. I'm in enough trouble as it is."

"Randy?"

"Yo!" The feisty policeman came to stand beside Jeff.

"Mr. Purdy needs a place of concealment for the next few days. Am I correct, sir?"

The late Jon Randolph's lawyer looked up at Jeff. "Who are you?"

"A friend. So is my associate, Mr. Ross. If you feel you are in danger because of something you did or did not do, we are prepared to offer you assistance."

"It's not what I did or did not do," Purdy said numbly. "It's what they think I did not do."

"And what is that?"

"Get rid of all the damn copies. But that one. Wherever it was when I was looking!"

"Well," Randy said softly, "that's pretty incriminating. You're in big trouble, buddy."

"No matter which way I turn, I'm in trouble."

"Tim," Randy called, "can you come over here?"

His partner, who was keeping a sharp eye on the doorway leading to the judge's office, quickly joined the small group.

"We need a safe house. Right now."

"I'll call Mac and Harris," Tim Murphy said. "They can arrange something."

Lorie saw a gleam of raw fear in Purdy's face. "You guys are from the police, aren't you? How long do I have? Can I call my wife and tell her goodbye? She's not well. This will kill her."

Randy Ross glanced at his partner, eyebrows raised, then back at Purdy. "We're from Marietta," he said. "Looking into another matter."

Hope sparked momentarily in Purdy's gray face. "Can you help me? I don't trust anyone at the station anymore. I don't know who they own."

"Who is 'they'?" Lorie asked.

"I don't want to talk about it."

Tim Murphy spoke quietly to Randy and left the room. Randy turned to Purdy again. "He'll be back with the car in a minute. Just walk out like everything is normal, like the three of us are going out for a drink. We'll all get into the car, and then you'll disappear."

"My wife?"

"Address?"

He gave it.

"We'll get her."

"Thank you." Color began to come back to his cheeks. "I don't know what happened to our secretary. Poor Louella.

She thought she'd be rich, just sticking a pill into the coffee-pot, but I suspect she's pushing up daisies somewhere around here. As soon as they're done with me, I'm next in line!"

"Or living in luxury in Switzerland," Randy suggested.

Purdy shook his head. "They're not that kind of people."

Phil Barnett and Lorie's aunt joined the group. "Trouble?" the doctor asked quietly, eyebrows raised.

"We're taking care of it," Randy said. "I'll check in with you later. Be very careful." They walked out with Purdy and the door shut behind them.

"Now what?" Lorie felt more than a little stunned. "I hate to mention it, but before we go into crisis mode, I need something to eat. Jeff, too. We got hustled out of the church luncheon before we could go through the line, and I'm starving."

"Our house," Sue said, coming up behind her, "and you can kick off those high heels, relax, and eat your fill. We've done what we had to do here, and to tell the truth, I think we're all curious…"

Carol cautioned her with a quick "shhh" and said out loud, "I'm ready to relax over a big glass of Georgia sweetened iced tea. Or some of that great coffee you make, Sue."

"Time to go," Sue responded in a very determined voice.

Carol looked at Phil. "Let's bring the car over here so we can make a fast getaway with Jeff. Until then, Lorie, take him into the 'Ladies.' Lock the door behind you. I'll come in when we get here and knock three times."

"Good grief," Lorie murmured. "This is seeming more and more like something out of a bad spy movie. Okay, mister, let's go hide."

No one was in the hallway when they left the courtroom. She led him quickly into the powder room and locked the door. He took off the dark glasses and handed them to her. She put them into her purse. He wasn't smiling. He seemed remote. Detached. She had seen him this way only at Riverside Plantation, and now it frightened her.

"The desk? Tell me."

"It was a gift for my father. I spent many hours building it and the chair with the help of my friend Moses, who was an artist as well as a master carver and carpenter. It was the office desk at Riverside." The hardness in his face had not gone away. He seemed more distant from her now than ever. "The people who robbed Sara's house before they burned it did the same thing at Riverside Plantation. Now I know that the people who tortured Moses and his friends were the same people who killed my father and the servants who tried to defend him."

"Someone associated with those events is living here in Randolph City?" Suddenly Lorie realized that the evil she had imagined as being far in the distant past was continuing to surround Jeff. "Can you give us an inventory of what was in both houses, maybe some sketches, so we know what else to look for?"

He looked at her, now alert. "A practical, useful idea, Lorie. Thank you, dear love, for pulling me back into the world as it now is." He put his arms around her and leaned his cheek against her hair. "Lorie, help me! Revenge is eating at my heart. But I have to keep telling myself: those people— the ones who destroyed my family—are long dead. And these people are not the ones to blame."

She strongly disagreed. "Whoever they are, we know they're still willing to kill to get Jon Randolph's estate. *These* people have a close connection with *those* people, Jeff. But who are they? Do you suppose someone is trying to intimidate Judge Cragin, too?"

"Lorie, what is your keen-eyed assessment of the judge?"

"I haven't seen enough of him to know one way or another. He's full of himself, but that doesn't make him any different from a lot of people. Do you recognize anything about him?"

"He looks like no one I've seen before. And the name is unfamiliar to me."

"Then maybe he's okay. We'll keep our eyes open."

Three knocks sounded on the powder room door. Lorie unlocked the door, and with the fierce protectiveness of mother bears, she and Carol flanked Jeff as they left the building. Phil had pulled his car into the parking lot at the courthouse. In short order, they were inside and on their way to the Baileys' home. No one said a word.

The house was full of people. Bailey kin. Neighbors and their relatives. Business associates. Church acquaintances. Even Judge Cragin dropped in for a short time, unwilling to discuss the business of the day, but otherwise chatting with people and telling amusing tales stemming from his long friendship with Jon Randolph. Nice people all, Lorie thought. And food. Lots of food, iced tea, coffee, wine, beer.

And no place for privacy.

She had to admit to herself, however, that she was having a better time than she had figured she might. She thought Jeff, still wearing dark glasses, quietly listening to conversations all around him, was at least diverted. On the other hand, all her senses were tingling. She, too, wanted to examine what Jeff had retrieved from his hidden storage compartments. Carol was walking around with a haunted look on her face as if she might explode if she were touched. And even Sue and Sid seemed abnormally animated as if they wished they could hurry people along.

Patience won.

All of the visitors left at last, and the big comfortable house was left in disarray, but it was quiet, with no one remaining but Jeff and herself, the senior Baileys, Carol, and Phil.

The Baileys' temporary guard, Randy Ross, had not yet returned from dealing with Will Purdy's needs. Sue closed all the shades, dimmed the lights, and offered everyone a goblet of wine, a mug of beer, or a glass of tea to take with them into the kitchen. There the light would focus on what was now spread out across the table: a green metal file box about the size of a large shoebox, three journals, and a small notebook.

"Don't spill the drinks," Sue cautioned as they all assembled around the table.

Sid Bailey took charge. The first documents examined were the items in the green box: a copy of the will signed by Jon Randolph Third, original deeds to several properties, promissory notes from people to whom Jon Randolph had made loans, a typewritten list covering the locations of all the properties, a list of items secured in Jon Randolph's bank box: stock certificates and the like. In addition, a list of the more valuable items on display in Randolph House was found, including their appraised valuations. Items on display in museums were also listed, along with the locations and valuations. The box contained many more documents in a similar vein. Most of the documents were copies.

"No letter to his son." Sue's face showed her disappointment. "I was sure we'd learn who you are, Jeff."

"I suspect Will Purdy was in charge of the originals of these documents," her husband mused. "I wonder what will happen when the judge finds out he's missing?"

"I expect," the doctor said, "that the judge will order the office searched and all documents in Jon's file brought to the courthouse. Executors require this kind of information to appraise the estate."

They then turned to the books Jeff Preston had found in the hidden compartments. Jeff opened the smaller book first and scanned the first few pages. "Coded," he said. "I'll work on this one tonight." He then pulled open the gray cover of one of the journals and showed it around. The date at the top of the last used page was July 16, 1864. In a crabbed scribble in black ink, the word "Riverside." Then a list of accounts. Food purchased. Wages paid. Repairs made. Animals sold and purchased. Wagons worked on. All the workaday expenses of a working plantation.

"These obviously came from Riverside Plantation," Carol said in a quiet, awed voice. "How did they get into that compartment?"

"Both of these books," Jeff spread two of the journals open on the table, "are account books from Riverside. The desk was obviously moved from Riverside before the house was burned. The other journal," he opened it and laid it beside the others, "is from Sara Randolph's farmhouse, Fox Haven. Here's her signature at the bottom of the page. Apparently someone stripped both houses of valuables before they set the fires."

"Not an act of war," Phil Barnett said, his voice grim. "Thievery, arson, and murder!"

"The two properties in question," Sid Bailey put in, "are miles away from Randolph City. And although I've never been to what you called Fox Haven, Jeff, I think it's completely in the opposite direction from the plantation. So the question is"—now he turned to Sue—"how did these two pieces of furniture, evidence of major crimes against your ancestors' families, my dear wife, get into our courthouse? And how do we go about finding out?"

"You have to be very careful," Lorie warned. "Will Purdy implied 'they' might own people on the police force."

"Will said that?" Sue looked up at her, shocked. "Who is 'they'?"

Lorie shook her head. "He wouldn't say. Or maybe he doesn't know. Randy and Tim have him secreted at a safe house by now. I'm sure they'll try to get answers."

"My God, who can we trust?" Sid said. His eyes were very large.

"Who works at the courthouse?" Jeff asked. "Anyone you know well?"

"The cousins. Martin Dewey and George Garnett. They're in the public defenders' office."

"Ask one of them where the furniture came from," Jeff suggested. "Casually."

"I see George and his wife a lot at the grocery store," Sue said. "I can quiz him the next time I see him. He won't think a thing about it."

"Here's the next question," her husband said. "Is Maratti a part of it? Or is 'they' someone we don't even know?"

"Mr. Ehrlich is helpful," Carol put in, "and we've decided he isn't an Italian gangster. But do we trust him?" She turned to Lorie. "What do you think, hon? You're pretty good at reading people."

"I tend to like Mr. Ehrlich," Lorie said carefully. "But trust is something else. His loyalty doesn't have to extend any farther than his client."

"What about fairness?" Sid said.

"Laws don't always seem fair," Phil Barnett put in. "And sometimes they just aren't."

"How do we assess the judge?" Sid asked.

"I don't like the people who've been hanging around him," his little wife added. "But they've been hanging around

Maratti, too. Sandy's a fixture in town. Most people like him well enough. But I was really disturbed by what happened today."

"The guy with the cigar," Lorie put in. "We know he's one of them. But who are those other two men?"

The expression in Sue's eyes sparked. "Let's ask Judy over at the hotel. She knows everything."

Her husband went immediately to the phone. He came back five minutes later to report. "The big guy is a lawyer from Atlanta. His name is Johnny McDaniels. The other two are developers. Ernest Merrill and Clint Samuels. They represent two different firms that want to buy property here in town."

"Are they part of our alleged conspiracy?" Carol asked.

Phil Barnett spoke with heat. "I thought they were pretty crass to actually show up at Mr. Jon's memorial service, kind of like vultures waiting for the red meat. I wouldn't put it past any of them."

Lorie glanced at Jeff. His face had hardened again. "Phil's right. Don't trust any of them."

"Are you remembering?" Carol asked gently.

He looked at her, seemingly a little confused, and shook his head. "It's just…a feeling. A strong suspicion. The names…they're familiar."

Carol pulled out a notebook and added the three names to one already there, the name of Randolph City's current mayor, Archie Hood. "Do we add Rolf Maratti's name to this list?" She looked at Jeff.

He seemed to be thinking deeply. "I had a notion this morning at the church that he thought he recognized me." Lorie looked at him, startled, and then remembered her own assessment of Maratti's reaction on seeing Jeff. "I'd like to speak with him directly before we decide where he stands."

"How?" Carol said. "And where?"

"Randolph House," he said softly. "I must talk with him privately inside Randolph House. Apart from those men who seem to surround him everywhere he goes."

Sue frowned. "And how do we arrange this improbable meeting?"

He was quiet for a time. "I'm not really sure. Let's think on it."

Phil Barnett stood up. "That's a good note to leave on. I don't know about you people, but this day has been utterly exhausting to one old man."

"Phil's right," Carol said. "Jeff, what do we do with the journals? And the storage box?"

"Miz Sue," Jeff asked, "can you keep them here?"

"Of course, Jeff. We'll put them in the pharmacy safe at the bank. Along with the will."

"I'll take a closer look at the notebook tonight," Jeff said, "and let you know in the morning if I can make any sense out of it."

The dramas of the day were discussed at length during the long drive through the night back to Phil Barnett's secluded home. Lorie listened with intense interest. Jeff would ask her assessment.

"Our man Rich seems to fit very well into the Baileys' circle of friends," the doctor remarked at one point as an aside. He chuckled. "I saw some very interested female glances. Even from some of the older women, young man. If you wished, you could cut a swath a mile wide. If you'd been able to show those baby blues…"

"I have a feeling," Jeff answered carefully, "that I never had much time for the ladies in my past life." Under cover of darkness, he was gripping Lorie's hand tightly.

"It's obvious you're beginning to remember people and names. Do you remember anything personal—who your parents are or what your relationship to Jon might be?" Carol turned around to face him in the darkened car.

"I know without question that I'm related to Jon Randolph Third," he said. "And that I've been in his house. It was many years ago. And I know some of the family history. Beyond that, I'm not so sure."

"But that's good," Lorie's aunt said enthusiastically. "It's starting to come back. Perhaps you'll also remember who was after you and who shot you."

"The most important thing," he said, "is to find out who is trying to muddy the waters in Randolph City."

"I agree," Carol said. "I'm beginning to think we're not simply facing an incompetent court system and some greedy people—we're fighting against someone who's purposefully willing to destroy people in order to grab the Randolph estate and shatter Randolph City's way of life. But who? And why?"

"Who indeed?" Jeff said softly.

"All we have to do," Carol said ruefully, "is figure out who that person is."

"Or persons," Lorie added. And then they were turning into the driveway at Phil's house. Talk was rapid for a while around the kitchen table, with conspiracy theories thrown left and right. But exhaustion finally wore everyone down, and they headed upstairs to bed.

Again Lorie slipped into the big tub, leaning back into the hot soothing water, letting it wash over her tired body, wishing she knew what the future might hold. There hung over her a strong sense of foreboding. She looked at the ring she now wore on the third finger of her left hand. She and Major Jefferson Richard Preston were promised to each other as surely as if they were formally married. There could never be another love like theirs, bridging time itself.

But how long could it last?

He came to her again in the dark of night, waking her from troubled sleep. She wrapped him in her arms, pressing her body close against his, wishing she could protect him and keep him near her always, fearing the choice was not hers to make.

This time they made love properly. Sweetly. Slowly. With the deepest of emotion, as if they might never be together again—and then with increasing passion, until all the fires were tamed and banked, at least for the moment.

Cradled in his arms, Lorie ran her fingers through his hair and down the deep scar that crossed his forehead. "Who hurt you, my darling?"

He lay quiet for a time. "Back in the spring," he began, as if it were still the year 1864, "I went to Chattanooga to report to General Sherman on the situation in Georgia. I was in Federal blue, my regular army uniform. There were questionable merchants at the camp that night, looking to sell moonshine and other contraband garbage to the Union troops. All I can think is that one of them recognized me. He came at me suddenly with a Rebel yell and a Bowie knife, and had it not been for the stiff brim of my hat and a quick back step, I would have been dispatched at that moment." Again he paused. "I shot him. He died instantly at my feet."

"Oh my God, Jeff!"

"From documents on his body, it seemed he was a citizen of Georgia, someone whose name I was familiar with. John Clint. His land bordered Riverside. To my knowledge, I had not seen him before, but I didn't know all our neighbors. His partner had been standing beyond the campfire. I didn't get a good look at his face as blood was running freely into my eyes. But now I think that person was someone whose form at least was familiar to me. Another neighboring planter. One who until then knew me only as a Confederate irregular. He left quickly, and we didn't see him again.

"But the names of the men who were at the church today, one sounded very familiar to me. A variation on a name."

Lorie sat up. "Good grief, we've got to find out more about those guys!"

"If I am right," he said softly, sadly, "it means that I may have been the direct cause of my father's death. And Moses's as well."

"Why?"

"I was talking with General Sherman when it happened. My attacker named me a traitor. The other man must have carried the news back to Georgia."

"But, Jeff, how then do you explain the deaths of your brothers and sisters and your mother so many years before?"

He was quiet for a time. "You are right, love. Of course. This enmity is of longer standing than what happened at Chattanooga. A hidden foe of my family. Perhaps former associates of my father who felt he had betrayed them by marrying my mother. Or perhaps they found her out."

"Your mother?"

"She was from Massachusetts, daughter of a New England family of Puritan descent. A beautiful, strong lady, abolitionist at her core. My father was handsome and dashing and very much in love with her. She didn't know until she moved south with him that he owned properties serviced by slavery. She and Moses, almost from the time she came to Georgia, helped slaves escape to the north. Many thousands of dollars were siphoned from the plantations around us and down the coast by our actions. By the plantation owners' lights, according to my mother, those enslaved people were valuable only as specie to be jingled in their pockets. But by her reckoning, those slaves were first of all human beings who each deserved a life of his or her own choosing."

"I think I would have liked her very much," Lorie said softly.

"And she would have loved you as much as I do." He kissed her gently. "Will and I were her helpers from the time we were small children, and after their deaths, her work went on without pause."

"Will?"

"My older brother."

"How old were you when that happened, Jeff?"

"Almost fourteen. And away at boarding school. Which is why I survived. Sara lived only because she had charmed Moses into taking her with him when he went to Atlanta on chores the same day that a slave infected by a contagious disease—a fatal disease—was brought back to Riverside by my father. Father was immune for some reason, and he made sure the three of us didn't return home until the contagion burned itself out."

"Oh, Jeff, what a horrible tragedy."

Again he lay quiet. "Yes," he said finally. "But I suspected from the start that it was murder. And so did Moses. After that, he was even more determined to take as many of his people as he could to the Promised Land. I think Father realized then what had been happening. But he was a shattered soul, losing my mother and so many of his children all at once. He was so consumed by guilt that we thought he had lost his mind to madness. But he would never have betrayed us, even had he known."

"The little book," Lorie said. "You didn't look at it yet. Would it hold some answers?"

He laughed quietly. "It's my book. My code. I kept track of every operation. I know who worked with me and how much we lifted from the wagon trains, courtesy of the Federal government. I know the names of every man and woman we helped to reach the abolitionists' network in the north. It is all in the book. I think my 'translation' will be very discrete."

"My God! You were a devious soul."

"Keep that verb in the present tense." He chuckled. "I am still a devious soul, and I have some ideas as to how to get our friend Rolf Maratti into Randolph House to meet with me—without any of those outsiders who seem to be taking an unnatural interest in him."

Lorie leaned up on her elbow. "Tell me."

"The circumstances will determine our action, but once we begin, we will have to act very swiftly before they suspect what we are about. First, you must find out what the judge decides about the two wills."

"That's scheduled for the day after tomorrow. I think we have to persuade our one remaining witness to Mr. Jon's signature to be there with us. I hope he won't be too frightened to help."

"We'll find him tomorrow if we can, and give him courage if he lacks it."

"Jeff?" Lorie said a moment later, after thinking about it.

"Yes, my love?"

"One word that I never hear in real life was spoken today twice: contraband."

"The little African table and the roll-top desk?"

"Yes, but also the goods your larcenous traders were selling to Union troops. You said it to be derogatory, I think, but might that have been exactly what they were selling?"

He was silent for a time. "Not merchants. Bushwhackers. Selling stolen goods to Union troops while they spied. Laughing up their sleeves at the same time. Why didn't I make the connection? Damnation, Lorie. John Clint, the man who slashed me, the man I killed, was always after my father to sell him property on the river. He wanted to put in a mill so he could weave cotton into cloth as the mills down-river did, making their owners very rich. We might want to find out if anyone claimed that piece of property after my father was killed."

"He could never have had clear title," Lorie reminded him softly, "because the property belonged from that time forward to your sister—who had been whisked away into hiding in Illinois by my multi-great-grandfather Marshal."

"Who also changed her name." Jeff chuckled and added, "I read in Jacob Cox's book that the Federal army burned the mills and dispersed all the workers. So even if someone tried to grab the property for himself, it would have gained him nothing."

"Jeff, one of those men hanging around the judge was named Clint Samuels. Might the bushwhacker who escaped have been related to the man you killed? Perhaps he was a relative."

He was silent for a time. "This is indeed the same man I think bears watching."

"Background checks. The police are very good at that."

"It is very hard to keep a secret in your world," he said thoughtfully.

"I guess the trick is not to have secrets," Lorie said, "but it's not going to stop me from keeping you in my bed tonight."

He chuckled again. "In case you're concerned about the proprieties, my dear one, your aunt won't give you any problems. She and the good doctor are sharing his bed—and have been since I've been under this roof."

"What?" Lorie thought about it, giggled, and said, "Good for her. It's about time. I hope she's as happy tonight as I am!" She snuggled even deeper into his arms.

CHAPTER 14

Wednesday, July 23, 2014

Lorie woke refreshed and discovered Jeff missing. She pulled on her robe and, following the delectable odor of frying bacon, found him in the kitchen. Dressed in jeans and a pullover, still barefoot, he was standing at the stove, cracking eggs into the skillet.

"Good morning, wife," he said. "Breakfast is almost ready."

"Call me that again." She said it very quietly and smiled up at him.

He pulled her close to him with the one arm he wasn't using. "Wife. Wife. Wife. I love the word. As much as I love you. More than the blue sky. More than the sunshine. More than the world itself!"

"Do you think we should at some time repeat the ceremony so everyone else knows, too?"

"You said a quite proper 'I do' when you accepted my dear mother's ring, Lorena Manning Preston. What need do we have for more formalities? Paper is to establish bloodlines or determine property rights. I have no property to leave you. And now that I know, thanks to the computer, what that little pill was that you swallowed yesterday morning, I can only

assume we won't be having fat little babies any time soon."
He grinned at her.

Emotion welled inside her, bringing tears to her eyes. "I
knew we were married the minute you put that ring on my
finger, Jefferson Preston."

"And I, my love." He leaned down and kissed her again
as he turned the bacon.

"No matter what happens in the future," Lorie said
fiercely, "you will always be my beloved husband."

"We are half souls apart," he said it very softly, "and
complete only when we are together." He moved the skillet
away from the burner and pulled her tightly against him.
"Husband and wife. Forever."

She snuggled inside the crush of his arms, warmed head
to toe with the love she felt for him. If only it could last forever…and the nagging sense of foreboding would go away.

She heard the clatter of shoes on the staircase and pulled
back, smiling through her tears.

Carol came sweeping into the kitchen, still in her robe.
"I just heard from Randy. Mac and Harris have persuaded
Mr. Taylor to talk with us. We're meeting them in about an
hour at the freeway intersection. We'll follow them to his
hiding place." She looked at Lorie. Then at Jeff. "Oops!" she
said. "I think I'm interrupting something."

"It's okay," Lorie said. "Aunt Carol, Jeff, and I are officially engaged."

Carol swept Lorie up in a big hug. "I was so hoping you'd
say that. I love you both to pieces. I know you just met each
other, but you seem so right for each other. Like peas in a pod.
My dears, I couldn't be happier." She turned back and called
over her shoulder. "Phil, honey, they discovered each other."

Jeff grinned at Lorie and mouthed the words, "I love
you."

Carol released her hold on Lorie, turned to Jeff, put her hands at either side of his face to pull it down to hers and gave him a big kiss on the cheek. "Welcome to the family, young man. Whoever you are is fine by me. Okay," she said decisively, "we're out of here in an hour. Jeff, continue as you were. Lorie, it's time to get dressed. This is going to be a big day."

She went clattering back up the stairs.

Lorie started to giggle. She couldn't help herself. A glow had come over her world. She went back into Jeff's arms.

"Better get a move on, wife," he said, sharing her laughter. "General Carol has given her orders. And the eggs are congealing."

"Yes, sir, husband, sir!" She moved to obey orders.

*****

A black unmarked police car, its small antenna jutting up from the trunk lid, was sitting at the entrance to the freeway when Phil's Town Car arrived at the designated rendezvous point. Randy, dressed informally, stepped out of the Crown Victoria momentarily and spoke with the doctor, giving him rough directions. "Follow us as closely as you can," he said. "But don't make it too conspicuous."

"Gotcha," Phil said. He pulled onto the freeway, headed toward hill country. The black car quickly passed them and settled into a comfortable speed.

Traffic was sparse on the chosen road, so no one was in sight when the two cars turned at an unmarked crossroads and headed into closely woven forest land on a graveled road.

Several long miles down the road, the driver of the police car flicked on the turn lights, slowed, and pulled onto a dirt road that meandered through sun-dappled woodlands. Phil followed at a distance, not wanting to get swallowed up

in the dust cloud. Soon Lorie saw evidence of human habi-
tation. A substantial white rail fence had been installed along
the right side of the road. It enclosed a large wooded area
which eventually opened onto a meadow bordering a lake.

"Someone keeps horses here," she said, pointing to a
handsome black stallion standing beside the lake, drinking
his fill. A small herd was cropping grass in the distance.

"I'm relieved to know they still exist," Jeff said quietly.
"I was afraid they had gone extinct."

Lorie chuckled. "Not exactly."

The house that they finally came to was built with logs.
It resembled a one-story cabin from the distance, but as they
approached on the long and winding private driveway, Lorie
realized that the house was far more extensive than the usual
log cabin, and much of it was concealed by trees.

The graveled parking area in front was larger than would
be expected, and indeed, Lorie spotted a helicopter secreted
within a relatively inconspicuous hangar tucked back into
another wooded area. Lorie pointed it out to Jeff. "This must
be the landing pad," she said. His eyes widened at the sight.
She could see his curiosity growing as he examined the craft.

Four men had emerged from the police car. They stood
in a loose group, chatting with each other. Four familiar
faces. All informally dressed.

"Jeans Day," Lorie remarked with a chuckle. Everyone
in their car was similarly clad.

Randy Ross and his white-haired partner, Tim Murphy,
joined them as they pulled to a stop and shook hands all
around.

"Nice to see you again, Detective," Phil Barnett said
as Alan Macdonald also came forward to shake hands.
Macdonald was wearing a handgun in a holster attached to
his belt.

"Call me Mac." Even in casual clothes he was unmistakably a policeman, tall, straight, well-muscled, and disciplined. His high forehead gleamed in the morning sunlight, and every hair on the remainder of his head was in its rightful place. He smiled warmly at Jeff as he took the extended hand. "Nice to see you looking so well, young man."

Dean Harris, the black detective, also shook hands with everyone before turning to Jeff. "Anyone recognize you yet, son?" Harris was also armed.

Jeff shook his head. "So far, only one person has blinked."

Harris's eyes widened. "Who was that?"

"Rolf Maratti."

Randy spoke out. "Jon Randolph's stepson. The Northerner. You really think he recognized you, Jeff? That's very interesting. It kind of keeps this in the family, doesn't it?"

"How is lawyer Purdy faring?" Carol asked the detectives.

"He's much relieved," Harris said. "He and his wife are at a safe house. He hasn't told us much yet. Only that this conspiracy has been cooking for a number of years, ever since Jon Randolph came up with the idea of creating a 'historic town.' A few extra people have come to town since the word went out...one by one. Archibald Hood is one. Hood is the mayor now. Former president of the Chamber of Commerce."

"Have you done a background check on him?"

"Yes. He's a successful businessman from Atlanta. He sells office supplies. Pretty innocuous stuff. He's never been involved in anything suspicious. His *bona fides* are on the up-and-up. Science degree from Georgia Tech. Nice family. Apparently the Hoods originated in Randolph City, and he came back to take over his grandfather's business when Grandpa died."

"His arrival could be a coincidence," Phil said. "Anything else?"

"A couple of new policemen have come on the small force," Harris went on, looking at his notes. "They weren't locals. Purdy doesn't trust them." Harris looked up at Phil. "I wouldn't either, quite frankly. We couldn't find that either has been qualified as a cop, and in the brief time we've had to work on it, we haven't been able to pin down exactly where they came from, or even if the names they go by are legit."

"Uh-oh!" Carol said. "So Purdy is right to be worried. Whoever hired them must be a plant, too."

"The red flag here is that the recommendations for employment of these guys included Hood's and Judge Cragin's names, among others. So we thought we'd better check out the judge as well. He came to town, also as a businessman, about twenty years ago. That's when Jon Randolph started advertising for people who had expertise in historic recon-struction. Cragin had been a successful lawyer in Savannah, but he was always interested in historic homes. Since he came to Randolph City, he's done a lot of work with locals who want advice on how their houses can look old-fashioned but still be up-to-date, if you get what I mean. He's one of the most respected people in town. And because he's very good at what he does, he's done very well for himself."

"The Baileys used a lot of his expertise in their reno-vation," Carol said. "What's curious is why he'd want to go back into law now. What qualifications would he have to be a judge?"

"At least seven years as a qualified member of the bar," Mac said. "And in his case, you have to know someone who'll appoint you to the position when the elected judge gets sick. Respect goes a long way in these parts."

Lorie said, "But what about the three guys who were hanging around him at the funeral? McDaniels is one. Another was named Merrill. What's the other name? Clint Samuels, I think. We were told that McDaniels is an Atlanta lawyer and the other two are developers."

Harris wrote down the names. "We'll check them out. Thanks."

"We'd best talk to Mr. Taylor now," Mac reminded them. He turned to Carol. "Did you bring a copy of the will you found? Mr. Taylor asked if he could see it."

"We did," Carol said, indicating her briefcase. "Ewen Taylor's name is typed below the witness line, but of course, this is only a copy. Jon's signature is the only one we have. But we can vouch for its authenticity."

"Well," Harris said. "Let's find out how this guy knows Jon Randolph."

Ewen Taylor answered the door himself. "Welcome to my hideaway."

*****

The term "dynamite in a bottle" suited this man. Lorie could almost see the energy radiating from him. He was no longer young, probably closer in age to Rolf Maratti, in his sixties, than to Phil Barnett, still in his early fifties. In top physical shape, he was almost as tall as Jeff and—with the exception of Randy—the rest of the policemen now surrounding him. His hair was pure white and hand-raked, his skin tanned and lined from hard outdoor use, and his intelligent eyes an unusual shade of brown. He was wearing a designer white knit shirt, high-quality khaki trousers, and boots. He shook hands as introductions were made and paused when he met Jeff.

"I've seen you somewhere before," he said softly. "Don't tell me. Let me think about where it was." Lorie's attention shifted to fast alert.

He invited them into his large study. It was a man's room with leather couches and deep armchairs, and lots of electronic equipment, its purpose obscure to Lorie. He asked everyone to have a seat and offered sweetened iced tea, which was brought to them by a quiet young man in dark clothing.

"Thank you, Jaime," he said. "Please let Clarissa know that there will be eight more for lunch." Carol demurred, but he insisted, and Lorie was fascinated and amused by the manners exhibited so correctly and discretely.

"So now we know why I was being tailed," Taylor said when Lorie's aunt showed him the will. He chuckled. "I'm relieved to know I wasn't simply imagining these things. I was beginning to think I was having flashbacks to my old days in the clandestine services." He looked up. "I always know when there's a tail on me, and I'm very skilled at shaking them off. These guys aren't amateurs, but they're not top professionals either. Still, it's enough to make one very nervous. I've sent my entire family to our Swiss compound until we get this figured out."

Carol glanced at Lorie, who nodded briefly, instantly relating to the term. "Nervous" was only a pale description of the feeling.

"Chances are good," Mac said to Taylor, "that since the provisions of the will are now going to be public knowledge, whoever is behind this malevolent little conspiracy will realize that silencing you is no longer a useful option. But we think you will be even safer once you have publicly testified."

"Of course I'll testify," he responded. "Jon was a good friend of mine. We worked together many times in parts of the world I'm unable to tell you about, despite the fact that the Berlin Wall has long since fallen. I was the electronics expert on his team. We shared some pretty hairy adventures and always emerged alive, even when it wasn't altogether certain we would. He was a good man."

All of the policemen seemed impressed.

"Sounds like a great book in the making," Phil Barnett said.

"Not in my lifetime." Again he turned to examine Jeff's face. His eyes narrowed. Lorie had seated herself beside Jeff on one of the comfortable couches. What could Taylor know, really? She slid her hand into Jeff's, and he gave it a reassuring squeeze. "I'll remember," Taylor said, shaking his head a little. "Old age creeping up on me. Just give me time." He flung his arms up behind him to rest on the soft leather of the couch, leaned back and crossed his right leg over his left knee. "Now tell me, what are these brigands up to?"

"There is talk in Randolph City about dismantling Randolph House," Carol said, "and replacing it with a Five Star hotel."

"No!" His hands came off the couch with a snap. He sat up, both feet on the floor, totally engaged.

Carol continued. "City council members are already debating options, and the town is in an uproar. Since nothing has gone to probate yet, and probate issues take time, someone is obviously stirring the pot to see what trouble can be caused."

"Why would anyone want to destroy Randolph House?" As he spoke, Taylor's hands moved in concert with his rapid words. He leaned toward them to emphasize what he was saying. "That house was constructed before the Civil War by free blacks as a station on the Underground Railroad. It should be on the Historic Register. I personally will stand in the way of its destruction!" Again he looked at Jeff, and a sudden spark livened his intense eyes. "That's where I saw you. At Randolph House. By God, you bear a remarkable resemblance to a painting I saw there of the man who built the mansion. Who did you say you were?"

Randy spoke up quickly. "He's suffering from amnesia, Mr. Taylor. He was shot and left for dead at one of Jon Randolph's properties, the South Wind Suites hotel. He calls himself Jefferson Richard Preston. And we're sure he's a relative, although we don't know how."

"By God, he's a relative all right!" Taylor shook his head. "What the hell is happening over there? At least the Chamber of Commerce should be wanting to save that old mansion. It's a marvel of engineering. Jon showed me through it several times. He didn't think he'd found all the secret compartments and passageways yet, although he was always looking. But the engineering in just the rooms and compartments he'd discovered so far was remarkable. That painting"—he pointed now at Jeff and looked from one of his guests to the other—"was of a Confederate soldier who looked an awful lot like this guy here, blue eyes and all. Jon found it in a large concealed chamber just off the drawing room. He laughed when I chided him about his Confederate ancestor. He confided to me his relative wasn't a Rebel at all, but one of the best agents the Yankees ever had. I could see how he'd been inspired by the man after I heard some of the hair-raising tales Jon's grandmother had told him about her older brother."

"See, what did I tell you?" Randy said forcefully, looking at Carol. "Whoever is doing this stuff to you folks has probably seen the same picture, heard the same stories, and was aware Major Preston was a Yankee spy. By damaging Jeff and dropping him into your laps, presumably dead, they were warning you to lay off or meet the same fate."

"That may be," Jeff interjected quietly, and Lorie listened with intense interest because she had no idea what he was planning at this point, "and my true identity may or may not play a part in their plans. But I've seen that picture, too, and it's clear to me now that I lived in Randolph House at one time. These people certainly overplayed their hand when they brought me back to Marietta."

"Wait a minute," Taylor said, staring at him. "You were left for dead at the South Wind? You look pretty damn healthy to me."

"Well, I had to climb a bit of a hill to get there. But once I did, I had the good fortune to meet a brilliant nurse." He turned to Lorie, smiling. "She knew what to do to keep me alive, and then the doctors took over, and here I am."

"Damned lucky!" Taylor said. He looked at the policemen seated around the room. "Any idea what's going on here?"

"It's a conspiracy of long-standing," Detective Harris said. "Randolph's lawyer, Mike Neil, was the first victim we're aware of. Possibly his secretary as well. We're not sure what the motives are, except that whoever is involved seems to want Randolph House and as many of Jon Randolph's other properties as they can get. They stole the will, destroyed all the copies they knew about, and tried to pretend it had never existed."

"I'm not sure how that would benefit anyone," Taylor mused, "because if Jon died intestate, the property would be split evenly among his heirs.

"And he has quite a few blood relatives left," Carol said, "what with Sue and her kids, and a few cousins scattered around the country who we're trying to find and warn."

Randy pointed to Jeff. "He's undoubtedly an heir. What happens if, God forbid, they're all knocked off?"

"Georgia law would kick in," Taylor answered. "I somehow doubt that developers would inherit the property, though."

"But guess what?" Lorie's aunt put in, with a sudden flash of clarity. "All of a sudden Jon's stepson shows up, after many years of absence. And he has in his possession an original will Jon wrote years ago, leaving almost everything to him."

"Rolf! Goddamn! Jon would never have suspected that kind of betrayal. He really loved his stepson, despite the differences between them."

"The developers," Carol said, "are swarming all over Rolf Maratti."

"One more person to investigate," Harris said, pulling out his pad and pencil.

"He lives in New Jersey," Carol pointed out to Harris quietly, and the detective added another note. "And someone keeps talking about Mafia connections, although we haven't pinned down who's saying it."

Jeff Preston spoke again, with such authority that everyone turned to him. "Our most important objective is to unmask the key players in this drama and determine each of their motivations." He looked directly at Taylor. "Because Rolf Maratti also lived at Randolph House for a time, I'd like to meet with him there. Privately. With your help, Mr. Taylor."

Taylor bent forward, listening. "Go on."

"Maratti made sure the house was locked tight the minute Jon Randolph died. I want to find out why. We need to know where his loyalties lay. Everything we do after that hinges on this meeting."

"I'm still listening."

"There are guards at the house," Jeff went on. "They're country boys, tough on the surface but easily spooked. We can be rid of them in an instant if they think the house is haunted."

A short sharp laugh issued from Taylor's throat. "You need ghosts?"

"Ghosts. To scare the guards away and make people curious. Since as far as Maratti knows he is the only person who has access, I suspect that when he hears there's something afoot inside the house, he'll be there—the sooner the better. If he comes with a crew of roughnecks, we'll know he's working with our adversaries. If he shakes them off and comes alone, or with his lawyer, it's another story altogether. In that case I need to talk with him."

The expression in Taylor's eyes hardened. "If there are guards, how the hell do we get in ourselves?"

Jeff squeezed her hand, and Lorie grinned, knowing what he wanted her to say. "There's a long, dark, spider-infested tunnel. We went in right under their noses. That's where we found the copy of the will."

"By God," Taylor roared, slapping his hands on his knees and rising to his feet. "I knew there must be a tunnel. We were never able to find it. I'll help all right."

"I think we all want to help," Harris said, his brown eyes alight, and his normally stoic partner Mac concurred with equal enthusiasm. Randy had been grinning the whole time, and Tim Murphy laughed out loud.

"Hold it, boys," Carol said. "That little expedition Lorie and Jeff made scared me to death. How many of those guards have guns? People who are spooked tend to shoot first and ask questions later."

Jeff turned to Carol. "They won't even know we're there, Miz Carol." He looked back at Harris. "Any chance I can get my uniform back? I want to look as much like that portrait as I can."

"Your uniform?" Taylor asked.

"He was dressed as a Confederate soldier," Randy put in, "when they shot him. Very spooky stuff going on here already. And boots," he added enthusiastically, "that are authentic Federal cavalry officers' boots. The real McCoy. Which means," he said, now in an intense tone, "that the people who dressed him knew the original Jefferson Preston was a Yankee spy."

Taylor turned back to Jeff, bemused. "Are you a horse-man, perchance?"

Jeff nodded. "It's been a while."

"What would you think..." Lorie could visualize gears turning in Taylor's brain. "What would you think about gal-loping up to the house on horseback. That old Rebel yell was pretty intimidating in its own right."

"You are wicked," he said to Ewen Taylor with a quick grin. "How about the black?"

"Just what I was thinking, young man. But you'd have to be a good horseman. That horse can be a devil."

"In my recollection, there was never a horse I couldn't ride...sooner or later."

"Let's see about that," Taylor said. "Come on, everyone. Let's see if this brash young man can handle Ravenwing." He turned and strode through the house toward the back, the men following. Lorie helped Carol out of the too-soft leather man's chair she was struggling with, and they hurried along behind. The men had gone out a side door and were walk-ing quickly across a wide yard toward a cedar-sided barn, trying to keep up with Taylor's long strides. A shrill whistle echoed through the air. Lorie saw, in the distance, the black horse pick up its head, turn, and come at a gallop toward his master.

"My goodness," Carol said. "I've never seen the like. What a beautiful animal."

Within minutes Ravenwing was at the fence. Taylor stroked its muzzle. The horse rubbed against his hand and took the offered treat. "How about it?" he said to Jeff.

"He's magnificent!" Jeff climbed the fence and watched as Taylor picked up a bridle and slipped it over the black's head.

"There's a saddle in the barn," he said to Jeff.

"No need." Jeff dropped down into the barnyard, wrapped a hand in Ravenwing's mane, and in one smooth move was mounted. The reins almost magically appeared in his hand.

"Well done, sir," Taylor said, obviously impressed.

Jeff saluted him and, with a slight motion of his moccasin-clad feet, took Ravenwing backward. Lorie's mouth dropped open. She had never once thought how Jeff's talents would translate into the modern world. With no seeming effort, he turned the horse and began to travel around the barnyard in slow loops. The tempo picked up until he was galloping slowly around the yard in ever-widening circles. Then he turned Ravenwing's head toward the lake and let out a banshee-type yell, and man and horse went streaming across the pasture at top speed, flying like the wind.

"By God, he's a horseman all right!" Taylor said, a big smile nearly splitting his face. Lorie saw Randy grinning ear to ear as well, leaning over the fence, waving his arms and yipping. The other men were only a little less restrained. Carol and Phil were both seated on the fence, excitedly crowing about the bravura display of horsemanship on Jeff Preston's part.

"You didn't tell us you could do that," Phil Barnett said when Jeff brought Ravenwing back to the fence.

"You didn't ask," Jeff said, laughing. He bounded to the ground as athletically as he had mounted and handed the reins to their host.

"You must have spent some time as a cowboy," Taylor said.

Lorie almost spoke out, wondering if Jeff's computer exploration had even touched on the subject of cowboys, but his answer sufficed. He shrugged. "I grew up on horseback."

Over a sumptuous lunch, sandwiches, salads, sweets, and fruits, plans were suggested and discarded. Ideas were brought up and thrown out. "I don't need anything too complicated," Jeff told them as he browsed his way through a fruit salad. "I'm not as good with wires and plugs as I am with horses."

"We need something so awesome they won't even think of sticking around," Mac said.

"What he did!" Harris said, pointing to Jeff. "If I saw something like that coming at me screaming like hell, I'd move out of the way real fast."

"Wouldn't you shoot?" Lorie asked, suddenly frightened by the idea. She set her tea glass on the table, afraid the unexpected tremble in her hand would cause her to spill it.

"They won't be shooting," Jeff said, laughing. "Trust me on this." The other gentlemen agreed.

"People moving past windows. Looking out. Then disappearing. How does that sound?" Ewen Taylor seemed to gain in enthusiasm by the moment.

"How do we do this?" Mac asked.

"Holograms!"

"I didn't think that was real." Carol's eyes widened. "I thought it was just sci-fi movie stuff."

"It's a science still in its infancy," Taylor said, looking up and past her as if he were seeing into a different dimension. "We can have people in Civil War-era clothes looking out of the darkened windows. Just flashes, nothing prolonged. We'll have portable equipment in each of several rooms, and have it all out quickly if Maratti, or anyone else, decides to come investigate." His eyes focused back on Carol's, and he grinned.

Officer Tim Murphy was chuckling. "I'm already getting goose-bumps," he said enthusiastically. "Will it be easy for us to install?"

"We can make it easy for those of you who aren't experts," Taylor said. "But we'll have to bring our equipment into the building and show you how to use it. How hard would that be?"

"The other day when we were at Randolph House," Lorie said, suddenly remembering. "Sue Bailey told us that a lawn service comes out to care for the gardens."

"Great idea," Taylor said. "Find out which service. We'll co-opt their trucks and bring our own equipment in, along with some technicians. How easy is it to get into the house during daylight hours?"

Lorie looked at Jeff. He grinned back and turned to Taylor. "We've discovered that the lawn equipment is stored in the summer kitchen."

"The tunnel starts there?" Ewen Taylor put the fingers of one hand through his white hair. "Good God, we searched that place so many times!"

Jeff lifted his eyebrows and smiled his crooked little smile.

"How long do we have to prepare?" Taylor asked.

"Tomorrow," Carol said, "we have a meeting with Judge Cragin. He's going to take a look at both wills. And at whatever proof of authenticity we have—your testimony included, I hope—we'll take it from there. Sorry we can't be more specific, but we're kind of playing this by ear."

"I understand. I'll get a crew working on something preliminary this afternoon. Once we know what we're facing, we can move forward rapidly."

*****

"I think," Lorie told Jeff privately as they were driving back to Phil's house, "that you're right. Between you and Mr. Taylor, the conspirators have surely overplayed their hand."

He smiled down at her sadly. "We must never underestimate them, my darling."

"And I will never underestimate you again. Why didn't you tell me you were a horseman?"

"I thought you knew." He seemed surprised.

"How could I know?"

"The cavalry uniform? I was a cavalry officer."

"Oh." She thought about it. "Sorry," she said contritely. "Even if I'd been remotely aware that was a cavalry uniform, horses would never have entered my mind."

"We have a lot of catching up to do, don't we?" He sighed.

She took his hand to her lips and echoed his sigh. Would they have time to catch up before their joined world came crashing down, as surely it was bound to do? Once more she was swept up in the sense of melancholy and loss.

CHAPTER 15

Carol was so tired by the time they reached home midafternoon that she headed for her room. "Wake me up when it's time to fix dinner," she said. "I'm exhausted."

Needing to see a patient at the clinic, the doctor excused himself. Lorie and Jeff were left alone. They wandered out to the screened-in porch and sat on the swing close together, holding hands. The day was heating up, but it didn't matter.

"I have a confession to make, Lorena," Jeff said after a while. "I took a few things from the green box before we left Oak Hill."

"Something besides your mother's ring?" She gazed at it. Flashing in the sunlight, it was a beautiful piece of jewelry. Worth a small fortune to others, but to her, it was now the whole world, and she would never let it leave her finger.

"There was more." He pulled from his back pocket a small journal. "My sister's journal. Do you mind if I read from it? I haven't had time, what with certain distractions."

She smiled at him and touched his cheek gently. "Of course, my dear love."

"I'd like to know how she handled...afterward."

"I understand, Jeff. Please go ahead."

He opened the book. The cover showed signs of age, but the paper inside was not brittle, and the handwriting was dainty and precise. Lorie watched him as he read…silently for a time, sometimes scowling, sometimes chuckling. Suddenly, without warning, he closed the book and looked up. "I don't know if I can go on."

"Do you want me to screen it for you?" she asked softly. "I can leave out the bad stuff."

Silent, he handed the book to her. He had stopped at the page dated July 15, 1864. She looked down at the neat script and softly began. "'I am going to Fox Haven, no matter what Father says. Jon has sent me a letter saying he needs me urgently. Moses doesn't like it, but he will take me.'"

The next date was August 4, 1864. "'Brother is gone,'" Lorie read, tears springing to her eyes whether she wanted them or not. She looked up at Jeff. His expression was stoic. He gave her a quick nod. Reluctantly, she continued. "'Captain Manning has talked with the soldiers who found Sergeant Ross's body, and they told him the officer who was with him was surely killed as they have no record of holding a Confederate prisoner. Nor have they found his body. But they really did not have time to look, what with the push toward Atlanta.

"'If he is found, we will have a proper burial. Captain Manning says to be brave, that might never happen. Father is gone, too, burned to ashes along with the house. My husband's death has also been confirmed. How can I bear this? Everyone in my family is gone now all at once, even my best friend Moses on whom I relied for everything.'" Lorie paused, seeing the expression on Jeff's face. "Are you sure you want me to continue?"

"I must." Tears were welling in his eyes, streaming down his cheeks.

She wiped her own eyes and once more looked down at the small tragic volume. "The next page is dated August

18, 1864. 'My little Jonny is a month old today. He is so beautiful, and he is growing so fast. He is my dearest hope for the future. Captain Manning has been extremely attentive to my needs. He brought me to Jeff's summer home at Oak Hill when I showed him where it was. Then he found Sergeant Ross's wife, Ellen, and she has been here to cry with me and care for me, bringing some of her many children to fill our lives with much-needed lightness and laughter. I believe Captain Manning wants to move us all north, far out of the war zone. He is a wonderful person. I don't know how I could have been so lucky as to be placed in his capable care. It was Brother's doing, of course.'" Now Lorie's voice began to choke up, and tears blurred her eyes. "Crap!" She handed the book back.

"It's okay." Jeff put his arms around her.

They were very quiet for a time. Finally, Jeff cleared his throat. "Okay, let's see what she says next. It can't be much worse."

He opened the book again. "'August 19, 1864. Here I recount my memories of those dreadful days.'" He handed the book back to Lorie.

She took it, cleared her throat one more time, and said quietly, "I'll try. 'The attack began the minute we reached the house at Fox Haven. They were laying in wait for us. There were probably a dozen or so men. Except that it was getting dark, I would not have had a chance. Moses told me to run as fast as I could up the hill to the spring house, and then to open the doorway he had put in the rock wall against the hillside, and into the cave that was there. He told me to wait until Brother came for me, as Rastus had been sent from Riverside to find Jeff. If it had not been for the baby inside me, I would not have left Moses. But he insisted. He had brought Caleb and Ezekiel with us for our protection, but there were too many of them against us.'"

Lorie looked at Jeff. She could see the anguish on his face. "Should I go on?"

"Please. I must know."

"Okay. But I'll quit if you tell me." She cleared her throat. "'Even as far away as I was from the house, I heard terrible screams that seemed to go on forever. I held my hands over my ears, but it did not do any good. The screams went on and on. And finally, there was nothing to hear. Later I heard people outside, cursing and talking rudely, and tearing down the spring house shelter. But they did not find the entrance to my refuge, and they finally left. I sat there for hours and hours in the dark, not knowing if it were day or night, afraid to come out. Then I heard Brother's voice calling, and Sergeant Ross's voice, and I came out and called back, and there they were. I crawled out and fell into Brother's arms. I must have fainted. When I opened my eyes, I was wrapped in blankets and lying in the wagon bed. The horses were taking us past the house. I wanted to look. Jeff did not want me too, but I was stubborn, as usual. I was wrong. I will never ever forget the horror of what I saw. Brother had cut Moses down to prepare him for burial, but I saw his naked body lying there in death. He had been beaten horribly. His wrists and ankles were covered with blood where they had tied him up. They had cut the shape of a diamond on his chest, and worse yet, they had cut away his manhood.'" Lorie stopped. "I can't..."

"Please." Jeff spoke quietly.

She cleared her throat and read, very softly. "'I fainted again at the sight.'"

"Is there more?" he said.

"Yes."

"Go ahead."

"'The next time I woke,'" Lorie continued very softly, "'Brother was handing my care over to Captain Manning. The captain tried to help them escape by giving them his personal mount and that of Elijah Benning, a young miracle worker. He had found Elijah treating war wounds on the battlefield and was taking the boy to the field hospital to help serve somewhere away from the front when Jeff and Sergeant Ross, in Rebel uniforms, stopped them at gunpoint to ask for help. It was great good luck that Jeff knew Captain Manning already. Their paths had crossed at West Point, and they had long since developed a mutual admiration for each other, even before they met on the trail. The horses were retrieved eventually, but not the men who went away on them.' Jeff, I'm not sure—"

"I can handle this part." But his face was very white.

"Okay, here goes. 'Jeff told Captain Manning how to take me home to Father. But when we reached Riverside, there was even worse waiting for us. The house had been burned to the ground and was still smoldering. Father had been stripped, beaten, and killed, and his body had been burned in the fire. When I saw Father, I fainted again. That kindly old man who hardly knew what he was doing, that once-strong man whose sharp mind died the day he had to bury his beloved wife and five of his children because he had, in a weak moment and under the influence of his so-called friends, purchased a slave who brought contagion to Riverside—they had strung Father up and beaten him and carved a diamond on his chest. And they had cut his manhood, too. I will never forget what those fiends did to my father and my true friend Moses and all the others. If it is ever in my power to destroy them, I will. Even if I have to return from the grave!'"

"Lorie," Jeff said very softly, "now I know why I am here. You were right. These are truly the same people. Pirates in the past. Slavers. Vicious criminals. I suspected my father had been one of them—until he met my mother. And I had thought it might be revenge against me they were after because they saw me as a traitor. I do know that played a part in their timing. They would not have moved against my family as long as they thought I was a genuine Confederate hero.

"But it is the diamond they're looking for—still looking for. They thought Father had it, or that he had given it to Sara, and they could cover up their crimes by blaming the Yankees for the destruction. But, Lorie"—he turned to her and took her hands—"Moses told me the diamond never reached my father and he would have known."

"That's why they burned two houses to the ground and tortured and killed human beings? To find a diamond?"

"There is no diamond, Lorie. If there had been a diamond, Moses would have been a free man."

"Maybe you'd better tell me a bit more about Moses."

"That wasn't his given name," Jeff began. "He tried to teach me a few of the African languages, but I could never pronounce his African name the way he did. He spelled it for me. U-kuh-la-kani-pho." He tried to pronounce it in a halting voice. "It's a Zulu word that means 'wisdom.' He was the son of a king. He was very tall and fit, very black, very handsome. He spoke English as an Englishman. It was because Moses was so elegant, my father used to tell us, that he bought the big black man for his new bride, thinking to please her.

"But Mother was horrified. She was a New England Unitarian, and she hated slavery with a passion. She wanted to free Moses. But there were strict laws against manumission in Georgia, so she kept him rather than letting him fall into unscrupulous hands. He respected her and called her Sister, and he did anything she asked him to. He was the planner and the chief guide when she established her section of the Underground Railroad right under Father's nose. After Mother and the other children died and our father had his breakdown, Moses became my tutor and guardian as well as Sara's. Moses had studied engineering and carpentry in France. Most of what I know about it, I learned from him. My West Point education added only the military aspect to what I had already learned from that wise man.

"We heard from some of the other servants that Moses's father tried very hard to get him back. He was willing to pay a king's ransom for his son. The price was a large uncut diamond cluster from Africa. We also heard around the quarters that someone had come from Africa with the diamond.

"But no one ever saw it. Most likely, the emissary from Moses's father was robbed and killed somewhere along the way. Father's business associates had apparently heard about it and assumed my father had received it. Father swore the diamond cluster never reached him. When I asked Moses, he confirmed that Father was telling the truth."

Lorie's mouth had dropped open. She shut it. "Good grief!"

Jeff smiled gently. "After one hundred fifty years without it, I guess it's a little hard to understand the concept of human slavery as well."

"You got that right!"

"I never once questioned the evil of that institution. I am sorry to see remnants of it intruding so prominently into new centuries. It should have disappeared with the Confederacy."

"Jeff, you've had a very hard life."

"Theirs was so much harder."

Lorie shook her head. Jeff put his arms around her, and they continued to rock quietly on the swing in the soft warmth of a late summer afternoon. The little book had gone back into Jeff's pocket to be read more thoroughly at a later time.

"Lorie," Jeff said after a time. "I need to think about something else. Would you tell me about your life?"

"It's dull and boring compared to yours," she said softly.

"Let me be the judge of that, my love. Please tell me. Where did you grow up? Why did you want to work with the ill and injured?"

She was quiet for a while, wondering what she could say that he could relate to. "My father was an officer in the army when I was born," she finally began. "Marsh and I were army brats. We moved often and lived on army bases or in small towns. It was fun and disruptive, and we learned a lot.

"But there was no continuity to it. Marsh and I were never in one school system for more than two years at a time. Our parents finally decided we were getting too wild, and my father was increasingly disgusted by fighting what he called rich men's wars. He got out so he could become a science teacher. We settled in a quiet river town in Illinois, where Aunt Carol had bought a home. It was a good place to finish growing up. We both graduated from high school there. I took pre-med, beginning medicine, at the University of Illinois and then went into a nursing program because of Aunt Carol."

"Why, because of your aunt Carol?"

"When she was young, she lost her husband and new baby in an automobile accident. She escaped without physical injury and always felt that if she had known something about emergency medicine, she could have saved her family. Probably not. But she felt very strongly about it. So she fought her way through school and finally got her degree as a physician assistant. It brought her back to life. She's a wonderful, strong person. I want to be just like her. But…"

"You faint." He smiled. "Lorie, this 'failing' of yours will pass. And when it does, you will exceed all expectations."

"You really think so?"

"I know it, Lorie." He reached for her hands and brought them to his lips. He kissed each fingertip in turn. Then very quietly, he asked, "Have you ever had a special… man in your life?"

She started slowly, knowing it had to be said. "Well, you've seen the little pills, and you know what they are for and why I am taking them, so you know there was someone serious. He was an intern at the hospital where I was finishing my certification—on his way to becoming a very rich doctor. Everyone thought I was going to be a good nurse then, if not a great one, and I think he figured I would be a steady source of income for him while he went through his training. When I started to have trouble"—she frowned, still irritated—"he dumped me and found another starry-eyed minion to support him." She stopped speaking, realizing that instead of her usual anger, she was experiencing a great surge of relief that her difficult affair had ended. She grinned broadly. "I escaped that trap just in the nick of time." When she looked at Jeff, he was grinning too.

He put his arms around her and kissed the top of her head and then her lips, lingering there. Love enveloped her.

Inside the house, the phone rang. Lorie heard Phil's voice, and then the doctor came to find them.

"Mac and Harris are on their way over," he said to Jeff. "They found something in the ravine they want you to see. And they'd like to get a DNA sample from you. Come on, let's eat a little something before they get here."

Phil had already heated up a lasagna casserole. He prepared a fresh salad and brought out the ever-present iced tea. Carol came down from upstairs wearing a colorful Caribbean print caftan and looking much fresher than when she had gone up. "Phil," she said, "again you have created a miracle meal."

"All in a day's work, beautiful lady." He smiled lovingly at Lorie's aunt. He reached for her hand and escorted her to the table.

As Jeff took his seat, he asked the doctor, "What is a DNA sample?"

"Nothing to it," Phil said, not quite connecting with the question asked. "They'll take a swab of saliva from inside your mouth and send it to the lab. For some reason, they want to check your identity against this item they found. They'll tell you all about it. Probably."

Jeff looked at Lorie and frowned. She tipped her head briefly, her signal that she would explain later. Now she was really curious.

*****

Sunlight was glittering in the leaves at the tops of the western trees, dinner was behind them and all the dishes washed when the Crown Vic pulled into the driveway. Mac and Harris emerged from the car, dressed as usual in suits with ties, although both ties were pulled loose and hanging askew. Mac was carrying a large white box.

Everyone gathered around the kitchen table. "Jeff," Harris said, his dark face unsmiling, "we've been doing a pretty extensive search of that ravine you climbed out of—that's where Randy is, in case you've missed him—and we've found a few things we'd like you to take a look at. Tell us, please, if you recognize any of them."

Mac pulled on some thin latex gloves, opened the box, and lifted out a series of ropes. Some were knotted fragments with frayed ends. "Does this mean anything to you?"

Jeff reached for one of the ropes.

"Don't touch them, please," Mac said. A sharp warning.

Jeff looked up at him, surprised.

"Contamination," Lorie said to him softly. "I'll explain later."

"I've never seen anything like this before." Jeff shook his head. "The ropes look chewed. I can't think what it would be."

"Restraints," Harris said. Lorie cringed.

Mac pulled another item from the box. Sweatpants. Gray. Discolored by grass stains, ground-in mud, and something that looked suspiciously like blood. Again Jeff shook his head.

"One more thing," Harris said. He pulled out a long-sleeved sweatshirt, muddy and as bloodstained as the pants. The only distinguishing feature was a name screened across the left side of the front in black ink: MARATTI.

Phil Barnett stared. "What the hell?"

"Our words exactly," Mac said.

"You know what these look like?" the doctor said, indicating the clothing. "Like something worn in a rehab hospital. On an army base. We see lots of them here. Any explanation?"

"We hoped Jeff would know. There's one more item." From the box, he pulled a soft hospital slipper, also gray, also stained.

"Only one?" Carol whispered.

"The other could have got lost somewhere along the way," Harris said. "We're looking for it."

"Randy's wacko explanation," Mac said, "is beginning to make a little more sense." He turned to Jeff again. "Does this ring any bells with you?"

Silent, Jeff shook his head. Lorie could feel his confusion. That was very unlike him, and a nagging unformed worry arose deep within her.

Mac said, "Let's get some DNA, and if we get any hits, we might be on the track to finding out who you are."

Jeff's saliva was taken very quickly. When Phil asked the detectives if they'd like to linger over a cup of coffee, they both declined. "We're hot on this thing," Harris said, "and we want to get back out to the site. We've still got people ripping up bushes, trying to find things that shouldn't be there." Harris turned to Jeff. "We'll keep you informed. If you can shake any information from Maratti, we'd like to know about it. Until then, we're keeping these things under lock and key."

"We will try to ask the proper questions," Jeff said quietly.

"We see the judge tomorrow morning," Carol said to the men. "We'll call you with the outcome as soon as we leave the courthouse."

"I wish we had some contacts over there in Randolph City," Mac said, "but as is, we have to keep a very low profile. We don't want them to know we're investigating what should be their case."

They left. "Now what?" Lorie said.

The phone rang. Phil answered quickly. "Sid. What did you find out?" He was silent for a moment, frowning. "That's not very helpful, is it? Well, we'll have to dig deeper." He hung up the phone and turned around. "Sid checked with George Garnett about the furniture at the courthouse. Garnett doesn't know where it came from. He says that any one of the judges could have brought it. The city council doesn't like to allocate tax funds to furnish the building, so often judges bring their personal furniture to spruce up the place."

"Did he give you the names of the other judges?" Lorie asked.

"He's going to call me back on that. Sid says he doesn't have much to do with judges in his line of work unless they have an earache or a sore throat and a properly signed prescription."

Lorie spoke softly to Jeff. "It's time for you to write out a list of items or furniture to look for. We may have to creep around private homes looking in windows." He nodded.

Again the phone rang. This time it was Ewen Taylor. Phil answered and handed the phone to Jeff. Seeing him fumble, Lorie remembered that this was the first time he had actually used the phone. "Put it to your ear and say hello," she whispered.

"Hello?" He seemed startled to hear a voice talking back. "Yes," he said and placed the receiver where it needed to be. He looked at Lorie and grinned. The conversation was largely a series of yesses and nos and the occasional "interesting idea," and finally he said "Thank you" and handed it to Lorie, who hung it up.

"Okay. What did he say?"

"He said he had an enthusiastic crew working on the holograms and that they should be ready any time now. He asked me about ideas, but I think his are fine. He has an old woman in one window, a child in another, and a man and woman dancing in one of the other rooms."

"Which means," Carol put in, "that we have a little homework to do this evening. I'll call Sue and find out if a few extra people can join the lawn service crew next time they go out to the house."

"And we," Jeff said, including Lorie in his team, "will work out what questions we need to ask our anticipated guest or guests."

"Very curious," Phil said, speaking under his breath, and everyone knew he was talking about the sweatshirt marked with the name Maratti.

"I think that might be one of the primary questions." Jeff then added to Lorie, more softly, "And I have a few questions to ask you, wife." They wandered back out to the porch. "How do the voices get into the machine?"

She stared at him, speechless; thought about it, then hurried back into the house to retrieve the computer. "Ask away," she said, seating herself on the swing. She opened the case. "If this little sucker doesn't know the answers, nobody does."

It was a productive evening, and the horrors of the journal were put off for another day.

During the night, however, when he came to her bed, she saw again how disturbed he was by the detective's report, saying, "What if this body, my body, belongs to someone else?"

"I think you've just asked me something the computer can't help us with." She moved more tightly into the circle of his arms. Then she began to get worried, too. "Jeff, you look just like the portrait at Randolph House. How could you be someone else?"

"I haven't been able to make out why I'm functioning in my own body. My flesh died a long time ago. My bones lie scattered. Jim Bailey looks enough like that picture that he could easily have posed for it. Am I inhabiting someone else's body, someone else who resembles that picture? Someone I don't know? Who?"

"Let's not go there," Lorie said quickly. She unfolded his arms from around her and sat up. "Okay, say you're borrowing someone else's body. Wouldn't you be able to tell if that person was still in it with you?"

He was quiet for a time. "I don't hear anyone telling me to go away. And surely this would be the moment. With this beautiful unclad woman looking down at me." He turned on the bed light. He was smiling his dear crooked little smile.

"Maybe he's…Jeff, I don't think we ought to talk about it. It makes me nervous." She turned off the light and returned to the warm spot she had staked out earlier. But now she couldn't get quite comfortable. If he had doubts about who he was, what if there was something to what he was thinking? Sue's son, Jim, certainly bore a resemblance to that painting in Randolph House. Except for the eyes, she thought. And the scar. Still…

"Jeff," she said softly, "you won't get angry, will you, if I ask you a few questions?"

"Lorena, ask any questions you like."

There were things only the real Major Preston would be privy to. Things that hadn't been written up in journals and eagerly read by those who were curious about the way life was lived many years before. Especially during the war. "What happened after you left Ben with the Yankees?"

"I wasn't sure what I was doing right then, Lorie," he said very softly. "I think I was in shock, losing Ben. I should have surrendered and told them who I was, but that thought didn't even occur to me. I just wanted to finish our mission!" He paused for a time. "Let me back up several days to tell you more fully why we were there.

"Federal troops were still engaged with the Confederates at Kennesaw Mountain when the general called for my assessment of the situation in Atlanta. Ben and I would have had plenty of time to get to Atlanta and back. But Rastus, my father's caretaker, caught up with us at Oak Hill just as we were moving out. He told us that Sara had received a letter from her husband, Jon, at Fox Haven, asking for help, and that she was on her way there with Moses and two of his strongest men, both Zulu warriors like himself.

"Fox Haven is in the mountains northeast of Oak Hill. I strongly suspected that the letter she received was a ruse, a trap. Ben concurred. So we headed northeast, thinking we still had some time.

"Lorie, now you can travel a long distance in an hour. Across the state in less than a day. It took us most of a day's steady riding to get to Fox Haven from Oak Hill. By then, it was too late to do anything except hand my little sister over to Captain Manning, who happened upon us only by blessed chance. Of course, we would have had no way of knowing that Riverside had been targeted at the same time and that everyone there had met the same fate!"

He paused for a time, trying to find his voice. Then, more softly. "We tried to salvage our assignment. But too many Federal troops were already on the move. Now that I've read General Cox's book, I understand that it was an unanticipated order that caught us, one we had not received. We didn't have a chance in the world to get past those Federal troops. Not wearing Confederate uniforms." He was very quiet.

"Moses had been my mentor," he finally said, "my teacher, the rock under my feet after my mother and Will and the babies died, and my father started acting like he'd lost his mind. Why was my friend Moses slaughtered like an animal? I can't get that picture out of my mind, the way he was strung up. And now I know the same fate befell my father on the same night!"

He paused, his words fading into nothingness. Lorie waited.

"As far as we knew," he finally said softly, "we were still under orders to find out what we could about Confederate activity northeast of Atlanta. But as we approached the river, we saw that some of our troops were moving up faster than we had expected. If we'd known they were under orders, we would have surrendered, told them who we were, and got updated orders ourselves. Instead, we hid, trying to assess the situation.

"But our true death sentence was those Confederate uniforms! It might have been July, but as the day got darker and the rain came down, we got more and more wet and miserable. We kept them on for warmth!

"Ben was the smartest man I knew and my best friend. He had a loving wife and eight children waiting for him at home. But both of us still thought we could reach Atlanta and finish our mission." Now he began to sob. She held him in her arms for a long time. She didn't need to hear anything more.

He slept hard for a time as she held him. When he awoke, his arms went around her, and he found her lips. "*Carpe diem*," he whispered. "I won't worry about whose body I'm inhabiting right now. No matter what happens in the future, I am going to love you right now, right here, my dear one, with this body and this mind. And we will live each of our days to the fullest while we have them."

Lorie thought she wanted to cry, too, but not right now, because his lips were working their way across from her ear and her cheek to her own lips, she had some idea by now of where they would go from there, and she really didn't want to interrupt the real progress they were making toward seizing the day.

CHAPTER 16

Thursday, July 24, 2014

Lorie stretched when she woke at daybreak. She snuggled closer to Jeff's muscular body, relaxed now in sleep. It was a treat to see it, to feel it with her fingertips, to become one with it in the dance of love. He was an athlete the likes of which she had never known. She thought how many people of his era must have been equally fit. They didn't have all the labor-saving devices she and her family had. They had to walk if they didn't have animals to ride or pull carts. They had to care for those animals, carry heavy loads, build their own homes, and raise their own food. A jarring revelation entered her thought-pattern: some people just didn't like doing those things for themselves. Get a slave to do it!

He opened his beautiful eyes. "Give me a kiss, wife." She giggled and complied. And once more, the slow erotic dance commenced.

"I love you so much."

"Enough to give me a fat little baby?" His voice was wistful.

"I wish," she answered softly. "But how could we, not knowing...?"

His voice was tinged with sadness. "I know. It would not be fair to you, when…"

"Maybe we shouldn't think about it," she said softly. "The future may not be to our liking."

"There's that odor again." He sat up, sniffing at the air. "Bacon. That and coffee are the only things that take precedence over my lovely Lorie."

"Not likely!" She grabbed his arms, wrestled him back down to the bed, and lowered herself slowly onto his hard, beautiful body. "Carpe diem, mister."

Both the bacon and the coffee were cold when they finally came down to the kitchen.

Carol, well dressed as usual in slacks and a lacy white overshirt, discovered them in the kitchen, making toast and talking. "Our meeting is at 9:30 a.m. in Randolph City," Carol said. "That's an hour's drive. You kids have about fifteen minutes to be ready. Get a move on."

"Yes, ma'am, General Carol." Jeff rose sharply from his chair, clicked the heels of his shiny black shoes, and gave her a quick salute. She laughed. He was wearing his suit trousers and a white shirt with a blue tie. "Correct uniform of the day?"

"You look spectacular, Rich. Who did your tie? Ah yes, our Lorie. She always had to do Marsh's ties when he was a kid. Maybe she'll remind you how to tie them. Don't forget the dark glasses. And bring your jacket."

Lorie was wearing white slacks again and a summer blouse that had caught Jeff's eye, swirled with blended colors. Her jewelry and makeup were understated. He told her she looked astonishing. She told him he looked smashing.

Before they left Phil Barnett's house, every one of them, including the doctor—who had managed to move enough appointments to be with them—put a bag of work clothes, sturdy shoes or moccasins, and black jackets and hats into the trunk of the car.

They entered the courtroom just as the nine thirty chime sounded. As before, the judge was sitting at the big polished table rather than the podium. "Good morning," he said, looking up at them. He smiled briefly.

Rolf Maratti and his lawyer, Arthur Ehrlich, were already seated at the table. Maratti had a stack of papers in front of him, which he was leafing through. Arthur Ehrlich smiled warmly at Carol and Lorie. When he saw Jeff, however, he frowned. "Who is this?"

"My fiancé. Rich Jefferson. He's from Atlanta."

"Good mornin', sir." Jeff reached for Ehrlich's hand. "Sorry about the glasses, but I have an eye condition that makes it necessary." Ehrlich pulled back. "Oh, it's not catchin'," Jeff said. "It's just mighty annoyin'. Too much light is painful to me." Ehrlich shook hands briefly.

Rolf Maratti was watching Jeff's every move. "Your name is Richard Jefferson?"

Jeff nodded. "Very nice to meet you, sir." He reached his hand toward Maratti, who took it quickly and as quickly released it.

"You're with her?" Maratti asked.

"She's goin' to be my wife very soon." Jeff put his arm around Lorie's shoulders and smiled at her. "Honey," he said in one of the broadest drawls she had ever heard, "let's go sit in that row of chairs and get out of their way, shall we?"

"Of course, darling."

Lorie watched with intense interest as Sue and Sid Bailey, clad in their best and appearing very businesslike, walked into the room about two minutes late. Judge Cragin frowned at them. Pointedly ignoring the frown, Sue seated herself directly across the table from the judge, which situated her next to Arthur Ehrlich. Her husband sat down at her other side. She pulled out her copy of Jon Randolph's most recent will and slapped it down on the table in front of her.

"Is your lawyer present?" Judge Cragin looked up at her.

Sue looked around, frowning darkly. "Do you see him, Sandy? I don't see him. And I'm damned if I ever want to see him again!"

"And why is that?" Cragin said sharply.

We've had some words," Sue snapped, "and we've discharged Mr. Purdy. We're going to do this without a lawyer, certainly not that unreliable son of a bitch!" She looked directly at Cragin, scowling.

The judge should have reacted with much more surprise, Lorie thought, to the profanity that had issued from Sue Bailey's mouth, but she saw no reaction at all. He seemed instead to be examining the faces of the people assembled at the table: the Baileys, with their obvious anger. Maratti and his lawyer, both sitting with carefully frozen expressions. His eyes shuttered. His jaw tightened. "I've read over both of these wills. One of them"—he nodded at Maratti—"is quite specific. It gives all of Jon Randolph's properties, except one or two small bequests, to his two sons: Thomas S. Randolph and the legally adopted Rolf Maratti. If one or the other of these sons is deceased and without heirs, all of his property goes to the living son. It's pretty clear that means all of his property goes to you, Mr. Maratti. Is that your understanding?"

Maratti turned to Ehrlich. "Art, is this our understanding?"

"It is, Judge Cragin."

"The will is signed and witnessed by two people whose names are written in blue ink, thereby proving this is not a photocopy. This is a legal and valid will."

"Are those people still living?" Sue asked. "The witnesses?"

"It doesn't matter," the judge said, not looking at her. "They signed, and that's all that's required."

He then turned to face Sue directly. "I've looked at the copy of the will you presented to me, Mrs. Bailey. It's more current than Mr. Maratti's will, that's true, but it's not the original."

"Dammit, you know we haven't even had a chance to search for the original, Sandy. We have one of the witnesses who signed the original willing to testify that this is the same document he looked at when Jon Randolph signed it. And we're looking for the second witness. Give us a break!"

"The witness doesn't have to know what's in the will." Judge Cragin said with a visible display of impatience. "All he has to do is testify that the will was signed by the testator. Georgia law is very specific on that point. This photocopy may have borne Jon Randolph's true signature, but no witnesses have signed it, and by law, that's required. I'm going to have to rule your will invalid."

Sue sat for a moment, genuinely puzzled. "Rule? We thought we were just discussing things here. Informally. You're making a ruling? At least give us a chance to find the original will."

"If you haven't found it by now, you won't find it. There's no point in putting off the inevitable. A written order will be drafted this afternoon."

Sue rose to her feet. "We'll sue!"

"It won't do you any good. The laws are quite clear."

Without another word, Sue picked up her papers and swept out of the room, followed by her obviously outraged husband. Maratti and Ehrlich watched them leave and then looked at each other. Lorie noted raised eyebrows.

"You're free to move ahead," Judge Cragin told Rolf Maratti. "It shouldn't take long once an executor is appointed."

"Thank you, Judge Cragin," Arthur Ehrlich said. He signaled Maratti, and they, too, picked up their papers and left the room, followed in short order by the judge, who retreated to his quarters without a glance behind him.

"Well," Carol said, "that was short and sweet."

"Very interesting," Lorie said.

"Maratti gets it all," Phil said with quiet fury.

"Almost," Jeff said just as quietly, "as if it were planned well in advance."

Carol got on the phone with Ewen Taylor, saying, "Plan B is now activated."

Lorie couldn't believe Sue had actually used profanity. She knew Sue's anger was part of the game plan—to give their lawyer, Will Purdy, a way out—but even mild profanity, coming from her, had been a little risky. If Cragin had known her well, or had been a truly discerning judge, he would have realized Mrs. Sue Bailey was playing a game. His focus, however, had been somewhere else.

On the other hand, Lorie's focus had zeroed in on the judge's handling of what had been billed as an "informal discussion." Would the judge be even-handed in his treatment of the two parties, as any judge worth his salt would be? He could have suggested there was still time to search for the original copy of Jon Randolph's latest will. He could have facilitated the search by allowing Randolph House to be opened. Why didn't he? The answer was obvious.

He knew the original will would never be found.

"He's working with them," she said to Jeff. "And he's trying to move everything along as fast as he can. Something very powerful is forcing his hand. I hope we can discover what it is."

*****

They discussed the encounter at length when they met at the Baileys' house fifteen minutes later. Lorie was seated across from her aunt and next to Jeff at the long kitchen table. She reached for a cookie to go with her coffee.

"I just checked with my lawyer back home," Carol said. "He tells me Judge Cragin was way out of line. He couldn't make a legal ruling on something that hadn't yet gone through the court system. But he could easily have signed an order letting the Baileys into Randolph House to search for the will since there was proof it existed. It was well within his discretion."

Sue was genuinely angry. "They're in a big hurry, aren't they?"

Lorie said softly, "Because something happened they didn't anticipate."

"Also," her aunt went on, "he felt the judge had no business reading the provisions of Maratti's will to everyone in the courtroom, even if all of us knew what it said. Theoretically, that's private until all the principals have been notified. I suspect he simply wanted us to know that Maratti is the new owner in town, the only principal who counts, and there's nothing we can do about it."

"So," Sid Bailey said, "does that prove to us without a doubt that Judge Cragin is in on the conspiracy?"

Carol grimaced. "Unless he's stupider than he looks."

"He may be under some pressure," Phil suggested, "as Will Purdy was."

Sue looked around at her husband. "How'd I do on the 'hate Will Purdy' score?"

"Great!" her husband said with a quick grin. "I could have given you some more colorful words to use, though."

She winced.

"The most important thing," Carol put in, "is that no one is going to come to you to find out where Will Purdy is."

Carol's phone rang. "Mac, what's up?" There was a pause. "Up by the road? Good God, that's at least a mile and a half from the South Wind. Maybe two." Again Carol was silent. Finally, she said, "That poor fellow. Old bones but no body. Well, that's good."

Jeff's quick glance at Lorie was one of alarm.

The phone conversation continued with perfunctory answers on Carol's end and concluded with her saying, "We lost without ever taking it to court. So plan B is going into effect immediately." A pause. "Sure, we can use all the help we can get. I'll call you later with the specifics."

"What did he say?" Under the table, Lorie gripped Jeff's hand.

"They found the matching hospital slipper." Carol shook her head. "It was at the edge of the northbound side of the highway, down by the bridge over the Chattahoochee. That's a couple of miles south of the South Wind hotel. There's clear evidence, Mac says, that someone either jumped or was thrown out of a vehicle there. He thinks, in view of the frayed ends on those pieces of rope, that it was an escape attempt. Anyway, bloody tracks lead down into the ravine and north toward the South Wind. They've looked up and down the ravine from there all the way to the South Wind, and Randy even arranged for search dogs. They've found no bloody body, alive or dead, only some old bones they're thinking date back to Civil War times. They're going to check whether the blood type is the same as the blood trail Jeff left behind at the hotel." She looked hard at him. "They're looking at you, Jeff. Do you remember anything at all that might lead you to believe that escapee was you?"

Jeff's face had blanched. "I don't remember any of it. And I was in a Rebel uniform when I came up out of the ravine."

"You could have been recaptured and dressed in an appropriate costume," Phil said quietly. "Randy has been suggesting that all along. I didn't quite buy into the line that they're trying to intimidate Carol, but Randy knows how much a part of the Preston-Randolph story the Mannings are. And our bad guys just might know it, too. Carol, between this and those people who were following you, I do think you have to take Randy's suspicions more seriously."

"I don't know what anyone would want with me," Carol said, frowning. "I'm just the interfering Northerner. I know nothing!" And to Jeff, she said, "Don't worry, hon. The incident they're looking at could be completely unrelated. The DNA in both cases is being sent to a lab. We'll have to wait until those tests are run, and often that takes a great deal of time." She turned back to Phil. "What bothers me is the name on that sweatshirt: Maratti."

"It indicates to me," Phil said, "that Rolf Maratti might be vulnerable. Does he have children?"

"I really don't know," Carol said.

"When we met him at the hotel, he said he had a number of heirs," Sue reminded them. "And as far as I'm concerned, that means children. I haven't been keeping track since he's not a blood relative."

"Perhaps we should have the detectives run a background check on him," Carol said.

Lorie said softly, "I suspect they already have."

"Wouldn't it be ironic," Phil said, "if our Jeff Preston is related to Maratti."

"Then why...?" she began. She stopped. Jeff's hand had tightened on hers. She had told no one she'd seen the painting in the hidden room. Its provenance might complicate an already complicated situation.

"Why what, honey?" Carol asked.

"Uh, Mr. Taylor said he'd seen a picture at Randolph House that looked a lot like Jeff."

"That's true," Carol said. "But he also said he hadn't seen it for some time. Memory gets distorted over the years."

Phil cut the speculation off. "Let's just wait until we get the results of the DNA tests. Right now, it's better to focus on what we're planning to do next."

Jeff's hand dropped away gently, and he sat at the table for a time in silence. Lorie began to feel uneasy. "How soon can we get our equipment into the house?" he said suddenly, to her vast relief. He'd been calculating and planning. "Lorie, can you find me a pad of paper, please? And a pen and some ink? We need to keep them off guard, to act immediately, before they can mount a defense." Lorie turned to Sue, eyebrows raised. They hurried to find what he needed, including a ballpoint pen.

"The next scheduled appointment for Clark's Lawn Service is this afternoon," Sue told him when she saw he was devising a time schedule. She frowned. "That's cutting it awfully close. Is Mr. Taylor ready?"

Carol called to find out. When she hung up, she was smiling. "They are ready and eager."

Sue put in a call to the lawn service. "Ginny, can we use one of your extra trucks today to bring the equipment I was telling you about into Randolph House?" Her face brightened. "Thanks, Ginny. Warn that talkative crew of yours to keep mum about this. I know they're all relatives of yours, so we can trust them. What time are they scheduled to go in?" She turned around and said to Jeff, "Two this afternoon. Just to be sure, they called the judge for permission. They usually have four trucks to do the service. This time five. The guards won't know the difference."

He started writing. Checking the clock, he said, "It will be tight. It's quarter to eleven right now. That means we have to coordinate with Mr. Taylor to get the equipment here at least within the next two hours. Is that at all possible?"

Carol called Taylor again and immediately reported back: "Ewen has found a small airfield about fifteen miles from here, at one of the private resorts. He gave me the coordinates so we can go pick them up. He already has permission to land, and his ETA is about twelve thirty." Jeff made more notes. "The equipment was assembled at his cabin," Carol went on, "so no one but select people know about it. He's bringing everything, including his crew, in the helicopter. We'll meet him there. Let's get going, girls and boys. Time to change into your work clothes."

Lorie brought the bags of clothing in from the car. She glanced at Jeff. He was still writing, thinking, writing again. He looked up at her, too serious by half. She understood the feeling. A resolution was close. What might that mean for the two of them? He smiled sadly. She saw resignation in his beautiful eyes and knew that whatever happened, it was not their choice to make. So much more was at stake than their own personal desires.

There was work to be done and in a hurry. She retrieved the laptop from Phil's car and pulled up the satellite map. With Carol calling off coordinates, it was easy to locate the airfield. The satellite view showed it to be on a flat piece of land next to a lake. A long runway lay between the lake and the slope of a mountain range. Easy for a fixed-wing plane more than enough for a large helicopter.

Carol was still running the operation. "Sid, can you take your minivan out to pick up Ewen's people? Did you check with him about what kind of equipment he's bringing? Is there enough room in the back end?"

"Yes, yes, and yes. If we take the back seats out, it should work," Sid replied. "Phil can help me."

"I'll take the Town Car to carry people," Phil said. "Ewen tells me he has room for three besides himself."

"That leaves the rest of us in the classic clunker," Sue said. The antique car. "There's an old empty service station at Walker's Crossroads, about ten miles from here. You know where that is, don't you?" When Sue looked up at her husband, he nodded. "That's going to serve as our staging area. Ginny's trucks will meet us there. She has a key to the old garage. It's where she sometimes stores equipment. Call to alert us when you've transferred everything from Ewen's helicopter into your cars, and we'll probably all reach the crossroads about the same time."

Phil frowned. "Are we all planning on going into the house?" he asked Carol, who was lacing up her hiking boots. "Honey, that's dangerous!"

"You're a fine one to talk, Doctor," Carol said to him with a wry smile. "Right there on the front lines yourself, big guy!"

Lorie didn't know when she'd been so proud, not only of her courageous aunt, but all the rest of Jon Randolph Third's loyal friends.

CHAPTER 17

A t one forty-five, they were at Walker Crossroads Garage and Canteen, a tightly built, now defunct relic of an older way of life. It sat resolutely on an isolated piece of mountain property left behind when the big interstate highways were cut across less problematic lands far away to the west. Jeff Preston, dressed in black, his feet clad once again in soft moccasins, stood ready to take over the operation. Lorie was wearing similar clothing, including the moccasins he'd given her the first time they'd gone into the house. Carol had chosen jeans and a dark shirt. Sue had seen no reason to change clothes. She would be their outside contact. Despite a forecast of rain, fair weather was holding, cooler than usual, with only scattered clouds above the mountains. Lorie wondered what they would have done if the day had begun with rain. Lawn service would have had to wait. It seemed providence was in charge and, in this case, at least, on their side.

The Baileys' minivan arrived first, closely followed by Phil's Town Car. The largest pieces of equipment had been tucked into the back of the minivan in rectangular boxes about the size of large tabletops. They were handled exclusively by white-haired Ewen Taylor, clad in a black jumpsuit. He greeted everyone and introduced three intense young men, Ivan, Bill, and Jared, who were similarly dressed.

"This is good stuff," Taylor said. "I'm curious how it will work in practice. We're breaking new ground here." He looked around. "Where's our transportation?"

"Should be here any minute," Sue said. "Ginny called and said they're on their way."

"Terrific," Taylor said.

The first of the service trucks, "Clark's Lawn Service" blazed across its side in bright red paint, arrived a moment later, driven by a short tough-minded redheaded whirlwind of indeterminate age who was introduced as Ginny Clark. Wearing the same blazing logo across the front of her shirt, she was introduced all around. "Glad to be able to help," she said. "Such an injustice going on in this town."

Jeff took one look at her and said, "There was an Ebenezer Clark in your family tree, wasn't there?"

"Why, my word, however did you know that?" Lorie saw the surprise on her face. "He was my great-great-great-grandpa. We don't like to talk about it much, but he rode with the original Jefferson Preston back in the day. That's why we're so hot on helping Jon Randolph, him being Major Preston's kin, you know."

"Old Eb helped on the Underground Railroad, didn't he? A conductor for many years."

"How did you know that, young man?"

"I've got a book," he said, "that belonged to Major Preston. It's coded. But I'm beginning to make it out. I just wanted to confirm."

She gave him a big surprised grin. "Good night, that's amazin'!"

Jeff went on in a soft voice. "Did you know that his red-headed children kept a hard eye out for Confederate recruiters during the early days of the war? Warned everyone by running through town waving their caps when they saw uniforms coming up the road toward town, so the able-bodied men could take off into the woods, hunting or the like."

"Well, golly me, I did know that! But it's not something we talk about openly. We don't know what our neighbors might think. It was all hush-hush stuff back then, and sometimes we don't think that much has changed in all those years since."

"Maybe that's why the book is written in code. But I can tell you right now that there are plenty of notes about him that show, what a good loyal Union man he was."

A smile lit up her face. "I'd like to see that book sometime. I can tell you, we're proud of old Ebenezer ourselves, even if we don't talk about him in front of people who aren't family."

"Thank you," he said softly, "for your help today. He would be very proud of you."

More cars could be heard coming along the road, and then four more white Clark's trucks pulled in to park at the old service station. The black Crown Vic was already there. Mac parked the unmarked police car, and he and Randy emerged, both dressed in dark clothing.

"We're ready to go any time you are," Randy said, grinning at Jeff. He held up a box. "Major Preston rides again. Here's the uniform, cleaned and pressed. Couldn't get all the holes out of it," he said cheerfully, "but I guessed you wouldn't mind. And here's those boots. Hope they still fit. And look, I got you a gen-u-ine Cavalry hat with a feather in it. How about that?"

Mac dug around in the back of the car and pulled out something else. "The saber." He handed it to Jeff. It was still sheathed, and the belt dangled beneath. "Be careful with it."

"Thanks, Randy, Mac." Jeff grinned broadly. "I knew I could count on both of you."

"Ravenwing will be here about sundown," Taylor said to Jeff. "My trainer will park the van where you told us, out by the entrance to the nature trail."

"Excellent," Jeff said. He looked around him and smiled. "The company is assembled. Gather 'round, troops, and let's coordinate plans. I understand the guards are expecting the lawn service trucks at 2:00 p.m., and it's almost that now. Ginny?" Her head popped up. "Do you have Clark's shirts for these extra fellers and gals?"

"A whole stack," she said. She reached into the back of her vehicle and pulled out fresh clothing. "Help yourselves. I've got some pants, too, if anyone needs 'em. And here's Clark's caps. Those of you without red hair, take one. The Clark cousins already have 'em." The red-billed caps went quickly. Lorie snatched up a shirt, pulled it over her own, and made sure her cap fit tightly.

Jeff spoke again. "On the off chance one of the guards actually knows the difference between electronic equipment and lawn equipment, we're going to distribute these wrapped-up boxes around all the trucks. So when we get to the house, if you have an extra box that doesn't seem to correspond with what task you have selected, please leave it at the summer kitchen. Ginny tells me she has the key to the lock on that door. She'll be there to monitor and make sure everything gets unloaded." He handed her the sheet of paper Ewen Taylor had given him, listing every piece of equipment. Ginny nodded at her kin, and a general redistribution of boxes was quickly made by the eight young people she had brought with her, assorted redheaded nieces and nephews.

"One more thing," Ginny said. "If this excitement's gettin' to any of you and anyone needs a john, there's facilities available in the summer kitchen. Mr. Randolph don't like folks to piss on his lawn, no matter the emergency."

Tension broke for the moment, and amid general laughter, everyone found a place in one of the trucks. Lorie squeezed herself between a bag of fertilizer and one of Ginny's younger less-talkative nieces in the back of the lead truck, just behind Ginny. She was too nervous to make any kind of small talk.

Jeff had been invited to ride in the van with the technicians.

Leaving the passenger cars parked at the service station, the convoy of white trucks found its way back to the highway. When the truck she was in came to a brief halt, Lorie knew they had reached the driveway at the estate. Ginny called out, "Sam, get the gate, will you?" Sam did his duty, and then they were on their way again, up the winding road to the house.

Again they stopped. Lorie heard Ginny arguing with someone. "Don't you tell me I can't bring my trucks in! We got a long-term contract here, bought and paid for by Mr. Jon, bless his soul. Open this damned fence and get outta my way!"

"I'm making a call," a man said in a loud truculent voice, and a moment later, sounding even more grudging, he admitted he had to concede. "Okay, Herm, it's all right to let 'em in. It's just the weekly lawn service."

As the truck finally rolled ahead, Lorie could hear from the front a choice collection of growled epithets concerning someone's ancestors. And then the truck turned into the parking lot and stopped.

Lorie crawled out and readjusted the cap, tucking her hair inside. She looked around. She hadn't remembered a second gate. But there it was...a substantial gate taller than a man, put into place across the road just outside the parking lot. It opened out of a wire mesh fence already installed, beginning in the forest on one side of the road and ending in similar woodlands on the other. It would take some time to enclose the entire property, she thought, but construction equipment now on-site showed the seriousness of the effort to keep Randolph House inaccessible.

Seemingly unperturbed, the young Clarks were pulling out machines and organizing their chores. One of them, a tall gangly boy with a thatch of unruly red hair, backed a lawn tractor out of one of the trucks by means of a portable ramp, then hooked it to a matching trailer already filled with brown boxes. With supreme indifference, he drove directly across the broad lawn to the summer kitchen far beyond. He waited until Ginny got there to unlock the door to the building, whereupon he proceeded to unload his precious cargo. Five burly guards, firearms attached to their belts, were spaced around the yard, watching carefully. Since no one challenged the redheaded boy, he came casually back to the truck convoy and repeated the process. In fifteen minutes everything Ewen Taylor and his crew had transported to the mountain airport by helicopter was stored away.

"Well done, Micah!" Taylor said quietly to the young man upon his return. "Anytime you need a job, just give me a call." The boy grinned mischievously.

Bored by the unloading process and tired of watching grass being cut and gardens weeded, the guards finally drifted back to the house. Lorie wondered which one of them was Moultrie. If he spoke, she would probably know.

Jeff motioned to her, and at his request, she took him across the grounds to the garden in which once stood a stone monument commemorating his life. Taylor followed them into the garden a few minutes later. "We'll replace this stone, by golly," he said, outraged at the destruction done by unknown hands. He had seen the monument, he told them and knew its history.

"This is where I'll bring Ravenwing afterward," Jeff said.

"We'll be waiting," Taylor told him.

At random intervals over the next half hour, Lorie watched as certain irregular members of the Clark crew, rakes and cutting tools in hand, disappeared into the summer kitchen. She was the last. Ewen Taylor, Sid Bailey, Phil Barnett, Officer Randy Ross, and Detective Alan "Mac" Macdonald were clustered around Jeff as he revealed the opening to the tunnel. "By God," Taylor said, "we never would have found it. How did you?"

"I have this book," Jeff said, by way of explanation.

"I heard about that," Taylor said. "You really know a lot about the Randolph family, Jeff. I hope we can sort out the relationship fairly soon."

Flashlights were brought out, loads were assigned, and the men descended carefully, one by one, into the dark tunnel. Jeff led the way, followed by Ewen Taylor, Phil, Sid, and the two policemen. The three technicians struggled for a time with the larger packages, which needed to be lowered by a sling to the bottom of the ladder. But everything finally fit through the opening, and all the boxes were passed carefully down to the bottom rung. It was because of Jeff's careful advance planning, Lorie realized. He had left nothing to chance, not even the dimensions of the equipment.

It was time for the ladies. Lorie followed her intrepid aunt Carol, leaving Ginny the task of shutting the secret doors. "You've got two hours," the tough little lady whispered as daylight faded away behind them. "Good luck!"

Jeff met them at the bottom of the stairs. "Everyone's down okay," he said softly. "They're all waiting in the tunnel. Lorie, you and Carol are responsible for seeing that all the doorways are properly shut behind us, and all the lights are off. I'll see you upstairs." He took her into his arms and kissed her. A kiss of love and longing, and perhaps farewell.

His hand brushed hers lightly as he left to move to the head of the column, a lump began to form in her throat. She took a deep, steadying breath.

"Should I have come?" she heard Carol say softly. "I might just be in the way."

"He wouldn't have let you come if he hadn't needed you," Lorie whispered. She understood exactly what Carol was experiencing. "Don't worry, he'll let you know what to do and when."

The tunnel seemed longer this time. There was the inevitable scraping sound of shoes moving across stone. Lorie could see spots of light on the floor ahead, jerking along, disappearing, but the passage was passably quiet. A breeze hit her, momentarily dispelling the odor of decayed vegetation and pools of stagnant water. She knew the large swinging door at the other end had just been opened. A light came on in the distance. Carol turned around to Lorie, who put a finger to her lips and, in the dim illumination of a small flashlight, mouthed the words "We're almost there." Carol nodded.

By the time Lorie and her aunt stepped through the turned panel into the root cellar, most of the crew had already passed through the mechanical room and were carefully making their way up sturdy wooden stairs with their bundles. Jeff had asked everyone to reassemble in the drawing room.

They would have to be very careful now. Lorie pulled the tunnel doorway shut and heard the latch click. She directed Carol through the mechanical room, followed her up the stairs into the large pantry with its many cupboards and closets, turned off the basement light, and closed that door behind them. The men had vanished silently into the house. Lorie pushed open the door to the hallway and beckoned to her aunt. With the help of flashlights, they made their way through the darkness and quietly entered the drawing room.

Enough daylight was seeping through and around the big drapes that the picture over the fireplace was illuminated in a beam of sunlight. "Maratti's mother," Carol whispered, pointing, and Lorie nodded and put a finger to her lips. Lorie looked up at the portrait. Maria Maratti Randolph, bedecked in diamonds, almost seemed to be smiling down at them.

The men had quietly placed their loads on the floor. Jeff twisted the gaslight fixture beside the glass-fronted cabinet. The wall opened silently. He entered the hidden storage room, pulled the chain on the florescent light, and motioned for everyone to enter.

Once the door was closed, soft conversation could begin.

"I've been here before," Taylor said excitedly. "This is where I saw the picture of the Confederate soldier who was a Union spy. Is it still here?"

"No time now," Jeff said in a hushed voice. "Everyone, please gather 'round." From a large umbrella stand in one corner, he pulled an ancient scroll of paper, knelt down, and spread it across the floor. He motioned to Lorie and Carol to help hold it flat. It was an architect's drawing of the main floor of Randolph House.

"Here we are." He pointed. "The drawing room is here. Two double windows at the front." He then deferred to Ewen Taylor, who examined the drawing carefully.

"The old woman," Taylor said, "can go here in the first window with the laser lights here and here." He moved his finger across the drawing to a smaller room close by the front door. "This is where the child can be placed." He then pointed to a room at the farthest side of the front portico. "The music room. Our dancers can be here. Looks like there's plenty of room for multiple lights."

"Are there electrical outlets in all these rooms?" Randy asked quietly.

"No need," Taylor replied. "Everything we have has its own power source. We wouldn't want anyone pulling the plug in the middle of a performance."

Randy, also kneeling, smiled up at him. "Brilliant!"

Taylor turned to Lorie and Carol. "I'd like you to rig up the draperies in each of these three rooms so they open when the music starts. Can you do that?"

Lorie nodded and squeezed her aunt's arm, whispering, "See?" Aloud she said, "Show us what to do."

He opened one of the smaller boxes he had carried in with him and pulled out a pale silken cord. "Drapery tie-backs. One end must be securely fixed to this anchor"—he held up a complex piece of aluminum with holes drilled into it—"which you will then attach to the window frame with this." He held up a small power screwdriver. "Then the cord must be wrapped loosely around the drapes, going through this little O-ring, which you will affix to the edge of the fabric halfway up at the center, and finally it must be pushed through the opening in this second device, which will catch it securely back at home base." The second device was a small motorized pulley meant to grab the cord and reel it in, thereby bringing the curtains smoothly open like stage curtains. The pulley device slid easily into the back end of the anchor. "It's run by remote control," he explained. "If I attach the first one for you, I think you'll be able to do the rest by yourselves."

Carol grinned at him and then at Lorie. "Piece of cake!"

The men were given their assignments. Randy and Mac were with Ivan in the drawing room, Phil and Sid were with Jared in the small entry room, and Jeff and Ewen Taylor were with Bill in the music room. Bill's group would work on the dancers, Taylor said, which was a more complex device involving a modest degree of motion.

Jeff checked his watch. "It's half past three. We have until five. Then everyone who's leaving with the trucks has to be out. Let's go."

Very quietly they spread out through the house, following their assigned duties. Carol and Lorie worked as quickly as they could. "If you feel like fainting," Lorie whispered as they knelt in the drawing room, wondering if the guard outside could hear the whirr of the drill as acutely as they could, "take a deep breath."

"I'm supposed to be telling you that," her aunt whispered back.

But there was no hue and cry from outside the window. Occasionally they heard men's voices outside and froze in position until the guards walked away.

At a quarter to five, everyone came together again in the secret room. "Any problems?" Jeff asked.

"Smooth as silk," Taylor said. "Everything is working fine. All you have to do is turn on the equipment at the proper time."

"Ginny will be waiting for us," Carol said. Lorie could tell she was getting a bit nervous. "We'd better go." She looked toward Phil Barnett, who nodded.

Jeff rebriefed his company of volunteers. "Randy, Mac, Lorie, and I are staying. Everyone else leaves now. Ewen, I'll meet you on the road as soon as it gets dark."

"Ravenwing will be saddled and ready," Taylor replied.

"Good. Nothing in the house will be activated until I charge the house, and all hell breaks loose. Afterward, I'll disappear into the memorial garden." He grinned.

Taylor added, "We'll keep Ravenwing quiet there until we can get him back to the horse van."

"If anyone except Maratti comes to the house, we'll disappear. By that time, all the equipment will be taken apart and hidden. No one will know we were here. Now move out, all the rest of you." Jeff looked around at apprehensive faces. "We'll be in touch by phone."

Her worried aunt gave Lorie a big hug. "We'll be fine," Lorie said softly. "Jeff knows what he's doing."

His arm went around her. He took the Clark's cap off her head, brushed her hair into its proper place and pressed a kiss atop her head. Then he was gone, helping his crew retreat to safety.

"What a guy," Randy remarked to Lorie sometime after the door had swung shut behind the last man out. "I bet the original Jeff Preston was exactly like that."

"I'd like to have met that one," Mac said with admiration, "but he couldn't beat this one. Did you see how he ran this operation? Precise timing. Not one thing off-key. The guards didn't tumble that we were here. And everything is in place and working. They need more officers like him in the US Army."

"And do those officers," said Jeff, returning through the wall panel wearing his Confederate uniform, "also serve lunch to hungry troops?" He was carrying a large box filled with sandwiches and the works. Enough for everyone, courtesy of Sue Bailey.

"See?" Mac said, laughing. "What did I tell you?"

CHAPTER 18

They all found places to sit while they picnicked. Jeff leaned against the wall near Lorie and drew his knees up. The high boot tops provided a prop for the paper plate, which bridged his knees. The sun would take its time going down, he told them. Courtesy of the computer, he had earlier confirmed sundown at just about eight forty-five.

The hands on Lorie's watch showed it to be exactly 5:00 p.m. She knew the Clark crew's trucks were even now passing through the new gate to begin the roundabout drive back to Randolph City. She hoped none of the guards had been smart enough to count the number of workers Ginny had brought in as compared to the number that had left. But then, some of those workers had been concealed in the trucks. And she thought, probably the guards weren't very bright to start with.

"When do the guards change out?" Randy asked.

"Good question," Mac said. "I'm sure the same five guys aren't here twenty-four/seven."

"Ginny Clark just happened to ask them," Jeff said with a mischievous grin. "They work twelve-hour shifts. Five new men come out at eight for night duty. Apparently it was hard to find locals who wanted to be here at night, so they upped the paycheck. Hopefully they'll all be on-site when we put on our performance."

"Ten people? Will it be dark enough by eight?" Randy asked.

Jeff said with a grin like a little boy with a frog in his pocket, "Oh, they won't be here until after it's dark."

Mac grinned back. "I won't even ask. Surprise me."

As they were eating, Randy asked the detective, "What have you turned up on the weapon used on Jeff? You should have seen him, Mac. He was bleeding like a stuck pig. I still don't understand why the guy's so healthy now." He grinned at Jeff. "Must be that beautiful nurse lady sitting beside you."

Jeff winked at him and nodded vigorously. Lorie grinned.

"We still don't know what he was shot with," Mac interjected. "The only thing close to matching those fragments of shot the doctor picked out of your side, Jeff, was old-fashioned minie balls. Thank God those aren't used any more. If it had been a real one, you'd have been dead!"

Lorie reached for Jeff's hand. It was warm. "What if," he said softly, directing his question to Mac while he slid his arm around her shoulders and pulled her closer, "a theoretical soldier jumped out of a car going at highway speed and rolled into a deep ravine?"

"You're talking about our investigation, I assume?" Mac said sharply.

"If I'm to ask Rolf Maratti certain questions about the shirt with his name on it, these are things I should know. Would that soldier have broken limbs?"

"Not necessarily." Mac was careful with his response. "It would depend on how he landed. If he were a trained paratrooper, and if he landed correctly on soft dirt and it slid under him, which seems likely in this case given the evidence, he could have escaped major injury."

"If, in this theoretical case," Jeff said with equal care, "he had a pretty good idea where he wanted to go, how far could he have gone barefoot in that ravine at night, say, the night of the eighteenth, with very little to cover his body?"

"It's pretty wet in some spots down there because of the terrific storms that came through last week and the flooding that came with it. But despite that," Mac said, just as carefully, "if he had been wearing heavy socks, it would have been easier on his feet, and he could have moved pretty fast… if he'd been trained to do that kind of thing. And in fact, I understand we found that type of item this morning, Randy. Two GI issue reinforced socks, at places far distant from each other. One was fairly close to where you came up the bank, Jeff."

"Now I'm not saying it was me," Jeff said softly, "because I don't remember doing any of these things. But if…"

"Go ahead," Mac said. Randy was listening intently.

"If he was very cold and he felt something under his hand, perhaps an old battlefield grave that had opened up during a washout because of a sudden rainstorm, and that grave held a Confederate uniform?"

"You mean the real Major Preston's uniform?" Mac sucked in his breath. "If you're asking if clothing would last that long, I'd say it would be very unlikely, unless it had been buried pretty deep. Cotton degrades quickly." He was quiet for a few moments, thinking. "Wool, on the other hand," he said slowly, tentatively, "and leather, animal products, might last for a while under the right conditions. In museums, I've seen clothing that was buried that long, or longer, reconstituted so it's almost as good as new. If the clothing is sewn with cotton thread, though, it would pull apart. And likewise the shoes."

"But if the wool clothing were sewed with woolen thread because the seamstress had a feeling against using Southern cotton picked by slaves, and the shoes were hand-sewn with thin strips of leather because of the same reasoning?"

"It's something to think about," Mac said softly. "We haven't examined the uniform and shoes with that in mind. Would you like us to?"

"I'm not saying that's what happened," Jeff said quickly.

"We haven't found a grave, exactly," Randy said very softly. "A few bones, old ones, so we didn't get very excited, although we kept them for the professors to date. We like to rebury soldier's bones, out of respect. I suppose it's possible. Could we have just found...?"

"I'm just theorizing," Jeff said. Lorie leaned her head against his shoulder and closed her eyes. A lump had come into her throat once again, and she was beginning to tear up, whether she wanted to or not. She knew exactly what he was thinking.

There was quiet in the room for a time. Then Jeff said, "If you fellows want to catch up on your sleep before the show begins, there are rooms upstairs with comfortable beds in them. And I know of an inside staircase so you can get there without being seen."

"Sounds tempting," Randy said. "I'm on leave, but old Mac here's been doing double duty because what he's doing here is on his own time."

"I wouldn't wanna be anyplace else right now," Mac agreed with a grin. "But even if we don't nap, I sure as hell want to see this inside staircase!"

Randy chuckled. "So do I. This is the most interesting house I've ever visited."

Grinning, Jeff pushed himself to his feet and offered Lorie a hand up. "Right behind me," he said, turned, and with a few motions of his hand, freed a previously unnoticed panel in the wall he'd been leaning against. It swung outward, revealing a narrow staircase going steeply up into the darkness.

"Good grief!" Lorie said.

"Who goes first?"

Mac put up his hand. He pulled out his flashlight and started to climb. "There's a big latch on the wall up there," Jeff said.

"I see it," Mac said softly. "Very cool." His voice faded into emptiness.

Randy was next, followed by Lorie, with Jeff just behind. For some time, they quietly explored the many rooms of the mansion's second floor. Many were bedrooms, beautifully furnished. Some were modern workrooms—for the use of staff, they supposed. And there were a couple of bathrooms that, everyone agreed laughingly, might prove useful.

"Don't flush," Jeff cautioned. "Someone close outside might notice."

"Good point," Randy concurred.

Each policeman picked a room with a single bed. Jeff left Lorie in a beautiful large bedroom at the front. The four-poster was elegantly canopied. She walked to the window and pushed the draperies open...just far enough to discover that what she had thought was a window was a door opening onto the filigree balcony just outside.

On Jeff's return, he informed her he had been handing out blankets and towels. He handed her a lightweight blanket. "Will you join me?" she said. She had already dropped her moccasins to the floor and was now stretched out on top of the lacy white coverlet, her head resting comfortably on a soft pillow. He spread the blanket across her.

"I can't allow myself to fall asleep, precious wife."

"Programmable cell phones with alarms are one of the finer luxuries of modern life." She held hers up, smiling.

He sat on the edge of the bed, thinking. Then wearily he pushed the boots off his legs and feet, dropped the belt and jacket onto a chair, and came under the blanket with her. He was wearing a black close-fitted long-sleeved knit shirt, but she knew every muscle of his chest and arms by heart. He held her tightly against him at first. As sleep took him, his arms relaxed, and he slumped away from her onto his back. She couldn't close her eyes. She needed to keep him in her vision as long as she was able. His straw-colored hair was tousled like a little boy's, his face handsome even in sleep, but the scar across his forehead was as ominous as a warning beacon. And strangely enough, in the light that was coming through the window, she thought she saw the remains of another scar on his face. Right across his cheekbone. She would have to ask him about that. When his deep breathing became very regular, she finally allowed herself to drift into an uneasy twilight doze.

She woke at once when the phone alarm started to vibrate. She moved to turn it off, and he came awake instantly. "What time is it?"

"Seven thirty. Do you feel rested, my darling?"

He turned to look at her. Even through the lowering shadows, she saw the smile in his blue eyes. "I do, wife." He came up on his arm, leaned over, and kissed her lips very tenderly. "There's work to be done," he said. He pushed himself up. A moment later, he bent down again and whispered, "You're so much softer, and prettier, than Randy's three-times-great-grandpa. He had whiskers. And you smell better, too."

She didn't mean to, but she laughed out loud.

He whacked her with a pillow. "Up, woman. I need help."

In shadowy darkness, she folded the blanket, tucked it away in the closet, and smoothed the bed. Together they woke Randy and Mac, who both yawned and stretched, then smoothed their own bed coverings and quietly stashed the blankets in closets so no evidence of anyone having been there was apparent to potential searchers.

"Just to make sure," Jeff told them, handing out cereal bars and bottled drinks, "as soon as you've finished eating, could the two of you run checks on the equipment and see that everything is still working?"

"Yo, boss," Randy answered. He unwrapped one of the bars and started to munch.

"Ewen Taylor is a genius," Mac said. "These holograms he put together are like something out of science fiction movies. But they're only three-quarters large as life."

"Ivan told me it's all in the perception," Jeff explained. "It will be dark outside. We're only opening the curtains a crack. At a distance, given the circumstances, everything will loom larger than life. Lorie," he turned to her, "come with me, please. We have to switch a picture and place some lights."

In the semidarkness of the upstairs hall, she watched with fascination as Jeff paused and simultaneously pressed the centers of two blossoms in the ornately carved chair rail. The door to a hidden staircase, concealed in plain sight in the wall itself, swung open. She saw Randy glance at Mac. Both grinned and shook their heads. "Awesome," Randy said under his voice as he pulled out a small flashlight. He sounded like a kid with a favorite toy. "They want to tear down this house? No way!"

Randy and Mac descended to the storage room, Jeff following to show the men how to maneuver through the house without his help. He opened the concealed doorway to the drawing room and, following a short tutorial by Jeff, Lorie saw the two men step carefully out, flashlights in hand.

Once the door had closed behind them, Lorie also descended. Jeff once more uncovered the oil painting of the Confederate Major. He held it up. "Not so bad," he said appraisingly. "It was good cover while everyone thought I was a hero."

"You were a hero," Lorie answered defensively and then modified her words, "*are* a hero. Just not a Confederate hero!"

He grinned. Turning off the lights, he once more opened the concealed door, and quietly he and Lorie came out into the drawing room. "One spotlight on Maria Maratti." Jeff handed Lorie a small sheathed light. It was also attached to its own electrical source, a heavy battery. She had been told by experts where it was to be placed to illuminate the picture over the fireplace, the portrait of a beautiful woman with sparkling diamonds at her neck.

She helped Jeff take down and store the picture of Jon Randolph Third and replaced it with the large portrait of a blue-eyed Confederate officer. "Second spotlight," he whispered, handing it to her. "Maria should be revealed the minute he comes into the room. You will know when to turn on the second light. Do you have the remote switches?"

"I do."

"I want all three of you to be witnesses to what happens here if visitors come from town. Beside the fireplace, there's a viewing panel. I'll show you where it is. Don't reveal yourselves by making any sound or by coming out, unless I ask you to or until everyone is gone. Do you promise?"

Lorie's tension increased. "What if someone has a gun, Jeff?"

"We will take this one step at a time, Lorena. You are going to have to trust me now. We will have help tonight far beyond what we can sense with our mortal bodies."

Her breath stopped short. She felt her body going cold and raked in a deep breath of fresh sweet air, wondering when she would faint. "Are they here? Who are they?"

"They are." He put his arms around her. "Don't be afraid of what you don't quite hear and see, my darling. The life forces in this house are all allies. Old battles will be fought out in the next few hours, loyalties will be tested, and if we on the front line can only stand bold, justice has a chance." He pulled from the pocket of his uniform a folded piece of paper and handed it to her. "If anything happens to me"—he put a finger to her lips to silence her immediate cry of distress—"you, Carol, her good doctor, and the Baileys must continue the fight. I have made some sketches and a list of some of the things that might have been taken. Riverside here, Fox Haven here. The only thing of great value that I would like you to reclaim if you find it, no matter what happens to me, is the African vase Moses made for Sara when she turned sixteen. It is very large, very heavy, and covered with paintings of African animals. He called it his 'ancestor' vase, and he took special pains with it."

"Would raiders have thought it valuable?" she asked. "Maybe it was destroyed."

"Moses's African artwork was purchased by many of the planters. He was an artistic genius and they knew it. He had studied with masters in France and in England. It's obvious these bushwhackers are aware of Moses's worth. They would not have let a piece of his artwork slip through their fingers when they burned Sara's house. It was far more valuable than his little African table. I want you to have it, Lorie. Now, what time is it?"

"It's 8:00 p.m.," she said. Nerves she didn't realize she possessed were beginning to vibrate throughout her body.

"I'm going out," he said. "You will see me in about an hour. Do not faint at what you see, Lorie. It is very important that you do not faint tonight."

She swallowed hard. "Jefferson Richard Preston, I swear to you that I will not faint." She held up her hand in true Girl Scout fashion, three fingers standing straight, and he smiled.

"Whatever that means, I'll take it as a positive sign." He pulled her close to him. She could smell every varied scent of him, his skin, his breath, his hair. She put her arms around his body, and he tilted her head back with soft fingers and lowered his lips to hers.

"Come back to me," she whispered. "Please come back to me."

"Here's something to keep in your mind while I am gone, Mrs. Lorena Manning Preston. I am determined to give you that fat little baby."

"I know." Tears welled in her eyes even through the unbidden laughter. She tried to brush them away, but still they came. "Be careful, husband."

"I love you more than life, Lorie. You be just as careful." He saluted her. And then he was gone.

Shortly thereafter, the door opened, and Randy and Mac reentered the drawing room, flashlights in hand. "Jeff said we should watch for our cues from the upstairs window," Randy said. "Let's go."

Back they went up the hidden staircase and through the big house to the elegant bedroom at the front. The window faced to the west, toward the setting sun. In forty-five minutes, the sun would slip behind the trees. True darkness wouldn't come earlier than nine, Lorie figured. Maybe a little later. They still had time to wait. Very carefully Lorie folded the edges of the draperies back, just enough for the inside watchers to view unobstructed the watchers outside.

They sat quietly for a time, watching guards pace back and forth in front of the house. "Boring job in sweltering heat," observed Randy. He waved his hand lightly. "I hope they're getting lots of money for letting us sit here in blissful air-conditioned comfort."

"I hope they're not," Mac said. "It'd be easier to quit."

"Good point!" Randy said.

"Are either of you guys married?" Lorie asked them, suddenly curious. They both turned toward her, surprised. She shrugged. "Here we are, locked in an epic battle between good and evil, where any one of us might get shot or otherwise harmed, and I don't know anything personal about you at all."

"Point taken," Randy said. "I'll go first. One brother, one sister. Both married and living in far places. I'm free as a bird right now with only my parents to care, or care for. I've had my share of girlfriends. But right now I'm pretty focused on this case." He paused briefly and then added with irony, "Women don't like that."

"Likewise," Mac said. "My wife of 20 years and mother of my two great kids jokes that she's ready to divorce me because I'm so obsessed by this case. And except for the divorce part, I think she's right. Those names you gave me, Lorie—Johnny McDaniels, lawyer; Ernest Merrill, developer; and Clint Samuels, developer—they're pretty shady characters. All three of them. They're known even within the local community of developers, which is rough at best, as totally corrupt. But very wealthy. So they have power."

"Of course," Lorie said. "Have you found out anything about the two policemen?"

"Both bogus," Mac said. "And someone in city hall must know it. As we supposed, something very bad is going down in Randolph City. We don't have jurisdiction there. So if anything needs to be done, we'll have to call in the state cops. Or federal agents, if it warrants that."

"When would we do that? And how?"

"We could alert them right away," Mac replied, "and have them ready to move if anything gets out of hand. Once we have something specific to tell them."

"Like what?"

"I really don't know."

"That's kind of vague, isn't it?" Lorie said.

"Well," Randy put in, "that's the problem with this case. It doesn't make a lot of sense. For instance, how do we explain 'haunting a house' to somebody? As far as I can see, we're the only people who've broken any laws. Trespassing, for instance. Except the murderers, of course. And we haven't even proved conclusively that anyone was murdered. Or who the murderers might be."

Lorie nodded. "I see what you mean."

"But there is the problem of the guy who went into the ravine," Mac added. "That's very real. And in our jurisdiction. Jeff's wounds were real, too. Perhaps tonight we'll discover if there's a connection. I don't believe in coincidences any more than Randy does."

They continued to chat and speculate softly as the sun went down in the western sky, leaving beautiful gold, red, and white streaks behind. As the sky got darker, however, Lorie began to see clouds rising just above the tree line. "Rain?" she asked. The clouds started to scud low across the sky from southwest to northeast.

"Is that what the weather forecast called for?" Randy said. "I hate to think we'll lose more evidence."

"We're in the mountains," Mac reminded him. "Marietta's a different weather system."

"Oh, sure," Randy said in a low voice. "I'm getting rattled."

Lorie glanced at her watch. "It's nine. Look how the guards are checking out the road. No replacements yet. They're an hour late."

The night was even darker when Lorie saw the lights of two cars driving up to the new gate. Angry voices were heard from below. Randy cracked the balcony door open so they could hear what was going on.

"We couldn't have got here any sooner," one of the arriving men said. He was illuminated by the car headlights at the open gate. The yard light in the parking lot finally came on. "The road was blocked."

"With what?" another voice said.

"Kids with dogs goin' coon huntin'," another voice said. "They was prob'ly a dozen boys an' about forty dogs, and they'd got a coon treed in a big ol' pine, and to git the coon they'd chopped the tree down, and it fell right acrost that there road. They wasn't a'gonna help us git the tree outa the road neither, 'cause them dogs started off again, bayin' like crazy, and the boys just rushed along after 'em, and they left us with the tree to chop up and clear the road. We only just now got finished haulin' the tree off."

"Well, that better not happen again," someone said. Lorie recognized the voice. Moultrie.

"Officious son of a bitch," she said under her voice, but Randy was chuckling softly beside her, while Mac was trying with a lot of effort to keep his laughter under control.

"I bet about half of them thar boys had red hair," he said in a smothered voice, and all of a sudden, Lorie started to giggle.

Suddenly the voices of the men below went silent.

"What was that?" one of them said.

Her giggles stopped abruptly.

"Showtime," Mac said softly.

"Sounds like a horse comin' up the road." Another voice. "What's a horse doin' out there in the dark?"

A wind commenced, swaying the tops of the trees, causing the branches to rub against each other with strange, gentle moans. Strange thing, Lorie thought, the way the weather was playing this game with them. Could Sara influence the weather? Well, they would see!

"I still hear it." The man outside sounded a little uncertain. "It's pickin' up speed."

"That's our cue," Randy said. "The party is about to begin."

Since it was obvious no one was now watching the house, Randy and Mac headed quickly toward the main staircase. A drum of hoofbeats could be heard, very softly at first, but without question approaching the house from the depths of the dark forest. Flashlights were brought out. A searchlight pointed toward the forest and then the road. Nothing. The searchlight went out suddenly. Then, one by one, all the flashlights failed.

Even the yard light failed. In utter darkness, there was now only the sound of hoofbeats, faster, nearer, and then the wind rose, wailing and sighing. A bolt of lightning flashed across the sky. The shadowy figures of the guards at the tall gate seemed to move closer together. Thunder rumbled. Somebody got back into one of the cars, and headlights came on...then blinked out.

"What the hell's wrong with the lights?"

Panic. Car doors opening. Slamming shut.

Swirling gray clouds continued to move in from the west, threatening to consume the sky.

Over the wind, the hoofbeats could again be heard. "What is it?" The tempo picked up. Then out of the dark came a high-pitched, wild, nerve-shattering scream. Lorie gripped the edge of the bed. She had never heard anything that sounded quite like that.

A moment later, a black horse glowing with eerie green light burst through an opening in the trees far below, racing toward the fence and the parking lot. The rider was unmistakably a Confederate officer, plumed hat firmly set atop his head, saber at ready. Ragged lightning illuminated the sky behind him as he mounted the hill. He reined in his black horse only for a moment when he saw the men waiting at the open gate. He thrust his saber aloft. Sparks flew off its edge. Once again, a wild high cry echoed through the night. The guards backed away and began a quick general retreat toward the house.

"Shut the gate!" someone screamed. It was swinging open very slowly. Two shadowy figures ran back to try. At that moment, a blinding flash split the sky, thunder cracked, and both halves of the gate exploded into the air. The men went down, picked themselves up, and then sat down again. Finally able to regain their footing, they bolted for the cars. One car regained its lights. Spinning dirt, it headed out of the parking lot.

"Hey, wait for me!" another man yelled, stumbling in his haste. The car paused, and the man disappeared. With the snap of a car door shutting, it sped away, giving a wide berth to the approaching horseman.

The other men scrambled toward the house. Stopped cold. "What's that?"

Now Lorie heard music reverberating through the old house below her, melancholy music, an old Civil War dirge. "Who is that?" A panicky voice. Men turning.

"That's a lady sitting there in the window."

And then words tumbled about.

"No one was inside there."

"She's there. Look."

"No, look there. It's a little kid."

"Oh my God!" Almost a scream.

Two more men stampeded toward the parking lot. A second car took off with a screech of spinning tires.

As the charging horse passed through the gate and approached the house, the rider rose in his saddle. Once more, the banshee scream. Horse and rider broke away toward the gardens to the south, toward the memorial.

"Oh shit!" someone yelled. "It's the Major. It's the Major. He'll see the monument's broken. Let's git outta here! He'll think we done it!"

"Ah din't break it!"

"He won't ask questions!"

The sound of hoofbeats faded. An instant of quiet before shocked words erupted again.

"Somebody's dancing in there."

"Somebody's in the house. Look there."

Through her half-opened drape, Lorie saw the glowing black horse sweep suddenly around to the front from the north side. It skidded to a halt in front of the portico, rearing, its high whinny cutting through the air. Front hooves dropped, and the Confederate officer could be seen once again, sitting straight in the saddle, glowing saber now lowered and pointed toward the remaining guards, who backed away slowly, step by uncertain step as the horse moved toward them. From somewhere in the house, soft, eerie music wavered through the night.

"We're leaving! We're leaving! Please! Don't hurt us!"

"We didn't bust your monument. It warn't us!" `

Again the horse reared. The rider raised his saber high. A shaft of lightning illuminated the sky. Crashing thunder echoed across the hills.

"We're going!" In sheer panic, all who had been left decamped at full cry toward the parking lot. Was that her Jeff now sitting watchful on the black horse below? That was not her Jeff. That soldier belonged to another time and place. Lorie felt a deep cold settling inside her bones.

Man and horse suddenly vanished from her view. She thought she heard muffled hoofbeats, quickly swallowed by the high wail of the wind. But she wasn't sure. All she knew was that he was no longer there. Several of the men looked around when they reached their cars. "Where is he?" someone said, looking back. Terror!

A man pointed toward the spot where Lorie stood, mesmerized. "Who are those people up on the balcony?"

Could they see her? She was in deep shadow. They were not looking at her!

"Let's get the hell outta here!"

A car motor started up, lights came on. Lorie saw that three people got into one car, two into the last. Both cars turned sharply and sped down the road faster than safety allowed, reflected headlights retreating through the trees.

People on the balcony? Right outside her window?

She backed up. Ran into the bed. Sat down suddenly. As she watched, paralyzed, a sudden gust of wind blew the balcony door open and the heavy draperies apart. A beautiful young woman, illuminated by an unknown source of light, stood just outside the door on the filigree balcony. She was dressed in a ball gown dating back to the mid-1800s. Her blond hair was bound up with fresh flowers. She turned to Lorie and smiled. Her eyes were blue as the skies. At her side was a tall black man in flowing African robes. He, too, had turned and was smiling at her, his teeth very white in his black face. The girl blew her a kiss, and Lorie felt a whisper of air against her cheek. The man raised his hand, as if in greeting. Or in blessing.

There was a scent in the bedroom that had not been there before, of roses and lilacs.

"I won't faint," Lorie said to herself. "I promised Jeff I wouldn't faint." She closed her eyes just for a moment, and when she opened them again, the apparitions were gone.

She flopped back onto the bed. "I'm not fainting," she said under her breath. "I promised not to faint." She picked herself up, straightened the bed, and shut the balcony door. Flashlight in hand, she scurried down the main staircase to find Mac and Randy in the music room. She was breathing very hard. All her nerves were tingling.

"It was great, wasn't it!" Randy said. By flashlight, he and Mac were quickly disassembling the equipment, getting it ready for packing.

She didn't answer him. Couldn't if she had wanted to.

"Phone," Randy said. He pulled it out of his pocket. "It's Ewen." He put it to his ear. "Great show!" he said with enthusiasm. "Horse and rider came through fine. How the hell did you do the green light thing? And the lightning sparks coming off the saber?" A pause. "You didn't?" When the conversation ended, Randy was quiet for a moment. Then he laughed. "Wow! Jeff's one step ahead of us every time we turn around."

Silent, Lorie sat down until the trembling subsided.

CHAPTER 19

B y the time Jeff returned, all the equipment had been
recrated, and the two policemen were busily moving all
the boxes into position under the summer kitchen trap
door for quick pickup when transportation became available.

"Is Ravenwing okay?" she asked him softly when he
came into the drawing room. She didn't quite want to touch
him. She had seen him enter a world where she could not
follow.

"Ravenwing is doing splendidly." He grinned at her as
he removed the saber, belt, and gray jacket and put them
down on one of the sofas. He tossed the hat up and caught it,
chuckling. "What a grand animal. Ewen says he's a registered
thoroughbred. Arabian. Was everyone impressed?"

She nodded, not able to articulate the proper words.

He frowned. "What's the matter, Lorie?"

She didn't want to say his ghostly aura had shaken her
to the core. "I saw your sister," she said very softly. "And
Moses, I think."

He put his arms around her and rested his cheek on her
hair. He seemed so real. Solid. Warm. Human in every way.
"Unnerving, I expect. Did you faint?" His voice sounded
slightly amused.

She looked up into his smiling face. Maybe this was still the man she knew. "I took the Girl Scout oath not to faint, and by golly, I did okay."

"Well, good for the Girl Scouts." He put an arm around her shoulders and led her back into the hidden room. "Let me show you their pictures, Lorie, and you can tell me if this is who you saw."

He rummaged about a bit and finally pulled out a large oil painting of the young woman she had seen on the balcony. She was wearing the same ball gown and flowers had been braided into her long blond hair. "This is Sara. She was sixteen when Moses painted this portrait. Isn't she lovely? And look there at the big floor vase behind her in the picture. It's Moses's ancestor vase. See all the African animals on it? That's what I want you to have, my love, if you can find it."

He brought out another oil painting, which depicted a handsome black-skinned African chief in flowing robes. "That's him," she said, awed. "They were smiling at me, and your sister blew me a kiss."

"Don't be afraid of them, Lorie. They are here to help us." He grinned broadly. "You should be pleased that Sara likes you. Without exception, she was critical of every girl I set my eyes on."

"I feel that way about Marsh sometimes," she said quietly, soothed by the compliment. "No one is really good enough for my baby brother." Lorie felt her cell phone vibrate. She pulled it into her hand. "Yes?" It was her aunt, telling her that several cars had just come into town at high speed, there were rumors spreading wildly that Randolph House was haunted and that Major Preston was mighty unhappy because his monument had been broken. She grinned at Jeff. "He will be happy to hear that. You should have seen him, Aunt Carol. He and Ravenwing were...well...pretty darned spectacular!"

"Judy at the Imperial Hotel called Sid to alert him that Maratti just received a couple of visibly shaken visitors," Carol added. "I expect you're going to get some more action very shortly."

"Thanks for letting us know, Carol. I'll tell Jeff." She looked at him. "Act Two is beginning right on time."

"Now we shall see who is in charge," Jeff said.

During cleanup, the draperies had once more been tightly drawn across the windows. Jeff called down the cellar steps to Randy and Mac. They both emerged from the tunnel and hurried to join Lorie in the drawing room. In the dim light of the single-bulb floor lamp they had allowed themselves, she saw they had both affixed holstered guns to their belts.

"Use those only if it's absolutely necessary," Jeff warned.

Lorie stayed near the windows, checking every now and again for movement or lights outside. Within half an hour, car lights could be seen coming rapidly up the long access road to the house.

"Only one car," Lorie said, again securing the drapes.

"That's good." Jeff picked up the gray woolen coat from the sofa where he had dropped it. He switched off the light. "That makes it much more likely it's Maratti. And hopefully his good friend Arthur. Okay, troops. Into the hidden room with you." Entering with them, he showed them a discrete mesh-covered panel beside the fireplace through which they could watch what was happening. "I'll try to keep all dialog within this area." He rebuttoned the jacket and strapped the belt around his waist.

"Do you want anything recorded?" Randy asked.

Jeff answered thoughtfully. "Only we will ever need to know what is said and in what context. We will divulge only information that needs to be told and keep the rest to ourselves. I will not deviate from my ghostly persona. Lorie, you know the cues for the lights."

She nodded. The remote keys were in her hands.

He left, and they stood silent, shoulder to shoulder, in the darkened room, watching through a narrow horizontal opening in the wall at a comfortable eye level. For a brief moment, Lorie saw the flare of a flashlight in the drawing room. Then the room went dark.

Long minutes passed. Finally, there was a rattle in a lock and a brief rush of air through the viewing slot indicating that an outside door had come open. Murmurs of voices could be heard from the hallway. Then the door to the drawing room opened, and in the glow from the hallway light, Lorie could see Rolf Maratti entering the room. He was followed closely by Arthur Ehrlich. Ehrlich was holding a small pistol in his outstretched hand.

Maratti reached for the light switch, disabled by Ewen Taylor not too many hours before. As his fingers moved, Lorie pressed the remote that illuminated the picture above the fireplace.

He stepped back suddenly. "Art," he said softly, "someone has rewired the house, and they may yet be here."

"Show yourselves," Ehrlich said, his voice quavering. "I have a gun, and I know how to use it." Lorie would have been willing to bet that Ehrlich had never held a gun until this night. He was clearly shaken.

"Rolf Maratti," Jeff said, his voice soft and deep.

Lorie pressed the second switch. The light illuminated Jeff, and although she couldn't see it from where she was standing, she knew it simultaneously illuminated the oil painting they had just hung on the wall close beside the fireplace.

She heard the sudden intake of breath from both men.

After a long silence, Maratti spoke. "Who are you?"

"You have known of this painting for many years, Rolf. You know exactly who I am."

"Major Preston." Maratti looked at Arthur Ehrlich.

The gun hung from Erlich's hand. Then it dropped to the floor. "Art." Maratti turned to him instantly, concerned.

"Please be seated, Mr. Ehrlich," Jeff said. "Explanations will all come in good time." He helped the large man to one of the sofas and saw that he was comfortable, if stunned beyond words. His eyes were focused on Jeff's face.

Rolf Maratti appeared to be tongue-tied as well. He kept looking at Jeff and at the picture behind him on the wall. "You...you look exactly like him."

"There is a reason for that," Jeff answered.

"You're really Major Preston? That's not possible."

"Suspend your belief system for the moment, Rolf," Jeff stood tall once again, "and listen to me very carefully. I am here because of the late Jon Randolph, your father."

Now it was Lorie's turn for surprise. She sensed it also in the subtle body language of the men on either side of her.

"He wasn't my father. He was Tommy's father. He was only my stepfather."

"His last words were a request to his friends to find his son and give him two letters that had been left for him in the clock room. Your father said that you would find in these letters all the answers you were seeking. He wanted to let you know that his grandchildren had a far better father than you had and that he was very sorry about failing you."

Jeff had not been part of the conversation when Lorie had heard essentially those words repeated by her aunt. She thought she would never ask him how he knew.

"It wasn't his fault entirely," Maratti protested, strangely enough defending the man he was supposed to have hated.

"He kept bringing these things up every time we got together. He wanted to talk about it. But I knew who my real father was, and I didn't want to discuss it with him."

"Who do you think your father was, Rolf?"

He was silent for a long time. Finally, Arthur Ehrlich spoke up. "Tell him, Rolf. What's the difference now? He probably knows anyway."

A long moment later, he began to speak very softly. "His name was Pietro Toschi. He was a member of an Italian army unit under Nazi command. They were ruthless. They tortured and killed Italian partisans during the Second World War. My beautiful mother, Maria"—his gaze shifted to her picture—"was the daughter of a count. She was also a fierce partisan. She didn't know what Pietro was when she married him. She thought he shared her beliefs. But he was only using her to get her money and to unearth the names of her friends and relatives who were fighting for Italian freedom. They were all rounded up and shot. Everyone she knew and loved. The only reason she survived is that she bore him a son. Me." There was intense pain in Maratti's expression. "Imagine searching for years to find your real father—a war hero, my mother always told me—only to discover that he was a sociopath, a despicable war criminal who was hung without a trial by his own people the minute they could get their hands on him. I've had to live with that truth for most of my adult life. I can understand why Jon Randolph didn't want to tell me my father's real name, but why did my mother lie to me about what he was? It put me on a search that was in the end so humiliating I could never come back to Randolph House."

"Rolf," Jeff said softly, "there is a letter here Jon Randolph wanted you to have. Will you read it now?"

Maratti turned away. "The old words. He always said them: he will always love and admire me for myself alone, not for the man who was my father. I owe Jon Randolph so much. Every time I turned around, I found myself surrounded and assisted by his friends and associates. Even if I'd wanted to fail, he wouldn't have let me. I've been successful at everything I did: my schooling, my teaching, the little jewelry shop, the retail store, even the gem import/export business. I'm not worthy of that care. Especially now, when I have to betray him."

Lorie had sensed at the beginning that Maratti was playing a role. But this was surely his true self. And he was under pressure, or he would not be talking about betrayal.

"If you will not read the letter, Rolf, I will read it to you." Jeff opened the envelope and drew out several thin sheets of paper.

"Please don't," Maratti said, his voice breaking. Tears were pouring down his cheeks.

"It is a letter from your mother, Rolf."

Jeff had taken a great deal more from the green box than he'd told her, Lorie thought. But perhaps this message was too private to be passed around to outsiders, even friendly outsiders.

Maratti's head came up. His luminous brown eyes were dilated in the dim light. They were beautiful eyes, Lorie saw. As beautiful as Jeff's in their own way. "My mother?" His attention shifted to the painting above the fireplace.

"'Dear son,'" Jeff began softly. "'I'm dying. You know it. I know it. And my beloved Jon knows it, too, even more acutely. Let me tell you something about him. He is one of the best men I know. And he is your father, my dearest child.'"

Maratti gasped and sat down suddenly on the sofa beside Ehrlich.

Jeff continued reading. "'One of my most difficult assignments during the war was to help Jon make his escape through the mountains to safety in Switzerland after his plane went down. We shared many harrowing adventures during that journey. And we fell in love. My dear boy, he was already married. As was I. Some might say we sinned against the church and man. But for that brief time in both of our lives when neither of us knew if we would live or die the next day or the next minute, we were living our lives to the very limit. We made love, my son. We loved each other well. I will never deny that knowledge to you. Jon brought me tenderness I had never known, and that was the love I felt when you were conceived. I was never so happy in my life as when I knew I was carrying you, his son.'"

Maratti sat silent, his mouth slack, listening to his mother's words. He whispered finally, "Why didn't she tell me?"

"All in good time," Jeff said and, looking back at the old letter, continued. "'My pregnancy was a problem for me when I got back home. Pietro had been long gone when I took the assignment, and I hoped he had been killed. But he was there waiting at the villa.

"'He liked to beat me, Rolf. It was very exciting for him to pummel a woman with his fists and then rape her. I thought I had lost you once, but you were stronger than he was. I was terrified that when you were born, you would be blond like your father, with blue eyes. We would both have died in that instant. But it was our great good luck that you were a small baby, and you inherited my dark skin and dark hair, and he thought you were his. So we were spared. But it was always by your eyes I knew you were Jon's. They are just like his, wide-spaced, with those beautiful long lashes and classic eyebrows. So I named you Rolf. An abbreviation of his last name, *R* and *olf*. And no one ever knew.'"

"Ahhhh!" The cry of anguish went on and on. Maratti leaned his face into his hands, now weeping from deep inside his soul. "Why didn't he tell me? He must have known."

"He knew," Jeff said when Maratti had finally gained control of his emotions. Teary-eyed, Arthur Ehrlich handed his friend a large white handkerchief. Maratti wiped at his cheeks and blew his nose. "Here is his letter," Jeff said. "Do you want to read it?" He handed it to the humbled man.

Maratti read aloud, softly, with hesitation. "'To my son Rolf. Here is your mother's letter. I didn't give it to you when she died, my child, at first for a very selfish reason—I didn't want Tommy to ever find out I had been unfaithful to his beloved mother while I was married to her. That was very wrong of me. I think Tommy would have accepted you fully as a brother. My weakness was that I didn't want to test him. He had taken her death so badly. I think now he would have understood. But you are the one who had to bear the pain of my failure to trust my oldest son. And your mother and I, in trying to protect you from the nightmare that was hers but still give you a father to admire, did you a huge disservice by telling you your father was a war hero. We never supposed you would try to find the man she had been married to during those war years. But you have always been stubborn. It's a trait in our family, that stubbornness. And you went on to discover his identity. It must have been a terrible shock. But, Rolf, nothing about you is any part of the evil that he was. You are my son entirely. I see it in everything you do.'"

"Jon Randolph," Jeff said to him softly, "was the war hero who was your father. Do you now understand?"

Maratti nodded, mute for a time, and finally turned back to the letter. "'I've met your son, Carl,'" he read, and looked up at Jeff, again surprised, "'I asked him not to tell you I had sought him out, because I didn't want you to forbid my seeing him. I am proud of my grandson and his sister, Constance, who is a wonderfully talented artist. But I have special words for Carl's son, Jeffrey. He stayed with me at the South Wind for a week after he graduated from Ranger School at Ft. Benning, just after his graduation from West Point. I was so proud of him, becoming an airborne ranger. He has stayed with me many times since, there and at Randolph House.'"

Lorie felt the grip of Randy's hand on her shoulder. "No coincidences," he breathed.

Maratti went on reading. "'He and I have explored all the cracks and crevices in this old house looking for secret panels. I don't think we've found them all yet. I know how much you and Tommy liked to do that during those early years. I used to hear you laughing and whispering behind the walls. I knew then you were learning to admire, if not love, each other. I didn't want to damage that fragile friendship, Rolf. It was too precious to me."

"'And now, in my later years, my dear boy, after I met your Jeff, I discovered a more compelling reason to keep you from taking your true surname. Your grandson looks too much like my side of the family. His bright blue eyes are a dead giveaway.

"'You see, on her deathbed, my dear mother, Sara, warned me that our family was being targeted by the same predators who had killed Moses and his men. She said that I should never let down my guard because they would surely try to destroy me and my family. I thought she was merely becoming delusional as she approached her ninetieth year. But in the years since her death, I have learned that she was not only serious, she was correct. Rolf, my reluctance to reveal you as a Randolph has for many years protected you from an unseen enemy that has our family in its cross-hairs.

I have been careless, and I think they have found me. I am becoming very wary about whom to trust.

"'Remember this: Maratti is your mother's family name, not the name of the man she was married to. Please continue to carry that proud name. Guard yourself and your family and especially your wonderful grandson.

"'I love you, Rolf. Please forgive the old man who has loved you always. Your father.'"

Maratti looked up into Jeff's face. "He knew my son and my daughter. He knew my grandson, Jeff. Why did I try to keep them from him all those years?"

"Because you were hurt. And for good reason, Rolf. He had lied to you about the most important thing in the world, and despite his fears for your safety, it was not easy to back out of that deception."

"I see that now." The words were spoken very softly.

"To his credit, he wanted to tell you, but his second thoughts kept him silent."

"But I rejected him, too," Rolf put in forcefully. "I'm equally at fault. I thought for a time he murdered my mother, and I was determined to destroy him. Until I found out about my...her bastard of a husband. I knew then that I had been wrong. But I didn't have the strength in me to apologize to him. Not me, the son of that same bastard. Why would he ever forgive me something like that?"

"Whatever made you think he murdered your mother?" Jeff asked. Lorie heard deep surprise in his voice. This was an entirely new element, something he had not anticipated.

"The will he wrote," he said simply. "It left nothing to her."

"Why didn't you ask Jon about it?"

"Because he didn't know I'd seen it. Someone showed it to me and suggested that Jon was not the man I thought he was. He told me I should be very suspicious that perhaps Jon had married my mother only for her connections and to get control of her estates through controlling me."

"Someone showed it to you? When you were a child?"

"I was almost eighteen. Not quite a child."

"Too young. And not familiar with the law, Rolf. Vulnerable. Your brother had been away at school and was now in the service. Jon was preparing for a mission away from home once he got you enrolled at a good university. You were completely alone at that time with no one to turn to but the man you now suspected of murdering your mother. Who would do such a cruel thing to you?"

Maratti thought for a time. "It was cruel, wasn't it? It was one of Mike Neil's law clerks. A young man named Clint. A year or so after Mother died, he called me to come over to the office, and he pulled it out and showed it to me."

"Clint Daniels?" Jeff asked.

"I never knew his last name," Maratti said. "Just Clint. He gave me the will to keep and put a copy back in the file in its place. He said I could use it as evidence whenever I wanted to, as there is no time limit on murder investigations."

"He expected then that you would turn on Jon Randolph?"

"I think he did. I took two of my mother's diamond broaches and left home. I was very angry. The diamonds paid my way through school, and afterward, I started my own business, focused on getting as rich as Jon Randolph. It was all revenge. Revenge is a relentless motivator.

"And then I started to research the man I thought was my father. The more I found out about him, the less I could believe that damned lie Clint told me about Jon Randolph. I finally remembered how Jon had protected us both and how he had cherished my mother. He would never have harmed her. Or me."

"But it was too late to go back," Jeff said softly. "Or so you thought."

"I wish now we had talked."

"He understood," Jeff said gently.

"But it's not over yet," Maratti cried out as he lifted his eyes from the letter in his lap. "They've got my grandson, Jeff. Carl's son. And they won't give him back unless I turn Randolph House and all the other property that belonged to Jon over to them."

Jeff frowned. This was obviously a surprise. "Who has him?"

"Shadowy people. It must be these same people my father is talking about!" He stood up, then sat down. His face had blanched. "I don't know who they are. But they're all around me. They won't leave me alone. First, someone called me to ask if I still had the old will. He told me he was Jon's lawyer and said he was just checking up on estate issues. I should have destroyed that damned will years before when I discovered the truth, but like a fool, I admitted to that caller I still had it. I didn't know what he was getting at. There wasn't a repeat call, and I completely forgot about it.

"Then someone started calling me again right after Jon had his first stroke, reminding me about the will. He said to keep it handy because my grandson's life might depend on it. It was shortly after that the people at the rehab hospital told me that Jeff had walked out of the hospital right after he'd had reconstructive surgery on his face, and they couldn't find him. I didn't know he was able to walk. But these people sent me pictures, so I knew they had him."

"Rehab hospital?" Jeff asked, frowning. "Why was he in a hospital?"

"He'd done multiple tours in Iraq and come back safely," Maratti said, his voice expressing the strain he was surely feeling. "Then he was sent to Afghanistan. While he was there, an explosive device went off under his truck. He's been in a military rehabilitation facility ever since, six months now, suffering from traumatic brain injury and post-traumatic stress disorder. That poor dear boy. We weren't sure if he was even aware of us the last time we were there. So much pain he was suffering.

"And then these heartless people kidnapped him from under the noses of the hospital staff. Jeff barely knows his own family, and they're holding him hostage until I betray Jon Randolph and everything he stood for. And now I find out that Jon Randolph actually was my father. And he was being targeted. What can I do to get out of this mess? What can I tell my son and his poor wife? And my own wife. His grandmother?" Again he began to weep.

Arthur Ehrlich finally found his voice. "We were trying to be tough guys." He put a comforting arm around Maratti's bent, shaking shoulders. "We were trying to make these people think we had connections to organized crime so they'd lay off. But they're relentless. Who would know that Rolf had the old will? And who would be so heartless as to use it against him? Especially now."

"What is your connection to Rolf Maratti," Jeff asked Ehrlich gently, "aside from the fact that you are his lawyer?"

"More like a brother," Ehrlich said, wiping at the tears streaming down his own face. "He was so alone when he left home. We were roommates in college, and I took him home with me on vacations. My family loved him, took him in. He's one of the finest people I know. The Mafia fabrication was just to keep the wolves at arm's length until we could figure what to do about them."

"Lorie," Jeff said. "Randy. Mac. Would you join us, please?"

Lorie felt the squeeze of Randy's hand on her shoulder. He turned the flashlight on and opened the doorway to the hidden room.

"Let me introduce you to my crew," Jeff Preston said to Maratti and Ehrlich, who rose in surprise when the silent watchers filed into the room. "Lorena Manning, whom you have met. Officer Randy Ross and Detective Alan Macdonald of the Marietta Police Department. Mac and Randy have been investigating an incident that involves someone whose last name, it appears, is Maratti. Since the clothing they've found is government-issue, I would not be surprised to discover that it is your grandson we are talking about, in which case he may well have freed himself from the custody of your enemies through his own efforts. He may have been trying to reach safety with Jon Randolph, not knowing his great-grandfather was dying."

Maratti's head lifted abruptly, his eyes wide. "Where is he? Is he safe?"

"Both those questions," Jeff said, "are as yet unanswered. But let us ask a few other questions before we begin. Mac, I think our sequestered lawyer, Mr. William Purdy, knows more about this situation than he has told us."

"Purdy's in on this?" Ehrlich's voice reflected suppressed venom. "Why am I not surprised?"

Mac said, "Perhaps we should ask him some more specific questions."

Jeff held up another piece of paper. "Here is another note I found in the green box." He glanced at Lorie with almost a hangdog expression of apology for not having shared it with her. "It says that Maria Maratti's diamonds have been transferred to the bank vault along with the will and that if anything happens to Jon Randolph, the diamonds should be given by his lawyer directly to Rolf Maratti, as they are his legacy from his mother, unclaimed until now and not part of the estate. Unfortunately, Rolf, your friends have found neither the will nor the diamonds."

"They're not here at the house?" Maratti cried out. "I had assumed they were here. I asked for locks and guards only to keep those bastards from getting my mother's diamonds, the ones I left behind. I was too proud to ask Jon for them after walking out with those two broaches. But I've always felt they were safe here, safer than anyplace else I could think of."

"Will and diamonds gone in one fell swoop," the detective said grimly, "never to be seen again. And the lawyer who had access to that bank vault won't fess up even though he's safe in protective custody." He walked out to the hall, punching in numbers on his phone.

"Did they ask you for diamonds?" Jeff said, frowning.

"They said they knew I had the diamonds, and they demanded them. They said the diamonds were their birthright." The hopeful expression that had been growing on Maratti's face transformed into one of deep anger. "They were obsessed with diamonds, and I was just as determined to keep them hidden. If those diamonds were anyone's birthright, they were mine. They were a symbol to my mother of her family. She tried to find her relatives after the war, but it wasn't until Jon Randolph found us living in the ruins of her family's home that she was able to contact anyone from her old life. Most of her family had been killed by that bastard she was married to. But the diamonds had been saved by the family solicitor. She was going to trade them one at a time for food for the two of us. But Jon told her to keep them in remembrance of a brave and remarkable family. He promised her that he would be the one to feed us both for the rest of our lives. And he surely kept his promise. For my mother's sake, I will not give them up easily. But if I have to, I will, for my grandson." He seemed for a moment, almost on the verge of collapse.

"He is no longer in the hands of the slavers who captured him," Jeff said firmly.

Arthur Ehrlich, who had reached for his friend, turned to Jeff, eyes wide. "Slavers?"

"I'm sorry." Lorie could tell Jeff was chagrinned that he had used the word. "That's what they were called in my day. Hoodlums. Gangsters. Criminals. Do I have it right, Lorena?"

"All of the above," she said softly.

Mac came back in. "Purdy still won't talk. He says if he tells us anything, they'll hunt him down and destroy him. He's terrified. Dean Harris is trying to get through to him, though, and Dean's good. He'll call us."

Jeff turned back to Maratti. "Rolf, gather your courage. We will fix this problem. We will return your grandson to you."

Lorie looked long at Jeff, who was gazing at her with unmistakable emotion, knowing the feeling of deep anguish she now felt in her heart was the reverse image of the emotion now beginning to animate Maratti. To make things right she would have to give up the man she loved even more than life itself. Worse yet, she had never been more certain of anything that her sacrifice was necessary. She took a deep breath, swallowed hard, nodded, and smiled at him.

He had come for a reason. This was it. Her life would never have been complete without knowing him, even for these very few days. But oh, how could she bear the loss? She looked down at her beautiful ring and then again at the man she called "Husband." *Gather your courage*, he had said. If anyone knew the true meaning of courage, it was Jefferson Richard Preston.

"Go back to town," Jeff said to Maratti. "Tell whoever asks that you found nothing here. We will be in touch with you."

"Thank you, Major," Maratti said. "Thank you. All of you. My heart is light tonight for the first time in more years than I can remember. I am a new man, Art." There was a brightness in his voice that had not been there before. He laughed lightly, as if the world were once more a place of happiness. "My wife won't recognize me. My children won't know me. If you can now send my boy back to me…"

"We will try," Jeff said softly. "But even though he got away from his kidnappers, he may not be as mended as you wish him to be. Can you deal with that?"

"Do whatever you can do for him," Arthur Ehrlich said, almost pleading. "I've known Rolf for many years, and his wife, Pat, and I know what good people they are. Please help them, Major Preston. They will do whatever they can to see that their grandson has the best of care."

"We will try to make everything right."

They turned to leave. Lorie followed them to the door, and Rolf Maratti put the padlock and its key into her hand. "Thank you," he said again, looking into her eyes with an awed expression of deep relief and thankfulness.

She closed the door behind them and leaned her head against it, trying to pull all her thoughts and emotions together. So much had happened in the past days, afternoon…hour…almost too much to process. But one thing had become very clear. Jeff had been right from the beginning. There was evil here. Rolf Maratti, a reasonable man, had been rendered helpless by the abduction of his grandson.

It was his grandson's escape from those captors that had precipitated such furious unplanned-for activity on the part of Jon Third's most implacable enemies and finally made those enemies visible.

She lifted her head. Jeffrey Maratti. A brain-injured soldier.

Nothing could be the same now. She took a deep breath and walked back to the drawing room.

CHAPTER 20

A s she came through the door, she saw Mac looking up at the oil painting of the Major. "By golly, Jeff, in that uniform you sure do look a lot like him!"

"How recently was that painted?" Randy asked. He, too, was examining the portrait with great interest.

"It's an original oil from the 1860s. I agree, there is definitely a likeness. But the hair is all wrong. And that's not my nose at all." Jeff quickly lifted it off the wall and asked Lorie to help him carry it back into the storage room. Once again he put the soft cover across it. The painting of Jon Preston Third was returned to its original place on the wall beside the fireplace.

"Now there was a nice man," Randy said, looking up at the strong, determined face. "He wasn't here much, but when he was, he spread his money and goodwill around and made everyone's lives easier."

But because of the evil that had come, his final illness and death had thrown the town into a frenzy of discord. "What kind of town is Randolph City?" Lorie asked Randy as Jeff disappeared back into the storage room. She had promised to stand beside him against whatever evil he had to face, and she would do that to the best of her ability. What they needed now was as much information as they could get—information a computer could not access.

"Small," Randy said, answering her question about Randolph City. "But big enough for most people. Between two and maybe three thousand people live here, depending on what's going on. It started with about thirty or forty families. Scotch-Irish and French Huguenot settlers, sometimes the same thing, veterans of Indian skirmishes and the Revolution. Most of them had ancestors who'd come to this country as indentured servants or who were escaping from indenture. They'd all had firsthand encounters with the evils of religious intolerance and slavery.

"Are the same families still here?" It could make a world of difference.

Randy thought a bit. "Yeah, I'd say the largest percentage of the people here are related in one way or another to the original settlers. There were blacks here for a time after the Civil War. But those who didn't go north mostly intermarried, even before it was legal in this state. Maybe that's the reason the people in this town kind of kept to themselves. They got a little clannish and darker-skinned as time went by. No one ever dwelled on the past. Didn't think about history much. It wasn't until Jon Randolph came back to town that anyone really paid attention. He brought an influx of creative-type people, artists and writers, who appreciated the mixed heritage. I think that's helped people to put it into context."

"From what I've heard," Lorie said, "a few of your ancestors were Union people."

Randy laughed sharply. "No one ever asked the people in this town to vote on whether they wanted to leave the Union. They still had patriotic memories of the Revolution, and a lot of them were angry about Georgia joining the Confederacy.

Angry enough to fight back. They did that very effectively with the Major's help. But after he and Granddad Ben were killed by the Yankees, everyone shut down and became super secretive about what they'd been doing."

Lorie frowned. "Everyone still seems to want to keep that heritage a secret."

"No one knows for sure who was involved. Some of us are real proud of our great-granddaddies, but we keep our mouths shut. Some may have had people who sat the war out and don't want to admit it. Or fought for the other side. And no one wants to push it, because up till now, everyone in town has been on real friendly terms. Tight. Something bad has happened recently. We're just not sure what."

"I bet they were all on the same side," Lorie mused, thinking about it.

"For the most part," Jeff Preston agreed with a grin. He walked out of the hidden room dressed once again in jeans and his black long-sleeved shirt.

Through a crack in the draperies, Lorie spied the pin-prick headlights of a car turning into the long driveway down by the country road. "Lights off," she snapped. The room went dark. Almost immediately, her phone rang.

Ewen Taylor was on the other end. "I'm bringing lights to illuminate that airfield out beyond the house. I'll have my pilot bring the helicopter in while eyes are focused elsewhere. That way, we can be packed up and out by first light."

Moments later, Lorie opened the door to him and his three helpers. After discussing plans with Jeff, Taylor and his young technical crew eagerly agreed to stay in the house overnight to guard it, since the gates, they had discovered, were no longer functional. "How did you do that?" Taylor asked.

Jeff grinned. "Chance lightning strike."

"Good God!"

"And some small charges of explosive," Jeff finished, laughing.

It was decided that Lorie would drive Taylor's van back to Randolph City by way of Walker's Crossroads, where she and Jeff would drop Mac and Randy off at the unmarked police car. Then they'd get some food and much-needed sleep at the Baileys' house and check with Taylor in the morning. "The chopper will be tucked away by then," Ewen Taylor told them. "And we won't leave if you think we can help you here."

"I'd like to go to the Baileys' with you," Randy said apologetically to Lorie, "but I think it's more important now that I get an updated briefing on what's being found out by the highway." He turned to Jeff. "Doesn't any of this ring a bell somewhere? I really don't believe in coincidences, and you're my prime suspect for our newly discovered 'Jeff Maratti.'"

Jeff shook his head. "The memories just aren't there."

If any memories are left, Lorie thought sadly.

"DNA will tell all," Mac said. "Maybe we can get the process speeded up a bit. I'll give it a try."

Lorie was almost sorry to see the policemen leave the van once they got to Walker's Crossroads. Now alone with Jeff, she wasn't sure what to say to him. He might be Jeff Maratti. But he had known things tonight he couldn't have known unless he had been at Jon Randolph's death bed. Jon Randolph's cousin Sue, who knew him well, had talked rhapsodically about the old man's buoyant "life spirit." How many souls might that same life essence have entered over the centuries? Had the spirit of a dying Jefferson Richard Preston entered Sara's newborn baby on a night of fire and murder long years ago and preserved Jon Randolph Junior's fragile life? Had it passed then to Jon Randolph Third in its turn, when Jon Junior's beloved wife was having difficulties with her pregnancy after her husband's death? Sara had been at her daughter-in-law's side when she learned her precious son would not be coming home from his hazardous night flight through the mountains. Might she have summoned that essence of awareness to her newborn grandson? Had that same spirit now entered the battle-broken mind of Sara's great-great-grandson, grievously damaged in the service of his country, and facing death at the hands of the murderers who were threatening his grandfather?

The headlights flickered across tree limbs and branches alongside the rough road. Now and then, a fence would come into view, or a postal box, and Lorie realized she was surrounded by living human beings, a vast civilization, the whole real world. But Sara was still nearby. And Jeff had been operating in a different dimension, one he seemed to flow through when he needed to, one she could not enter. The time for their parting was very near.

As if he understood what she was feeling, he reached his left hand to her right across the space between them in the van. "I love you," he said softly. His hand was warm. "I will always love you. Through all time and in all places."

She glanced at his face, so beloved to her, but he seemed more a stranger, not quite, she now understood, a part of her reality. He was not hers to claim. She thought her heart would break.

"My life will always reflect yours," she said simply, through pain. She hoped he understood those words to be the deepest, most important vow she had ever made. She would never fail this beautiful soul. No matter the cost.

At the Baileys' house there was much commotion. "What happened?" Sue said as they got out of the car. "Come on in. We've got chili on the stove. Phil's stirring it even as we speak. Tell us everything."

Carol put her arms around Lorie, who clung tightly to her aunt. "You're not laughing, Lorie. You scared the bejesus out of those country boys. You should be tickled pink. What happened?"

Jeff came up beside her and put a hand on her shoulder. "It was very intense, Miz Carol. She's tired."

"A big glass of iced tea." Lorie unwrapped her arms from around Carol and smiled at her. "That's all I need. And some of that chili. It smells wonderful."

Carol sat on one side of Lorie and Jeff on the other. Once Phil and the Baileys were seated at the table across from them, Jeff made his report. "Rolf Maratti and Art Ehrlich were able to break away from their watchers and come out to the house. We talked with them for a good long while. We have found your love child, folks. It's Rolf."

A long whistle issued through Sid Bailey's lips. And Phil Barnett said, "You've got to be kidding!"

"It's true," Lorie added tiredly. "Jon Randolph Third didn't want to confess he'd been unfaithful to Tommy's mother while he was in Europe during the Second World War. So the relationship has remained a secret all these years. Even to the product of that affair, Rolf Maratti himself."

"Soap opera stuff," Carol said.

Jeff frowned at Lorie. She smiled. "Tell you later," she mouthed.

"Did you find the letter Mr. Jon talked about?" Sue asked.

"It was in the storage room all along," Jeff said evenly. "On the table beside the green box. There were two letters. One was from Rolf's mother, confirming that he was Mr. Jon's biological son. The other was a letter of apology to Rolf from his father, explaining why he hadn't said anything."

Carol said with a flare of anger, "Shame on Mr. Jon! Nothing could explain that! After Tommy was killed, there was no reason to withhold the information."

"A mutual lack of trust," Jeff answered carefully. "It compounded over the years. And when Jon Third wanted to open up to his son, he realized the occasion had passed them by."

"A wedge had already been put between them by a third party," Lorie put in. "And we think that person is still involved in what's happening right now in Randolph City. We just have to find out who that person is."

"Well, now that Rolf Maratti knows he's Jon Randolph's son," Sue asked, "is he still going to sell out the town?"

Lorie sighed. "He's being blackmailed. He's in total lockdown, except for a brief instance of ghost-induced confusion when he and Mr. Ehrlich were able to break loose and drive out to the house."

There was complete silence in the room. Finally, Sid Bailey said, "Who's involved?"

"That's the problem. He doesn't know who he's dealing with. They've been holding his grandson hostage for several weeks now until he agrees to turn all the property he inherits over to the kidnappers."

"Damn it to hell!" Sid exploded, pounding the table with his fist, with no adverse remonstrance from Sue.

"And the grandson," Lorie continued slowly, "is a West Point-trained officer who was brain injured by an explosive device in Afghanistan, which also left him with post-traumatic stress disorder."

Phil whistled sharply, and now it was Carol who exploded. "PTSD? This gets worse and worse."

"There is evidence," Lorie went on, "that somehow he escaped his captors. He was a tough soldier, an Airborne

Ranger." She paused a moment and then continued softly. "Randy and Mac think it's Jeff."

All eyes focused on Jeff. "Whoa," he said, straightening up in his chair. "I don't remember anything like that."

"But," Carol said, "your memory—"

"I know." He shrugged helplessly. "I know."

Sue Bailey asked quietly, "So does this help Randolph City? Or what?"

"Let's think about it," Jeff said. "And let's talk about it tomorrow. I don't know about anyone else, but I'm so tired I'm falling asleep in my soup."

"Chili," Lorie said quietly, without much thinking what she was saying, "con carne."

When he grinned at her as if everything was still the same, she almost wept.

"To bed with you all," Sue said. "Lorie's in Marianne's room upstairs. I'll show you." She led the way, calling back to her husband, "Jeff's in Jim's room. And Carol's in the big guest room with Phil."

"Oops," Carol said softly. "How did they know?"

Lorie just smiled.

Jeff found her bed that night. First, she cried softly into his gentle whispers. And then, quietly, she loved and was loved, with more passion and intensity than she had ever experienced.

CHAPTER 21

Friday, July 25, 2014

He was gone when she heard the knocking at her bedroom door. It was bright midmorning. "Lorie," Sue was saying. "You have a phone call."

She sat up and grabbed the blanket to cover her nakedness. "Who?" she said, confused.

"Rolf Maratti. Can I bring the phone to you?"

"Of course." The door opened, and Sue stepped in. She handed Lorie the mobile unit and went back out, gently closing the door behind her.

"Hello?"

"Miss Manning?" She recognized the voice immediately. He sounded anxious, excited. "How can I get hold of the Major? I need to talk with him. I think I know who's behind this."

"The Major?"

"Please. I need to talk with him. One of the developers came to see me this morning. I think I recognize him. I think he's the same person who gave me Jon's will. He's a lot older now, of course, but he has the same look in his eyes. Not quite on the level, if you know what I mean. He doesn't like to look a person straight in the eyes."

"Mr. Maratti," she said, her brain now beginning to function, "can you meet me at Randolph House in about thirty minutes?"

"I can. Do you mind if Art comes with me?"

"Of course not."

"We'll sneak out and be there in thirty minutes."

Lorie leaped out of bed and pulled on her clothes. "Where's Jeff?" she asked Sue as she raced down the stairs.

Sue pointed down the hallway.

"Which room?"

"Last on the left."

She pulled out her cell phone and was phoning Ewen Taylor as she burst into the bedroom where Jeff had been peacefully asleep a moment before. He sat up. At Randolph House, Taylor picked up the phone. "Yes, Lorie?"

"Rolf Maratti is on his way out to the house with Arthur Ehrlich. They want to meet with the Major. Rolf thinks he knows who one of the kidnappers is. We'll be there as soon as we can get there."

"Thanks for the warning, Lorie. What do you want us to do?"

"Just stay hidden for a time. Let's play it by ear."

"I'll leave the front door open, girl. Get here fast with 'the Major.'"

"We're on our way."

Jeff was already up and pulling on his clothes. "I'll need time to get into that uniform."

"I'll get the car started."

"Honey," he said, staring down at her feet. "Shoes?"

She looked down. "Oh." And she pounded back through the house and up the stairs.

"We'll have breakfast waiting when you get back," Sue said to them as they headed out the front door, the keys to Carol's car in Lorie's hand.

Carol was at the front door watching them as Lorie turned the car onto the street and headed toward Randolph House, Jeff at her side.

Once they reached the mansion, he grabbed up his uniform and boots and made the fast transition to "Major." Maratti was parking his car as Jeff seated himself before the fireplace in the drawing room. He drew a deep breath and rose with no sign of haste as Maratti and Ehrlich came into the room with Lorie.

"Good morning," he said with a smile.

Lorie went to the window and pulled the draperies back. Light spilled into the room.

"Are you real?" Maratti asked as Jeff reached for his hand, then Ehrlich's. Arthur Ehrlich still looked rather shaken.

"Not quite," Jeff said softly. "Can you accept that?"

Maratti nodded. "I don't know how, or why, but I accept that you are who you say you are, Major. My grandson Jeff certainly does take after you. He's a major, too." He spoke quietly. "He used to carry himself the way you do. He's tall. Strong. There are differences. His skin is dark. His hair isn't as light as yours, it's golden brown, I'd say. His nose and cheekbones were messed up by the explosives, but he used to be a handsome boy. I always wondered where those beautiful blue eyes came from. Now I know. You were at the funeral, weren't you?" Jeff nodded. "And at the courthouse." Jeff nodded again. "You are here because of me, aren't you?"

"And your grandson. For right now, think of me only as a distant relative, gentlemen. Now, please sit down and tell me what's happened to change the picture."

The two men seated themselves on the sofa in front of the fireplace, the picture of Maratti's mother looking down at them. Jeff stood beside the fireplace, under the portrait. "I had a visitor this morning," Maratti said. "It wasn't an ordinary thug like the ones who have been harassing us. It was one of the Atlanta developers. Clint Samuels, he called himself. We've done a background check on him. He's a lowlife, to put it bluntly."

"We are aware of that."

"If you hadn't reminded me why I took that damned will, I probably wouldn't have been alerted to his name. But it's the same man, Major. The same man who told me my real father was capable of murdering that beautiful woman"—his eyes turned up to the portrait—"whom he adored more than anything in the world." He looked back at Jeff. "I know now that she was slowly dying of injuries that bastard left her with. There was no need for her name to go into the will. And even if she hadn't inherited, he must have known I would always care for her. I was a stupid boy."

"What's done is done," Jeff said. "Put it behind you, Rolf."

"Easier said than done. Because I took the will and they used it to guarantee my inheritance, they have me where it hurts."

"Rolf, I can assure you that Jeff Maratti is not under their control. You will see him again. I'm not sure when or where or under what circumstances, but it will be soon."

Maratti took a deep breath. "So I can act freely and we can unmask these bastards?"

"Rolf, we are all working toward the same goal. May I introduce you to another associate?" He asked Ewen Taylor to join them. Taylor pushed the cabinet doorway open and came into the room. Jeff introduced Taylor to Maratti and Ehrlich, who rose to greet him.

"I'm so sorry to hear that these brigands have kidnapped your grandson," Taylor told Rolf Maratti as they seated themselves under the watchful eye of Maratti's mother. "These same idiots have been trying to intimidate me, if not destroy me. I want them put away. Permanently."

"How do we do this, gentlemen?" Jeff asked. "Do you have any suggestions?"

"Let me tell you what I've been told." Maratti leaned forward. "I'm to be at a special council meeting tonight. The chief item on the agenda is the future development of Randolph City. At that point, I am to get up, introduce myself, tell everyone I now control the property, and let everyone know that a new hotel and resort will replace Randolph House. A *fait accompli*. I'm to put a spin on it to the effect that there will be plenty of jobs for everyone, if not in the construction of the new development, in the administration of the new facility."

"In other words," Taylor said, "suck it up or leave town."

"Pretty much."

"Do they have a problem with the council?" Jeff asked.

"The major problem the developers face," Maratti answered, "is a strict zoning law set in place years ago by some very forward-looking council members, probably at the insistence of Jon Randolph. Randolph House and much of the other property he owned have been designated as historically significant and, as such, can't be touched. The citizens of Randolph City will have to vote to change the zoning and the designation. My job, on pain of my grandson's death, is to get them to change their minds by bribing them with jobs and tourism."

Ewen Taylor winced. "How do you think these people will vote?"

"I don't know." Maratti frowned. "I've had people following me around giving me advice one way and the other. Right now I think it's about even."

"Would you be willing to take a chance on that?" Jeff asked.

"In what way?"

"How about taking a straw vote among the people attending the meeting? Can we propose a discussion of the issues, followed by a nonbinding vote?"

"You're planning something, aren't you?" A smile hovered on Maratti's lips.

Jeff sat back, grinning. "Always."

"Let's run it past Sue," Lorie put in. "She knows everything there is to know about how politics runs in Randolph City. Let's go back to her house and get her and Sid in on this discussion."

"My boys will keep an eye on this house," Ewen Taylor said, and Lorie grinned. Mr. Taylor's "boys" would be pleased as punch to "keep an eye on this house."

*****

The war council had grown by three. The trestle table in the Baileys' kitchen was spread with breakfast makings— fruit, cereal, beverages, breads. They sat at either side of it, Carol and the doctor, Sue and Sid Bailey, Ewen Taylor, Rolf Maratti, Arthur Ehrlich, and Lorie, with Jeff Preston, now out of uniform, but still very much the officer in charge, seated at the head of the table. He had found a pad of paper and a pencil, and he began to write.

"Sue. Sid. How do council meetings work?"

They briefed him on the general procedures for running the open meeting. Lorie watched him take notes in some kind of code only he knew. She thought of the little book that told of his wartime operations and would have been devastatingly invaluable to an enemy if they had been able to crack his code. She was willing to bet even the vast computer banks at the CIA wouldn't be able to do that.

"So," he said, repeating what they were telling him, "each council meeting starts with open discussion. If someone gets up to speak, he or she is given that opportunity."

"It doesn't happen very often," Sid explained, "but when it does, things go to pot very fast. It's like a town hall meeting but with no direction. If we have a good mayor, he generally takes over and brings the discussion to a resolution very quickly."

"Do you have a good mayor right now?"

"Not particularly," his wife answered. "It's Archie Hood. He's a nice guy, but he's not very effective."

Jeff grinned. "That's what I like to hear."

"He ran for the position," Sid added, "because the Chamber of Commerce wanted him to. He looks nice. He's got a moneymaking office supply store. But he knows zip about running a meeting."

"Rolf," Jeff said, "do you mind if I preempt you on talking about development?"

"Mind?" Maratti answered. "You can take over the whole meeting if you want to. If I don't have to say anything, I'll be a happy man!"

"Good, because I plan on consuming most of the evening."

"And how is that?" Phil Barnett had been watching the proceedings with interest, focusing, Lorie could see, on the way Jeff was organizing his thoughts. He was thinking of brain damage, she knew, and seeing no evidence of it. Quite the contrary.

"I'm going to tell everyone what their ancestors did in the late war."

Sue Bailey gasped. "It will tear this town apart!"

"Or heal it," her husband said firmly.

"I'm betting on that," the doctor put in quietly. "Jeff has this little book. It's all written in code. But he's almost got it licked, and I think he already has his answers, and he knows this will bring the citizens of Randolph City together against the forces who are trying to tear it apart."

Now Ewen Taylor spoke up. "Brilliant! I want to be at that meeting."

"Your pursuers will see you," Lorie reminded the entrepreneur.

He was defiant. "Let them! I will not allow them to intimidate me any longer. I have other things to do."

"And perhaps," Rolf Maratti added, "they will reveal themselves, and we will finally be rid of them."

"And you will have your grandson back," Jeff said softly.

Lorie's heart turned over. She reached out to Jeff for reassurance. He took her hand in his, lifted it to his lips, and let it linger there.

She saw Maratti watching them. He smiled, approving. Arthur Ehrlich was watching his friend. For the first time since Lorie had met him, Arthur Ehrlich truly smiled.

CHAPTER 22

When Ewen Taylor returned to Randolph House with the van Lorie had commandeered the night before, he took two baskets of Sue's finest breakfast treats with him. His young companions and his pilot were hungry, as they had been reminding him. Jeff had given him lists of concealed compartments and passageways to look for, and Taylor was eager to return. He would be exploring most of the rest of the day, he said, with his enthusiastic crew. He asked to be included when the council meeting started. Lorie told him she would call to remind him.

Jeff, clad in jeans and a blue shirt, was still copying from his book notes to be used that evening. Sitting on the floor, leaning comfortably against the couch, Lorie was giving Phil and Carol a humorous account of some of the livelier aspects of the Randolph House haunting when she received a phone call from Detective Dean Harris. It was close to noon. "We're going to question Will Purdy again," the black detective told her. "Would you and Jeff like to be there?"

"Do you think he'll say anything in front of us?"

"We're doing it at the safe house where he feels comfortable, and he won't know he's being observed. You'll be behind mirrored glass in the next room."

"Can Rolf Maratti and Mr. Ehrlich come with us?"

Harris was surprised. She briefed him on the liaison that had been forged between the two formerly opposing forces.

"Bring them along," Harris said. "Their take on his answers should be exceedingly interesting."

Lorie called Maratti at the hotel and arranged for him and Ehrlich to join her and Jeff in the Escort at the rear of the hotel in half an hour. She'd never seen them in anything except business attire, so the idea that both would have donned chinos, knit sport shirts, and golf caps jarred her until she realized the clothes they were wearing would make them less recognizable to the watchers in Randolph City. They seemed more relaxed when they realized the car was not being followed. But during the hour-long ride to Marietta, there was very little conversation. They were both clearly on edge. Understandable, she thought. A precious life was on the line.

Once they reached the Barnett Orthopedic Clinic parking lot, Lorie pulled the Escort into place beside Randy's unmarked black Crown Vic. "You're all going with me," the young policeman told them, opening the doors of his car to them. Maratti sat in front with Randy. Ehrlich sat in the back seat to Lorie's left, Jeff at her right. Again, silence. Lorie could feel the same tension in Jeff that seemed to afflict the others. She kept his hand wrapped tightly in hers.

Their final destination was an unassuming house in a quiet residential area of Marietta. Randy pulled the black car into the attached garage and waited for the overhead door to close. They entered the house silently and followed Randy to the room from which they could observe. Four chairs had been provided in front of a two-way mirror. Lorie seated herself beside Jeff, who again reached for her hand. Nervous and edgy, Maratti positioned himself near the mirrored window.

Arthur Ehrlich grasped his arm. "Breathe slowly," he whispered and finally convinced his friend to take a seat.

"I have my list of questions for the late Jon Randolph's lawyer," Dean Harris told them quietly before he went into the room. "Let us know if we miss anything. Mac's here. He'll give me a signal."

The interview room was furnished with an office table and several chairs. The detective was seated when Will Purdy came in. "How is your wife doing?" Harris asked quietly, kindly. His gentle brown eyes turned up to Purdy's face with genuine concern.

"She's been under so much pressure," Purdy said, almost smiling. "She's feeling better every day now. Thank you for asking." Purdy himself appeared more rested, more at ease than he had when Lorie had seen him the day of the funeral. He was wearing casual clothes that actually fit, and he moved with a gracefulness she had not previously seen in him. He seated himself at the table. "I think we've pretty much covered everything I know about," he said to Harris. "What else can I tell you?"

"Well, for starters," Harris said in a slow nonconfrontational drawl, "we'd like to know what you did with the diamonds."

Purdy recoiled, stood up abruptly, and turned toward the door. Mac stepped inside, blocking it.

"What…what makes you think I had anything to do with diamonds?"

"We found a note written by Mr. Randolph," Harris said, holding Purdy's attention with laser intensity, "saying that the will and the diamonds were in the bank vault and that his lawyer should give the diamonds to Mr. Maratti as they were his inheritance from his mother and not part of the estate. And since you have already admitted you took the original will from that vault—"

"Oh shit!" Purdy said. "Oh shit! I didn't know they were his!"

"I think," Harris said sternly, "you are in serious trouble, my friend."

Purdy sat down at the table again, leaning his head into his hands. "I didn't mean to steal anything."

"What do you call it?"

"Recovery. I was recovering them for Ernie. He told me I should be keeping an eye open for the diamonds belonging to the Compact. He said Isaac Preston had stolen them. Years ago." Lorie felt Jeff's subtle reaction. "I was so relieved to have found them because these people are obsessed with diamonds. Totally obsessed! I thought, thank God I'll be done with them forever. But now," he looked up at Harris, "I'll have the Mafia after me, too. Shit! Will I ever be able to live a normal life?"

"Ernie? Who's Ernie? And what's the Compact?"

"Ernie Merrill. He develops property. He's my cousin on my mother's side."

"Can you get them back from him?"

"Are you kidding?" he said, his voice rising. "I don't ask Ernie or Clint to do anything for me. They tell me! And then I do for them! That's the way it works in our family."

"Clint?"

"Samuels. He's another cousin on my mother's side."

Lorie wondered how Will Purdy had wormed his way into the law office of Jon Randolph's genuine lawyer. Purdy must have come highly recommended by someone he and Mike Neil trusted. Cragin, perhaps?

"And have your cousins," Harris went on, "been asking you to find and destroy all the interim wills Jon Randolph wrote since Mr. Maratti left town? He must have written several. People do that."

Purdy hung his head. "It had to be the will that left the estate to Maratti or nothing. They were simply fixated on it. Have been for decades. What's happened now has thrown them into a shit pile!"

"And how long has this conspiracy been going on?" Harris asked.

"Years. Many years. But lately? Probably twenty-five years. They'd lost track of Jon Randolph until he started pushing the historical project in that little town of his, and it came out in some magazines. He should have stayed hidden. I'd have been better off. They use me when they need me, and they're just as likely to discard me. Permanently."

"Nice relatives, Will. Why didn't you turn them in?"

"They have contacts in police departments when they need them. They buy officials. They are officials. They have very long fingers. They know everything. They probably know where I am right now." His voice was rising, panicking.

Harris said calmly, "You're safe with us, Mr. Purdy. But you'll have to face the consequences of what you've done."

"I'm willing to testify against them and spend jail time if you'll keep Gloria safe."

"We'll consider it, Will. Now, we've got a few other questions for you."

Again Purdy dropped his head into his hands. "It's the soldier, isn't it?" he said softly. "I had nothing at all to do with that. When I heard what they'd done, that's when I decided it was time to break away from that crowd. I even bought plane tickets to Argentina for Gloria and me. But we couldn't ever catch a break. They were watching one or the other of us all the time." He looked up at Harris, a hopeful expression on his face. "The soldier got away from them! They thought he was brain-dead, but he still had a little something left up there. And he was strong, even if he didn't know exactly what he was doing or why. He looked like a cripple, the way he was all balled up, sitting in that wheelchair. But he'd been fighting them. So they had him tied when they put him in the back of the van when they were taking him up to Randolph City. But they didn't think they had to watch him. He chewed away at the ropes they had on him and managed to get the van door open just after they crossed the Chattahoochee River."

The van! Lorie thought, stunned. He was talking about the van that had followed Carol and herself from the South Wind to the pharmacy in Marietta. The people in the van were looking for a kidnapped soldier who had escaped.

"I don't know what's happened since then," Purdy went on. "They've been trying to find him or his body. The drivers were both carrying, and they tried to take him out. But they didn't know if any of the bullets hit him. Clint told me the police have been beating the bushes out along the road where he dropped out so they can't do any more looking there." Suddenly he went silent. Perhaps it was the look in Harris's eyes. "You? You're the one who's been looking for him? Oh shit!"

Lorie saw the grieving grandfather rise to his feet. Ehrlich held one arm, and Jeff stood up and put his hand on Maratti's shoulder. "He's safe," Jeff whispered. "Don't speak."

"Mr. Purdy," Harris said in the room outside, "you are in very serious trouble."

"I know," the man said. "I know. But I was never involved with kidnapping that soldier. I have too much respect for servicemen!" He took a deep breath and straightened up in his chair. "I always admired Jon Randolph, too. I hated every minute what I had to do to him." He looked directly into Harris's eyes and squared his shoulders. "I'm already a dead man, just by disappearing. Even if I go to jail, I'm dead." He took another deep breath. In Lorie's eyes, he seemed to gain in stature. "They're very good at using people to intimidate other people," he began. "I've known that game all my life. So if you can promise me you will keep Gloria safe, I'll tell you everything I know about them. All I ask is that you keep them from hurting Gloria."

"Mr. Purdy," Dean Harris said solemnly, "we can give you that promise. And we will do everything we can to protect you as well as your wife."

"I believe you," Will Purdy said in a deep, emotion-choked voice. For a moment, he bowed his head. Then he straightened up and looked Harris full in the face. "Ask me what you want to know."

Jeff reached down for Lorie's hand. His other hand was still on Maratti's shoulder.

The black detective sat silent for a short time, giving Purdy space to organize his thoughts. Finally, he asked, "Who is Johnny McDaniels?"

"He's the Quartermaster."

A surprised pause. "Quartermaster of what?"

"The Compact," Purdy said. The word came out as a long whispering sound between his teeth, almost as if he couldn't speak of it out loud.

"I wouldn't mind," Harris said after another long moment of silence, "if you explained."

"The Compact," Purdy said again. "The Compact. The damned Compact!"

"What the hell does that mean?"

"You've heard of the Mayflower Compact? That's what it is. It's a written compact among a group of men saying that they all agree to certain terms and rules for the benefit of all. When the Mayflower people did it, it became a government.

When the Blackheart people did it, it became a terror organization. If any one of the men breaks the rules set down by the majority, they're subject to punishment, to be decided on by the majority of the members and acted upon by the quartermaster."

"Blackheart people?"

"A pirate ship. I know. I know. It sounds like something out of a movie. I'm sorry, but there's nothing funny or adventurous about this Compact. One of my ancestors signed it a couple of hundred years ago, and my whole family is ruled by it. Still. With no possible way to break free! The quartermaster makes sure of it!"

Jeff Preston sank down into his chair, still grasping Lorie's hand. He was trembling.

"Let's take this from the beginning," Harris said. Mac was still in the room. His face showed that he was listening intently, taking in all that was said, understanding all too well.

"My family roots," Purdy said softly, "include pirates. A fact of life for me, unfortunately. The way they tell it, all the sailors who were crewmembers of a ship called the *Black Rose*—this was way back before the Civil War began—they had to sign the Blackheart Compact. It meant they had to steal when they were told to, they had to take prisoners when they were told to, they had to murder when they were told to. And if they broke any of the rules, they were punished. The ultimate punishment was death. That was the only way to break the Compact."

"So these people still tell you what to do?"

He nodded. "If I don't do what they tell me, that's it! I'm a walking target right now."

"And this affects Jon Randolph and his family how?"

Purdy sighed deeply. "One of his ancestors signed the Compact. When the guy got married to an uptight, religious woman he tried to leave. The quartermaster didn't like it then, and he doesn't like it now. The Compact can't stand whole unless it is upheld by all the signers. At least that's what they tell us. They drum it in. Like gospel."

"Which ancestor?" Mac said, very softly, with a hint of retribution in his voice.

"A man named Isaac Preston."

"My father," Jeff whispered.

"Surely this man is dead by now?" Harris said.

"Yes, of course, but he had kin. Worse yet, one of Preston's kin killed another member of the Compact. That's a death sentence for the whole family."

"But the family survived?"

"The Preston who killed John Clint was a traitor to the Confederacy. But he was killed in the war, so the way they see it, justice was done there. And Isaac Preston's daughter, the last family member, disappeared. But then, years later, who should turn up but Jon Randolph, part of the family the Blackhearts thought had been wiped out. Worse yet, he was intervening in things that were none of his business. I guess the captain decided that in this day and age, with so much surveillance equipment and high-tech law enforcement, grabbing the family property was easier than killing an old man who was still improving the property, and should die soon anyway, although he sure took his time doing it, which I didn't mind," he added hastily, "because I really liked him. But they were getting impatient. Besides which, they're still looking for the diamond, or diamonds if it's been cut up."

"Diamond?"

Harris was trying hard, but the answers didn't make any sense. This man, Lorie thought, is either nuts or demented.

"I know this'll sound crazy to you, too, but it's what I've been told since I was a little boy," Purdy went on. "The diamond was ransom for a black slave who'd been a king. A big uncut diamond from South Africa. The Blackheart crew knew it had been sent by emissary from Africa, and they had proof it had reached the shores of this country. The guy who was captain of the Blackhearts at the time of the Civil War thought Preston had it and was holding out. Preston denied it. They didn't believe him.

"So when he wouldn't tell them anything, they killed him, which I always thought was a pretty stupid thing to do because a dead man can't tell you anything, period. But the quartermaster is sure it's somewhere on Jon Randolph's property because Randolph inherited all the Preston property. And that's why the captain went after Rolf Maratti. Maratti is adopted, so he's an outsider. In fact, he's Mafia-related, so they're keeping hands off, although I'm not so sure they'd be that kind with the soldier, at least not now since he escaped. But the captain thinks the diamond is hidden somewhere on or in Randolph property, and when he gets hold of the property, he'll search inch by inch until he finds it. It's probably worth twenty million by now."

"Who's the captain?" Harris asked, his voice deep with suppressed anger.

"No one but the members of the inner circle know that."

"And who are they?"

"No one knows that either. At least not me!"

Harris took a deep breath. "Un-be-liev-able!" he said, drawing out each syllable of the word.

"I know," Purdy said, "but these people think different, and they play by different rules. Always have. Always will."

"Not," Detective Macdonald said in a deep, slow cop voice, "if we can help it."

Harris looked at Purdy again. "Anything else we should know?"

Purdy shook his head. "I've been out of the loop since you took me away after the funeral. I'm sure they're planning something for the council meeting tonight, but I don't know what. I do know they carry concealed if that makes any difference anywhere anymore. So any metal detector at the courthouse in Randolph City will be disabled. Does that help?"

"Yep," Mac said. "Mr. Purdy, we understand it took a lot of guts for you to tell us all this. You have shown a great deal of bravery today. We thank you. And we'll do what we can for you."

The man slumped in his chair with an expression of sheer relief on his face. "Can I go back to my wife now? She's right upstairs, and she's terrified that we're going to be killed now that I've talked with you!"

Harris reached out to Purdy, took the man's hand with both of his, and held on to it. "Please reassure her we're still watching your backs and tell her that you both will be able to stay in protective custody as long as is necessary! We'll talk about future options, if you like."

Harris came into the observation room after Purdy left. "What do you think?" he asked them. He was still shaking his head.

"Offhand," Lorie said, a bit under her breath, "I'd say you have a good reason to call in the FBI."

"Mac is talking to them, even as we speak. They'll be with us at the courthouse tonight."

Randy had heard the conversation from the hall outside. When they finished discussing plans with Mac and Harris, he took his uncommonly quiet passengers to a local restaurant, where Mac caught up with them. Over a round of burgers and drinks, they finally were able to discuss the interview.

"Hard to believe we're dealing with pirates," Mac said, his voice almost a whisper.

Lorie wished Jeff would speak out, but he didn't seem to have a voice. "Apparently, they were slave traders during the Civil War era," she said into the silence, "and smugglers."

"And bushwhackers," Jeff added softly, finally saying, "Some of the people Purdy named were planters who owned the property surrounding Riverside Plantation. My...my ancestors were boxed in by them. No wonder Sara Preston's father was so ineffective. He couldn't back out of this... Compact, even if he wanted to. I had no idea."

"You saw this evil in the journals you've been reading?" Randy asked.

Jeff answered, "Sara Preston Randolph's journal is beginning to make a lot more sense to me now."

Arthur Ehrlich said, "It's a blessing to Rolf that they don't know of his genetic connection to Jon Randolph."

Maratti sighed. "I don't know if that relationship is a blessing or a curse now. Goddamn! I understand Purdy's dilemma all too well."

"I don't suppose either Jon Randolph or his grand-mother knew about the Compact," Lorie said.

"It seems," Ehrlich added, "our Mafia fabrication was helpful."

The law enforcement officers all chuckled. "Stick with it," Mac said, "as long as it works."

"And what about me?" Jeff said to Lorie when they were finally alone, back at the Baileys' house, talking quietly in the upstairs bedroom where Lorie had spent the previous night.

She grinned at him. "You died! Your screwy allegiance to any Compact is paid. And, Jeff, I'd say that goes for the rest of your family as well."

He reached for her and held her so tightly for a moment she could scarcely breathe. "You are life! My life!" His kiss was long and very erotic. Lorie turned the lock on the bedroom door, and the next hour, while immensely satisfying to herself and to the most unselfish man she had ever known, went far too quickly.

CHAPTER 23

T hen it was time to think about the council meeting. It was to start at seven that evening. Sue served a light dinner at five thirty, and at six thirty, Lorie, Jeff, Phil, and Carol, dressed as they had been for the meeting with the judge, left for the courthouse. They met Maratti and Ehrlich there, both clad again in sober business suits, and spoke briefly.

The city council convened in a good-sized room on the lower level of the big brick courthouse. Rows of folding chairs filled nearly two-thirds of the room. A long table had been set up on a platform at the front of the room. Five chairs at the table were designated for council members, and their nameplates were already in place. At the left end of the table was a separate chair for the mayor. A few city officials were located at a table located to the side, off the platform—city clerk, comptroller, city attorney.

Maratti and Ehrlich chose to sit at the back and on the opposite side of the room from the rest so as not to alert Compact members, wherever and whoever they might be, that a liaison had formed. The four Marietta lawmen, all in civilian business attire, arrived at various times: Randy, Tim, Mac and Harris were each accompanied by a well-built, well-dressed "friend." They took seats at random positions around the room.

"The feds are here," Lorie whispered to Carol, who nodded knowingly.

"More outside, I understand. Just in case."

Sid and Sue Bailey finally arrived with a few of their neighbors who had been informed that their presence might be necessary. The word had apparently been passed, as more and more people showed up. Soon the room was full. Standing room in the hallway outside the council room also began to fill. Looking at the Bailey contingent, Lorie noted that their son, Jim, had joined them, filling in the seat they had held for him. He sat next to his mother. Again, the resemblance to Jeff Preston was remarkable. Many people seemed to know him. They greeted him with handshakes or waves.

A few minutes past seven, several men in business attire, all wearing white shirts and ties, walked through a side door and mounted to their seats on the platform. The council was called to order by a bearded young man named Archie Hood. The pledge of allegiance was recited, a few announcements were made, and a local Boy Scout who had just been awarded his Eagle badge was given a hand.

Then Mayor Hood asked for Open Comments. It was obviously a pro forma request, and he didn't expect anyone to respond.

Dark glasses once more in place, Jeff stepped up to the microphone at the front of the room and said, "I have a comment." Everyone looked his way with surprise and there was a good deal of whispering. Lorie thought he looked quite professional in his blue suit and very handsome despite the eye-concealing shades. "I'm called Rich Jefferson," he began. "You may think I'm a stranger here, but relatives of mine used to live here a long time ago, and I visited frequently when I was very young. I love this town and would like to live here myself. But only if it stays exactly the way it is. Small. Friendly. Beautiful."

A deep quiet had come across the room. Jeff looked around. No one on the council platform challenged him to ask more specifically who he was, and in fact, had probably got some sense of his connection to the Baileys at the funeral, so he continued. "I've found"—he held it up—"an old notebook containing historical records of the people of this town. I'd like to read some of it to you, if you don't mind."

Mayor Hood smiled with a fair amount of surprise and nodded at him. The officials of the Chamber of Commerce, whom Carol had pointed out to Lorie, began to preen. Obviously the history of the town's accomplishments—the history, at least, not hidden by the fog of war—was its pride and joy.

Jeff opened the book. "This is an account of the activity of members of this community a few years back."

A few people started to whisper, but none of the men seated on the platform seemed disturbed. Lorie read the nameplates sitting on the table in front of each council member: Martin Dewey, George Garnett, Oliver Jennings, Sam McIntire, and Lyman Thomas. All were present.

"Let's start with the family of a friend of mine, Ginny Clark," she heard Jeff say. She saw him look around, saw recognition in his expression. The feisty little red-haired lady was located in the center of the room. Jeff asked her to stand up. She did, her face showing confusion and a little anxiety. He smiled at her. "Miz Ginny, I think it's time to fess up that your great-great-great-granddaddy was Ebenezer Clark." He held up the little book that was open in his hand. "There's a lot about Ebenezer in this book," he said. "Some people called him a conductor, but Ebenezer always said he was a guide. It was a difficult, dangerous job, but someone had to do it, and Ebenezer was one of most daring, courageous men in this small community back in those days before the Civil War. He managed to spirit many poor souls to the north along the Underground Railroad, and neither they nor he were ever caught. I understand he died in bed after living to a ripe old age, with the blessings on his white head of many lucky souls who were now living in freedom north of the Mason-Dixon line."

An undercurrent of surprised comment began to pass around the room. Ginny Clark sat down, looking a little stunned.

Jeff continued. "There were others on his team. Sam McIntire," he said to one of the council members sitting on the platform in front of him, a tall, rangy man with two-days growth of dark beard, "your great-great-great-grandfather, Elias, was another courageous member of Ebenezer's team of guides. He didn't lose a soul on those long, arduous journeys to the north. There were some close calls, but everyone made it over the border into the hands of the Abolitionists. And he always got back home to his large, loving family." McIntire's eyes grew large.

The undercurrent of comments from the assembled citizens grew stronger.

"These were the other members of that team." Jeff read off a list of about ten names. "Jones, Connor, Coshow…" As he read, the swell of voices increased. Jeff looked around and smiled. "Are any relatives of these people here tonight?" A number of people spoke out. "Stand up, why don't you?" Many people rose in their seats. "If you don't mind," he said, "would you all move over there to my left? Let's see how many of you are in the room."

Lorie noted a few people talking on their cell phones, and when she turned her head, she saw more townspeople coming into the room, some walking briskly to join the standing group at the left.

Again Jeff turned to the book. "Once the war began, there was a unit that was called the Eyes and Ears." Again an undercurrent of comment arose. "Citizens in that unit served on the front lines in the fight against slavery and disunion. They were, for lack of a better word, spies for the Union. Oliver Jennings?" He looked directly at the tall, lanky, bald man whose eyes, behind the glasses, reflected sudden shock. "Your great-great-great-granddaddy, Daniel, was one of the best spies in the group, followed closely by Michael Thomas." Again he looked up at the table on the platform, at the rotund, red-faced man labeled Lyman Thomas, who was seated at the opposite end of the table. Jeff turned back to the book and began to read more names aloud. "Murrow, Landry, Andrews...is there anyone here related to these brave men, and women, who by their activities risked hanging or worse? They were the bravest of the brave." Again hands went up and, surrounded by a soft babble of voices, a large group of people started moving to the side of the room, where already stood the descendants of the guides.

Lorie noticed more and more people coming into the council room. She saw cell phones in evidence, especially among the younger people.

Jeff grinned, pushed the dark glasses more securely up his nose, and looked around. "Then there were the Raiders. They operated in Confederate uniform, and if anyone had known they were other than what they appeared to be, they would have been shot in a minute." Another swell of exclamations erupted. "These were the men who rode with Major Preston and Master Sergeant Ben Ross. Martin Dewey,

George Garnett," he said, looking up at the two council members who had not yet been named, "you share a great-great-great-granddaddy, Barton Thompson. He was a reckless son of a gun, and he always got exactly what he was going after. He was one of the most valued members of that brave bunch of selfless men who fed the people of these hills while war was swirling around them." Again Jeff read off names. And many more excited people rose and moved to his left. In fact, Lorie saw with surprise, three-quarters of the many seats in the hall were already empty. To her left stood a burgeoning crowd, people murmuring among themselves, eagerly comparing notes. The crowd spilled outward to the entry hallway, where Lorie saw more people coming into the building.

"Your ancestors," Jeff said quietly in his slow Southern way, and again the room became quiet, "made this town what it is. The headquarters of all this activity was called Oak Hill Plantation. It is now called Randolph House. Do you really want that symbol of everything your ancestors stood for to be destroyed?"

"Who said Randolph House was going to be destroyed?" someone called out. Another voice said, "George? Martin? Who's gonna take down Randolph House?" The reply was loud, ragged at first, and then a solid cry. "Nobody's gonna take down Randolph House!"

Among the still-occupied seats were the developers. Lorie saw them staring at Jeff Preston with raw hatred in their eyes. Clint Samuels was there. So was Ernest Merrill. And the quartermaster, whatever that was, Johnny McDaniels. A few more—big men, well dressed, all glum, some obviously simmering with anger—were clearly trying to figure out the identity of the tall man in the blue suit standing at the microphone.

Judge Cragin was sitting alone, his face emotionless. He looked around him, saw Lorie and her aunt, and turned away.

Jeff looked around the room. "Anyone else?"

"I don't have a dog in this fight," someone said. He was a small man with large glasses and a full head of dark hair. "I'm just an artist." He nodded at Jeff. "I think I'm going over there, though. It looks like they're having more fun." A large number of nodding, smiling people got up and followed him across the room.

Lorie spotted Ewen Taylor sitting in the back row, leaning back in his chair, grinning. He was thoroughly enjoying himself.

Mayor Hood came down from the podium to talk with Jeff. "Is there anything about my family in the book?" Lorie heard him say quietly.

Jeff replied in an equally soft voice, "I think your great-great-great-granddaddy tried not to take sides, Mayor."

"I was afraid of it," Hood appeared crestfallen. "Our family was kind of shunned while I was growing up. My daddy left because of it. I decided to come back and see what I could do to restore our honor."

"I'm sure you'll be able to do that very well." Jeff's voice was gentle. "You've taken a big step just by getting involved."

"We won't let them have the properties," Hood told him forcefully. "I don't think there's anyone in town who'll vote to change the zoning. Maybe some newcomers who don't know the history. You know, I'd really like to see that book you were reading from."

Jeff shoved the glasses up on his nose again as he handed the book to the mayor. He was smiling. "It's written in code. Kind of hard to make out. I've been studying it carefully."

"Who did it belong to?" Mayor Hood asked, passing it back into Jeff's hands.

"Major Jefferson Preston."

Hood's eyes opened wide. "He's always been my hero. I just wish my great-great-great-granddaddy had ridden with him. I would have!"

"And he would have welcomed you." Jeff clapped him on the shoulder.

The exchange was overheard by Judge Cragin, who turned to watch them, his face impassive.

Lorie looked around to see Rolf Maratti and Arthur Ehrlich sitting quietly in the back of the room. Lorie wondered if they were intimidated by the block of builders sitting at the front of the room and then realized by the studied lack of expression on both faces that they were simply biding their time.

"Is there still going to be a meeting tonight?" Jeff asked Mayor Hood.

"Oh golly, yes!" The mayor strode back up to the podium. He banged the gavel several times, but the sound was drowned out by excited voices coming from even more people pouring into the meeting room. He turned up the sound system and got a squeal, which brought people's attention to the council members, still sitting at their table, talking among themselves.

"We were going to discuss changing the zoning in this town to allow historic properties to be taken," Mayor Hood reminded everyone. "Can I get a vote on whether anyone's in favor of doing that? All in favor?"

Only the builders held up their hands, and since they weren't residents of the town, that didn't count.

"How about a vote against?" Mayor Hood said and didn't have to wait for an answer. Hands went up all over the room, with a great roar of approval. "Then I think we don't have to proceed," the mayor said. "Meeting adjourned." He banged the gavel.

"Wait just a minute," one of the builders said loudly. It was the big man who liked cigars, Johnny McDaniels. He stepped up onto the platform. "We've got someone else here who might like to have a say in this matter." He looked toward the back of the room, at Rolf Maratti and Arthur Ehrlich, sitting silently side by side. "Mr. Maratti. What's your vote on this issue?"

Rolf Maratti stood up, more dignified than he had ever appeared before. "Mr. McDaniels," he said in a strong voice. "I'm not a registered voter of this community. But if I were, my vote would be with the majority!" He turned to leave, and the crowd roared even louder.

CHAPTER 24

s Archie Hood came back across the room, Jeff stopped him. "Mayor Hood," he said deferentially to the young man, "do you have any idea who owns the roll-top desk that's sitting upstairs in the courtroom?"

"Sure, It's Judge Cragin's desk. It's a beauty, isn't it?"

"It is," Jeff agreed. "But are you aware that it's civil war contraband?"

Lorie saw Cragin swivel around to follow the conversation. There was a scowl on his face. "What makes you think so?" He rose to his feet.

Jeff turned to face him. "Because that's where I found this book I'm holding in my hand."

The judge looked as if he might explode. Some of the builders were alerted to the rising voices. "You opened my desk?"

"No. There is a hidden panel in the desk. That's where I found it."

"Prove it! Prove it!" Cragin headed out of the room, looking back at Jeff, who fell into step close behind.

"Don't go," Lorie said softly. Fear crept over her, frozen fingers playing down her spine. She got up to follow but was pushed rudely out of the way by several of the builders headed up the steps behind Cragin and Jeff. She heard Carol's voice at her elbow.

"We can't let him be pinned in by those guys!"

They followed the men up the steps into the lobby of the courthouse and then into the courtroom, where sat the roll top desk.

The crowd surrounding Jeff and Cragin consisted primarily of people self-identified as builders, but Lorie saw, pushing up behind her, at least two of the men she had tagged as Federal agents. Randy and Mac were also pressuring their way through the crowd.

"Now show me where you found that book." Cragin's voice was deep and angry.

Lorie saw Jeff crouch, as he had before, to open the panel at the rear of the kneehole of the desk. "It was here." Securing the dark glasses once more, he held the solid wooden panel as he stood up and pointed into the darkness. Randy had finally made his way through to Jeff's side. He crouched down under the desk and, with some effort, because it had adhered to the interior wall through long years of humidity and heat, peeled away the third gray journal, companion to the two Jeff had retrieved earlier. "Here." He handed it to Jeff, who in turn passed it into Judge Cragin's hands.

There was no expression on the man's face. He looked down at the journal. "So what?"

"Open it," Jeff said.

"Go ahead," someone behind him said. "Open it."

Reluctantly he did so.

"Read what's there, right at the top of the first page," another voice called out. This time it was Sid Bailey. "If you don't, I will."

"It's dated 1862."

"And what's that other word?"

"Riverside."

"Riverside Plantation," Sid Bailey repeated loudly so everyone could hear. "Down on the Chattahoochee. It was burned by Southern bushwhackers in July 1864. This piece of furniture was stolen from the house before it was burned, and everyone who lived there was murdered in cold blood."

"How do you know?" the man called Ernest Merrill called out. He was Ernie to Will Purdy, Lorie thought. His cousin. A member of the Compact.

"Because of a journal." Little Sue Bailey pushed her way forward to stand beside her husband. "The journal of Sara Preston Randolph Manning, who lived at Riverside Plantation when she was a child. The roll-top desk was made for her father by her brother, Major Jefferson Richard Preston."

"Who was a traitor!" yelled one of the other men, the one named Clint Samuels. "He dressed as a Confederate, but he was a spy for the Union." When he heard the angry growl emanating from the surrounding crowd and concluded his sentiment wouldn't make much traction in a town that had always sympathized with the Union cause, he shut his mouth and took a few steps back.

"Where did you find this journal?" the judge asked.

"At Randolph House," Sue answered. "It's part of the legacy of Randolph House, and this furniture should be as well."

"It's mine," the judge said firmly. "I bought it, and I have a receipt for it. And you..." He turned to Jeff. "Who exactly are you? Where did you come from? What's your connection to this town?"

Jeff ignored the question. "May I see the receipt, please?"

"It's in my chambers. Come on in, and I'll show you."

"Don't go in there, Jeff," Lorie said under her breath, trying to work her way through arms, shoulders, and chests, to get closer to him. The courtroom was becoming more and more crowded. He and Cragin were moving toward the door. She wished she could just scream it out. But she was working with him. This was what he had come to do.

"Sandy Cragin," Sue Bailey called out in a final reckless attempt to keep the men from disappearing into the other room. "We'd like you to prove you're not involved in some kind of criminal conspiracy to take Randolph House away from us."

Lorie saw one of the men near her draw a small gun and aim it. Carol saw it too and stepped in front of her cousin. The *crack* reverberated throughout the room, and Carol went down. The crowd separated as she fell. Blood began to spread across her white shirt, her sleeve. Phil Barnett was with Carol in an instant, kneeling beside her. He looked around at Lorie. "I'll take care of her," he mouthed to her. "Get Jeff."

The attention of everyone in the room was focused in silent shock on Carol and the doctor kneeling over her. Frantically searching the crowd, Lorie saw Jeff following Cragin through the doorway to the judge's chambers.

Lorie pushed her way through stunned onlookers toward the chamber door and entered. A dark opulent room—she saw only one thing! Positioned between two windows, framed by heavy draperies, stood a tall floor vase covered from top to bottom with exquisite paintings of African animals. Jeff had whipped off his dark glasses. His eyes were also focused on the vase. He moved toward it, stood before it, and whirled to face the judge with fury written across his face.

Cragin jerked open his desk drawer, pulled from it an antique pistol—pointed at Jeff. "You left us before we could find out how good a job the Army had done on that nose and your cheek once the bandages came off! Somebody got a little cute with the peroxide, too, didn't they? Did they think it would make you disappear into the woodwork? Well, the eyes have it this time, Major Maratti. No mistaking those baby blues. Your grandfather loses this game!" He pulled the trigger. The sound was like a cannon, leaving Lorie's ears ringing.

Jeff dropped. The vase exploded. Diamond jewelry tumbled from it, bouncing in every direction. Lorie recognized a necklace as it skidded across the polished wooden floor, the one Maria Maratti had been wearing when her portrait was painted. She saw blood spreading away from under Jeff. He tried for a moment to push himself up. He looked at her, longing and farewell in his beautiful eyes.

Another gunshot resounded through the small room. Jeff's arm flung outward, and his body skidded across the floor. His head bounced hard off a heavy sideboard. His eyes closed.

Lorie looked around frantically. Too late, Johnnie McDaniels, the quartermaster, was being handcuffed by Federal officers who had forcibly removed a small gun from his hand. Sudden activity erupted at the back of the room and in the courtroom outside. Loud voices. People being asked to leave. All the extraneous noise faded from Lorie's senses as she focused laser-like on what she now had to do.

Kneeling at Jeff's side, working with concentrated precision, she pulled his jacket down his arms and jerked it out from under him, then loosened and threw aside his tie. Without hesitation, she ripped his shirt and white T-shirt apart to get to his chest. She grabbed a pillow from a nearby settee and shoved it under his knees to raise them against the flow of blood. "Not high enough," she murmured and grabbed for the companion cushion.

"They're priceless antiques," someone screamed. She looked up, straight into the eyes of Judge Sandy Cragin. His arms were already pinned behind him by one of the Federal officers. His face was distorted by an emotion she couldn't even fathom.

"Tough!" she said coldly and dragged the second cushion through pooling blood before shoving it under Jeff's knees. "Get me some scissors," she barked to the person whose legs had just come up beside her. Randy. He handed her a knife, and she set to work. She saw the bloody wounds on Jeff's left shoulder and chest. She knew these wounds too well. Quickly she tied off the shoulder wound with a portion of his T-shirt, saying grimly, "You're not dying of these suckers on my watch, Jeff Preston." She looked up into the few faces that still surrounded her, even as she sensed movement of people being evacuated from the building. "I need packing. Towels. Or clean shirts."

Randy shucked out of his jacket and slipped off his tie, then his shirt, which he folded quickly, and handed to her. She held the bundle tightly against Jeff's gaping wound. "More. And call an ambulance."

"Already called." Randy slipped his jacket back on over his undershirt. "Carol's down, too. But she's going to be okay. It's her shoulder. Clean wound."

He handed her another shirt, one that had been handed to him. Blue. Then another. White. And another. Red. She packed them against the chest wound as best she could, trying desperately to stem the heavy flow. A plaid wool shirt came into her hands.

She sniffed at it, looked up into the face of a redheaded teenager she had seen before. Micah Clark. He seemed chagrined. She smiled gently and handed it back, saying softly, "Thanks!" Another shirt quickly replaced it.

Jeff's face was white and unresponsive. She checked his eyeballs. They were beginning to roll back into the sockets. "He's dying." She turned to Randy. "Hold the pack tight against his side. I'll try resuscitation." She cleaned out the blood welling in his mouth, leaned over him, blocked his nostrils, put her lips across his, and began to blow. Over again and over again she gave him her breath, let him exhale, again and again and again, until finally he was breathing, albeit shakily, on his own.

"He needs blood." Rolf Maratti was kneeling beside her now, his voice reedy and anxious. "He's so white."

She heard Phil Barnett's voice calling from the other room. "Have the hospital put out an immediate call for donors. He's got a rare type, O negative."

"That's my type." Maratti looked at Lorie, startled. "That's my type! I have some blood stored for situations just like this, but here I am. Can someone do a person-to-person transfusion?"

Ewen Taylor had come up behind Maratti. "I've got the helicopter on the way. My pilot was a battlefield paramedic. We have an emergency kit aboard the copter. I'll fly. He can do the transfusion. I've already notified the hospital that we'll be there as soon as we can."

"Ask people if they'll clear out of the parking lot," Lorie called out. Micah Clark had been lingering in a dark corner of the room. His face lit up. Calling out orders to his friends, he ran outside, plaid shirttails flapping.

"Randy," Lorie said. "Have you secured the diamonds? Did you get those men?"

"The diamonds are safe, kiddo," he told her gently. "And the Feds and state troopers are rounding up a lot of people. Cragin's headed to lock up. So is McDaniels. And the guy who shot Carol. And everyone who came into this building armed. Including some local police officers. We'll sort them all out later."

Taylor had left the room. He returned a moment later. "The chopper is almost here, Lorie. It won't be long."

"We've got to take Jeff out very carefully without jarring him. We don't have a gurney."

"We have a door," she heard Mac say. He and Harris had removed one of the closet doors in Cragin's office. It was laying on the floor.

"Four strong guys," Lorie said, getting to her feet. "Make sure he's not jiggled. I've got the pack secured with the sleeves of someone with very long arms."

"We'll lift him onto this oriental rug," Mac said, "and from there to the door. Come on, guys, let's get him outside. I can hear that chopper."

She went with them down a short flight of stairs and out the big doors of the courthouse into a warm summer night filled with the sound of a helicopter's whirling blades. The parking lot was illuminated by a brilliant light descending from above. It had been emptied of cars and people in record time. But everyone who had come to the courthouse was still there, waiting, silent, hair whipped by the wind of the rotors. The many flashing red and blue lights around the perimeter of the courthouse illustrated how serious law enforcement had considered this confrontation to be.

With skilled expertise, Ewen Taylor's pilot put the large chopper down in the middle of the lot. Taylor and Maratti got in first and helped the others move the makeshift stretcher into position. "Ready to go." Lorie couldn't hear Taylor's voice over the whopping sound, but she could see his lips moving. She waved. Moments later, the helicopter lifted off. Flashing red lights receded into the night. She watched until she couldn't see it anymore.

She turned back to the courthouse. Even after the thump of the blades had faded away, she heard nothing. Her mind focused entirely on her beloved husband. Would she ever see those beautiful eyes again? Feel his strong arms around her? This time she thought not. He had done what he had come to do—unmask the evil that had tried to destroy his family, the town and the people he had loved and admired, the way of life he lived for. There was such a lump in her throat she could hardly swallow.

Randy touched her arm. "Lorie, what should we do now?"

She looked at him, surprised. "What do you mean?"

"You're in charge of this operation."

"I am?"

He laughed. "You've been throwing out orders right and left, Babe. I've never seen you like this."

"Where's Carol?"

"Inside, with Phil. He says it's not too bad as gunshots go. Nothing vital hit. But I know from experience that gunshots aren't fun. She's a very brave lady, your aunt. You, too, kiddo!"

"Let's check out the judge's chambers," she said. "There's something there I very much want to see before we go."

He accompanied her through the building and into the chamber where Jeff had gone down. Federal agents had put "CRIME SCENE" tape across the doorways. They ducked under the tape to get in and turned on all the lights. The large room had been tastefully furnished with antiques of every sort. The desk, the chairs, the long sideboard on which sat wine and liquor bottles, and every variety of glass. Lorie pointed to what was left of the shattered vase. "It was beautiful, Randy. Jeff told me he wanted me to have it if we ever found it."

"It was pretty spectacular, wasn't it? I only caught a glimpse."

She walked to the place where it had stood. A spotlight had been directed toward it. She turned the switch, and light flooded the area. All that remained of a major work of art was its heavy base. The rest was lying in shards around the room. Much like the monument at Randolph House, she thought.

She picked up a piece. On it was painted with a deft hand a dainty likeness of an African gazelle. She shook her head at the loss.

Again she looked at the base. Something had caught her eye, a glint within, a faint sparkle. One of Maria's jewels must have lodged there. She bent down to look, scraped at the clay with her fingernail, and then sat down suddenly on the floor.

Instantly Randy was at her side. "What's wrong?"

"Look." She picked up his knife, dropped thoughtlessly in the intensity of an earlier moment, and scraped away more of the heavy clay. Another sparkle. And another.

"It's a big diamond," Randy whispered. "A great big diamond. A cluster of diamonds—Lorie!"

"The captain of the Blackheart wanted his Zulu diamond," she said. "Randy, he had it. Here it is. Moses fired it into his gift to Sara. He didn't want to be set free, because he was already free. He had never been a slave. He was working with Jeff, and probably Isaac, to set others free." She remembered the black man's smile and his blessing and knew she was right.

She stood up. She looked back at the place where Jeff had fallen. Remembered his body stretched out, the light fading from his eyes. The floor was dark with spilled blood, his blood. "Not now!" she said. "Please not now!" Her knees buckled. Her eyes clouded. Everything went black.

This time when she awoke, it was Randy holding her as he had the first day she had met him. She turned her face into the rough fabric of his jacket, hung on to him, and started to bawl.

"It's all right, kiddo." He cradled her tight, rocking her. "It's all right, honey. Let's get you out of here. The emergency people are done with Carol, and the doctor is taking her to the hospital in Marietta where Jeff is. Let's get you into the car, too. You hit the edge of that sideboard on the way down, and your forehead is bleeding like crazy. Here." He dug into his pocket and brought out a white handkerchief. "Hold this on the cut." He helped her to her feet. "God, you're gonna have a hell of a headache tomorrow."

His strong arm around her, Randy helped her move through the throng of people still milling around outside the office. "Wait, Phil," he called out to the doctor as they went out the door and down to the parking lot. "Another patient coming through." Phil Barnett had brought the Town Car up to the building. Carol was already in the front seat, wrapped in bandages. Phil got out and opened the backdoor for Lorie. She climbed in, still feeling woozy. Randy folded into the back seat beside her and put his arm around her, saying soothing words.

"What happened to her?" Carol's anxious voice.

"She passed out," Randy said, "and hit her head on the sideboard in Cragin's office. She's got blood all over her. First from Jeff, now from her own forehead. Relax, Lorie," he said. "We'll get you to the hospital. You can sit beside Jeff, kiddo. For better or worse, you'll be there with him."

The doctor exceeded every speed limit getting to the hospital in Marietta. In the front passenger seat, Lorie's aunt was trying very hard not to cry. Lorie had already lost that battle. She didn't know if she would ever stop crying.

At the hospital, Phil Barnett whisked Carol off one direction while Randy aimed Lorie toward the emergency room. "It's going to leave a scar, I expect," he said to her later as she lay on an examination table covered by a warm blanket. Her forehead had just acquired several stitches, set in place by a competent woman doctor who didn't even smile when Lorie told her how it had happened.

Lorie looked up into Randy's kind gray eyes. "Can you find out if he's still alive?"

"Already did, Lorie. He's had emergency surgery, with some more scheduled. He's still alive, but he's not anywhere near out of danger. He's sleeping, drug induced. Do you want to see him?"

She nodded, very carefully.

He was in a room in the intensive care unit, surrounded by life-support devices—tubes, wires, monitors. His eyes were closed, his color looked much better, but she saw a pack of blood being infused into his vein and knew that accounted for the pink flush in his cheeks. Randy stood beside her, his hand on her shoulder. "What a brave man," he said. "I just knew he was Jeff Maratti. I don't believe in coincidences."

"Jeffrey Maratti?" She stared at Randy.

"Everything came back as a fit. Fingerprints. Finally. The first time they tried it, they didn't find the match. But we checked with the army, and they confirmed. The DNA double-check? We had to pull in a lot of favors to get it so quick. But it was the blood type that sealed the deal right off the bat. It's Maratti all right. The same blood type as his grandpa. The boots were the only anomaly. They were Major Preston's boots.

"Jeff really did find the Major's grave, Lorie. It saved his life because then he was able to climb out of the ravine and find his dark-haired angel." He smiled at her gently, and tears came to her eyes. Randy went on softly, "Now that we know Rolf was Mr. Jon's true son, it's no stretch that our Jeff looked so much like that painting of Major Preston. Someone must have bleached his hair to keep him from being recognized."

She looked back at the man lying in the bed. Although it was difficult to see his features clearly through the respirator, there seemed to be only a few differences from the Jeff she had come to know so intimately. His hair was darker at the roots than she had noticed before. His nose looked the same, she thought. There were new scars on his face. The rest would have to wait.

Would he remember her when he woke up? If he woke up.

She wanted to weep again, but now was not the time. She and Randy returned to the waiting room where Rolf Maratti sat, exhausted and worried. He looked up. "Thank you for saving his life, Lorie."

She put out her hands to him. She couldn't keep the tears from streaming down her face now. Her white slacks were soaked in his grandson's blood. He rose and pulled her into a tight embrace. "We've saved him, you and I," he said softly, into her ear alone. "I know what you're thinking. I don't understand it, but I don't doubt that he was for a time exactly who he told us he was. We'll know in good time, you and I, who he is now."

Arthur Ehrlich came into the room with two coffee cups and handed one to Maratti. "Miss Lorie," he said, "do you want anything? Officer Ross?"

She shook her head, as did Randy, who found a chair and sat down. She sat beside him and mopped the tears away from her eyes. They waited. It was all they could do.

More people came into the waiting room. Sue and Sid Barnett came, with Sue weeping copiously into a large handkerchief. "Carol could have died," she kept saying. "Damn those people to hell! Damn them, damn them, damn them! The bastards! The bloody shitty bastards!"

"It's okay," her husband said. "Honey, you were so brave! It could have been you!"

They saw Lorie and came to her. Both hugged her tightly. "He's got to be okay," Sue said. "You kept him alive during those first golden minutes, Lorie. That's got to count for something."

"And now we know who he is," Ewen Taylor said, coming up to them. "He's the soldier they kidnapped. He's Rolf's grandson. What a brave, talented guy. Look, Lorie, we'll do everything we can to bring him back to you and to Rolf. If there's anything at all you need..."

"Thank you," she said to him, looking up, and for the first time he noticed the bandage on her forehead.

"What the hell happened to you?"

"I faint," she said, "in times of stress."

He looked at her, startled, and then let out a booming laugh, causing everyone in the room to look around. "You faint? Well, I must say, you make sure to take care of business first. I guess you're entitled to a little faint. But you shouldn't hit sharp objects on the way down. Does it hurt?"

"Pretty much," she said, touching it, suddenly realizing she really did have a hell of a headache!

CHAPTER 25

Saturday, July 26, 2014

They waited all night and most of the next day. Part of the time Lorie sat beside Carol's hospital bed. Her aunt was in a great deal of pain but didn't want anyone to know. Chiding gently, Lorie called for a nurse and made sure her aunt took an appropriate painkiller. "Go back and see how he's doing," Carol told her impatiently. "I'll still be here when you get back, honey." As Lorie was walking out, Carol called out to her. "Lorie your folks are on their way. I think my brother is going to beat me up on this one."

Lorie laughed in spite of herself. "Let's just tell him we're both big girls now, and we kind of knew what we were doing."

She went back to the ICU waiting room. Other people came in and out, law enforcement people including Alan Macdonald, Dean Harris, and Tim Murphy, all concerned, almost teary-eyed, but alternately excited about their haul. "A major bust, Lorie," Mac said. "These guys are into so much corruption it almost boggles the mind. Completely unknown to us until now. Bigger than the Latino gangs and the black street gangs. Drugs, stolen goods of all kinds, kidnappings, construction site intimidation—you name it, they're into it.

We got a lot of 'em cold this time. Not all of them, more's the pity. But these on-site folks? Hands in the cookie jar!"

She tried to smile. Still her protector, unwilling to leave her side, Randy beamed.

"How is he?" Tim Murphy asked.

Randy answered, "He went through another operation this afternoon, to repair bone and tissue that was damaged by that damned minie ball. Thank goodness the powder had degraded. If it hadn't, Jeff would have died on the spot."

Dean Harris exploded with rage. "What the hell is someone doing with minie balls in this day and age?"

"Cragin was a collector. Civil War stuff."

"I hope they throw the book at him," Harris said.

"More so," Tim said, "because he's been pretending to be an officer of the court."

Lorie thought about it. "He wasn't pretending unless he made the original judge sick in order to get the position."

Randy said thoughtfully, "We might want to look into that, too."

"But it was so…useless. He was a successful lawyer. He was successful as an architect doing historical reconstructions, a respected member of society. What more did he need?"

"He was," Mac reminded her, "a member of the Blackheart Compact. It was his duty to do as he was told, no matter his obligations to a greater society."

That was a sobering thought. Were there other Compact members somewhere operating under the same vows of allegiance to evil? Her head throbbed as she thought about it. Quickly she pushed all thoughts of the Compact to the back of her mind.

Dr. Phil Barnett walked into the waiting room. "Any word?" Mac asked.

"They took the respirator away," the doctor answered.

"He's dying!" Lorie's voice rose.

"No, honey. No. He's doing better. They've got good docs here. Would you like to see him?"

She nodded. He motioned to all of them to join him. "Be as quiet as you can," Phil said. "He's sleeping naturally." He paused for a moment. "You have to remember, folks, when Jeff left that vehicle out on the highway a week ago, he was a brain-injured patient with post-traumatic stress disorder. The docs at the rehab center tell me he'd had little to no idea where he was, or even who he was, for months. They're shocked he's been so highly functional in the time he's been with us. They're thinking maybe the violence of his capture, and then the physicality of his escape did something in the interior of his brain that brought it back into a workable range for a time. But that progress may not last. You've got to be prepared. One way or other, we may have lost the Jeff we've known so well for the last week."

"That would be a damn shame!" Mac rumbled.

They walked into the hospital room. Rolf Maratti was standing by the bed looking down at his grandson, still attached to monitors and IVs. His Jeff was lying quiet, eyes closed, breathing with the help of a small split oxygen tube inserted into his nostrils.

Maratti was silent for a time. "I'm his grandfather," he said softly, "and I didn't recognize him. But I should have, and I should have insisted that he stay away from that meeting. There were assassins in every aisle."

"It was his show," Mac said. "How could you tell him not to be there? Don't blame yourself, Rolf. Jeff turned that whole situation around in a heartbeat. He knew what was at stake and he was courageous enough to take the chance."

"What his family has been dealing with the past few months," Maratti answered, "was a young man who couldn't speak, could barely walk. It was hard for him to hold up his head. The same blast that injured his brain also broke several bones in his face. They were being repaired. He was snatched from the hospital before the bandages had even been removed." He turned to Lorie. "How was I to know this athletic, articulate young man was the same person I had cried over at the rehab hospital? How did Cragin know who he was if I didn't?"

"I've thought about that." Lorie looked up at Maratti. "I understand Cragin was a good friend of your father, Rolf. He had probably met your grandson when he was visiting here. Maybe more than once. The face may be somewhat different now. But the eyes…"

He nodded, understanding, and sighed deeply. "His parents are on their way. I'll go wait for them outside, with Art."

"A good soldier. A great man," Randy said. He put a hand on the sleeping man's right shoulder.

Mac, Dean Harris, and Tim Murphy all clasped Jeff's uninjured shoulder in the same fashion and then left the room, allowing Lorie to be alone with him.

"Hi, Jeff," she said to the almost familiar face. "Are you still here, my darling? I need you back." Tears started to pool in her eyes. "If you're Jeff Maratti and if we're not married anymore, I guess I can live with that. But if you're still my Jeff, I really need to talk with you."

She turned to walk out.

"Where's my kiss, wife?" It was no more than a whisper.

She whirled around. Jeff Maratti might look a little different from his birth family. But aside from some additional scarring on his face, he didn't look that much different to her. His beautiful blue eyes were open. He smiled.

There was no mistaking his smile.

CHAPTER 26

When at last he managed to lift his heavy eyelids, Preston saw electric lights above him and was thoroughly confused as to where he might be. In a dream, he had been having a companionable chat with another young man named Jeff, a rather insistent person. Their far-ranging conversation had ebbed and flowed. But he thought at last he was beginning to see the logic of the other Jeff's arguments, unimaginable as those arguments had first sounded to him.

He wasn't sure where he was. Tubes were attached to his arms. Wires seemed to surround him. Gauges above him tracked his heartbeat. Feeling returned with the pain in his chest. It hit him hard. But pain, he realized with sudden splendor, meant life! He could scarcely believe it. He was in a hospital. The last thing he remembered clearly before the dream was being ambushed in the judge's office, bullets exploding into his body.

Then he heard her voice. His Lorie. She was here. Tears came to his eyes as he caught a glimpse of her through partially lifted lids. Her dear sweet face. It looked worn out, dreadfully tired. She would never be considered a classic beauty. The beauty she had was far more desirable, the kind that would last through the years, coming as it did from deep inside her soul. It rose through her enthusiasm, her sense of humor, and her grasp of all that was important to being human. The way her eyes lit when she saw him or when she was helping him with a problem. That funny little grin she'd give him when they were sharing a secret. The rapture that transformed her when they were making love. Her body was perfect, would always be perfect. She was undoubtedly the most beautiful woman he had ever known. His wife! How could he have been so lucky?

Why did she look so bereft? She turned to leave.

He didn't want her to go. He tried to speak. He needed to feel her lips on his. To his ears, the words sounded like nothing more than a croak. But she whirled about, held out her arms, and came back. She touched him very softly with gentle fingers as if he might break. Then he saw the bandage on her forehead.

"Lorena," he whispered as she bent to brush his forehead with her gentle lips, "were you shot?"

She grinned sheepishly. "I saw your blood and hit something on the way down. We have matching scars."

He wanted to laugh. The attempt ended in a groan. She put her cool hand on his forehead. "You're hurting, love. Maybe not the right time for humor." She was correct, as usual.

"Is my grandfather outside?" he asked her then. "I must speak with him."

"Your grandfather?"

"I'll explain."

She disappeared and came back a moment later with Rolf Maratti, who was smiling and crying at the same time.

"Jeff, Jeff, you're back!" The man leaned over him, stroking his forehead, touching his shoulder, his arm, wanting to hold him, to hug him, not knowing how through all the tubes and wires. "Your parents are on their way. They'll be here very soon. We've all been so worried about you."

"Grandpa…" It was a different voice now, a different cadence, a Northern accent, coming from somewhere inside, somewhere very deep, through his mind, but not of his mind. The other Jeff. The one he'd been arguing with. Yes, it was better if the other Jeff explained his position. "I'm tired." He knew this was going to be very hard for the much-loved grandfather to hear.

Maratti fell silent.

"I've seen too much," the other Jeff said. "I've done things I didn't want to do. I can't stay, Grandpa. If I stay, this body, this mind, will be my prison." He saw the smile fade on the beloved face looking down at him.

"Are you dying?"

"I'm waiting for another chance. A fresh start."

"Jeff…"

Preston took over as the other presence shifted, momentarily fading. "He's been a soldier too long, Rolf." He cleared his throat, and his voice strengthened. "He is a genuinely good person. He says he has seen too much, followed too many unconscionable orders. His brain has been damaged by blows of many kinds. If he stays, he will be trapped in a shell, a burden for caregivers and for himself."

"Major?" Maratti lifted his head sharply.

"Yes, Rolf. I am here. We are both still here. He has allowed me access to memories which I can use to give comfort to his parents. And to his grandfather. Your Jeff wants you to know how much he loves you. But…he feels…to stay would be intolerable. He is asking your forgiveness and your blessing."

Maratti stood with bowed head for several minutes, then looked back at the beloved face of his grandson. "It really is your body, isn't it, my boy?"

"It's my body, Grandpa," the other Jeff said. "But I need to go. Major Preston comes from a different place. He's strong enough to rebuild what needs to be healed, and if the Compact raises its ugly head again, he is the one who can beat it down."

"But only if you are willing," Preston said softly to the good man looking down at him. "The decision is yours."

Rolf Maratti bowed his head and closed his eyes, tears streaming down his cheeks. Lorie put her arms around his shoulders, crying with him. Finally, he turned back to the bed. "I must honor my grandson's wishes," he said. "Art will know, of course, and Lorie."

"Thank you, Grandpa," Jeff Maratti said.

"His life force," Preston then said to the two anxious faces above him, "is still here but fragile, awaiting a fresh start." He smiled gently at Lorie. And then at Rolf Maratti. "What do you say, both of you, to a fat little baby? It's what he most wants."

His Lorie grabbed a tissue and wiped at her eyes. A sparkling smile emerged.

"A great-grandson?" The glimmer of a smile appeared through Rolf's tears. "Named Jeff, for his father? With a refreshed life spirit? That wonderful boy can start over again? Lorie?"

"I am quite in tune with this solution," Lorie said to the grandfather, who gave her a tight hug. Then purposefully leaving them alone to talk, he excused himself to go find his friend, Art. Maratti's mood, Preston knew, was in agony but hopeful. Bittersweet, entirely appropriate. Perhaps this would work after all.

"Everyone will be coming in to see you." He felt the touch of Lorie's cool fingers on his lips. She was still wearing the clothes she had put on for the council meeting. He didn't know how many hours, days ago, that had been. Everything was stained with blood, her white trousers, her colorful shirt. Even the bandage on her forehead.

With all that, she never looked more desirable to him. "Before they come back in, my darling," she said softly now, "there are a couple of things I really must talk with you about."

"What is so important, my love?"

She smiled at him. A hopeful smile. "Randy and I found Moses's diamond."

He spoke as firmly as he could. "Moses would not lie to me. He told me…"

"The truth, Jeff. Moses told you the truth. Your father never received the diamond because it was delivered to Moses by someone loyal to him. And Moses, in turn, fired it into the base of the African vase he gave to Sara on her birthday."

"The ancestor vase?"

"If that's what you call the big vase the Compact stole from her home. To possess it, the Blackhearts would have had to destroy a priceless work of art."

As he thought about it in all its implications, a smile grew and blossomed into a laugh. Wasn't that just like Moses! He could see the broad slow grin now as Moses was thinking about it, white teeth contrasting with that beautiful black face. He had learned that very kind of deviousness at Moses's knee. His beloved mentor had been the master of more than one craft.

Then another notion struck him. He frowned. "Why? With that diamond, Moses could have finally gone home. He'd been away for far too long!"

Lorie put a finger to his lips. "He had another mission far more important to him. Freeing his people from slavery. Besides the other thing."

He frowned. "What other thing?"

"He would have had to leave you and Sara. You were his family, too, Jeff."

He lay silent for a time, stunned. But he knew she was speaking the obvious truth—so obvious he had missed it! "What a rare human being he was."

"If you like, husband, we can bury the diamond with all the broken pieces of the vase under the new monument to the Major, to keep it away from them forever. Randy and I are the only ones who know about it. And we are sworn to secrecy."

He realized again why his love for this woman was so profound.

An involuntary groan overtook him then. "What godawful pain. It's not going to be so easy this time around, wife."

"Maybe not, but you'll have a nurse to care for you, hand and foot, day and night. We'll manage, husband, no matter how long it takes."

He smiled, pressing the pain aside, realizing what delights might come of the arrangement she was describing. "Lorie, you haven't given me my kiss yet." She took the oxygen tube from his nostrils and pressed her sweet lips to his. "By God," he said with relief. "Things may hurt like the very devil, wife, but all the essentials in this body continue to function splendidly. I'll still be able to give you that fat little baby."

She kissed him again and said with the little giggle that had become so dear to him, "I stopped taking those pills, my darling, when we talked about it because I had this overwhelming need to keep a part of you with me if I ever had to let you go. Little Jeff Junior might already be on his way."

He lay silent now, gazing up at her, love and wonder flooding every part of his being, easing his pain, then heard a chuckle from somewhere deep inside.

"Jeff Maratti," he said softly, now understanding a great deal more than he had before, "you sly dog. You've been here all the time!"

This time, pain or no, he did laugh. Right out loud. He and Lorie were still grinning at each other when Rolf Maratti and Arthur Ehrlich came back into the room.

Damn the pain. He was beginning to feel just fine.

THE DIAMOND

(BATTLE OF WILLS BOOK 2)

Squib: What do you do if the bad guys in your life grab you to get back a priceless diamond—which, by the way, you don't have—and they're willing to kidnap, torture, and kill to obtain it? After you make your escape, you help devise, with the assistance of the most devious people you know, a totally improbable plan to reproduce the lost treasure. Then you get real sneaky! Lorie and Jeff Preston and their devious friends go full tilt at the Blackheart Compact in the follow-up to Battle of Wills.

APPENDIX

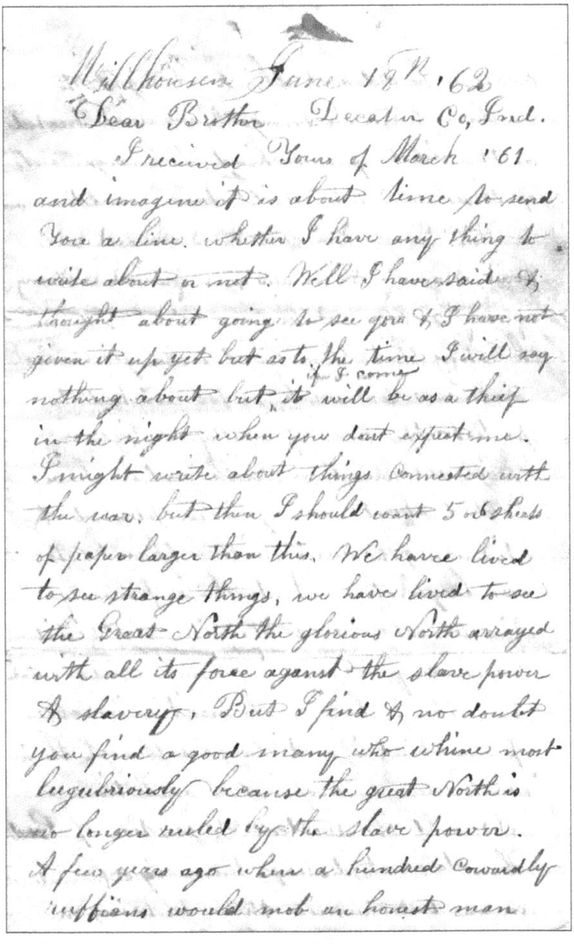

Millhousen June 18th '62
Dear Brother Decatur Co, Ind.
I received Yours of March '61
and imagine it is about time to send
You a line whether I have any thing to
write about or not. Well I have said &
thought about going to see you & I have not
given it up yet but as to the time I will say
nothing about but if I come it will be as a thief
in the night when you dont expect me.
I might write about things Connected with
the war, but then I should want 5 or 6 sheets
of paper larger than this. We have lived
to see strange things, we have lived to see
the Great North the glorious North arrayed
with all its force against the slave power
& slavery. But I find & no doubt
you find a good many who whine most
lugubriously because the great North is
no longer ruled by the slave power.
A few years ago when a hundred Cowardly
ruffians would mob an honest man

because he did not think it right to
enslave human beings & we were treated
as the vilest of mankind. The arguments
of those men when boild down would amount
to this: "D—n You go to the South and talk
about Slavery & see how soon you will be strung
up by the neck and serve you right too." thus
boasting that they lived in a government
that was too weak or too wicked to
protect the lives of worthy citizens.
Well we have been South and we have
talked about slavery as we pleased &
did not get hung neither thanks to
our bayonets. And those princely
Nabobs who swore they would & did
hang every abolitionist they could catch
are like to become the most miserable
of mankind if not beggars through their
wickedness & disapointed ambition.
Behold the wisdom & justice of God
He does not destroy them by supernatural
means but permits them to bring on

thier own destruction
"So God ordains their punishment severe,
Eternally inflicted on themselves." Pollok
It is not likely you took up the subject
as I did & I must confess when I saw the
great mass of preachers & professers of
religion stand aloof or condemn us my
faith became weak, but now we see the
dawn of better times and are like to
be rewarded for the trials we have endured
through the long irrepessible conflict.
Let us thank God and take courage
In years that have gone by we prayed
that the issue at elections might be
the slavery question alone, our prayers
were answered to the letter when Fremont
was Candidate and the next time we
beat them, I know there are many honest
men who consider these speculations all humbug
But I see and take great interest in it
because it displays the justice of God
tempered with mercy and that he
will not longer permit the innocent

black man to be crushed under the
heel of a fiend in the shape of a man
and the honest man of the North who
sympathizes with the poor slave is no
longer to be treated as the offscouring
of the earth, You mentioned the
ages of the family Mother was born
in 1769 and father in 1775 you
must be near 60 and I am in my
seventieth I have nearly spun out
my three score & ten. I have been
remarkably healthy for one of my age
my eye sight fails some but I can see
to do the finest kind of shoe making yet.
I have some trouble with my fellow
men but I enjoy some of the choicest
of blessings for which I know I am not
thankful enough, I will note one
Item and you may construe it as you
please. I had so little confidence
in some of our religious teachers I wrote
to you that I could study the testament
Turn to the single Leaf

in the original for myself. Well about the time you got the letter the Greek Testament I had in the School house was burnt up school house & all, & I have not had an opportunity to get another since We have had bad luck in our little Free will Baptist church to which Roxana belongs, we had a good preacher, and I believe he was a good man but he and his wife parted and there was a hubbub in the church & he has left—. I can tell you nothing about B. Mattheuron I have not heard of him for years. Perhaps you know more of Smith Williams than I do, Calvin Parmore told me his post Office address is —

Franklin Johnson Co. Ind. We are all well at present Samuel is in Ohio & Isaac works out in the neighborhood

Elias & Wilmot are the main farmers and the clearing goes on slowly.

If you hear any one slandering and villifying the black man, You may tell him that I live on the underground railroad and have spent many pleasant hours in conversation with the fugitives, they have but little learning, but for common sense, humanity & piety they are far ahead of their masters & mistresses. To paraphrase a hymn —

Not all the blessings of a feast,
  Can please me half so well,
As when of bursting chains they speak
Or future prospects tell.

What a glorious Jubillee we will have when the Monster Slavery dies and the abolitionists can walk jubilant over its dead Carcass, that's what makes the pro-slavery democrats rave & gnash their teeth. Will let them rip. . Write from henceforth write soon. Yours &c Elias P. Williams

ABOUT THE AUTHOR

Marolyn Caldwell has been creating stories ever since she read a book her Grandfather Frank Caldwell wrote using an Alaskan wolf as the protagonist. If imagination can do that, she figured, ghosts should be easy! All the ins and outs of *Battle of Wills* emerged from a trip she made with her first husband many years ago from the Mississippi river town in Illinois where they were then living, to Marietta, Georgia, where his mother, a lovely little Southern lady—always an abolitionist—had been born. The Marietta ghost is only a product of her imagination—sorry!

The letter from Elias Williams, appearing in the appendix of this book, was found in a box of family bits and trivia. While many have sought to portray the roots of the War Between the States from differing angles, this real-time report from the front lines leaves little to the imagination.

A freelance writer living now in the Finger Lakes region of New York State, Marolyn is the author of two previous books, *Flight Into Danger* and *Whirlwind* (Walker). She is continuing the adventures of the Georgian ghost in two more volumes: *The Diamond* and *The Compact*. If Helen Faw Mull's spirit remains in Marietta, or even in Quincy, Illinois, this one is for you, Dearest Lady!

CPSIA information can be obtained
at www.ICGtesting.com
Printed in the USA
JSHW030725280622
27404JS00002B/5